The Shadow of God
A Novel

Steve Jackowski

EPILOGUE

Mike and May were stretching on the San Francisco Belle as it motored out towards Alcatraz. This would be their fourth Escape from Alcatraz. Next to them was a young man who looked extremely nervous. He suddenly clutched at his stomach, bent over the railing and heaved his breakfast over the side. "Are you okay?" May asked.

"Not really. First, I'm nervous. If you can believe it, this is my very first triathlon. Second, I get seasick. I surf and it doesn't bother me, but this boat and these seas, I just can't hold my breakfast down. Do you guys have any advice to help a newbie like me?"

"Well, my husband Mike, here, did this as his first triathlon too, four years ago. Mike, do you have any advice for this young man?"

Mike held out his hand. "I'm Mike Mckensey and this is my wife May. She might not look it, but she does Ironmans. This is about the most I can do."

The young man shook Mike's hand and introduced himself. "I'm Jim Henderson."

"Well, Jim, May coached me through my first Escape. Unfortunately, she forgot to warn me about the swim and I almost quit in the first five minutes. I jumped in with the pack, and even though I'm a strong swimmer, with the kicking, the punching, having my goggles knocked off, and the chaos of the start, I was ready to give up. So, my one piece of advice is to wait to jump in, and wait again for two minutes before swimming.

That will let the pack thin out and you can find your rhythm before you catch them. For the rest, take it easy on the bike, and when you get to the sand ladder on the run, don't stop, even if you have to walk. Just keep in mind that it's an easy downhill after that. You will finish."

"Thanks! I would never have thought about that on the swim. Foundering in the cold waters of the Bay off of Alcatraz after being kicked and pummeled and after losing my breakfast would have been too much. I'll definitely follow your advice. I'm not trying to win this thing, I just want to finish."

"Well, good luck!"

The race went off without a hitch and both Mike and May did their best times ever. Unlike the first year, May didn't stay with Mike. Instead, they met up at the finish line.

As Mike finished, May cheered him on.

"How long have you been here?" he asked, wheezing.

"Only a few minutes," she lied.

"Yeah, I'm sure. And you started five minutes after me too."

"Mike, you did great!"

"Yeah, right."

"Well, look who I found. Remember Jim from the boat?"

"Hey Jim, how'd it go?"

"Your advice was a lifesaver, both in the water and on the sand ladder. I almost gave up there, but I remembered that it would be all downhill if I made it to the top."

"And how was your time?"

"Ah I finished in two hours and thirty-four minutes. I don't know where that puts me in the standings."

"Are you fucking kidding me?" Mike groaned. "You've got to be in the top ten for your age group. This is your first triathlon? Christ, we've got another one."

"Another one?"

"Yeah, you're just like May. A natural. I'm just an old fart who can't keep up."

"Honey, you know you're great. Not many people who work as much as you do can even finish this race."

Mike started to grumble something else but May interrupted. "I've asked Jim to join us for brunch at the Cliff House and he's agreed. He and his wife will meet us there in an hour."

Ninety minutes later, Mike, May, Liz and Jim were seated at a table with a spectacular view of Seal Rock and the huge ships

DEDICATION

To Lynn Distefano

ACKNOWLEDGMENTS

I've dedicated this novel to my sister, Lynn Distefano, who has battled mental illness for most of her life. I'd like to thank Jo Minola who was the first to read the manuscript, my wife Karen, for her encouragement, and especially Sabrina Noel who provided valuable insight into the workings of psychiatric inpatient facilities.

Steve Jackowski

CHAPTER 1

"Sunlight is the Shadow of God"

- Michelangelo

1

Mitch Stern came to San Francisco for MacWorld at the Moscone Convention Center along with thousands of computer nerds, all fans of the resurgent Apple Computer. After spending the day in tutorials and meandering from booth to booth in the huge convention hall, chatting with many of the vendors and other attendees, Mitch decided on dinner at Chevy's just a few blocks down Mission Street.

Mitch hadn't been to San Francisco in twenty-five years, not since he married his wife. They came here for a passionate honeymoon and weren't disappointed. When they weren't making love in their hotel, they were wine tasting in the Napa Valley, hiking at Fort Cronkite, picnicking in Golden Gate Park, lounging on the Marina Green, having high tea at the Ritz Carlton hotel, high above the city on Nob Hill, or taking in shows and dancing afterwards. They walked the streets holding hands and loving one of the most romantic cities in the world.

But now, the city had changed. There were more towering hotels blocking the sunlight, imperious in their dominance of the skyline, many with an insidious, almost threatening feel to them. There were also more panhandlers. They called them homeless people here, but aside from a few who clearly needed psychological help, most looked able-bodied. You couldn't walk down the street without being accosted or having to step around groups of them lounging in the middle of the sidewalks. The smell of urine and grime was pervasive. What had happened to the city he once almost knew?

His hometown of St. Louis had a poor, ghetto section, but the downtown was pristine compared to the fabled City by the Bay.

Mitch didn't usually attend conferences. He had almost stopped traveling altogether after his marriage. Margaret really didn't like to sleep alone and she made it very clear that she didn't want him to travel. So Mitch had backed off on his career and focused on his wife and family. He spent hours with the kids, helping them with homework, taking them to school, dance lessons, singing lessons and sports practices, while Margaret pursued her teaching career. Funny how he ended up raising their kids while she taught so many others. How was it she didn't have time for her own kids?

Now both kids were away at college and Margaret had decided she wanted a different life, one without Mitch. He had given up so much of himself for her: his friends, his sports, his career, even the rest of his family. It seemed like a good deal at the time. They loved each other like no other couple. They danced, saw shows, had countless romantic weekends, and their sex life had not changed since their honeymoon. Lots of passion. Mitch was certain they'd be caring for one another into their old age until one or the other slipped away, that while their bodies would age and wither, their love never would.

Then, last fall, Margaret went off hormone replacement therapy. She'd been on it for fifteen years, ever since her early menopause. While most women went into menopause over the course of years, Margaret's body changed in a matter of weeks. Sex became painful, and while Mitch was more than willing to make love in alternate ways, Margaret felt her body had betrayed her. She was embarrassed by her inability to perform, even though she continued to have earth-shaking orgasms through their creative lovemaking. She refused to talk to a doctor about it. It was too embarrassing. Mitch felt guilty for wanting her as much as he always had and it seemed that she felt obligated to satisfy him, but resentful too.

One day she was gone. She moved out. Mitch returned from work to a house, not a home. Everything was in disarray. Unwanted clothes and personal items were strewn throughout every room except the kids', which were completely empty. Most of their prized possessions were gone, but she had left albums and pictures of Mitch. It was as if she just wanted to forget their twenty-five years together and start over. What had he done? Why did this happen?

The quiet and emptiness of the house was oppressive.

Worse, the kids supported their Mom's decision. When he talked with his daughters, they told him they thought their Mom had been too dependent on him. They said she had never really lived on her own or made her own way and that she needed to do this. He was strong and independent and would just need to move on with his life without Margaret.

Mitch realized that young women in their late teens and early twenties were trying to break away, to be independent, but why did they feel their mothers needed the same thing? He had put all of himself into his kids and his marriage and now it was all gone;

they'd all betrayed him.

A week ago he and Margaret had met to talk about finances. Of course the conversation started with the usual recriminations. Margaret seemed to want to vilify Mitch and their life together.

"I gave up myself to be with you. All women do that. I've taken a seminar on how women mold and model themselves after their men. We all become what men want us to be. I don't want to see you. I don't have time for you in my life. I need to reconnect with myself and with my daughters."

"Are you planning to see other people?" Mitch asked apprehensively, his stomach turning at the thought of her with someone else.

"I've decided I'm done with all that, thank God! I don't need men in my life, just women friends."

Mitch was too stunned to react. Their life together had been so romantic. Even after so many years married, they still held hands when they walked down the street or saw movies together. He sent her flowers at work and brought home surprise little gifts. And their dancing! They moved together like one person. It didn't matter what move Mitch tried or how creative he was in inventing new patterns and routines, Margaret could follow him. If she was off-balance or uncomfortable, he sensed it and compensated unconsciously. Her body and his were connected in a way that each could anticipate the moves of the other. God, how he loved her!

When he did have to travel, Margaret secretly slipped little cards into his luggage, one for each night he was to be away. The first usually talked about how much she loved and missed him. With each day they became progressively suggestive, with the last one describing the physical pleasures he would experience when he returned to her and their bed.

"She was done with all that?" he asked himself, completely confused. "Could she really live without romance in her life?" He could understand her fears and embarrassment about sex, but no romance, no long walks, shows, dinners out, weekends away exploring new places? And the sex could be worked out. He was patient. After all, it could have gone the other way. Wouldn't she have supported him if he'd had prostate problems and became impotent?

It didn't matter now. The life he'd tried to build, giving himself up to marriage and family, was gone. Could he really start over at fifty? Should he wait for her? They had needed each other for so long. Was this just a phase? Would she find herself and realize she missed what they had? Wasn't love supposed to transcend all? Didn't she believe in true love and the destiny of their being together?

He had cleaned up the house and thrown away much of the detritus that she'd left behind – fragments of their life together. He bought new pictures to cover the white spots on the walls. It was funny, he thought, years of exposure had changed the colors of the walls except where the pictures had hung. Now, there were white rectangles, surrounded by the darkness of the walls. They were like white shadows of his life.

When he came home from work, he usually fixed a quick light dinner. He was losing weight. It didn't make sense to cook for one. He'd grab a book or watch an old movie, the classics he'd neglected for years. He fell into a routine – get up, go to work, come home, eat a bit, read, go to bed. He was keeping time, waiting for his life to begin again or with luck, for the old one to resume. Some days he thought he'd be just fine. Then suddenly, he'd just burst into tears and cry uncontrollably. He never knew what would set him off. The turn of a phrase, a touching moment in a black and white film, or reaching for Margaret in the middle of the night and finding an emptiness next to him. Then the tears would stop and he'd sit there stunned, wondering where that had come from.

When he received the email about the MacWorld conference, he decided that a change of scene might help. At least he wouldn't be wallowing in self-pity, doubt and despair over his future. The first day of the conference had been interesting, but he was brooding a bit and hadn't yet opened himself up to meeting other people.

Mitch walked out of the restaurant after a superb Mexican meal. You couldn't get this kind of food in the Midwest. He staggered a bit after the three margaritas he had downed over dinner. The sun was setting out to the west, but it was too low to see over the hills and the skyscrapers cast long shadows across the streets like the ominous prison bars of the old black and white films noir.

Mitch turned south down Mission Street, away from his hotel. Maybe a walk would clear his head. Within a few blocks he found himself in the Tenderloin. Young black men eyed him suspiciously and prostitutes bent over, showing their breasts and asked if he wanted a date. He knew he should turn around, head back to the hotel, but something drew him deeper into this seedy world he'd never experienced.

As he rounded a corner he thought he saw Margaret. This seemed to happen a lot since she left. He'd see someone from behind and his heart would quicken with anticipation. He'd fantasize a romantic reunion. Of course when he saw their faces, none of them were Margaret.

This woman turned and he saw that she looked remarkably like his wife did when they first met. "Wanna date?" she asked.

Mitch ignored her and continued walking.

"I can do things for you your wife never did," she purred as he passed.

Mitch thought about it. He'd been married a quarter of a century and had been faithful to his wife. He'd never been with a prostitute. If not now, when? He could use some physical contact, it had been months since anyone had been affectionate to him, let alone made love with him.

"Okay," he replied sheepishly. "But I've never done anything like this before."

"That's okay sweetie. I'll take good care of you."

She took his arm and led him around a corner into an alley. She opened the back door to an old Chevrolet Impala and said, "Hop in!" Then she slid in beside him.

"Uh, what do I do?" he asked, clearly nervous.

"Honey, it's twenty for a hand job, fifty for a blowjob, a hundred for straight, I don't do backdoor and no rough stuff."

"What's your name?" Mitch asked, hoping to know this woman, realizing that he was looking as much for intimacy as he was for sex.

"Call me anything you want and tell me what you want to do. But you do have to pay me first."

Mitch looked at her and thought about his marriage and sex life. While he and Margaret had frequent sex, and although he loved to please her orally, she had given him a blowjob only three times during their years together.

"Margaret!" he almost shouted. "I'll call you Margaret. Margaret, I would like a blowjob!" he said laughing, trying to get caught up in the fantasy. He reached in his wallet and pulled out four twenties. "Keep the change and take a little time, please."

Margaret took his hand and slipped it up her shear black blouse. She was braless and her breasts were full, her left nipple hardening at his touch. She slowly unbuttoned his shirt, unzipped his pants, then began to stroke his chest. Mitch was hard and ready. She kissed his stomach, working her way down. She gently licked the sides of him then slowly took him in her mouth. Mitch almost lost it as the warmth and wetness surrounded him.

"Slow down please. It's been a while," he whispered huskily, overcome by sensation.

She did as he asked and Mitch began to relax. "Oh, Margaret! You don't know how many times I fantasized about you doing this. Suck me off! Suck me off!"

Margaret complied taking him deep into her mouth.

"Margaret, why did you do it? Why did you leave me? I loved you. We should be together. You've walked out on our future. I'm alone. Alone. I'm going to die a broken-hearted lonely old man. Take all of me, you fucking bitch!"

Mitch forced her head down hard, causing her to gag.

"Yeah, gag. That's nothing compared to what you did to me!" And he jammed her head down again, hitting her with open hands, grabbing her head and forcing it up and down hard. After a moment he realized what he was doing. Then he stopped and started to cry.

Margaret lifted her head, coughed, spit, and got out of the car, slamming the door. Mitch sobbed, unable to catch his breath. He felt sick. He'd never hit a woman or forced one to do anything before. Caught up in a maelstrom of emotion, disgusted with himself, and devastated again by his wife's desertion, Mitch leaned back and sat there sobbing and exhausted, trying to regain some semblance of control.

The car door opened and a streetlight cast the dark shadow of a woman across Mitch.

Without opening his eyes, Mitch said, "I'm really sorry Margaret. My wife just left me and I lost it."

"I'm not Margaret. She told you no rough stuff, you bastard. Now you've got to pay!"

"Sure, sure. How much? I'm really sorry!"

Jane leaned over him, her face only inches away. Her dark eyes flashed as she said, 'Everything!'

Mitch felt a sharp pain in his chest as he searched the angry brown eyes looming above him for answers. He wanted to understand, really understand what had happened. Why had Margaret left him? Why wasn't his love good enough for her? Why was she killing him now?

But he never got the chance.

2

Jane looked at the son-of-a-bitch who had hurt Dawn. She almost felt sorry for him – almost. He certainly got what he deserved. It was bad enough a married man sought out whores, but to rough them up? No! The world was better off without his kind.

She drove the car to a deserted parking lot in the former Presidio. Abandoned buildings with only a few streetlights provided dark cover for her task. She stripped the body, removing all its clothes. The wedding ring presented a problem, but makeup remover she kept in her purse finally helped it come off.

Jane took the one hundred sixteen dollars from the wallet and put it in her purse along with the ring and watch. She cut up the credit cards and driver's license and put them in a thirty gallon plastic garbage bag along with the clothes. She looked briefly at the picture of the middle-aged woman who looked a bit like Dawn, and the two young women at her sides. "You won't even miss the asshole. I promise," she said.

Jane tossed the pictures and wallet into the bag that she'd burn later, then lit a cigarette and waited.

After an hour, she double-checked her tide chart then made her way to Fort Point at the base of the Golden Gate Bridge. High tide was at 12:45 am. Now that it was almost two, the waters of the San Francisco Bay would be rushing out to sea. The current was moving several miles an hour and she could see the moonlit roiling whitecaps where the Bay met the ocean.

She dragged the john's body out of the car and lifted it over the railing. Jane watched as it slowly sank, then floated almost to the surface, and was finally caught up in the rushing tidal waters heading out to sea.

3

Detective Mike McKensey of the San Francisco Police Department looked at the naked bloated corpse that had washed up on Ocean Beach a few hours before and he knew had another one. This made the third found in San Francisco County in the last year, and four total. All were men and all shared the same mark – a puncture wound about an inch below the left nipple. They had died instantly from a knife slipped between the ribs directly into the heart.

The first was found floating in the San Francisco Bay by a couple who was sailing their Hobie Cat near Treasure Island. The second was discovered on Baker Beach, just outside the Golden Gate. Another body with an identical wound had washed up near Bolinas in Marin County two months before. Lieutenant May Reeves, the homicide detective assigned to the case by the Marin Sheriff's Department, recognized the similarity with the unsolved cases in San Francisco and she and Mike had decided to work together to find the killer.

In spite of the substantial decomposition of the hands, accelerated by the salt water, the Medical Examiners had successfully identified each victim through fingerprints. Mike shook his head at the thought of the science involved. He had seen the bloated victims' bodies and couldn't even make out a single ridge on any of the fingers. Like most of his counterparts in Homicide, Mike had attended FBI training on fingerprints and the techniques used for recovery. Some, like removing the skin of the hand, slipping it on like a glove, and then using a standard inking pad seemed quite grotesque. Others, like super glue fuming combined with ninhydrin seemed too simple to be true. Still others were so complicated that he didn't even begin to understand how they did it. But the MEs got results and that's what mattered.

Unfortunately, aside from the first body which had been in the Bay only several hours, the others had spent days at sea before washing up. Then, between scheduling the autopsy, getting the prints, and ultimately matching them, days passed. Even if they could identify people who knew or might have seen the victims, most of them couldn't remember much. Mike couldn't blame them. He couldn't remember what he'd had for lunch a week before, so how could he expect someone to remember what for them was probably an even less significant event?

The first victim was a student from City College of San Francisco. The second was a tourist from Cincinnati, Ohio. The third was a Silicon Valley executive. All were men and all had been in downtown in San Francisco shortly before their deaths. Other than that, and the facts that they were killed in the same way and their bodies had spent some time in the water, there didn't seem to be any pattern to the murders or connections among the victims. Only the student had a criminal record and that was a minor possession charge though from what the investigators could determine, he was also a small-time dealer at the college. The murders weren't increasing in frequency, nor were they regularly spaced. They seemed to be completely random. None of the victims' clothes, credit cards or belongings had been found. The FBI profilers had been called in and had come up with nothing. They agreed that the killer was smart, seemed to have some knowledge of anatomy, and had chosen an excellent method for hiding DNA evidence. Bodies that had spent days in the ocean didn't provide many clues. So thus far, they had no leads whatsoever.

Mike called May and asked her to meet him Monday at the city morgue for the autopsy. Maybe something about this body would make a difference.

4

Jim Henderson turned his Subaru off Highway 20 onto the narrow road that wound its way north through peach orchards laden with green unripened fruit. After nearly three hours on the road, there were only a few miles to go to reach the campground at Elk Mountain, site of the United States Hang Gliding and Paragliding Association's Western Regional competition.

The road narrowed as the orchards were replaced by scrub oak trees and scattered pines. A wide, dry, stone-filled creek bed radiated heat into the late morning air. A few wisps of nascent cumulus clouds were just beginning to form above Elk Mountain peak and Jim could feel anticipation start to take hold. He loved to fly and Elk Mountain was his favorite hang gliding site. In anticipation of his first competition, Jim had spent dozens of hours flying here and he knew the mountain as well or better than most of the local pilots.

Cumulus clouds marked the tops of the day's first thermals, warm bubbles of air which lifted off the ground like bubbles in a soda glass. If they contained any moisture and rose high enough, the moisture would condense and form a cloud. They were great markers for hang glider and sailplane pilots, making thermals much easier to find and enabling engineless flight for those so inclined. It was going to be a great day, and if the weather reports were right, the competition would have ideal conditions.

Jim pulled into the campground and was pleased to find that only two campsites were taken. He chose one as far from the road as possible, then completed the self-registration for the campsite. It was only eleven o'clock and the registration for the competition didn't begin until three.

He decided to wait another half hour to see if more pilots would show up. If not, he'd head up the mountain alone. The conditions were too good to pass up.

He walked out into the creek bed and set up a windsock. The most challenging feature of Elk Mountain was its landing area, the creek bed that generated most of the thermals for the mountain. You could be on a perfect path for landing, when all of a sudden, a thermal could lift off under you, thrusting you fifty or more feet into the air. Worse, if a thermal lifted off a few hundred feet in front of you as you were landing, the wind direction would suddenly reverse, filling the void left by the rising air, and you'd be landing downwind, a big mistake and a certain crash. Yes, this was going to be an interesting competition, especially for those who didn't understand the fickle conditions in the landing area.

At eleven thirty, no other pilots had shown up, so Jim took his Subaru up the mountain. He left the pavement at the top of the ridge and put the car in four wheel low, then slowly negotiated the treacherous dirt road to the take-off site. With its lower center of gravity, the Subaru was less likely to roll over than larger 4x4s. Still, Jim didn't like to take chances.

He stopped at the top of the rise before the launching area and tied a Dacron streamer to the tip of a tree as a wind indicator. He was pleased to see that the wind was still coming up the south side of the mountain. While you could launch from either the north or south side of the ridge, south wind days were the best, generating the biggest thermals as the creek bed and rocks on the south face of the mountain heated up in the morning sun. There were more trees and fewer thermals on the north side, and often when the winds turned from the north, the cooler air coming off the ocean a hundred miles away would cap the thermals and limit your altitude gains.

As he set up his glider, Jim remarked on the fact that he was alone again. He seemed to be doing this a lot lately, ever since he and Sharon split up. He felt lonely, but at the same time, independent. There were certainly advantages to not having to worry about hurting other people's feelings, always having to say and do the right things. Alone, you could do whatever you wanted whenever you wanted.

And yet, he had enjoyed flying with Sharon. She was never terribly serious about hang gliding, but she liked to get out. She loved the outdoors and camping at remote landing areas. Why wasn't she here? His gut clenched at the thought of her with someone else.

Putting Sharon out of his mind, Jim finished the setup of his glider, then did a careful preflight inspection, checking every wire for crimps or frays and making sure that each component was assembled correctly and in working order.

He put on his harness and helmet and clipped into the glider. Then he waited. The wind was blowing three or four miles per hour, but every minute or two a thermal would roll up the face of the mountain and the wind would gust with its passage. He scanned the bushes a few hundred feet below the take-off. After a minute or so, they started shaking fiercely. Jim picked up the hang glider and began to run down the hill.

As he gained enough airspeed to fly, his feet left the ground and then the thermal hit. It was strong and he felt the familiar jerk upwards as he wrestled with the control bar to maintain mastery over the glider. He entered the thermal and felt the surge as the power of the lift increased. His variometer chirped loudly and he looked over to see that he was climbing at over six hundred feet a minute. As he passed through the core of the thermal, the concentrated lift at its center, he gently banked the glider to the left and began circling. With each circle, he'd hit the core, then would increase the steepness of the turn. After a few circles, he was centered in the core, climbing at over a thousand feet per minute.

Round and round. Jim wondered why he never got dizzy doing this.

After a few minutes, the thermal was weakening. His rate of climb slowed to less than fifty feet per minute. Time to move on. He checked his altimeter and saw that he was at seventy-two hundred feet, more than three thousand feet above the launch. He was now higher than all of the surrounding mountains. The air had cooled ten or twelve degrees and he could see the sunlight glittering off the ocean far to the west.

To the north, twelve miles away, was Hull Mountain at nearly seven thousand feet. There were still a few patches of snow near the top. Just below Hull, he could make out Lake Pillsbury and the landing strip that serviced the ultra-private vacation retreats for the rich and famous.

To the east, Snow Mountain was the boundary between the coastal mountains and the great Sacramento Valley of California. The Sierra Nevada Mountains were visible further to the east.

Jim checked his drift and noted that he had exited the thermal just slightly north of the launch. This was good. The winds aloft were light southerly. If he headed south, he could fly downwind on the way back.

By the time he crossed the valley separating Elk Mountain and Pitney Ridge to the south, Jim had lost nearly three thousand feet of altitude. He hadn't encountered a single thermal along the way. As he reached the ridge, he started to look for bare spots among the trees and rock outcroppings, planning to position himself just downwind and above these thermal generators. Then it hit him. It had only happened a few times before, but it seemed to be occurring more and more frequently. He KNEW where the next thermal was. In fact, there were three nearby and he could FEEL which one was strongest.

In spite of his analytical personality, Jim trusted this instinct and was soon climbing again in a large, strong thermal. What was it? You couldn't see, hear or taste the thermals, though people said that hawks and eagles could see small bugs and dust particles rising. Sometimes you could smell a thermal, but that was when you were in it. Once in a while you could catch the scent of fresh breaking pine. But what was this? Was it some kind of sixth sense about thermals? It certainly wasn't logical, but it was working for Jim, so he decided not to question it.

Climbing with thermals, then gliding downward after exiting, Jim flew south past the small town of Upper Lake along the east shore of Clearlake and then past the village called Nice. An hour and a half into the flight, he decided to return. He waited a while at the end of Pitney Ridge to be sure to gain as much altitude as possible before crossing the valley back to Elk Mountain. Then he scratched his way back up Elk Mountain. Just as he was about to crest the ridge, a red-tailed hawk took off from a tree and joined Jim in the thermal. They circled opposite each other for a while, then the hawk flew directly under Jim's wing, less than fifteen feet away.

Jim had heard stories of pilots being attacked by hawks, of talons aimed directly at their eyes. Fortunately, Jim knew this hawk.

"Hey, Sam!" Jim called.

The hawk turned its head briefly towards Jim and then ignored him. It was strange. 'Sam' had started joining Jim in thermals about a month before. Now on almost every flight, they shared at least one thermal together. Jim had never seen Sam do this with anyone else.

They crossed eight thousand feet together. Jim checked his watch and decided he should land and go check in for the competition. Looking over at Sam, he realized that these birds flew for the sheer joy of it. It wasn't like Sam was going to spot and dive at some prey several thousand feet below. If not pleasure, why would he fly so high?

Jim left the thermal and pulled himself forward past the

control bar as far as he could. The glider started to dive. As he gained speed, the dive recovery capabilities of the glider made it more and more difficult to hold the bar in. Just when he couldn't hold it any longer, Jim shifted his weight to the left, then pushed the bar outwards and the glider did a wingover – Jim had just banked it over one hundred thirty degrees. He was almost upside down for a second. As the glider dropped through the wingover into another dive, Jim repeated the maneuver to the right. Ten wingovers later, he had lost several thousand feet and was only a few hundred feet above the ridge. He noticed a four wheel drive truck approaching the takeoff. He checked the wind direction on the streamer he'd tied to a tree and landed on the road at the top of the ridge. The truck pulled up and Jim heard cheers.

"Hey, I've never seen anyone land up here," a voice called from the truck.

Jim set his glider down and unclipped. A young man of about Jim's age, height and build stepped from the truck. Startling blue eyes with black rings around the irises were the most prominent features of a sculpted, somewhat aristocratic face. He approached Jim and held out his hand, introducing himself, "I'm Steve Franklin. The guy stepping out of the truck is Bill England, and our good looking driver is Liz Leahy."

"Hey, I'm not a driver. I'm a pilot!" Liz shouted in feigned outrage.

"I knew that would get her." Steve said laughing. "We first spotted you south of Upper Lake and you were coming up Pitney when we signed in for the competition. Do you always land on top?"

"There were no other pilots when I got here and the conditions looked good. I figured if they weren't, I could always hitch a ride back up. Or, in the worst case, which did happen once, I could hike back up to get my car. But yes, if possible, I land on top. Not only can I save myself the need for a driver, I can also avoid that landing area. I think I have it down, but it can always surprise you."

Bill turned to Steve and said, "Steve, I think you may have some real competition here."

"Yeah. But the pros are going to be here too. Jim, have you been flying long?"

"About eighteen months, but I have spent every weekend for the last two months here and I think I know the site well. I'm not looking to win since this is my first competition ever, but I'm hoping to do well."

"If you fly during the competition like you did today," Liz interjected, "I think you'll place in the top ten without a problem. You could make it to the Nationals."

"Thanks for the kind words," Jim responded. "I'd better head down the mountain and get registered. I guess I'll see you guys tomorrow."

"Hey," said Bill, "Our first night we have pizza in Upper Lake. Want to join us?"

"Sure. What time?"

Steve jumped in. "It's almost three now, give us two hours to fly and an hour to clean up and get into town. How about six thirty at Upper Lake Pizza?"

"See you there!"

Jim broke down his glider. He waited and watched as Liz helped Steve and Bill set up, then assisted with their launches, just in case there was a problem. There wasn't. He watched as they each grabbed a thermal after taking off and as he got in his Subaru and headed down the mountain, he saw that they were rapidly climbing above the launch circling up together, sharing a thermal.

5

Liz looked after Jim as he pulled away. Not only was he an excellent pilot, he certainly was good looking. Blond hair, blue eyes, and swimmer's shoulders. This trip might be more interesting than she thought. She got into the truck and followed him down the mountain, trying to stay in his track on the treacherous four-wheel drive road. She, like most people who drove off-road, knew that going downhill was more dangerous than climbing.

Just a month before, an inexperienced driver had hit the brakes hard on a very steep downhill section of the road rather than downshifting. The overloaded rear end fishtailed, turning the vehicle perpendicular to the slope. With the raised body, several gliders on the top and 5 people inside, the 4x4 tipped over sideways and tumbled several hundred feet down the hill, luckily stopping when it hit a small stand of rocks and trees just above a precipitous drop off. The gliders and the 4x4 were totaled. Everyone in the truck suffered multiple contusions, lacerations and broken bones and they were airlifted to the hospital in Ukiah. Four had died of their injuries.

Liz loved her high risk, aggressive lifestyle, but she certainly wasn't going to kill herself doing something completely stupid. She was her father's daughter, and like him, she wasn't planning to check out until she too had made a mark on the world.

Her father was a classic success story. Raised in the Castro of San Francisco long before it became the famous gay district, Michael Patrick Leahy had started with nothing, and had become one of the most famous lawyers in the country if not the world. Both his grandfather and father were working class Irishmen who drank themselves to death at early ages. His mother died of cancer when Michael was six and his grandmother took him in.

The young Michael spent most of his early youth on the streets with his friends or, depending on your perspective, the gangs of the district, perpetrating petty crimes and mischief. His grandmother's fiery temper, tongue lashings, and expertise with a belt helped keep him in school.

In seventh grade, he developed a crush on his Civics teacher. Recognizing some potential, Miss Reevers began encouraging the boy who quickly became caught up in her enthusiasm for the subject. Over the following years, Michael graduated high school as class valedictorian, served a brief tour in the Navy, received a full scholarship to the University of California at Berkeley, and then excelled at Hastings Law School in San Francisco, graduating first in his class. He worked several years for the San Francisco District Attorney's office prosecuting criminal cases, but then jumped ship to become a defense attorney. While many in the DA's office considered him a traitor to the cause, Michael's consideration for his opposition, even in the course of a heated trial, earned him their respect. Still, having been schooled in most of their strategies at the DA's office, Michael became a formidable adversary, rarely losing a case. His obvious charm and non-stop banter made him a media favorite.

He married Janice Giardina, a small, shapely, fiery, raven-haired woman of Sicilian descent. Janice tried to keep the extravagant Michael under control, but it was part of Michael's nature to be generous, to make loans to friends, and to throw lavish parties. Michael often brought home interesting strangers that he'd met on the street or in a bar. Sometimes they just stayed for dinner. Sometimes they stayed for months while they searched for jobs to get back on their feet.

Michael and Janice lived in high style, but never became rich, seeming to have just enough money for the next party or major expense.

While they often brushed elbows with the old money of San Francisco, largely because of their 'modest' backgrounds, they were never accepted as members of the elite. This irked Janice, but didn't bother Michael at all. He felt much more connected to a homeless person looking for a job than to people who never knew what it meant to be poor or to work to make ends meet.

Elizabeth Louise Leahy was born a few years into the marriage and to use an old-fashioned expression which certainly fit at that time, Liz became the apple of her father's eye. Michael worshipped his little girl and couldn't wait to get home to play with her and eventually, as she got older, to spar with her in political and legal banter.

Somehow, Liz inherited the best genes from each of her parents. She had her mother's dark hair, eyes, and eventually her remarkable figure, and received a smattering of freckles from her father along with his easy charm, intelligence, and good humor. Her charm was effective on virtually everyone, but most particularly on her father. If ever she saw the beginning of a dark mood, she'd jump in his lap, kiss him, and tease him into good humor.

The only discipline Liz received came from her mother. But in most cases, her father intervened and Liz got away with pretty much everything. This made her a bit of a scofflaw. She obeyed traffic laws only when they suited her, and having learned to debate and use charm from one of the best, she frequently talked her way out of traffic tickets, or if she couldn't, she took them to court where she was quite successful in getting them dismissed. She had no qualms about using her deceased great-grandmother's handicap placard so that she could park wherever she wanted. She saw no moral dilemma in cheating a bit to gain an advantage. In fact, Liz took it as a point of pride that she could talk her way out of just about anything.

Many called Liz spoiled. But Liz knew she wasn't. Spoiled people didn't appreciate what they had. Liz fully appreciated what she had and having watched her parents' financial situation go up and down, understood how precarious financial success could be. She had promised herself she wouldn't make the same mistakes they had and that she would use the advantage of her starting point to climb even higher than her father had. She'd make him even more proud than he already was.

Liz was on her way. She was about to graduate from one of the best law schools in the country, had several job offers, and was engaged to the son of one of San Francisco's old-money families. Yes, the future looked bright for Liz.

As Liz continued down the steep 4x4 road, she couldn't help thinking that she was about to make a big mistake. She wasn't spoiled, but she certainly had more freedom than anyone else she knew. The thought of stepping into the realm of old money and a law career with a big firm seemed so confining, and if there was one thing that terrified Liz, it was being confined.

6

"Did you hear? Liz is off to a hang gliding competition with Steve and Bill."

"No Dawn, I didn't know that. She's engaged to Mark Sinclair, that banker's son. What she doing with Steve now?"

"I think she's still sleeping with him from time to time. From what I hear, although Mark is VERY well endowed, he comes and falls asleep within two minutes. I understand that Steve is a much better lover."

"Well, Liz was always interested in good sex. But I'm surprised she'd be cheating on Mark. He's a really nice guy. And what's she doing with this hang gliding thing? When is she going to settle down?"

"Eve, I think her plan is to settle down with Mark. She'll be well taken care of as the wife of Jonathan Sinclair's son, and she'll become the perfect hostess to their old-moneyed friends. I think hang gliding and flings with people like Steve will finally fall by the way side.

"You know, she's not actually flying in the competition, she's just there to support Steve and Bill."

"Yeah, but who's tent is she sleeping in?"

"Eve, I'm sure she has her own tent. After all, she's engaged. Steve is a thing of the past. Actually, so is Bill if you think about it. I don't think she'd do anything to jeopardize the engagement. After all, Mark's family is rich and so is Mark. They're also incredibly well-connected. You know Liz's expensive tastes. I don't think she'd risk a solid financial and social future for another fling."

"Okay. I guess we'll see. Still, if she's not happy with Mark sexually, in spite of his big penis, I'd bet that she's still looking around for something better."

"Eve, I'm pretty sure that she's over Steve. We'll just have to wait and see what's happening.

"By the way, have you talked to Betty lately? I think she likes hearing from you. She's coming into puberty and really likes the advice of her older British cousin. I'm a bit too jaded to deal with such innocence. And I'm pretty much a pariah as far as the family is concerned. Please talk to her soon."

"Dawn, you are her sister. Even if no one likes what you do, you'll always be sisters. I think you should talk to her directly.

But I know you won't, so I'll see what she's up to. In the meantime, if you hear anything interesting from Liz, let me know."

"Of course!"

7

When Liz got back to the campground, she saw several people grouped together, obviously looking at something. Walking over, she spotted the object that had piqued everyone's curiosity: a large barrel, probably a former oil drum. It had been modified and now had a spigot on one side. A long pipe extended upwards several feet with a spray nozzle attached. There was an open door on the face of the barrel and a fire was blazing inside. As she looked closer, she could see coils of pipe amidst the raging flames. A grizzled young man of about thirty with long dreadlocks seemed to be in charge. He was stoking the fire with small pieces of oak.

Liz walked up to him and said, "What is that thing?"

He smiled and responded, "There's water here at the campground, but no hot water. This is a wood-fired water heater and shower. I'm going to sell hot showers to all the folks here for the competition."

With the coals now blazing, he took a long hose and hooked it up to both the device and a campsite spigot.

"Who wants to try it?" he asked the gathering crowd.

Having driven three hours to get here, then four-wheeling up Elk Mountain and down again through the dust and heat, Liz thought a hot shower sounded good. "How much?" she asked.

He looked her up and down, taking in her full breasts and shapely body and said, "If you'll be the first, you can go for free."

"Okay," Liz replied, "Let me get a towel. I'll be right back."

Two minutes later, Liz returned, clothed in nothing but a white towel, carrying bottles of shampoo and conditioner, a bar of soap and a loofa.

"Let her rip," she said.

He opened a valve and hot water started falling from the nozzle. He adjusted the rate of flow with the spigot until Liz nodded that the temperature was right. Liz dropped her towel and showered as several pilots from the upcoming competition looked on admiringly.

Jim was walking back to his campsite after completing his registration and saw the small crowd. Ignoring them, he continued past, but couldn't help seeing Liz standing naked, water pouring over her as smoke and flame roared in the makeshift water heater next to her. He stopped.

Liz leaned her head back into the water. Who could imagine a simple shower would feel so good? Maybe it was having hot water out in the middle of nowhere.

As she washed the conditioner out of her hair, water and white swept down her back and over her firm bottom, slipping between her cheeks and down the backs of her thighs. Her nipples hardened as her breasts were thrust upwards out of the warmth into the cooler air.

Looking on, Jim could hardly believe his eyes. She was a water nymph. Her perfect body was so relaxed. She appeared completely unaware of those around her, caught up in the sensation of the steaming water washing her down. When he caught a glimpse of the very thick patch of dark pubic hair, Jim felt a stirring. It had been months since he'd been with Sharon. This arousal was just normal, right? He was sure every other male looking at Liz felt exactly the same thing – desire. And then he felt ashamed.

Liz stepped from the shower, ran the towel quickly over her body and began drying her hair, tilting her head to the side and rubbing it furiously with the towel. After a few moments, she bent over at the waist and let her long dark almost black hair fall forward. Then she stood upright suddenly, flipping her hair back over her head. Wrapping the towel around herself, she said to the crowd, "Show's over!" And she walked back to her tent.

8

Upper Lake Pizza was a small rustic restaurant. The interior was dark even during the day and it served as the local hangout after school and on weekends for kids who loved to play its many pinball and video games. Its best feature was the fenced patio in the back. The fence itself was overgrown with blackberries and honeysuckle and by early evening, the patio was cool and fragrant. Dinner outside was served on one of several picnic tables.

Jim was playing pinball when Steve, Bill and Liz walked in. Their eyes were still adjusting to the relative darkness after a day in bright sunlight, so they didn't see him at first. They walked over and Liz put her hand on the machine, leaning in to say hello.

"Don't touch the machine!" Jim ordered.

Liz jumped back but her face flushed and she started to get angry. After all, she was just trying to be friendly. Steve put a hand on her shoulder and whispered, "Watch!"

It was impressive. Jim's slight movements of the machine gave him amazing control over the ball. He would catch the ball on a flipper, use that flipper to toss it to another flipper, then accurately flip the ball towards a moving target. Over and over, he'd catch, pass, shoot the target and repeat.

"He just passed the high score and he's only on his first ball!"

They watched for nearly half an hour completely transfixed, until it became clear that Jim was bored. When he finally lost the ball, he asked if anyone else wanted to finish the game. Not wanting to look completely incompetent, they all politely refused. Jim shot the remaining balls and let them drop through the machine ending the game with a new high score.

"Where'd you learn to play like that?" Bill asked.

"In college I managed a pinball arcade. It was pretty slow most weekday evenings, so after I finished studying, I played. I also watched a lot and learned quite a few moves from some real experts. I'm good, but I'm not competition quality.

"Liz, sorry I was so abrupt a while ago. I get in this zone of concentration and just a minor change to the machine will make me blow it. I hate to blow it."

"Ah, no problem," Liz replied, clearly still a little piqued.

They agreed on two pizzas, one veggie, the other meat, and ordered a pitcher of beer and a pitcher of Coke, then made their way to the patio where they took over a table. Two young parents were fussing over their crying baby a few tables away. Liz looked over at them and glared. The parents didn't notice.

"I've got to go to the loo," Liz said in a feigned aristocratic British accent.

The guys sat down.

""Liz caused quite a stir at the campground today," Jim began.

"Yeah, we heard about it," Steve responded. "That's Liz, give her an opportunity to take her clothes off, and she's naked in a second, especially if it's outside. She loves to frolic au naturel in nature."

"I know the pilots liked it, but I heard some grumbling from wives and girlfriends," Jim continued. "Is she always the center of attention?"

"Always!" Bill and Steve said in unison.

Liz stepped out on the patio and said, "Talking about me of course?"

"Why of course!" Steve replied. "What topic could be more interesting?"

"How about the legality of Bush's election?" asked Bill.

"Hey, he was elected fair and square!" replied Steve.

"Are you kidding?" said Liz. "He loses the popular vote and it comes down to Florida, where his brother is governor. There are countless irregularities in the vote count and the voting procedures. People were turned away at the polls, the ballots were confusing, the chads themselves bring the whole thing into question. I know we've been through this before, but you can't really believe that he was elected 'fair and square', can you?"

At that point the baby across the way let out a piercing wail.

"Can't you shut that baby up?" Liz seethed. "We're trying to have a conversation here."

"Wait a second and catch me up a bit here," Jim said in a not-so-subtle attempt to bring Liz's focus back to their table. "What are your backgrounds?"

Liz responded. "Bill owns a construction company in Berkeley along with a couple of other partners. Steve is originally from Chicago and has just finished his PhD in Economics at Berkeley, and I'm about to graduate from Boalt Law School.

"Bill and I have reasonable views, but if you can believe it, Steve is an arch conservative. What about you?"

"I'm Vice President of Engineering for a small software

company that builds database systems. I graduated from UCSB in Computer Science after surfing my way through college, worked for IBM for several years, then joined Macrodata Systems a couple of years ago. My politics tend to be socially liberal and fiscally conservative. But I must admit, I too think Bush was put in power by some significant forces acting behind the scenes. After all, he's an admitted alcoholic. Can you imagine giving an alcoholic the most powerful position in the world? What's the recidivism rate? Is it really worth any risk at all? He could start a nuclear war at a moment's notice. And he just doesn't seem bright enough to be President. I think he's a puppet."

"And who's pulling the strings?" Steve asked. "The Neocons who are supposed to be taking over the world? Skull and Bones? Karl Rove? Come on guys, you're just sore losers. They did a recount in Florida and the Supreme Court upheld the election. Do you really think the Justices are corrupt? Forget the conspiracy theories and let's just get on with business."

"Spoken like a true economist," Liz said, clearly angry. "And what about abortion rights, drilling in Alaska, Global Warming, and his standoff with Saddam Hussein? He's just looking for an excuse to go to war to fatten the pockets of his friends in oil and military equipment businesses. This country is on a major downhill slide and Bush is going to make the U.S. a pariah to the rest of the world. Mark my words!"

The baby's cries filled the patio and several other tables looked over, some distressed and some concerned.

"Kill that goddamned baby!" Liz shouted.

The parents looked at Liz, alarmed. They quickly packed up the baby, grabbed their pizza and drinks and moved inside. Liz smiled.

"Guys, we've been round and round on this for months," Bill said clearly in an attempt to distract Liz, "What about the meet tomorrow? What do you think about that?"

"We have different tasks each of the two days with points for landing accuracy," Jim said. "I like that."

"After seeing you land on top, I would think you would like landing points," Steve responded. "I haven't heard of anything like that in a meet in years. But maybe it makes sense to encourage pilots to take their landings seriously. That landing area has caused some serious damage to equipment and pilots."

"Yeah, and you've already more than run the out and back

course," Bill continued. "Though running it for time might be different. Also, given the conditions today, the endurance flight seems a bit ridiculous. Three hours in the air will be a piece of cake if tomorrow is anything like today, so it may well come down to the landing points!"

"Well, as I said before, this is my first competition and I just want to find out what it's all about and whether it's something I want to do seriously," Jim replied. "Are you guys seriously into Hang Gliding?"

Liz jumped in, the incident with the baby clearly forgotten. "Steve has some good finishes in most of the competitions and has qualified for the Nationals. Bill just comes to the meets to hang out with other pilots and see the latest. I've been flying for a year and love the people in the sport. I also like aerobatics. I've got a Stratus."

"What's a Stratus?" Jim asked.

"It's a bowsprit glider without a cross bar." Steve replied, "It's experimental and hasn't been certified by the Hang Gliders Manufacturer's Association. It lands badly because of all the weight in the front from the bowsprit, and I think it looks like a lawn dart every time Liz puts it down."

"Yeah, but the really good guys are pulling off barrel rolls and full outside loops," Liz countered. "Maybe you'll see me as the top woman finisher at Telluride someday."

Telluride, located in the Colorado Rockies, sponsors an aerobatic competition each year. The best pilots from around the world come to demonstrate their skills and insanity, and are judged based on degrees of difficulty of the maneuvers they attempt. The launch is at over twelve thousand feet, the highest hang gliding launch in North America, possibly the world.

"Liz, won't that new husband of yours object to your flying?" Steve asked. "I wouldn't think his crowd would accept a wife who participates in risky sports. Isn't bridge more their speed?"

Liz gave Steve a dirty look. "First off, he's not my husband. He's my fiancé and we're not married yet. If we do get married, I'm wearing the pants in the family. You've met Mark, he's a pussycat.

"And as far as what his society friends think, Liz Louise Leahy is going to bring new meaning to 'nouveau riche'."

"If we get married?" Steve asked, clearly surprised. "Is there trouble in paradise?"

"Of course not," Liz replied, looking at Jim with what could only be described as lust. "But a girl needs to keep her options open!"

Steve and Bill exchanged knowing glances, barely able to conceal their grins. They'd seen Liz in action before and knew that Jim was her next target. Poor Jim. He appeared oblivious as he happily sipped his beer and wolfed down the last piece of vegetarian pizza.

The next two days went well for the pilots. While many others damaged their gliders on landing and had to drop out of the competition, Bill, Steve, and Jim successfully completed the tasks each day and managed to survive the landing area. As predicted, Jim got a special award for the most landing points. Steve and Jim finished in the top ten pilots and were thus eligible for the U.S. National Competition to be held later that summer.

In spite of some obvious overtures by Liz, Jim expressed no interest, but the four exchanged contact information and promised to stay in touch after their returns to the San Francisco Bay Area.

CHAPTER 2

"During your life you will meet many people.
Each one significant."

- Unknown

1

Counting the forty-five minutes stuck in traffic on Doyle Drive after crossing the Golden Gate Bridge, it took over three and a half hours to get home from Elk Mountain Sunday night. Tens of thousands of people spent their weekends in points north of San Francisco, and from the City and the Peninsula, the Golden Gate Bridge was still the best route. In spite of the lane management, it still made for a huge bottleneck on Friday and Sunday evenings.

Thinking back on the weekend as he finally made it to Pacifica, Jim was pleased with his performance in the competition but a bit wary. He was on his way to the Nationals and didn't quite understand how that had happened. Jim had only been flying for eighteen months and while he knew he had some talent, he also knew he didn't have the skills and experience of the pilots he'd be competing with. For him, the competition was just a test to see how well he was doing in his new sport. It certainly wasn't his lifelong avocation. He was first and foremost a technologist and never intended to become a professional at any sport. Perhaps he was getting in a bit over his head with competition in hang gliding. In fact, he'd never really wanted to get into the sport to begin with.

Eighteen months before, four of his engineers had come into his office and asked him to join them for Hang Gliding lessons at Marina Beach north of Monterey. Jim had initially refused.

"But we get a great discount if we bring five people and Dan just backed out on us. He's going roller skating with his girlfriend in Golden Gate Park. He also says Hang Gliding is too dangerous. The wimp. You have to come. Think of it as bonding with your team. Don't you management guys call that teambuilding?"

The guys were just having a go at him with that last comment. They knew he was an engineer and they respected his technological prowess, but they also loved to get a dig in at his move into upper management.

"Guys, Hang Gliding is the last thing I want to do. I know people think of it as exciting, but for me, the idea of jumping off a high place and gliding downward just isn't interesting. Yeah, yeah, I do what you think of as risk sports. Surfing, whitewater kayaking - they are exciting. But for me it's about harnessing the forces of Mother Nature and finding that perfect harmony. I don't see that in Hang Gliding. It's just a controlled fall and gravity makes us do that every day."

"C'mon Jim," they replied in unison. "You have to help us out here. We'll lose our discount."

Jim reluctantly agreed. On Saturday, he took the long drive down to Marina Beach just north of Monterey. After getting instructions on how to set up and pre-flight a glider, they began to run with the glider on flat sand. The object was to control the glider so that the nose remained level and a wing didn't tip. On the first few tries, everyone dipped a wing and quickly found themselves eating sand as the glider caught a tip in the sand and the glider quickly turned around, smashing into the ground and dragging the helpless pilot with it.

About two hours into the lesson, they were finally ready to run down the sand dune. The instructor made it look very easy, walking, then running, then lifting off the ground and gliding a hundred feet down the sand dune, only two to three feet off the ground, then pushing out hard on the control bar, ending with a perfectly gentle stand up landing. Everyone else struggled, running crashing, and eating sand. Eventually, most all of them were able to get off the ground with the assistance of the instructor on one wing. Very few had graceful landings largely because they wanted to fly as far as possible and didn't flare the glider in time for a controlled landing.

Early in the afternoon, the wind started to pick up. Several people were getting five or six feet off the ground and it was clear the instructor was getting nervous. "Sorry guys, the wind is picking up a bit and a crash with the wind blowing this hard could get you hurt."

Jim was fine with this. While he'd gotten a bit of exercise carrying the glider back up the dune, from Jim's point of view, hang gliding was exactly as he thought: boring. Run down the sand dune, glide a little bit a few feet off the ground, then carry the damn glider back up. This certainly wasn't a sport he was interested in.

The instructor continued, "I'm calling a lunch break. Grab your lunches and rest for a while. The wind usually drops again later in the afternoon, so we can start up again after it does. In the meantime, I'm going to take a quick flight."

With that, he clipped into the glider, ran down the same dune they had all been training on, but near the bottom, he turned the glider to the left and began to rise over a small group of steeper dunes. He turned back, still only ten feet or so over the ground and gained a bit more altitude. Turning south again, he was now thirty or forty feet in the air and he continued flying away from them towards Monterey. Everyone got up and ran down the beach to get a better view. A quarter mile away, the instructor flew low in front of some very large dunes. Over the course of a few minutes, he made passes back and forth in front of the dunes, getting higher and higher with each successive pass. When he finally turned south again, he was at least one hundred and fifty feet above the beach. Fifteen minutes later, he was too far away to see.

Jim and his coworkers grabbed their lunches and stretched out in a somewhat sheltered area of the beach. After finishing his lunch, Jim picked up a novel he'd brought and kicked back in the warm sand. As he started to doze off, one of the guys shouted, "Look, he's back!" They all stood up as the colorful glider returned. The instructor flew out over the ocean and then started turning in circles. With each circle he drifted further over the beach. His last circle was only about twenty feet over the ground and as he completed it, he came to a standing position and landed the glider next to the wide-mouthed students.

"I've got to learn how to do that!" Jim said to the others.

As the instructor predicted, the wind eased later in the afternoon and they each got several more flights. Jim peppered the instructor with questions and the instructor answered them gladly. Two years before he'd been like Jim. He knew the look of the addicted. He invited Jim to join his class the next day and Jim agreed. In fact, Jim returned each day of the next four weekends and then bought a glider of his own.

When the team returned to the office on Monday, everyone wanted to hear the hang gliding stories. That is, everyone except Dan, the team member who had chosen to go roller skating instead. In the course of his much safer outing in Golden Gate Park with his girlfriend, he'd taken a bad fall and had broken his wrist in two places. He was teased ruthlessly for months afterwards.

2

Jim pulled into his driveway, opened the garage door and unloaded his glider and gear. He closed the garage and walked up the stairs to the small deck which looked north over the Linda Mar district of Pacifica. He could easily make out the lights of the Marin coast thirty miles to the north. Jim took a moment to savor the view and the cool marine air, a dramatic change from the dry dust of Elk Mountain. He opened his front door and stepped into his dark, empty house.

He'd lived alone for many years in college and had rented a modest apartment after he graduated and took a job with IBM. He really should be used to living alone and to coming home to an empty house. But it just didn't seem right. Sharon, his wife of fourteen months had moved out four months ago. This was her house too and he'd really only known it with her. It just wasn't right.

He remembered how they first got together. He was sitting alone in his apartment on a rainy night when the phone rang.

"Are you the Jim Henderson that landed his glider in a tree at the Pleasanton Site two weeks ago?"

Jim thought back to the embarrassing episode. He'd taken three flights from the top of the mountain above Pleasanton and had landed comfortably on the football field of the school below. On his fourth flight, he'd decided that he wanted to try to practice his landing skills by imagining that the landing area was quite small. One side of the landing area was bordered by trees and on previous flights, Jim had cleared the trees and glided safely into the landing area. On this disastrous flight, Jim tried to land as if the landing area were only one-third its actual size. He knew he'd have to set up behind the trees and make a final drop just clearing the trees to achieve his goal. Things went as expected as he made altitude-losing passes back and forth behind the rows of trees. He started his final approach and it looked like he was going to land in the targeted space. Unfortunately, he was unprepared for the effect of a small creek that ran through the trees. The chilly water cooled the air and instead of gliding smoothly towards his destination, Jim and his glider sank suddenly in the colder air. As a crash into the top of a tree was imminent, Jim flared the glider and was lucky enough to place both of his feet on a large branch. He landed standing up like a bird. He set the glider down, unclipped, and climbed down to be met by uncontrolled laughter from the crowd of pilots in one of the easiest landing areas anywhere. He didn't even try to explain what he'd been attempting.

Jim took off his gear and then tried to figure out how to get the glider out of the tree. He climbed back up and started disassembling the glider. At one point he slipped and grabbed ahold of the right leading edge to catch himself. It bent awkwardly under his weight. He slid the broken glider out of the tree, put it on his car and drove away more embarrassed than he'd ever been. He learned about the creek and the effect of the cooler air when he dropped off his glider at his instructor's shop. He didn't know that someone had put a picture of his tree landing in the local club's newsletter.

"Yes. That was me."

"I don't know if you remember me but we met a couple of months ago at Waddell Creek on the coast north of Santa Cruz. You were just landing and I came over to talk with you. We talked for a while about how you were able to fly the site with just a Hang 2 rating and how I was hoping to do the same at some point since I was a Hang 2."

Jim remembered the red-haired young woman with the stunning green eyes. She seemed very self-assured and in no way interested in Jim, just in flying. Most hang gliding sites required that pilots have at least an Intermediate rating before they can fly there. The club that managed the site at Waddell permitted pilots with Novice ratings to fly there if their skills were verified by the club and then only as long as a senior club member was present. In Jim's case, he had passed all the tests and far exceeded the required air time, and was now logging as many days as possible to get to the thirty required by the United States Hang Gliding and Paragliding Association. The senior club members saw him as a promising pilot and wanted to help him advance rapidly so they'd stretched their rules to allow him to fly whenever he wanted.

"Ah, yes. I do remember you."

"Well, you mentioned that you worked for a start up in the Silicon Valley and I'm thinking about moving into high tech. I was hoping we could get together and you could give me some ideas about how I could break into the industry.'

"Sure," Jim replied. "When would you like to get together?"

"How about tonight? You live in Pacifica and I live in Moss Beach, so we could meet at the Costanara in Montara."

They agreed to meet in 30 minutes.

Jim hopped in his reliable Subaru and took coastal Highway 1 south over treacherous Devil's Slide in the driving rain. He was glad for the four-wheel drive of the Subaru as he crept around each curve at the edge of the five hundred foot cliffs. Several people died on Devil's Slide every year and Jim was amazed that highway engineers managed to salvage the road, even after the tremendous slides that closed it for days or weeks at a time during California's rainy season. He'd read about plans to bypass the slide with a series of tunnels and bridges, but the multi-year project hadn't even started yet – at least not that he could see.

Jim pulled into a parking space in the large lot overlooking the Pacific. There were only four other cars there on this rainy weeknight. Jim looked admiringly at the new Subaru Outback a few spaces away as he rushed into the restaurant to avoid the pounding rain and wind. Entering, he hung his wet jacket on the coatrack and made his way into the bar. Sharon stood up and smiled as Jim entered. She offered her hand and said warmly, "Thanks for coming on such a nasty night!"

"Actually, it's nice to be here. I was sitting alone in my apartment as I do most evenings and this is a great change. One of these days I'll get used to driving Devil's Slide, but it is a bit challenging in this weather. Thank goodness for my Subaru."

"Oh, you have a Subaru? I just bought one a few weeks ago. I figured that now that I'm getting serious about hang gliding, I'll need the all-wheel drive."

"So, what are you drinking?" Jim asked smiling to himself at the thought of her Subaru outside.

"I'm teaching tomorrow morning early so I'll just stick with club soda."

Jim nodded at the server and she came over to take their order. She looked disappointed at their request for two club sodas and Jim promised himself that he'd tip her well. They were the only patrons in the bar and tonight probably wasn't terribly lucrative for the server.

"This certainly is a beautiful place," Jim began. I'm sure the views would be fantastic in better weather. I've driven by it but have never had a reason to stop."

"I live a couple of miles to the south and only came here for the first time about a month ago. The food is unusual. They call it Peruvian Fusion and it's quite good – a mix of Latin and California flavors. And yes, the view is amazing. We're perched right over Montara Beach with views of the ocean and Devil's slide. It's really pretty spectacular."

"So Sharon, you said something about wanting to break into High Tech?"

"Yes. I've been teaching German at Half Moon Bay High School for the past eight years and although I love teaching, the discipline problems now seem to take up most of my time. I have a few gifted students, but for the most part, the kids are just trying to get through High School so they can get back to their ranches. Most of them are never going to college. There are also issues between the white kids and the Hispanics. Of course very few of the Hispanic kids take German, but it creates a lot of tension in the school.

"I think I'm ready to move on. I'm pretty computer savvy and have taken a few programming and computer operations courses at San Francisco State. I'm really hoping to find an entry level job before school starts next year. How did you get into the industry?"

"Teaching, huh? I've always wanted to teach. I get to do a bit of it giving training sessions to our customers and I taught database programming classes when I was at IBM. I guess High School would be a lot more difficult. At least my students are all motivated to do well.

"As far as my career is concerned, I started working while in school. I graduated from UC Santa Barbara where I majored in surfing and Computer Science. My last year I worked almost full time for a small manufacturing company moving them to a new database system. Somehow I managed to get an interview with IBM and they hired me into a very unique group right after graduation. In addition to me, this division of IBM hired seven others right out of school and they immediately put us on our own projects. That was a far cry from the traditional entry level position where you spend a couple of years testing other people's code then a couple of years coding to other people's designs before you ever get real ownership. The head of this group at IBM took a big chance and it paid off. He made sure that each project had an experienced mentor who could help us if we got stuck and who could make sure that we did things the IBM way.

All of us were really motivated and since none of us were married, we worked our tails off and turned out some really cool products in very short times with quality that amazed the IBM old-timers.

"After nearly three years in development, I got the opportunity to move into the field – that's what IBM developers call the sales offices - where I worked as a system engineer and evangelist for the products I'd developed with the engineering group. I learned a lot about how businesses worked and how they used IBM and others' products to run more efficiently. I also got to see sales close up and although I swore I'd never become a salesman after I graduated from IBM sales school, ultimately when I worked one-on-one helping the real sales guys with the technical side of their proposals and presentations, I discovered that with my strong technical background, customers listened to me and indeed, bought from us because of my credibility.

"After two years in the field, MacroData, one of my customers, asked me if I could join them to manage their software development team and the rest is history. The company is doing very well and we may be looking at going public in a year or so.

"That's pretty much it."

"Yeah, but do you like it?" Sharon asked.

"The truth is that I love it. It's all about solving problems whether it's customer problems or problems in the code or problems getting engineers to work together. I love to solve problems and this job is the most fun I've ever had."

"It sounds too good to be true. I love problem solving too. I'm constantly doing puzzles, playing chess or Scrabble, and I've recently become hooked on a new Japanese puzzle game called Sudoku. It's actually not originally Japanese but a company there made it the craze and now it's starting to spread. I've heard the Times of London is about to offer a daily Sudoku puzzle and that the New York Times is not far behind. You should give it a try."

"A new puzzle game? Sure. I'd love to. But getting back to you breaking into the industry, it might be difficult."

Seeing her face fall, Jim continued in a more encouraging tone, "By difficult, I mean that because you're not the standard Computer Science or Engineering graduate, you're going to have to take a different approach.

"I do the hiring of engineers for MacroData and our standard base requirement is a B.S. in Computer Science or Engineering along with some experience. You're coming at this with no degree and no experience. I've actually recently hired a couple of people who didn't meet our official minimal requirements and I did it largely based on their cover letters where they convinced me to interview them. Once in the interview, they demonstrated that even without the Computer Science degree, they could more than hold their own. You'd need to do something like that. Another thing that occurs to me is that larger companies often provide training. If they see someone bright and motivated, they'll train them to their way of doing things. This often proves more efficient than trying to correct the bad habits of someone with experience. Maybe you can break in by targeting the right companies and ensuring that you have a cover letter that will get you in the door. "

"Jim, this is great. I've been looking at openings in the Silicon Valley. While Cisco and other high tech companies seem to have lots of open requisitions for people, I don't meet the minimum requirements. I have seen that some really huge companies like PacBell are hiring. Anyway, I'll get to work on my resume and cover letter. I'd really like to get your input on it. Could I fix you dinner at my place this weekend? We could go over them together and I can show you Sudoku and maybe challenge you to a game of Scrabble."

And that's how it started. Jim discovered how much they had in common. From their love of games to their socio-economic backgrounds, political views and goals, they just seemed to be in sync. While Sharon came to Jim's apartment from time to time, they preferred Sharon's place in the little town of Moss Beach, a mother-in-law cottage with panoramic views of the rocky beach below, wood paneled walls, and a huge stone fireplace.

One Friday night as Jim was about to leave after another great evening of Scrabble and lively debate, Sharon kissed him passionately and dragged him to her bed. Their lovemaking was the most intense Jim had ever experienced and went on for hours and hours. They lay together afterwards in the dancing light of the fireplace. Jim couldn't have been happier. Clearly Sharon was a perfect fit for him in every aspect of their lives. As he began to doze in the afterglow, Sharon suddenly shook him awake.

"Jim, you have to go! Now!"

"Is something wrong? Can I help?"

"No. Just get out now."

Jim was too stunned to speak. What had he done wrong? Did he say something during their lovemaking or in his sleep? Seeing the anger in Sharon's face and that she clearly wasn't going to talk to him, he quickly gathered his clothes, dressed, and slipped out the door.

The next day, Jim went flying at a little-known site in the Santa Cruz Mountains about an hour from his apartment. He had just landed on the side of the nearly full reservoir after a two hour flight. He was breaking down his glider when he heard Sharon's voice.

"Jim!" she shouted running towards him across the uneven slope.

She stopped just inches away from him smiling and clearly excited to see him.

"Jim, I'm really sorry about last night. I just get confused sometimes. I know it has something to do with my mother, but I can't always control it. We're so good together. I want to be with you. Can you forgive me? Can you help me with this problem? Can we work on it together?"

Jim took her in his arms and was overwhelmed with love for Sharon. She wanted him. She trusted him. She could talk openly about her problems and saw Jim as a partner to help solve them. Of course he could forgive her. And at this moment, Jim knew he wanted to spend the rest of his life with Sharon.

Jim packed up his glider and Sharon helped him lock it onto his Subaru. They hiked to a remote spot with a view all the way to San Francisco across the Silicon Valley and Sharon broke out the picnic lunch she'd brought along with a portable Scrabble game. After beating him mercilessly at Scrabble, she moved into his lap, kissed him with the same intensity as the night before and they made gentle love in the tall grass.

They started looking for a house to buy together and found one just before they were married, only one month later. Jim had met Sharon's parents and found them a bit unusual. Her father was a car salesman, overweight with a ruddy complexion and always ready with a story to tell. At the same time, it was clear that he saw women as inferior and expected them to serve him. In many ways, he was similar to Jim's own father, both products of a time when men ruled and women served.

You could almost feel the resentment and anger seething beneath the overly polite attitude that Sharon's mother projected. There was nothing specific Jim could point to. She didn't make snide remarks. She didn't tease or look hurt, but whatever it was, it was almost palpable. Sharon had begun to talk about her mother and the problems they had. Sharon's mother felt that women had a duty to perform. They were to marry, support their husbands and raise children. Sex was a necessary evil and a woman who enjoyed it was a whore. Women shouldn't work outside the home.

Sharon explained that her extreme reaction after their first lovemaking was due to guilt feelings. That she had enjoyed it so much that she knew she must really be the whore her mother sometimes accused her of being. And it was Jim that made her feel that way so he had to go. As intelligent as she knew she was, Sharon struggled with her guilt feelings and her relationship with her mother. They discussed counseling, but Sharon wanted to see if she could get a handle on this with Jim's support. So they moved forward as a couple thinking they understood the problems that faced them.

Unfortunately, things got worse instead of better. Sharon's mother called multiple times daily and berated her for working, for not having children, and for the unnatural things she was sure her daughter was doing with her new husband. Sharon would get off the phone drowning in tears and if Jim were home, he'd hold her and they'd talk until she calmed down. The rational side of her knew she should just ignore her mother, but emotionally, she wasn't able to get past her feelings.

Their lovemaking fell into a weird pattern. Sometimes Jim would come home from work and Sharon would leap into his arms wrapping her legs around him. They'd make love for hours, exhausting themselves. Afterwards, Sharon would cry uncontrollably and Jim would try to comfort her until they fell asleep. Then weeks would go by where they'd be affectionate, but wouldn't make love. Just about the time it got too frustrating for Jim, the pattern would repeat. Sharon saw the problem but just couldn't deal with it. They finally decided to seek counseling but after seeing three different therapists, Sharon gave up. On their first wedding anniversary, Sharon gave Jim a book titled 'How to do your own Divorce in California'. A few days later she moved out saying that she could never be a good wife to Jim and that she was sorry for having put him through the last year. Sharon initiated the divorce and now it was just a matter of waiting the rest of the six months required by the State of California before their marriage was officially over.

Sharon had also found an entry-level management position with Pacific Bell. They would train her and she could begin climbing the corporate ladder. She'd moved into an apartment in Walnut Creek about thirty miles to the east. They stayed in touch, largely about logistics for the divorce, and their few conversations were civil if not downright friendly, but every time Jim suggested they get back together, Sharon just shut him down and the conversation ended abruptly.

Jim missed Sharon in spite of the problems they'd had.

3

After dropping Bill off, Steve parked in front of Liz's house and helped her carry her bags inside. He dropped them on the bed, went into the kitchen and found an open bottle of white wine in the refrigerator. He returned to Liz's bedroom and handed her a glass.

"Thank you kind sir," Liz said, after taking a sip from the glass. "What did you think of Jim?"

Steve eyed Liz analytically. "You really like this guy, don't you?"

"Well, he's good looking, smart, a talented pilot, and there's something else. I'm not sure why, but I find him really attractive."

"Yeah, but you find a lot of guys attractive. I could list Bill, me, and Mark to name just a few. You're engaged now. You really should think about easing off a little bit. I know you want to 'grab for all the gusto' as some beer commercial once said, but you've got job offers at several good law firms, a fiancé that will get you into the best social circles, and a very bright future if you don't screw it up."

"True, but I have to tell you Steve, the more I think about my future - going to work for a big law firm, marrying into society, giving up the crazy parts of me that I enjoy, the more I think I just want to do something different.

"I went into law to make a difference. I wanted to follow in Daddy's footsteps. He blazed a trail and is looking at me to follow. I've always loved the law but I'm beginning to ask myself if this is what I really want or if I'm not just fulfilling the destiny that Daddy has laid out for me. Not that I don't love him or want to please him, but I'm just not sure I'm ready to take on all that I've been preparing for my whole life. I've never questioned where I was going before. But now, I'm starting to."

"I hear you Liz. When I think about you, me, and Bill, I'm sad to see us all going in different directions. We met what, seven or eight years ago in an Econ 1 class? You and Bill were an item and I was the outsider from the Midwest. You pulled me into your social circle and I loved it. I'd never experienced anything like what you, your family, and friends offered me. I had a great time!

"Now, even with his degree in Philosophy, Bill is running a

construction company; you're graduating from one of the top law schools in the country; and I'm headed off to the University of Chicago to teach. I'm really going to miss the life we've all shared together. I still think of you as my best friend. I'm not sure how that happened, but then again, you broke up with Bill too, and you're still great friends with him.

"Anyway, I can't help thinking that you're feeling nostalgic about the past years and are just apprehensive about moving into the life you've worked so hard to achieve."

"Maybe," Liz replied. "But I think this is different. Part of me feels like a fraud, like I'm about to be found out. Sure, that could be some sort of professional performance anxiety, but something tells me that if I go this route of ninety-nine hour days in a law firm and big social weekends with Mark's family and friends, a major disaster is just waiting to happen. Yeah, I know what you're going to say, but I'll tell you that this is a feeling I just can't shake. I've been having some really weird nightmares about it."

"Well Liz, you've been brilliant in stalling the law firms so you could have a summer off. I know you still haven't set a date for the wedding, so you've stalled Mark too. You're done with school in less than a month, so take the summer. Think it through, but be careful you don't burn any bridges along the way."

Liz knocked Steve onto his back and jumped on top of him. "I love you, you know," she said.

"I love you too Liz. Now get off of me before I try to start something we'll both regret."

4

Standing at her window above the quiet Berkeley street, Liz watched Steve drive away. Why couldn't she have fallen in love with Steve? He was handsome, athletic, brilliant, on his way to being hugely successful and the best lover she'd ever had. Why was she always looking for more? And why had she agreed to settle for Mark Sinclair? He wasn't terribly bright. He wasn't fun to be with. He never got into discussions with her. And the sex had turned mundane after the initial fascination with his huge organ had passed. No. Mundane was too kind. It was downright boring. Mark seemed to expect that just the sight of his organ would satisfy a woman. He didn't make any effort to go out of his way to please her. The money? The connections? It all seemed so pointless and certainly not worthy of Elizabeth Louise Leahy.

Steve was right. She had time to make up her mind. She'd decided to put off the bar exam until February and thanks to Daddy, who knew the principals in most of the firms that had offered her positions, she'd have a summer off. She needed the break after three years of Boalt with more than her share of setbacks and renegotiations along the way. It seemed like she was always playing catch up. Things would be going along smoothly and then she'd do something stupid and would have to recover. She still hadn't changed her partying ways. Even at twenty-five, she often woke up in the morning barely remembering the previous evening's drinking, drugs, and sexual encounters. She had to grow up sometime. One more summer. Then she could settle down and get serious. Or could she?

As Liz put her things away, throwing most of the clothes from the weekend into the hamper, Jim's card fell onto the floor. She picked it up and read:

James Henderson,
Vice President of Engineering

Jim intrigued her. He was well on his way in a career he seemed to love. When she looked at the people around her, she realized that most of her friends were students. Steve was just about to start his job; she was just graduating; and even Bill, who ran a construction company, was just biding his time while he tried to write the Great American Novel. Mark was given his job by his wealthy father and from what she could see, he didn't work terribly hard and certainly wasn't passionate about what he did. None of them was yet fully engaged with what they were going to do with their lives.

Jim was different. From what she'd gathered in their conversations at Elk Mountain, he was pretty much a self-made guy, coming from a relatively poor family, putting himself through school, finding his own job and taking control of his career. Daddy would certainly like him.

Although it was late, since they'd left Elk Mountain about the same time, she was sure Jim was still up. She decided to give him a call.

"This is Jim," he answered after the third ring.

"Hi Jim, this is Liz. We met at Elk Mountain this past weekend."

"How could I forget? " Jim teased.

"Did you have an uneventful drive back?"

"Aside from the traffic on the Golden Gate and Doyle drive, it wasn't too bad. How about you guys?"

"We come back through Napa so we get to avoid all that. Even though it's further, you might consider going that way next time and then popping over the Bay Bridge. I suspect on weekends, you might save some time."

"Sure. I'll give it a try. What can I do for you?"

"Well, my parents are having a big party next Sunday at our house in Orinda. Bill and Steve will be there along with fifty or sixty of our closest friends. It's an informal afternoon thing – just a reason to drink some champagne and sample lots of hors d'oeuvres. Would you like to come?"

"Well, I don't have anything planned other than possibly some flying, but sure. Why not? "

"Okay. I'll email you directions. Dress is nice casual and you can bring a bottle of moderately expensive champagne and something to munch on if you like. I'd like you to meet my parents, especially Daddy. I think you two have a lot in common."

"Well, please don't set the expectations too high. I don't go to a lot of parties and I'm not exactly a big-time social kind of person."

"Don't worry. You'll be surprised at the diversity of the

people at this party. My parents don't hobnob with the elite. Daddy likes anyone who can express himself intelligently no matter what his or her background. I guarantee you'll fit right in."

"Okay. I'll be there."

"We're all looking forward to seeing you again!"

"Me too!"

That was easy. Jim hadn't even put up a fight. He'd just expressed a bit of insecurity. Liz resolved to take care of him.

Liz finished unpacking, washed out the wine glasses, showered and got into bed. Her last thoughts before falling asleep were about taking Jim on as a summer lover. Maybe it could go beyond that.

5

Dawn looked around to make sure no one was following her, then stepped into the dark alley where she had parked her car. The streetlights didn't penetrate here and shadows from the surrounding buildings afforded her privacy and anonymity. Dawn unlocked her car and got in. It was late and she was tired. She opened her purse and counted out five hundred and fifty dollars. Not bad for a Thursday night. This would certainly help pay the bills and maybe provide a bit extra. Dawn was lucky. The johns liked her. She was younger than most of the girls and had managed to avoid drugs. More important, she didn't have a pimp to support.

Most of the other girls took home only a fraction of what they made after their pimps gave them their cut. If the girls wanted drugs, the pimps supplied them and deducted substantially from the take. Their Men encouraged the drugs, mostly heroin, which everyone on the street called chiva. It gave them more control. They'd hold out on drugs until the girls delivered the cash. More cash, more drugs. Most of the Men managed the girls' intake, not just to motivate them, but to make sure that they didn't become full-on junkies too soon. A real junky was not a profitable investment. The better paying johns didn't want a girl with obvious tracks or whose looks had suffered the ravages of long term use and life on the street.

There was a hierarchy. The young, pretty, and vibrant didn't stay that way for long, but they could make a lot of money in a short time. As the work and the street took their toll, they aged rapidly and had to turn more tricks to make much at all. And it just went downhill from there. Most ended up as junkies on the street only able to turn a trick now and then and usually just in exchange for a hit.

Yes, Dawn was lucky. When she'd first started, several of the Men tried to recruit her. They'd started by offering protection. God knows a girl can use the protection. But Dawn had refused. This was only a part time thing for her, a way to pick up some extra cash. But one enterprising Man had sent a nice looking polite john her way with instructions to rough her up a bit. He thought this would motivate Dawn to join his harem, as he liked to call his girls. But Dawn had lucked out. Her sister Jane had followed them and had stopped the john. He was never heard from again. Word on the street spreads fast and soon everyone knew that you just don't mess with Dawn. While her protection stayed in the shadows, no one doubted that Dawn was represented and they backed off, leaving Dawn as one of very few independent girls in the Tenderloin. Anyone who roughed up Dawn suffered the consequences. Yes, Dawn considered herself very, very lucky indeed.

She worried about Jane though. For as long as she could remember, Jane had hated men. Jane was always angry and would often become violent if confronted. The family had proposed counseling but Jane had refused. In fact, Jane refused to talk to anyone in the family. Aside from Dawn, no one had seen Jane for years.

Of course Dawn had refused counseling too. She didn't want some shrink poking around in her psyche. Yes, she had problems. Really, all of her sisters did. Only Betty, the youngest, seemed to have escaped. Jane was violent and crazy, Liz was wild and reckless and as smart as she was, didn't seem to be able to settle down. Dawn herself was a prostitute. Clearly something had happened to them when they were younger that had sent them all off in these aberrant directions, but none of them could really point out anything specific.

Of course they never discussed their childhood or teenage years. That subject was taboo. Even Eve, their British cousin who had come to live with them ten years before, didn't delve into their pasts. At least Eve was married. The rest of them had remained single. Then again, Liz was engaged and Betty was still just a kid, so maybe the odds weren't so bad after all. Still, aside from Betty, none of them was what you would call normal. What event or events had caused them to go off track?

Although she wanted to know, Dawn knew that she didn't have the courage to find out. Her sisters wouldn't talk to her about it and even if she could get over her fear of psychiatric help, she certainly wasn't going to do it alone. Maybe she could handle it herself. If she could just bank a bit more money, maybe she could quit whoring. Yes, that's what she needed to do. She needed to look at her lifestyle in the most graphic terms. Maybe then she could stop making excuses about it, stop justifying it as easy money with no harm done. She could get a regular job, settle down with a partner who loved her and start leading a normal life.

Even with Jane protecting her, the life was risky. There would come a day when Jane couldn't get there in time and she'd get hurt. Or maybe she'd get arrested. That would be horrible for the family. Dawn cringed at the thought. It would be much worse than Liz's arrest for cocaine possession a few years before. Daddy had gotten her off and had the charges dismissed. The event was written off as a college student's experimentation. But prostitution? That would make the papers. The family would be embarrassed. No. She really had to stop.

Didn't someone say that you needed to start by going through the motions and that your new behaviors would become part of you? Yes. She was sure she could do it. She was a strong person and could get her life on track without any help.

Dawn started the car and made her way to the Bay Bridge. As she drove home, she became even more resolved. She had enough saved to live on for several months so tomorrow she'd start looking for another source of income. Maybe she could find a real career, something she'd love to do. The problem was she'd never really thought about doing anything else. It just seemed so easy when she started. But she'd find something. She'd take the summer off, do some serious research on the Web, and get some job applications out there. This life would be over.

6

May Reeves stood up to greet Mike McKensey as he entered the café across from the Marin County Sheriff's Department.

"Thanks for driving all the way up here Mike. You could have just emailed me the reports."

"Well, as much as I love the City, sometimes I just need to take a break. The ride over the Golden Gate Bridge and a quick look at Frank Lloyd Wright's Civic Center seem to make me relax a bit. I feel like I've stepped into a different world."

"Hey, it's Marin. It is a different world. You know the reputation: peacock feathers and hot tubs, right?"

"Maybe in the seventies and eighties, but now it seems like an extension of the Silicon Valley. Plus you've got Lucasfilm. In any case, it's definitely a different atmosphere from the City and I'm glad to get away for a few hours. Plus, I wanted to discuss what we have in person. Maybe we can come up with some thread to chase 'cause I'll tell you, I've got nothing.

A server approached the table and asked if they were ready to order. She looked a bit impatient as the lunch crowd was beginning to fill in.

"Sorry, we haven't even looked," May replied. "Come back in two minutes and we'll be ready."

They quickly reviewed the menu and both decided on the seafood salad with greens, scallops, shrimp, calamari, and sea bass. May flagged down the harried server and they placed their orders.

Mike continued. "Here's the ME's report. As you can see, it looks just like the others. Death from a blade to the heart. This one spent about two days in the water before washing up on Ocean Beach. Other than that, nothing unusual.

"The ME did manage to get prints and we got an ID: Mitchell Blaine Stern from Saint Louis. He was here for the MacWorld conference at Moscone. We can't be sure exactly when he was last seen, though it appears he didn't go back to his hotel after the first day of the conference. We contacted his wife. They're separated. I asked what happened and whether Mitchell was depressed over the split, and she explained that she'd left. She'd put in her time as a wife and mother and now that the kids were grown, she wanted to start a different life. She confirmed that 'Mitch' was upset, but having been married over thirty years, she knew he was strong enough to get over it.

"She sounded upset that Mitch was dead and shocked by the fact that he was murdered, but at the same time, I got the impression she was relieved. I guess she won't have to go through the divorce now."

"You sound pretty cynical and a bit depressed yourself."

"Yeah. Well, it seems like I know a lot of guys, especially on the force, whose wives have left them. It catches them off guard. They're working hard. Maybe they're not spending as much time at home as they should, and with this job, I'm sure they're not always the best of company when they are at home, but they're dedicated to their families. Then wham! The wife has had enough. No counseling. No conversation. It's just over and there's no chance to get it back."

"Talking from personal experience?"

"Unfortunately, I am," Mike replied sheepishly. "My wife left me two years ago and I'm still not really over it. At least I didn't start drinking like some of the guys. If possible, I'm putting even more time into work, and during whatever spare time I have, I work out and run. Right now, I'm training for the Escape from Alcatraz triathlon. I thought that was appropriate for a cop."

Their lunches arrived and they ate in silence for a few minutes before May said, "Yeah. I did it last year. It was the best triathlon I've ever done."

"You've done it? How was it? Although I'm a strong swimmer, I'm a bit worried about that leg," Mike asked, noticing for the first time how fit May was.

"Well, you're not the only one who got dumped. My husband of twenty years left me eighteen months ago and married a woman twenty years younger. I don't get it either. It's not like I let myself go. What could he possibly have in common with a twenty-five year old? Of course it could be the kids issue. His new wife is pregnant. We never had kids. I was ready and willing, but he seemed too driven by his work – he's in high tech – and claimed we didn't have the time with our crazy work styles.

"I've been doing a couple of easy triathlons a year for the last ten years and after he left, I decided to put in the time to train for something more challenging. I'm thinking about doing an Ironman this year.

"As for the swim in the Escape, it's really not that bad. They drop you in the Bay near Alcatraz from the San Francisco Belle.

I'd never heard of this boat before, but it's gorgeous. It's an old sternwheeler, like what I imagine a Mississippi River Boat to be. From what I learned on the ride out, they also have dinner cruises and moonlight cruises. Maybe someday…

"Anyway, the organizers are good with the tide tables so there isn't a lot of water moving. Plus they have lots of chase boats and kayaks. If you get too tired, you can take a break on a kayak and they don't even penalize you. If I were you, I'd worry about the Sand Ladder. It comes after the swim, bike and the turnaround point on the run. It only takes a few minutes, but they're grueling, especially that close to the end of the race."

"Sand Ladder? What's that?"

"You should practice the bike and run portions of the course before the race. The sand ladder is four hundred sandy steps up the cliff from Baker Beach. I admit that I almost quit when I got to the top. Only the fact that I knew it was mostly downhill from there let me finish."

"Good advice, thanks! Sorry to turn the conversation back to a morbid topic, but it occurred to me when you talked about the currents in the Bay and tide tables that these bodies are probably dumped in the Bay and that the perp has some knowledge of the tides. One body was found in the Bay. It was the first one and it had been in the water the least amount of time. Maybe he got smarter after seeing the body recovered so quickly. The others all went out to sea and spent multiple days in the water before washing up. And as we've discussed, we really don't know how many there really were."

"He? There's really nothing that says this is a guy. It could very well be a woman. It's not like it takes a lot of strength to insert a knife between someone's ribs if you know exactly where to do it. Clearly our perp does.

"I know a professor at the Romberg Tiburon Center. They're a part of San Francisco State and I know they do research on the Bay and Ocean currents. Maybe they can help us narrow down where the bodies might have been dumped.

"Something else occurred to me when you described Mitchell Stern. He was separated and alone in the City. He was at Moscone which is a short distance from…"

"The Tenderloin! Of course. Maybe our perp is a hooker or a pimp. I have a friend in Vice. I'll ask him to get some photos out there. We've lost a lot of time, but maybe we'll get lucky and someone will remember one of our victims. At least we finally have a couple of things to pursue. Maybe we can get this case moving yet."

Finishing their salads, Mike asked, "So May, are you planning to do the Escape triathlon this year?"

"I hadn't quite decided. As I mentioned, I want to do an ironman and I do need to do a few warm up races. Why? What were you thinking?"

"Honestly, I was just thinking it would be nice to have someone to train with. I usually work out alone."

"Sure. I'd like that. Why don't we meet on Marina Green this weekend and I'll show you the run and bike parts of the course. Then we can figure out what level of training to pursue."

"Great! West end of Marina Green Saturday morning at eight?"

"Done!"

They split the check, leaving a generous tip and walked to Mike's car.

"I doubt we'll have anything from Vice by Saturday, but I'll update you on anything we have then," Mike began.

He looked at May who over the course of the last hour had transformed from the distant homicide detective he'd met a few times to an interesting woman.

For her part, May, too, suddenly found herself intrigued by Mike and how much they had in common.

"Yeah, I'll give my professor friend at Romberg the locations, dates and times that the bodies were found, but I suspect it'll be a while before he can get back to me."

They shook hands a bit more warmly than they had before and looked at each other objectively as they said goodbye. Each was wary but cautiously hopeful. Mike got in his car and drove back to the City as May crossed the street to her office.

7

Sunday dawned bright and sunny and after twenty minutes of stretching, Jim took off for a run up to the top of Montara Mountain just behind his house. Completing his run a half mile from home, Jim began his walking cool-down realizing that he'd be sore tomorrow. It had been almost two weeks since he'd run and long downhills always left his glutes sore if he hadn't run for a while.

After a quick set of final stretches, Jim went to the kitchen and whipped up a batch of his famous brownies. As a kid, Jim discovered that he loved to bake. For him, this was chemistry in action and he was always transfixed by the transformation of batter into something people couldn't wait to eat. He had developed his brownie recipe over several years starting with one his grandmother gave him, then substituting Baker's Chocolate for cocoa, later adding chunks of chocolate, then working on the texture to make sure that with the overabundance of chocolate, he didn't end up with a gooey mess or a chocolate brick. Now, he was truly proud of his brownies and if he ever went to a pot-luck event, he brought them and usually received rave reviews from the chocoholics present. Of course his brownies were too much for those who weren't true chocophiles, but in spite of his usually egalitarian views, Jim always found people who didn't like chocolate a bit suspect anyway.

Jim jumped in the shower while the brownies baked then dressed in a polo shirt, slacks, and running shoes and made his way to Safeway to find a bottle of champagne.

Jim didn't know anything about champagne. The few times he'd had it, it really didn't taste very good. As he examined Safeway's huge selection, he discovered that prices ranged from about five dollars a bottle to over a hundred and twenty dollars a bottle. What had Liz said? A moderately expensive bottle? What did that mean? If he took the mid-point of prices, he'd be buying a sixty dollar bottle. That seemed like a lot for a bottle of champagne for an outdoor party. In presenting himself to this group of people, he certainly didn't want to come off as cheap with a five dollar bottle and didn't want to appear to be stepping beyond his means with a very expensive one.

Ultimately Jim decided to remove the high end bottle from his calculations (there was only one over a hundred dollars), and to go for a twenty dollar bottle: Mumm's. The name sounded familiar. Hopefully they'd like it.

With light traffic on an early Sunday afternoon, Jim breezed through San Francisco and onto the Bay Bridge. San Francisco Bay was filled with dozens if not hundreds of sail boats, hobie cats and windsurfers. It was a spectacularly picturesque day.

Jim transitioned onto Highway 580 in Oakland then onto Highway 24 which led to the Caldecott Tunnel and Orinda to the east of the hills. He was always a bit nervous about traversing the tunnel. He knew its history. In the eighties, several people had died when a car struck a tanker truck and the tunnel channeled the resulting fire, incinerating everything in its path. It was fortunate that the accident had occurred after midnight. If it had happened during commute hours, hundreds would have died. Since then, they'd prohibited transport of flammable materials in the tunnel, but there had been many accidents with multiple car fires. Jim gripped the wheel a bit tighter as he entered the tunnel and had an uneventful passage.

Exiting the tunnel, Jim immediately noticed the temperature change. As usual, it was at least fifteen degrees warmer on this side of the hills. The fading late spring green hills of the Oakland side had become dry and brown on this side. Jim could appreciate the beauty of the golden California hills, but couldn't quite understand why people chose to live in this part of the East Bay which was very hot in the summer and usually cold and foggy in the winter. And yet, Orinda was considered one of the nicest, most expensive parts of the Bay Area.

Jim turned off Highway 24 and followed his Yahoo Maps directions onto smaller roads, eventually winding his way up a large hill. The homes here were widely spaced. Most were located down long driveways, hidden by lush hedges. The Leahy house was the last house on the road at the very top of the hill.

Jim followed the tree-lined driveway to a circle in front of a spectacular house. It was all glass and wood with unusual angles, more round than rectangular. He'd never seen anything like it before. Jim parked in a grassy area just off the driveway, grabbed the brownies and champagne and made his way towards the house. The top of the hill offered panoramic views of the East Bay hills to the west and the twin peaks of Mount Diablo to the east. He spotted a lake or reservoir to the north and looking further towards the east was able to see tops of cumulus clouds which had formed over the Sierra Nevada Mountains seventy or eighty miles away. He couldn't see another house within several miles.

Ignoring the note on the door inviting visitors to enter, Jim rang the bell. After waiting a few minutes, he decided to follow the directions and cautiously entered. He was stunned by the interior. A wide wooden staircase wound its way upwards and downwards like something out of an old nineteen thirties movie. Beyond the staircase was a huge rounded room with white carpets. The exterior walls were all glass and opened on to a deck that seemed to wrap around the house. About a dozen people in groups of two to four were sipping champagne inside while at least double that number were outside.

Jim walked past the staircase and discovered the kitchen with a large bar and side table to the right. He unwrapped his plate of brownies and put them on the side table, then looked around trying to figure out what to do with the champagne. There were several open bottles on the bar so he moved in that direction but was reluctant to just leave the bottle which had warmed quite a bit on the drive over. Seeing his confusion a small compact middle-aged woman approached him.

"Hi, I'm Janice Leahy. Let me take that from you. I'll put it in the fridge so it can stay cold. Oh, Mumm's – a nice choice. Thank you! And you are?"

"I'm Jim Henderson. Liz asked me to come," Jim stammered.

"Oh yes, Jim. Liz mentioned you. Welcome! Liz and most of her friends are out on the deck. What would you like to drink? As you can see, we have wine, soda, sparkling water, and of course, the ever-present champagne."

"A sparkling water would be nice. Thanks!"

Janice returned to the refrigerator and took out a bottle of San Pellegrino, then poured Jim a glass.

She took his arm and, leading him outside said, "I hear you're a hang glider. Whoops! Sorry. Liz has corrected me on that. You're a hang glider pilot."

"Yes. I took it up a while ago and really like it. It's not like anything else I've done. "

"Well it certainly looks dangerous to me! I know, Liz has told me that with the latest equipment and training, it's safer than General Aviation, but I can't bring myself to try it even though Liz has been arguing that I should take a lesson. She keeps quoting Da Vinci: 'For once you have tasted flight you will walk the earth with your eyes turned skywards, for there you have been and there you will long to return.' but I still can't quite bring myself to do it."

"Well, I can tell you from experience that Da Vinci was right. My eyes are often turned skywards and I do long to return there. I agree with Liz, even if you don't get hooked, just the experience of leaving the ground under your own power, even if you're just a few feet from the sand, is a life changing event. Think of flying dreams. The feelings you have dreaming don't even come close to the reality because the experience of really flying isn't fleeting. It sticks with you."

Seeing Janice smiling broadly, Jim apologized, "Oh, I'm sorry. I don't mean to get carried away."

"Don't worry. I must admit that I'm a bit intrigued. But my life is so busy. I really don't have time for something new. It's clear that you and Liz have a real passion for it as do Bill and Steve," she responded as the two young men turned around to greet them.

"Speak of the devil," Steve began. "Janice, thanks for bringing Jim. We were just talking about his top landing at Elk Mountain. If you saw Jim fly, I'm sure you'd be convinced to give it a try."

"You guys never stop," she said teasingly. "Have fun. Jim, I'm really glad to meet you. I hope we can have a non-hang gliding discussion later. And of course, you have to meet my husband Mickey. I'm sure he'll be making the rounds."

Janice left and went back inside to make her own rounds. She seemed the perfect hostess, stopping to talk to everyone she passed, reminding them of food and drink inside, and clearly in her element.

"This is quite a place," Jim began.

"It certainly is," Bill replied. "They've had this house for more than ten years. Back then there were no neighbors at all and as you looked out there towards Mount Diablo, you hardly saw any houses.

"Mickey certainly has vision. He had the house designed by an architect he's known since college and it was built by contractors who he's either represented in court or worked with in college. He worked his way through college and law school doing construction work. For all intents and purposes, he got the house built at cost. It's worth millions now."

"Yeah, and wait until Liz gives you the tour," Steve chimed in. It's one of the most impressive homes I've ever seen with interesting angles, lots of glass, and as you've seen, incredible views."

"So where is Liz?" Jim asked.

"Oh, don't worry. I'm sure she'll make a grand entrance very soon," Steve replied.

"So how do you guys know Liz?" Jim asked.

"I met her at UC Berkeley, Steve responded. "As a Teaching Assistant, I was running the lab portions of a basic Econ class, and met Liz there. I must admit that I, too am one of Liz's exes. We were together for about a year until she and Mark got engaged. "

"Well, I've known her since Elementary School," Bill followed. "My Dad's an attorney and used to work with Mickey in the DA's office. We were an item for a year in High School, and then another in college, but we both moved on. Oh! Here's another member of the Liz Ex Club. Bob, come over here and meet Jim."

A very muscular young man with short cropped blond hair approached and held out his hand. "Hey Jim, I'm Bob Builder, Bill's partner."

Seeing Jim's look of surprise, Bob continued, "Yeah, I know. You're thinking of Bob the Builder and yes, I'm in construction. It may be seem a bit funny, but it works well for business. People know the TV show and all the toys and games, and when they see Bill and Bob the Builders – our company name – they subconsciously associate us with the capable and knowledgeable Bob the Builder. Business is good and so far we haven't had any cease and desist orders because of the name. If we ever do, Mickey says he'll defend us and that we'll win."

"So how big is your company?" Jim asked.

"Including Bill and me we have four full time licensed contractors plus a full time admin person. Mickey has helped us with the legal side."

"At any given time we have between four and fifteen active jobs and we're looking to do about six million in sales this year, up from three last year. Of course we hire subcontractors for all the jobs so we can keep our overhead quite low. If there's lots of work we prosper. If there isn't, there are only the five of us to pay and Bill and I will forego salaries as necessary."

Looking at Bill, Bob continued. "Sorry. I love what we do and I must admit that I'm pretty proud of what we've been able to build, so to speak."

"And you're one of Liz's exes?"

"Yeah. I have the honor of being the founding member of the Liz Ex Club. Liz and I were together through Middle School and most of High School until she dumped me for this clown," Bob replied, punching Bill in the arm and knocking him sideways a few feet.

"Hey! Take it easy. You don't know your own strength!"

"Of course I do. That was a love tap."

"Some love tap. I hope you don't do that to your wife. Where is she anyway?"

"She's down in the playground with the kids."

Pointing at the swing set, slide, teeter totter, jungle gym, and sandboxes at the edge of a large lawn, Bob said, "Jim, that overly fit blond is Sharon and the two girls driving her nuts are my daughters Lynn and Stephanie."

"She certainly does look fit as do you. What to you guys do to stay in such great shape?" Jim asked.

"We met in college on the gymnastics team at Stanford. We're both gymnasts. Sharon made the Olympic Team but got injured right before the Games and had to drop out. I didn't quite qualify. However, we both have stayed active in it and in what little spare time we have, we work as coaches for local schools which can't afford their own gymnastics programs.

"I consider myself very lucky to be with Sharon. We're really a perfect fit in every way."

Jim thought back to his own Sharon. Somehow the fact that Bob's wife had the same name and that Bob's marriage appeared to be a happy one, made Jim reflect on how perfect his Sharon had been for him. He missed her.

"Are you married, Jim? Bob asked.

"Yes, are you married, Jim?" Liz asked teasingly as she approached them from behind.

Liz was wearing a bright yellow dress with a loose V-neck, full skirt, and short rolled sleeves. She spun around quickly and the skirt flared.

"Like it?" she asked flirtingly.

Liz hugged Bob, Bill, Steve, and then approached Jim and

said, "Why not?" and gave him a big hug which she held a bit longer than she had with the others. Jim could feel the heat from her body.

"You look fantastic," Steve replied to nods from everyone else once Liz released Jim.

"Why thank you kind sirs!" Liz responded. "So Jim, do answer the question. Are you married?"

"Actually, yes I am." Seeing the surprised look on Liz's face and the amused glances shared by Bob, Bill, and Steve, Jim continued. "But unfortunately, we're separated and just waiting on the final paperwork for the divorce. It's a sad story and really not fitting for this occasion. Let's move on, okay?"

"Speaking of marriage," Steve began, "Where's Mark?"

Liz glared at Steve and if looks could kill as they say...

"Once he and his parents received our invitation, his parents decided to host their own little party. Of course it's catered, not pot luck like ours. And none of us were invited though Mark did ask me to come as his 'date'. I refused."

Turning to Jim, Liz continued. "Mark's parents don't like mine. Ever since Daddy defended Jason Livingston in that intellectual property case, our family has not been welcome at the Sinclair Estate."

"Are you talking about THE Jason Livingston who was sued by MegaTrust after he started a business selling software that he had previously developed under contract for MegaTrust? That's a famous case that has set the standard for Intellectual Property law in the Silicon Valley. It changed everything. Who would have thought that without specific language in the contract prohibiting it, a developer owns what he or she creates even if someone else pays them to create it. Your father won that case?"

"He sure did and as you've probably figured out, Mark's father, Jonathan Sinclair, is the CEO of MegaTrust. Hence the bad blood. But realistically, independent of that case which really pissed them off, the Sinclair's have never appreciated our family. They think my father comes from the wrong side of the tracks, son of an Irish immigrant from a seedy part of San Francisco; they don't really like the Irish or Italians, let alone Sicilians like my mother's family; and they don't like the kinds of people my father tends to associate with. Ultimately, they don't consider me worthy of their son either. Quite frankly, with this latest snub, I'm really reconsidering the whole engagement thing."

Bob, Bill, and Steve nodded at each other conspiratorially.

"What are you guys grinning at?" Liz asked, somewhat irritated.

"Who us?"

Liz glared.

"Well, I'm not sure we want to welcome Mark Sinclair into the Liz's Ex Club," Bill stated flatly without a hint of humor in his voice. "I don't think he'd fit in,"

"Yeah, well, I guess not all of my exes have to like each other, though I'm sure Mark and I will remain friends. He may not be terribly clever, but he is a really nice guy. And you never know. The world is getting smaller every day. You shouldn't burn bridges. Mark may be someone we need to turn to someday."

The afternoon continued on a lighter note. People laughed and told stories, drank champagne, and ate hors d'oeuvres. Jim's brownies were a hit, with several people asking for the recipe which Jim refused to divulge. Liz flitted about exuding charm and chatting with people, very much the image of her mother who was doing the same thing. Liz would regularly come back to Jim, take his arm and lead him to a small group where she'd make introductions.

Jim couldn't help feeling like she was showing him off. He was impressed by the diversity of the crowd and the level of discourse taking place throughout the party. At one point, Steve had pointed out Mickey, but since he was engaged in a lively conversation, they decided not to interrupt.

As evening approached, the crowd began to dwindle. Jim thought that he should probably be making his way home. He approached Janice to offer his thanks for the invitation and to tell her that he'd had a great time, but Janice cut him off.

"Didn't Liz invite you to stay to dinner? You must stay. This crowd will soon be gone and Mickey will get the barbeque going. I know he really wants to meet you and this will be a good chance to talk to him outside of the superficially social environment. Please stay."

Jim agreed. He stepped outside where he found Steve alone on at the far end of the deck looking out at Mount Diablo.

"I love flying that mountain," Steve said.

"I just got my advanced rating and haven't flown it yet," Jim replied. "What's it like?"

"There are three launches. They're all from the top of the

mountain which is over thirty-eight hundred feet. It's usually above the marine layer so you don't see much of the ocean influence until you get closer to the landing areas. That means good thermals. The best days are in the spring. You've heard that Chris Arai flew over one hundred thirty miles from there, right? So far, I've done a few twenty mile out-and-backs, but haven't had the chase car to turn south and go for it. I think Chris got very lucky that day. Of course, he's one hell of a pilot.

"Anyway, it's a solid hang 4 site. The main launch is basically a cliff launch and is challenging when there's no wind. The landing areas are easy – they're huge, but they're all a long way from the launches, so you have to judge the conditions well or you won't make it to a designated landing area. Some of the ranchers aren't too happy about 'out' landings and neither is the park service.

"If we get a late season cold front through, we might still get a good day. Can you get off work if it happens mid-week?"

"Sure. I stay on top of the weather so I'll keep my eye out and I'll take my glider to work if it looks like there's any chance it'll be good."

They heard footsteps on the deck and turned to see Liz approaching.

"You guys are staying for dinner, right? Daddy's firing up the barbeque and most of the other guests have left."

Steve nodded and Jim responded, "Well I probably should be going since tomorrow is a work day and I have a long drive home, but I did promise your mother that I'd stay, so yes, I'll stick around for a bit."

"Great!" Liz replied enthusiastically. "Steve, why don't you join Daddy while I give Jim a tour of the house? We'll be there shortly."

Taking Jim by the arm, Liz led him into the house.

"Daddy worked with an architect friend to design the house. It's basically a three-story octagon. He had always liked dome homes but found the interiors impractical for most furniture. The octagon gives the sense of roundness without the constraints of round walls."

They proceeded up the wide curved staircase that Jim had seen when he entered the house. Reaching the top, Jim was overwhelmed by the views which were even more spectacular than those from the floor below. The sides of the rooms were composed of huge panes of glass separated by narrow columns of white walls decorated with vivid artwork. The room, if it could be called that, provided a two hundred and seventy degree panoramic view looking south, west, and north at the East Bay hills. One third of the open space was set up as a semi-formal living room, one third was a game room complete with pool table, and the last portion was a classic bar with dark polished woods, swiveling leather barstools, and lighted mirrored shelves packed with colorful bottles of liquors and glasses. After a quick walk around the room, Liz led Jim through the only doorway into her parent's master bedroom suite. Thick oriental rugs sat on top of a low-pile sand-colored wall to wall carpet. The head of the bed was against the only non-glass wall providing expansive views of Mount Diablo from the bed. French doors opened onto a narrow curved deck. From the side of the bed, it almost felt like the room was suspended in the air and in spite of his experience hang gliding, he felt a touch of vertigo and leaned into Liz.

"Sorry! I actually am a bit afraid of heights. It doesn't bother me in a hang glider where I have control, but to be suspended in air in a new place makes me a little nervous. I do get used to it though."

"No problem," Liz replied holding Jim a little tighter, touched by his confession.

"Let me show you my room downstairs. It's not quite as vertiginous."

Heading down the stairs, Liz continued. "You've seen most of the main floor. We do have a laundry room, powder room for guests, and a guest bedroom with its own bath. It's not terribly interesting and one of Daddy's friends is staying with us for a while, so I don't think we should invade his space.

"However, the bottom floor is the kids' domain. My parents felt strongly that kids should have their own space separated from their parents and from the main part of the house. This has worked well for me as I can escape parties if I want, give my parents privacy when they have their intimate times, and do my own entertaining down here out of view of my parents.

"There are four bedrooms, each with its own bath, and great views."

Jim glanced briefly into the first three and couldn't help but be impressed. All but one were decorated in feminine styles and although the views were more limited, all were spectacular.

"And here's my room. I don't spend much time at home anymore, and except when Daddy's friends stay with us from time to time, the rooms stay pretty much empty. I'm beginning to think the house is too big for just my parents and Daddy's occasional friends. But at the same time, I'm terrified that they'll sell it. I love this house."

Like her parent's room, Liz's bedroom looked out at Mount Diablo. The room appeared to encompass three sides of the octagon. An arched entrance on the right led to what Jim assumed was the bathroom. While he certainly wasn't beginning to take these overwhelmingly beautiful views for granted, Jim was struck by the contents of the room itself. Liz's canopied bed was covered in stuffed animals. Some looked quite old and frayed. A few dolls looked quite comfortable on a small table next to a delicate art-deco styled lamp. The artwork was romantic. Jim recognized two Monet prints. This certainly showed a different side of Liz. She came across as a strong, opinionated woman, but her room was something out of a little girl's storybook.

"You have to see my bathroom," Liz called.

Jim stepped into a large room with a claw foot tub, toilet, and bidet. It looked quite elegant, like something he'd seen in films of luxury hotels.

"Come see the shower!" Liz ordered.

Jim stepped past the thin wall separating the tub from the shower and gasped. The shower was itself an octagon cantilevered out beyond the side of the house and all of the walls were floor to ceiling glass.

"Oh! I forgot about the vertigo. Sorry! This must be pretty bad for you. When I shower here, I feel like I'm standing at the top of a mountain with rain pounding down on me. I love it."

Stepping back and recovering quickly, Jim couldn't help thinking about the other shower, the one outdoors at Elk Mountain with the white foam slithering down Liz's naked body. He flushed and was glad that he'd worn loose fitting trousers. But Liz wasn't fooled.

"Thinking of me naked in the shower?" she teased.

"Ah, ah," Jim stammered.

"It's okay. I like the idea of you thinking of me naked in the shower. Come on. Let's go meet Daddy. I'm sure he'll get you thinking about other things."

Jim wasn't so sure.

By the time they stepped out onto the deck, Jim was relieved that his ardor for Liz had cooled. At least the external manifestations of it were gone. There was something very attractive about her though and it wasn't just physical.

Liz led him around a corner of the house where the deck was much larger, probably twenty by twenty feet. It was built over some low scrub brush and like several other places in the house, had a great view of Mount Diablo. Mickey was holding court at the barbecue and five of his admirers were laughing heartily at something he'd said.

Seeing Liz and Jim approach, Mickey grew quite serious. Focusing his steely blue eyes on Jim, he challenged, "I certainly hope you've behaved yourself with my daughter down there young man."

Jim couldn't tell if he were serious or just having a go at him. Quickly scanning the group, he decided to bet on the latter. "Actually, I did everything I could to keep her off of me, but you know your daughter. She gave me no chance to escape and ultimately I did succumb to her charms."

Liz elbowed him in the ribs as everyone laughed hysterically.

"At your age with a fireball like my daughter, I couldn't have resisted either," Mickey replied smiling broadly and grasping Jim's hand in his bear-like grip. "I've heard a lot about you Jim. Welcome!"

"I've heard quite a bit about you, too. But it wasn't until today that I found out that you won the Livingston-MegaTrust case. It's made a huge difference in our industry."

"Yes, that was a good one. I really believe in what you guys do. You're changing the world in major ways and you need to be protected. I should note however that I've been on the other side too. I had a case about a year ago where a local Savings and Loan had hired a contractor to develop some special loan processing software. In the contract, they made a deal that the contractor could sell the software elsewhere but would pay the Savings and Loan twenty percent of his receipts. It was also understood that over time, the contractor's version of the software would evolve, so they agreed that once eighty percent of the software had been changed, royalties would no longer be due. The contractor paid royalties for the first two months, then stopped, claiming he had changed more than eighty percent of the code. He sent a copy of a report by an independent consultant that demonstrated that of all the lines of code in the product, more than eighty percent had been changed.

"Of course the S&L was suspicious. We brought in our own expert who ultimately determined that the contractor had –

"Done a global replace of variable names in the code," Jim interrupted.

Mickey grinned. "Exactly right! We should have hired you. It took our expert over a month to figure out what had happened to the code.

"Anyway, our judge wasn't the most technical, but I gave him an analogy of taking a piece of great literature and changing the names of the characters, but nothing in the story. He understood the argument and we won."

Mickey turned back to the barbecue, pushing several pieces of chicken away from the hot coals. He cut into a steak and moved four salmon filets and a pile of asparagus spears into the area vacated by the chicken.

"Okay everyone, grab your plates. The steaks are currently medium rare and cooking fast. The chicken is done and the fish and asparagus will be ready by time you load up with potato salad, green salad, and garlic bread. Meat eaters, start here. Fish lovers, start with the salads."

Jim watched as the five others grabbed plates and did as Mickey had suggested. It seemed quite orderly.

"Come on," said Liz, again taking Jim's arm and moving him towards the large round table which was covered in a forest green table cloth and had a lazy Susan in the middle with three open bottles of red wine, three open bottles of white wine in ice buckets, and two large pitchers of ice water. Each place setting had multiple glasses, gold napkins, and what appeared to be real silver cutlery.

Liz handed Jim a dinner plate, leaving the salad/bread plate on the table as the others had. She picked up two other plates and they made their way to the long table adjacent to the barbecue to 'load up' on salads and bread. Liz filled two plates. As they made their way to the barbecue, they passed Bill, Steve, Bob, and a frail-looking young man with stringy blond hair. All had filled their plates with steak and chicken. Liz handed one of her plates to her father who set it aside. He reached for Jim's plate and added a salmon filet and several spears of asparagus. "Want some chicken too?" he asked.

"No thanks, after the appetizers earlier, I'm sure this will be plenty."

Mickey filled Liz's plate, then his own and the three made their way back to the table. Liz directed Jim to a place between Steve and Bill, then walked to the other side of the table where she sat next to her father.

"I'm sitting across from you so I can gaze into your gorgeous blue eyes," Liz teased.

Jim could feel himself blushing again.

The lazy Susan turned and everyone filled their water glasses and poured their wine of choice. Jim selected a Mount Eden Chardonnay.

Mickey stood up and raised his glass.

"On this momentous occasion, I want to propose a toast to my lovely daughter who has just confided in me that she will be breaking off her engagement to Mark Sinclair. He's a nice enough guy but clearly not up to the standards of this family –"

"Daddy, that was told in confidence," Liz scolded.

"Yes, but we're surrounded by family and friends and I'm sure everyone would have found out very soon. So, I'll amend my toast. I'm quite proud of my daughter's decision so I toast Liz, family, and friends."

"To Liz, family, and friends!" they all chimed, each touching all the others' glasses with their own.

"Thirty-six," said the stringy blond-haired young man..

"Thirty-six what?" Steve asked.

"Thirty-six clinks: n times n plus1 over 2. Eight people makes thirty-six clinks," said Jim.

"Ah, a fellow mathematician," said the blond-haired young man. "I'm Marcus Johansen."

"Jim Henderson," Jim replied, shaking Marcus' hand. "How do you fit into this group?"

"Well, it's a bit of a long story," Marcus began. Seeing Mickey nod, Marcus continued. "I was working as a software developer in Billerica, that's in Massachusetts, off Route 128. I got a job offer from eSuperMarket, a dot-com startup based in San Francisco. They offered me fifty percent more than I was making and a small apartment in the building they'd acquired near China Basin. I convinced my girlfriend to quit her job and to move to San Francisco with me. This was in late 2000. The NASDAQ had peaked earlier in the year, but most of us didn't realize we were in the middle of a bursting bubble. Our company scraped by for the next few years. We almost got acquired several times, but in each case, the acquirer backed out. Our VCs quit giving us money, and revenue from our few clients really didn't come close to paying the bills.

"I managed to survive three rounds of layoffs, but the fourth one got me. This was in early 2004. They gave me a month's severance and said I could stay in the apartment for three months. I was sure this would be plenty of time to find a job in the Silicon Valley, but after sending out hundreds of resumes and not getting any interviews, I got pretty discouraged.

"My girlfriend decided to move back east. She missed her family and friends, and I think she was very disappointed in me. Since my parents had died three years before we moved out here, I really didn't have anything to return to and I didn't want to spend the last of my savings on airfare. I like California and love San Francisco. I'm a good software engineer and I know I can make it out here if I can just find a job.

"eSuperMarket" went under shortly after I was laid off. I was a bit lucky, because they didn't evict me from the apartment until they locked up the building at the end of the year. In the meantime, I looked for a job, any job, just to make enough to feed myself and pay for a cheap apartment. No luck at all. So, I lived on the streets for five months. I panhandled and made enough to at least feed myself some of the time. The shelters in San Francisco helped out and I worked there for as long as they let me in exchange for food and a bed. But they have limits on the time you can stay. About two months ago, I made a sign saying 'Will develop software for food'. I panhandled around BART stations, constantly moving since I was competing with the professional panhandlers. That's another story for another time. Anyway, one day, Mickey came up to me in his three piece suit, talked to me for a few minutes and then offered to buy me breakfast.

"We talked and I guess he felt I had some potential. He put me to work in his office designing software to help manage the law firm's documents and he's given me a room here until I get on my feet. We put together an agreement where I can resell the software to other law firms and I get to keep eighty percent. Mickey has made some introductions, and it looks like I may have my first sale in the next few weeks. If I do, I can afford to put down a deposit on my own place. I owe him a lot."

"I think we both got lucky this time," Mickey said. Then looking at Jim, he continued, "Don't think I'm a saint or infallible-"

"That's for sure," Liz and Janice said almost simultaneously.

"Ahem," Mickey corrected with false gravitas. "We've been very fortunate. Many others haven't. If we can do a little to help out, we should. Of course we have our failures too. One time I made the mistake of bringing home a closet alcoholic and another time we found out our guest was a coke-head. He was a brilliant guy, but as soon as he made any money, he dove back into cocaine. Most of the rest have worked out though. It makes me feel like I'm giving something back. Sometimes working with the law is less than rewarding. You win a case even when it's wrong. As much as I truly believe in the adversary system, sometimes I think it goes too far. We really should be looking for the truth more often."

"You mean like in the owl case?" Bill asked.

"Oh no, not the owl case again," Liz complained.

"What's the owl case?" Jim asked to the dismay of the others.

Seeing his opportunity, Mickey continued. "Well, a few years ago, a man drove off the road into a ravine. His car hit a tree and was pretty much totaled. He called AAA and they promised to get there as soon as possible, but that it would be nearly an hour. They asked if he was hurt and he replied that he didn't think so, but that his car was completely undriveable. Being cautious and concerned about possible injuries, AAA called the Highway Patrol to see if they could get someone on scene sooner, just to be safe. Thirty minutes later a cruiser arrived. The CHP officer asked the man what had happened and he replied that an owl had flown in front of his car, that he had swerved to avoid it, lost control of the car and crashed into a tree in the ravine, but that he was unhurt. AAA was on its way so there was no reason for the officer to waste his time on the scene. Certainly there were more important things for him to do.

"Sensing a bit of slurring in his speech, the CHP officer asked him if he'd been drinking. They man acted insulted and claimed that he hadn't. The officer asked for his license and registration and called it in. He found out that the guy had a DUI a few years before. He then had him perform the standard walk the line, touch your nose types of tests which the guy passed marginally.

The officer then asked the guy to take a Breathalyzer test, but the guy refused, saying he wanted a blood test.

"About then, AAA arrived and they waited until the car was pulled from the ravine and hooked up to the tow truck. The CHP officer drove him to their offices where blood was drawn.

"The blood test came back as point oh-seven, just under the limit. To most of us, it's obvious that he was well over the limit when he crashed his car sometime before, but since he was legal at the time of the test, they let him go. You'd think that would be the end of the story, but no. In our litigious society, people are always looking for a scam. Our intrepid driver decided to file suit against the county claiming damages to his car, back injuries which suddenly appeared, and loss of time for the diversion to the police station. He claimed the owl had caused the accident and the county had to pay.

"The counsel for the county asked me to assist, and after hearing the complaint, I filed a cross-complaint against the owl. Ultimately the court ruled against the owl and ordered the owl to pay damages to the plaintiff, which obviously never happened, so the county was spared.

"To put a nice ending on the story, I can tell you that although he wasn't specifically targeted, the story made the rounds of the local police and the CHP, and within a month, our hero was arrested on a DUI. Since this was his second offence, he served ninety-six hours of jail time, had his license suspended, and had to attend an eighteen month long DUI reeducation program. Sometimes it takes a while, but I like to think that ultimately the bad guys get caught."

Janice, who had stepped away during the story returned with a tray and served strawberry shortcake to Jim, Bill, Bob, and Steve, then brought four more plates for the rest of them. "Coffee or Brandy?" she asked.

She took their orders and returned with steaming cups of coffee and a few glasses of Brandy.

"So Jim, have you got some stories about your work?" Mickey asked.

"Yeah, I do. However, most of them are quite sad. In my short career, I've seen a lot of good people lose jobs, I've seen brilliant ideas stolen, and even worse, I've seen big companies quash world-changing technologies just to preserve their markets. Maybe someday I'll write a book about the Silicon Valley. But this really isn't the time. How about something lighter?"

"What did you have in mind?"

"How about a Shaggy Dog story – I know quite a few. I do need to work tomorrow, so we probably only have time for one, but I'd be happy to tell it over dessert."

"What's a Shaggy Dog Story?" Liz asked to the inquisitive looks of the others.

"Oh, you've probably seen at least one on television. A few years back one of the telephone companies did an animated version of one of my favorites as an ad. Does this ring a bell?"

Everyone shook their heads.

"In that case, I'll tell that one. Just so you know, Shaggy Dog stories are supposed to be quite long with lots of irrelevant incidences along the way. You're supposed to invent all sorts of misdirections, deviations, and drag it out as long as possible. Since I really do have to get home tonight, I'll give you a short version but you'll get the idea.

"Once upon a time in a land far, far away, in a lush green region at the foot of a spectacular mountain range with snow-capped peaks and – you get the idea – there was a kingdom ruled by a benevolent monarch. The kingdom prospered because of the rich lands surrounding it which provided sustenance for all of the local residents and for many of the neighboring kingdoms as well. The people were happy and lived in peace and tranquility. They lacked nothing and had rich lives – again, I could go on and on. One day a giant yellow dragon appeared. It had scaly wings, red eyes and huge forearms with long yellow fingers and sharp claws. The first thing he did was to attack the farmers. He caught them unaware. They'd be working in their farms when all of a sudden the dragon would appear. He'd chase the farmers down – there was no contest really – he just scooped them up in his giant yellow fingers and popped them into his mouth, crunching on them like pieces of popcorn. Again, I could go on...

"Those farmers who survived the attacks sought refuge in the castle as did the people of the surrounding villages. Many were lost on the way as the dragon scooped them up in his giant yellow fingers and they, too, became so much finger food."

The entire table groaned at the pun, but was rapt and encouraged Jim to continue.

"The King asked his most trusted knight to slay the dragon.

The brave knight exited the castle to do battle but the combat was lost before it started. The knight threw his lance which just bounced off the impenetrable skin of the dragon, then drew his sword. If dragons could laugh, this one almost did. He smiled greedily as he scooped the poor flailing knight up in his yellow fingers and crunched on him and his armor like an M&M.

"Sadly, the scene was repeated with all of the king's knights. As food supplies began to run low, even the squires tried to do battle with the dragon, but they, too were scooped up in the yellow fingers and devoured whole. "What's a squire?" Liz asked.

"It's a knight's assistant, who trains to become a knight," Bob replied. "Jim, please continue."

"The kingdom suffered. Several people tried to escape, hoping for refuge elsewhere, but there was no escape from the dreaded yellow fingers. As starvation began to set in a young page approached the king and said, 'Your majesty, let me go. I'm small and very, very fast. I can't slay the dragon but I think I can escape and get past him. If I can get to the sheriff, he can bring an army to slay the dragon.' The king looked at the young page and said, 'I can't let you do that. We've already lost too many of our best and most promising young people. You will one day grow up to be a brave knight.'

"Weeks passed and the kingdom was in dire straits. People were dying from starvation. Once again the page approached the king and in desperation, the king reluctantly agreed. He and most of his remaining subjects gathered on the parapets to watch the brave page make his attempt. The gates were opened and the little page ran like the wind. Sadly, he was no match for the larger, faster dragon who nonchalantly reached down with his giant yellow fingers and snatched up the little page. Those watching gasped in disappointment and began to resign themselves to their awful fate. The king buried his face in his hands. Not only had he failed again, he'd just sacrificed a brave young boy to this evil monster."

Jim paused.

"This is the Shaggy Dog Story?" Liz asked angrily. "I don't like it. It's horrible."

"He's not done yet," Mickey said smiling. "Let him finish."

"Okay. All of a sudden someone in the crowd shouted 'Look!' The king looked up and sure enough, the little page had slipped through the yellow fingers and this time was just walking onward. But the dragon didn't give up easily. He chased the little page and once again, scooped him up in his yellow fingers preparing to munch on this tender snack. But the little page slipped through his fingers again. I could go on and on with this, but I'll spare you. Ultimately, the page succeeded in reaching the sheriff who raised an army which slayed the dragon. The kingdom recovered and prosperity was regained. Do you know what the moral of this story is?"

"Let me think – pages, yellow dragon. No, fingers, pages..." Bob began.

"I've got it," said Mickey. Everyone turned to him expectantly. "Let your pages do the walking through the yellow fingers!"

Jim smiled.

"You're a true raconteur," Mickey said. "Got any more?"

"Yes. I have quite a few, but as you just heard, they take a while."

"Can you pick a short one and really just give us the gist?"

"Okay. It's not in the spirit of the Shaggy Dog Story to make it short, but I'll try. The other one was cute. This one is a groaner.

"There was once an evil violinist who employed an evil orchestra. They liked nothing better than modifying their instruments to include body parts. As you know, many string instruments include cat gut. The evil violinist loved to murder famous people and use their intestines for his strings and the strings of other instruments."

"This is really morbid. Are you sure you want to tell this?" Liz asked.

"Ah Liz, you've heard worse," Bill replied impatiently. "You even see slasher films from time to time. Let him continue."

"Okay. So one day he got a great idea. He'd travel to Africa and kill Tarzan. Of course I could go on and on about the voyage, the killing, the intestines, the stringing of the instruments, but I'll spare you.

"Thank heavens for that," said Janice.

"Anyway, I'll wrap it up. He and his evil band created instruments from Tarzan's intestines. They started playing and thought they sounded better than they ever had so they decided to just keep playing on and on. They were so pleased with themselves that they just couldn't stop.

"Do you know what they were playing?"

"Tarzan intestines, Tarzan band, Tarzan evil," Liz began.

"Tarzan's tripes forever," Jim said. "With that, I really need to go. Thanks for the wonderful day and fantastic company."

Liz walked him to his car and watched longingly as he drove away.

Returning to the house, she saw her mother and father waiting at the front door. "I really like him," Janice said. "He's a keeper."

CHAPTER 3

"All changes, even the most longed for, have their melancholy; for what we leave behind us is a part of ourselves; we must die to one life before we can enter another."

- Anatole France

1

During his drive to work Monday morning, Jim couldn't help but think about Liz's party. He'd really enjoyed himself. It had been a long time since he'd had so much fun with a group of people. He almost felt like part of the family. They'd certainly made him feel welcome. Looking at his life thus far, Jim realized just how much he wanted to be part of a family like that. What would it be like to have people around who cared for you, who stuck together to watch out for you and if necessary, defend you?

Jim certainly hadn't experienced family in the classic sense. He was the son of a sergeant in the Air Force. Their family had moved every one to three years and Jim attended fifteen schools before he graduated from High School.

His father was a strict disciplinarian, still of the generation that believed the old saying 'Spare the rod, spoil the child'. In his case, it wasn't a rod. It was a thin black belt. If Jim did anything wrong, his father grabbed the belt and forced Jim to drop his pants and his underwear and bend over a chair. Then, depending on his mood, his father would deliver between ten and thirty lashes of the belt, striking Jim's buttocks. Sometimes the belt would break the skin and Jim would get up bleeding, his mother rushing to his aid with a towel filled with ice. Sometimes, but rarely, his mother would try to intercede, "Joseph, for god's sake, he's just a little boy. He's had enough." But his father would just glare at her and her intervention usually just resulted in more lashes.

Jim's younger sister Annie was never subjected to the belt. Somehow she was always 'Daddy's Little Girl'. Her worst punishment was being sent to her room, a room she shared with Jim. Often, Jim would be punished when Annie blamed him for something she had done. Jim resented her throughout their entire childhood together.

His father usually went to work very early, before Jim and Annie got up for the day. Since their father would not allow their mother to work, she was home to pour them bowls of cereal for breakfast and to pack sandwiches in their bag lunches.

When Jim got home from school his father was waiting. Every day, Jim was required to give his father a massage lasting one hour. Jim hated giving the massages and grew to hate his father for making him give them. He felt like a slave. Over the years, Jim's hands grew quite strong and ultimately, though Jim hated to admit it, his skills at massage became a hit with the women he'd met in college.

Most evenings his father went bowling. He was a semi-professional bowler who bowled in leagues during the early evening while he waited for the 'pot games' to start close to midnight. Each of the late night bowlers would throw ten dollars into the pot and the winner took all. He also did reasonably well in professional tournaments, even appearing on TV several times. Jim's father was successful in supplementing his meager military income through bowling.

During the years that they were too young to stay home by themselves, Jim and Annie slept in the bowling alleys. Jim begrudgingly admitted that this too was a surprising blessing as he'd always been able to fall asleep anywhere, no matter how much noise, light or even motion attempted to disturb him. This had proven very helpful in his international travels.

Still, Jim couldn't remember a single time he'd spent with his father doing something fun together. Actually, that wasn't quite true. He remembered exactly one time. They were stationed in Japan and Jim was four years old. His father headed up a drill team which performed at major events on the base. On this particular day, his father brought Jim along to watch him drill his men. To his almost incomprehensible shouts, the group of twenty-four airmen marched in unison, turning, splitting into multiple groups, then remerging into one. It was quite impressive. After thirty minutes of practice with the team, Jim's father left the team standing at parade rest and approached Jim. "It's your turn," he said.

"What do I do?" Jim asked shyly.

"First of all, you have to be confident. Stand up. Stand up tall. Okay. You and I will march alongside them and I'll tell you what to say. Let's go."

They walked up to the team who stood waiting.

"Say Attention, loud and forcefully."

"Attention!" Jim shouted as loud and seriously as he could.

The men moved to Attention.

"Say Present Arms."

"Present Arms!" Jim ordered.

The men all raised their rifles in front of them.

"Say Order Arms."

"Order Arms!" Jim cried, beaming.

The men put down their rifles.

"Now say Right Shoulder Arms."

"Right Shoulder Arms!"

The men put their rifle on their right shoulders.

"Next, Right Face."

"Right Face!"

The men all turned to the right simultaneously.

"Now, Forward Harch."

"Forward Harch!"

The men started marching. Jim's father was at their side keeping step. Jim struggled a bit trying to keep up. He was happier than he'd ever been.

His father coached him through several marching commands, ending the drill after five minutes with "Fall Out."

Afterwards, several of the men came up and congratulated Jim. "He's a chip off the old block," they said. Jim was all smiles.

That was the first and last time his father and he had one-on-one time. No fishing, no hiking, no sports. They were stationed all over the world: Japan, Germany, Spain, even Omaha, Nebraska at the Strategic Air Command. Occasionally, they saw members of their extended family in passing while travelling from one base to another, but Jim and his sister never got to know any of them.

One day when Jim was twelve, he got home from school five minutes late. His father was angry. He ordered Jim to drop his pants while he went to get the belt. Jim felt this was unjust. He protested that the teacher had asked him to stay a few extra minutes so he couldn't help being late. His father didn't care. Jim got angry. He decided that he wouldn't cry. He wouldn't even cry out. He wouldn't give his father the satisfaction. He'd laugh instead. The more it hurt, the more he'd laugh.

And as the belt hit and the pain surged, Jim realized that he really could convert his cries into laughter. He laughed a lot. At first, this just made his father angrier. He struck harder. And still the laughs came. Ultimately the lashes grew softer and his father said, "Pull up your pants. It's time for my back rub."

With his next infraction a month later, Jim was bent over the chair waiting for his father to return with the belt. His father approached and said, "This is for your own good," and raised the belt over his head. As it travelled downward, Jim rolled out of the way and grabbed the belt as it struck the chair. He pulled hard and the belt came out of his father's hands.

"I'm done with this. You're not going to whip me with this belt anymore," Jim said staring coldly at his father, seething with hate. He turned and went to his room taking the belt with him.

A few minutes later, his father knocked at the door then opened it. Jim feared for the worst, but his father was smiling. "My son has become a man. I'm proud of him," he said. He turned and left.

That was the first and only time Jim's father had ever said he was proud of his son.

Jim did well in High School. Hoping to get away from home as soon as he could, he managed to graduate early, then got a full scholarship to MIT on the opposite side of the country. After two years of missing surfing, he transferred to UC Santa Barbara to finish his studies.

Shortly after he left home, his mother divorced his father. His sister, 'Daddy's Little Girl', remained at home cooking and cleaning for her father. She didn't date. She wasn't allowed to. One day, his father died. His heart just quit. Jim didn't attend the funeral though his sister begged him to. Jim had started his own life and just wanted to forget about the past.

At some point Jim realized that maybe his sister didn't have such a great life either. At least with his father dead, she was free. Unfortunately, the freedom seemed to be too much for her to handle. While she successfully charmed her way into some good jobs, she invariably lost them. For reasons not apparent at the time, she would just not show up for work. On some occasions, Jim found her at home, depressed and unwilling to leave the house. A few days later, she'd be normal again. Then she'd just disappear. No one would hear from her for weeks. In the midst of one of these disappearances, Jim's mother called him.

"Jim, Annie is in a psych ward in Sebastopol. She's been there a week. I don't really understand the way the laws work with these situations, but apparently they couldn't call us unless Annie asked them to or unless she called us herself. She finally did today. Can you come with me to pick her up? We'll also have to get her car from the police impound. I'll tell you more on the way."

Jim picked his mother up and they made their way to the

hospital. Annie was waiting for them.

"I'm really, really sorry," she said sheepishly. "I knew I had problems but I never thought I would lose control like this. It turns out I'm manic-depressive. They've put me on Lithium and now I feel fine. According to the doctor, if I stay on the medication, I can live a normal life and won't screw up as much."

And it was true. While she was on her medication, she did fine. Unfortunately every year or so, Annie would decide that she didn't need it, that it made her 'slow' and she'd stop taking it. For some reason, this always resulted in a manic episode and she would be picked up by police after some outrageous incident and placed in a psych ward for a week or two. After each release, Jim's mother would faithfully stay with Annie for several weeks to ensure she was back on track, desperately hoping each time would be the last. Once Annie seemed stable, Jim's mother visited or had Annie over to dinner several times a week hoping she could spot the symptoms of an impending attack before Annie disappeared. But invariably, it would happen again.

After one of these incidents, the attending psychiatrist sat down with the three of them.

"First, you should know that we now call this bipolar disorder," he began. "If you've known Annie, you've seen that she can be depressed or manic. These are part of a cycle which magnifies into either a deep depression or an uncontrollable high.

"Many people live with this undiagnosed because their extremes are not severe enough to require intervention. For others, like Annie, it's a dangerous condition. As I've explained to Annie, there is no cure. This is an anomaly of the brain. We see some hereditary links, but we can't always associate it with that.

"Before, I think Annie believed that she would get better if she took her medication, so once she saw her life in order and felt okay, she stopped it. I'm hoping she now understands that she will be on her medication for life. The medications will change as we get better at controlling bipolar disorders, but it doesn't get better by itself and the medications just control it. They don't fix it."

Annie nodded sadly.

"So, I've taken Annie off Lithium. We're seeing some side effects and in some people it can become toxic after time. Annie will now be taking several medications which will control the disorder, and which should have fewer side effects. The most notable for Annie will be that she won't feel as 'slow' on these."

Everyone felt relieved, especially Annie. Things looked good for almost two years. No one knows exactly what happened. It appeared that Annie was still taking her medication, but she was found dead of a drug overdose. She had taken sleeping pills and everything else in her medicine cabinet – clearly a suicide.

A year later, Jim's mother met an executive from an aerospace firm who was tired of the rat race of the Silicon Valley. They bought a truck and went into the moving business, carry loads of household goods across the country. Jim and his mother saw each other several times and she seemed to be a different person. She showed herself to be strong and independent once she was free of Jim's father and without the burden of caring for a daughter with a mental illness. Jim and his mother finally became close, but then tragedy struck. His mother and her friend were asleep in the cab of their truck at a truck stop in the Ozark Mountains during a wintery night. Another truck trying to pull into the truck stop lost control on the ice and slammed into the cab of their truck killing them both.

Yes, the thought of a real family was appealing to Jim. He would certainly see more of Liz.

2

Liz stopped at the gate in front of the Sinclair estate, rolled down her window and pressed the button.

"Hi, it's Liz to see Mark. He's expecting me."

Liz waited impatiently as the gate slowly opened. The security seemed pretentious to her. When she'd first met Mark Sinclair, she was fascinated by his family and connections. While Daddy knew a lot of people and had a lot of friends, even in high places, Mark's family largely belonged to those who didn't have to work for a living. In fact, it had been a couple of generations since anyone in Mark's family actually had to earn a living. That's not to say that they didn't work, as all of the men in the family actually did, but they really didn't have to. The women didn't have careers. Their work consisted of helping raise money for charities and coordinating associated soirees and fund-raising events. It certainly wasn't a crowd that Liz thought she'd ever want to be involved with.

But one night while having drinks at the Top of the Mark after a show in San Francisco, Liz's friend Amy pointed out Mark Sinclair across the room in what appeared to be a debate with an older man whose back was turned to them.

"That's Mark Sinclair, one of the most sought-after bachelors in the Bay Area. Isn't he gorgeous?"

Liz looked over at the very tall young man in black tie with his sculpted features and calm demeanor. She agreed. He was gorgeous.

"I bet you the next round of drinks that you can't get him to buy you one."

Never one to shy away from a challenge and much to Amy's dismay, Liz got up and walked over to Mark Sinclair.

"Excuse me, but I recognize you Mark Sinclair. I'm Liz Leahy and my father beat up your father in court. Want to buy me a drink?"

Turning to the older gentleman who looked surprised, Liz recognized Jonathan Sinclair and flushed. "Oh, I'm sorry. I just wanted to meet your son. I really didn't mean anything by that remark. I hope I didn't offend you."

"Aggressive, knows what she wants, but has manners too. No Ms. Leahy, I'm not offended at all. Your father did, indeed, beat me up in court. Ultimately, though, he helped us and the rest of the industry as we tightened up our contracts to avoid repeating that unpleasant history. I'll excuse myself. I think you two should get to know each other. Mark, I'll see you at home later."

Mark Sinclair looked lost. "I'm sorry, who are you again?" he stammered, breaking out into a sweat and spilling his drink.

"I'm Liz Louise Leahy. My father is Michael Leahy, the attorney who represented Jason Livingston in the lawsuit MegaTrust filed against him for theft of intellectual property."

"Oh, I'm sorry," he stammered. "I don't know anything about it. When was this?"

"It was a couple of years back. Basically, Jason developed some software for MegaTrust under contract which he later sold in a different form to other businesses. MegaTrust sued and lost. The suit changed how intellectual property rights are handled in software development contracts with independent contractors."

"I – ah – guess I was away at school. Still, it seems to me that if we paid someone to develop something for us, we should own it. Doesn't that make sense?"

"Well, at one level it would. If Jason had been an employee and MegaTrust had employment agreements that included granting intellectual property rights to MegaTrust, then yes. However, with independent contractors, the whole idea is that they work independently, use their tools, their expertise, and in some cases things they have already built to fulfill the contract. So, with this ruling, companies like MegaTrust now have to include more specific ownership and assignment language in agreements with their independent contractors."

Mark looked a bit lost. "I apologize again, but I don't completely understand this. Are you a lawyer?"

"I'm in my last year of Law School, and I've been raised in a household where I was fed the Law almost from the time I was born.

"What did you study in school and what do you do for MegaTrust? You do work for MegaTrust, right?"

"Ah, yeah, I work for MegaTrust. I finished my MBA at Yale last year and Da- my father brought me into MegaTrust. I work for the CFO. Right now I spend most of my time creating spreadsheets and PowerPoint presentations for him. I guess I'm getting a good view of the company from the top down. I'm sorry. Let me buy you that drink."

The bartender approached at Mark's nod. "What would you like?" Mark asked.

Turning to the bartender, Liz said, "A scotch and soda please."

"And I'll have another one of these," Mark added.

They watched as the bartender efficiently mixed their drinks and set them on the bar before them.

Liz raised her glass to Mark and said, "To new friends!"

"To new friends," Mark replied, touching her glass with his.

Liz took a sip, turned towards Amy and raised her glass.

"Who's that? " Mark inquired.

"Oh, that's my friend Amy. She bet me that I couldn't get you to buy me a drink."

"Are you always so straight forward?" Mark asked, a little miffed.

"I try to be. Don't be offended," Liz soothed, placing her hand on Mark's arm and smiling broadly. "I'm really glad I met you. Who knows, maybe we can be like Romeo and Juliette, but without the tragedy. Maybe we can bring our families a bit closer together."

As she finished her drink after what to her seemed an innocuous conversation, Liz explained to Mark that she had to get back to her friend Amy. She wrote her phone number on the palm of his hand which caught him completely by surprise. He in turn handed her one of his business cards and pointed out his cell number.

For his part, Mark was intrigued. While a number of the women he'd met at his mother's insistence were aggressive, none was like Liz. All they seemed to want to talk about were charities, who they knew in common, and what party was coming up next. His parent's crowd was so insipid. Liz, on the other hand seemed to be filled with boundless energy and a thirst for life. She challenged him from the first sentence and he felt that he'd have to work to keep up with her. In fact, he realized he hadn't done a very good job of that during their shared drink. He'd do his best to make up for his ineptness.

The next day, Mark called Liz and invited her to dinner, asking that she wear something dressy. He took her to Chez Panisse in Berkeley where Alice Waters greeted him personally by name. Mark introduced an astonished Liz to the legendary restauratrice and they shared an intimate dinner in one of the Bay

Area's top restaurants.

Over the course of the next several weeks, Mark applied a full court press. He invited her to several parties of his social set, and in addition to meeting many from the social register in San Francisco, Liz was overwhelmed by the whirlwind of celebrities that Mark introduced her to. Jude Law, Kiera Knightley, Beyonce, and countless others who knew Mark by name and told Liz how lucky she was to have Mark as a boyfriend.

Mark's father found Liz quite refreshing if a bit brash, but in spite of her charm, Liz was unable to crack Mark's mother's icy demeanor. Margery Sinclair remained distant. As she later learned from Mark, his mother didn't feel that Liz came from the right group of people to be included in their family. Mark shouldn't waste his time on her.

For his part, Mark's father enjoyed lively debates with Liz, usually leaving Mark far behind in the discussions. Unlike his wife, Jonathan Sinclair felt that Liz was certainly good enough for Mark, but knowing his son well, he predicted heartbreak. Mark would never be able to keep up with Liz, and while she was initially dazzled by their lifestyles and society, he also knew she wasn't after their money and would likely tire of Mark once the dazzle faded.

Liz became caught up in the world that Mark offered. Her only issue was that Mark didn't seem physically interested in her. She'd wear her most revealing outfits and would make suggestive proposals, but he seemed oblivious. Watching him at parties, she saw that he had very little interest in women. He certainly didn't seem to even notice a tight fitting dress, glimpses of cleavage, or beautiful legs walking by. If she didn't know better, she'd think Mark was gay. And yet, he was attentive, affectionate, deferential, and overall a genuine and wonderful person to be with. Mark seemed to be falling in love with her.

One night after a rich dinner and too much wine, Liz asked him to tuck her in. She lit candles in her room and much to Mark's surprise began to undress in the flickering candlelight, her back towards him. She asked him to hand her the oversized t-shirt hanging on the post of her bed and then turned around as he approached. Looking up at his flushed face, she stood on tiptoes and he bent over to kiss her. She pulled him down onto the bed and she helped him out of his clothes as they frantically groped each other. When Liz saw Mark's erect penis, she almost fainted. She'd never seen one so big, even in the few porno movies she'd watched over the years. As he moved on top of her, she was more excited than she could ever remember being, but a little frightened too. Would it hurt?

It did, but Liz experienced one of the most thunderous orgasms of her life a short minute or two later as Mark exploded inside her. She wrapped them in the covers and they fell asleep. Waking in the wee hours of the morning, she found Mark gazing at her lovingly.

"That was wonderful," he said. "Will you marry me?"

Without even thinking, Liz said yes. She thought that they would make love again, but Mark just smiled, kissed her warmly, curled up beside her and went to sleep.

Their engagement was announced, much to the dismay of Margery Sinclair. Jonathan Sinclair had several heart-to-heart conversations with Mark, explaining his concerns but hoping for the best.

Over the course of the next several months, it was more of the same: parties, social occasions, expensive dinners, trips to exotic places, the opera, the symphony. All of this was a step up from Liz's previous life. For her part, Liz still managed to attend classes, stay close to her friends and family, and pursue hang gliding. With the addition of the Sinclair's social circle, Liz's life was quite full.

Unfortunately, Liz discovered that as wonderful as Mark was in every way, he lacked something in bed. While their first encounter was thrilling, it was all downhill from there. Mark had no sex drive. Liz managed to seduce him roughly once a week, but even that was a struggle. After the first few weeks, the novelty of his huge organ wore off and Liz was disappointed to discover that Mark had no interest in going out of his way for her. He gladly accepted oral sex, but the thought of providing it was repulsive to him. He actually said that he thought his penis should be more than enough for Liz.

In many ways it was. However, sex was painful, and on those few occasions where Mark was overwhelmed by his own passion, he couldn't control the depth of his penetration, and Liz felt like he was damaging her internally. She no longer had orgasms from his brief penetration and since he immediately fell asleep afterwards, she was left unsatisfied.

As she thought about a lifetime with Mark, she realized that sex would always be a problem. The combination of lack of desire and no interest in pleasing her was going to be a disaster. She also had begun to notice that while Mark was charming and all her friends found him quite friendly, they also had to help him along in many of the intellectual debates that raged at get-togethers with her crowd.

Now with this latest slight from his parents, clearly engineered by Margery, Liz recognized that even the social aspects of her future life with Mark's family and friends would be a battle. All in all, it was clearly time to call it off. She really hated to do it; Mark was one of the nicest people she'd ever met. But Liz knew what she wanted to get out of life and it was clear that wasn't going to happen if she married Mark.

Coming out of her reverie, now prepared to go through with the break up, Liz climbed the marble steps to the Sinclair mansion. William, the Sinclair's butler, opened the door as she approached and led her to the game room where Mark was watching a Giant's game.

Mark jumped to his feet and rushed to greet Liz, kissing her passionately, nuzzling her neck. "I know it's only been two days, but I've really missed you," he said. "Would you like some champagne? We can watch the game together if you want."

Liz realized that this was going to be harder than she thought.

"Mark, would it be okay if we went up to your room? I'd really like to talk to you in private."

Without even a questioning look, Mark took her hand and led her upstairs to his bedroom. Passing William on the way, Mark asked him to bring a bottle of champagne and two glasses to his room.

Actually, it was more of a suite. Ornate, elegant, a bit too feminine for Liz's taste, but beautiful and comfortable, Liz took a seat on the canapé, a nineteenth century antique sofa made of exotic hardwood covered in a lush, forest green velvet. Mark sat beside her and before they could say anything, they heard a discreet knock at the door. William entered with the champagne. He opened the bottle silently – a pop would have been gauche - poured two glasses, expertly wrapped the bottle in a torchon and placed it in the ice bucket. "Will there be anything else, sir?"

"No, William. Thank you for your as-always impeccable service!"

William exited, quietly closing the door behind him.

"So if this is about your parent's party," Mark began. "I'm really sorry. My mother can be so unreasonable. I probably should have just ignored her and gone to your house instead. I'm really, really sorry."

"Mark, that's not it; at least not all of it. It did get me thinking though. My family is very important to me. While your father and friends have made me feel very welcome here, I just can't see our two families really coming together. I envisioned my married life as one where I gained another family like mine and both families enriched each other. It's pretty clear to me that that will never happen for us. Worse, I think there will always be a bit of a battle to be fought. I don't want to live that way."

"Are you saying you're breaking up with me?" Mark asked, clearly suddenly on the verge of tears. "I love you Liz. You're the most amazing person I've ever met. You make me better than I am. I want to marry you!"

"I love you too, Mark," Liz replied, taking him in her arms as he buried is head in her neck, crying softly now. "I've struggled with this, but I know it's for the best. Ultimately, we'd both be unhappy. You need someone who fits into your social circle. I really don't."

"Is it the sex?" Mark pleaded, grasping her left breast. "I know I can do better."

"No," Liz lied.

She slid Mark's hand under her blouse and felt him become aroused. They moved to Mark's bed. He was gentle with her and took more time. He looked at her deeply just as he finished and collapsed on top of her in tears.

"I'm sorry. I'm sorry," he said.

"I'm sorry too, Mark."

Liz held him until he fell asleep then slipped silently out of bed. She dressed then picked up Mark's clothes and laid them on the end of the bed. She took an envelope from her purse, placed it on top of Mark's clothes and left after saying goodbye to William.

As she drove away, Liz thought of other breakups. She was a bit ashamed to admit that she'd used the same formula. But she also knew that it worked. She was still friends with each of her past lovers.

Men had so much ego tied up in sex, even men like Mark who weren't obsessed with it. Most of her friends didn't believe in goodbye sex. When it was over for them, it was over. They refused to see their boyfriends or husbands. This resulted in suspicion, doubt and major damage to egos. Revenge was often the order of the day and more than one friend had found compromising pictures posted on the internet. Worse, it created division in the social fabric as people chose sides, usually men with men and women with women, although it wasn't unusual to find a competitive friend who went after the dumped male, suddenly an easy conquest.

Liz believed that goodbye sex was essential to a successful breakup. The breakup could be about anything but every man she'd known thought it was about sex in the end. With their bruised egos, they often counter attacked and what were once solid friendships and passionate love affairs became bitter battles and resulted in irreparable rifts. A little nookie was reassuring. It made the breakup about something other than sex and the man's ego was spared, at least on that front. If you could provide a reason that was unarguable, things got really easy. The man saw it as for the best, even if he was disappointed. Call later and ask for advice on something and invite them to a group function and things could go smoothly. Lovers became friends. Liz was sure that Mark would remain her friend.

3

Jim cursed the Friday afternoon traffic as he made his way to Berkeley. Surprisingly, the San Mateo Bridge had moved at the speed limit but once he turned north onto Highway 880, traffic came to a complete halt. It was going to be a long ride. It was only about twenty miles, but Jim guessed it would take him at least an hour. Dinner was at seven-thirty, so he'd still probably make it on time.

Jim was looking forward to dinner with Liz, Steve, Bob, and Bill at Liz's place. After the great time he'd had at the Leahy's the previous Sunday, Jim felt like he was finally developing some friends. It seemed like between work and his difficulties with Sharon, there hadn't really been time for friends in the last several years. Sharon wasn't the most social person and while he'd loved the endless games of Scrabble, Boggle and other made-up variations as well as their one-on-one time, in retrospect, he now knew that something fundamental was missing. Maybe his life without Sharon wouldn't be so bad after all.

And Liz. Liz was something else. She was socially adept, beautiful, confident, athletic, and smart. What a combination! Maybe she didn't have the raw intelligence that Sharon did, but didn't he read something recently about multiple intelligences? Liz certainly excelled in many different arenas. Even better, Liz seemed to be interested in Jim. He wasn't sure how all this was going to work out. Liz was still engaged; he was still married; and there was this circle of family and friends who, while intriguing, seemed to have visibility into everything going on. Did you have to give up privacy to develop these extended relationships? Maybe Jim would have to come out of his shell a bit. He and Sharon had lived a modest life. Their intimacy was not for others to know about. Of course, they never really developed any close friends either. Their lives seemed to consist of work and their time together. Not much else. The intimacy was unique, but really, could life be about just one other person? Shouldn't people have lots of friends and family that they could rely on?

Jim couldn't blame Sharon though. He knew that he'd always been a loner. It was probably his military brat upbringing. How could you develop close, long-lasting relationships when you moved every two or three years? You met people, became good acquaintances, then left, never to see them again. You might think that with a life like this, you'd pull closer to your immediate family, but at least in Jim's case, that never happened. He never got close to his sister and his parents were always occupied elsewhere. And then he chose to marry someone very much like himself. No, Jim only had himself to blame.

But with the divorce, the master reset button had been pressed. Or, in the terms of his industry, he'd just had a reboot. It was now his time to choose to be different and that's what he intended to do. Liz's crowd was intellectually challenging. They all came from much more money than he or his family had ever seen and clearly, none of them were afraid to live life. Jim vowed to be open to new experiences, less conservative than he'd been his whole life. If opportunities presented themselves with this group, Jim was going to go for them. No hesitation.

Jim pulled up to the address that Liz had given him and parked his Subaru in an open spot across the street. He rang the doorbell but receiving no answer cautiously opened the door and entered the small Craftsman-style house. Music was playing loudly and Jim found everyone in the small kitchen sipping champagne, of course.

"Jim, we were wondering where you were," Liz said smiling, rushing over to give him a hug.

"Sorry. Traffic on a Friday is a real challenge," Jim replied, handing Liz the bottle of Ridge Zinfandel he'd brought. "Something smells good. What's for dinner?"

"Ah, just like a man. The first question out of his mouth is about dinner." Seeing Jim blush, Liz continued. "I'm just kidding. We're having my signature dish, Spaghetti Carbonara along with a nice salad and a good red wine I see."

"Signature dish?" Steve snorted. "Admit it Liz, it's your only dish."

This time it was Liz who blushed. "Yeah, well we can't all be gourmet cooks like you are. Now that I think about it, why am I cooking?"

"All men loved to be served by a beautiful woman," Steve responded seriously. "My cooking certainly can't compete with that."

"Ever so gallant," Bill joked. "I can still remember the time Liz tried to cook linguine with clams. We all suffered through the meal only to spend the rest of the night kneeling before the porcelain alter – and it wasn't that we drank too much wine as Liz would like us to believe."

Seeing the dark look on Liz's face, Bob jumped in. "Guys, we're getting a free meal here. We know how good her Carbonara is. I'm certainly looking forward to it. You're crazy to insult our gracious hostess. She could send us home hungry and we certainly wouldn't want that, now would we? "Seeing Bill hang his head in feigned remorse, Bob continued. "Okay then. That's settled. Let's eat!"

Each of the guys grabbed a large dinner plate and lined up in front of the stove where Liz poured the Carbonara mixture into what had to be the largest pasta pot Jim had ever seen. She began tossing the spaghetti.

"I'll serve the pasta and then you can help yourselves to some salad. Dressings and grated parmesan are on the table and garlic bread will be out of the oven as soon as you sit down."

Once Jim had his plate, he set it on the table and came back to the kitchen to open the wine he'd brought. As he finished pouring the fifth glass, he kicked himself for not having brought another bottle.

"Don't worry about it," Liz soothed. 'Steve brought a bottle too. We'll drink that next."

"Yeah, but it won't be as good as this Ridge," Steve replied, swirling his glass and clearly savoring the aroma. "Unfortunately, I'm still on a student's budget and the best I could afford was this Cinnabar."

"I certainly wouldn't complain about that Mercury Rising," Jim answered. "It's definitely one of my favorites."

Once everyone was seated, Liz turned to Jim and said, "Jim, will you say grace please?"

Jim almost panicked. His family of ex-Catholics was never religious and he'd never said grace in his life. Jim looked around the table as everyone folded their hands and bowed their heads. 'Grace?" he asked sheepishly.

"Well done!" said Steve, slapping him on the back. Everyone laughed.

"To good friends!" Bill toasted.

"To good friends!"

Each took a sip of the Zin and smiled at Jim gratefully.

"This is really good," said Bob. "I drink red wine, but I must say, I've never really liked it that much. I'm surprised."

"You need to get out more," said Liz.

'The pasta is excellent," said Jim after taking a bite.

Everyone agreed and Liz positively beamed.

"One thing I should mention to clear the air," Liz began. "A few of you have heard but just so everyone knows," Liz said looking directly at Jim, "Mark and I broke up. In reality, I broke our engagement. As you know, while Mark is a really nice guy, he's not the smartest person around, and with his parents snubbing us and holding their own party after receiving our invitation, all I could see were the problems to come. Mark took it well and we'll continue to be friends."

Liz looked around the room expectantly.

Steve decided to break the silence. "Well I for one am really glad to hear it. As you said, Mark is a very nice guy, but he's not the right one for you. Worse, you're a social creature and his family's crowd, while certainly connected, is a bit pretentious for a practical woman like you.

"Plus, with his money, having Mark in the Liz's exes club means he can pick up tabs for a while. Good move, Liz."

"Thanks Steve. I hope you all feel that way." Seeing everyone nod, Liz continued, deciding it was time to change the subject. 'So putting that behind us, are you guys ready for the Nationals?"

"Actually, I've never flown Dunlap," Jim replied. "What's it like?"

"Turkey poop!" Liz responded laughing.

"Turkey poop?" queried Jim bewildered.

"Actually," Steve began, frowning at Liz, "it's a great place to fly. In many ways it's like Elk Mountain. The launch is at forty-six hundred feet and the landing area is at twenty-two hundred feet. What makes it special is that it's at the base of King's canyon. There's great potential for cross country flights to the north and south. A few people have thought about trying to cross the Sierra since Mount Whitney is pretty much a straight shot to the east, but I only know of one person who actually tried it, and it didn't go too well. He landed in the canyon, broke his glider, and had a nasty hike to the nearest road. As far as I know, no one has tried it since.

"It really is an ideal location for the Nationals since they can lay out cross country courses and there's plenty of room. I've flown there a few times and it's pretty intuitive, a combination of ridges and obvious thermal generators. Usually there's enough ridge lift to maintain altitude so you have plenty of time to search for thermals."

"Stinky thermals!" Liz interrupted giggling.

"Yes," Steve continued, "There are several turkey farms in the valley below the launch and since they've cleared ground in the middle of lots of trees, they tend to be the primary thermal generators near the launch. And yes. They do generate thermals that smell of turkey droppings. Sometimes you do need to hold your breath while climbing and then move on to better smelling ones."

"You don't really think that the cleared land generates those stinky thermals, do you?" Liz teased. "Everyone knows that the thermals are the result of thousands of turkeys doing a simultaneous fart! I'm not sure I'd want to fly in a giant turkey fart."

Liz took a sip of her wine and then couldn't control her laughter. She snorted and wine came spewing out her nose. Then she coughed uncontrollably while trying to contain her laughter.

"Now that was one of the most lady-like things I've seen in a long time," Steve scolded, clearly miffed at Liz's puerile jokes and lack of control.

"I've never claimed to be a lady," Liz responded with false aplomb.

"Anyway, Bill and I were talking about taking a trip up there weekend after next. Would you like to come along? Maybe Liz will come too if she thinks she can live with the smell of the turkeys. On the other hand, if she drives and doesn't fly, she wouldn't have to smell the thermals."

"No way Steve," Liz answered intently. "I'm a pilot and I'll fly just like the rest of you. We can take turns driving."

"Sure, I'd love to come," Jim replied. 'If we take two cars, we won't need a driver."

"Great, let's plan on it."

Dinner continued and discussion bounced between politics, the law, and the economy. After clearing plates, Liz said, "I have vanilla ice cream and freshly picked blackberries from my parents property. Anyone want dessert?"

Everyone did.

"I also have news," Liz stated enigmatically as she turned back to get dessert.

Once everyone was served, eyes turned expectantly towards Liz. Like the consummate actress she was, Liz let the anticipation build just long enough, then announced, "I took a job!"

"A job for Elizabeth Louise Leahy?" Steve joked. "You have a trust fund. Why aren't you just enjoying life until the Bar exam? Weren't you at least going to take the summer off?"

"As you well know, it's a woman's prerogative to change her mind if she wants to. I just decided that with all of you working, I really didn't want to just laze around all summer. Daddy and I had lunch with Mark Mansfield of Mansfield, Mason, and Williams, and they've agreed to take me on. They're hoping I'll fall in love with the firm and will stay after the Bar Exam, but I'm pretty sure that this is just a temporary thing for me. I still don't really know what I want to do with my law degree.

"Anyway, it's only three days a week so I have plenty of time to have fun. The good news is that I will get real legal experience. In addition to the grunt work, I'll actually be interviewing clients to gather facts, and drafting pleadings. I'll also get to watch in court if my cases make it that far. I start Monday."

Breaking the sudden silence that descended on the room, Jim stood up, raised his glass, and toasted, "To Liz. May she get everything she wants out of her new job!"

Everyone chimed in, "To Liz!"

Once the conversation about Liz's new position wound down, Bob turned to Jim and said, "Hey Jim, do you have any more of those Shaggy Dog stories?"

"Yeah. I have quite a few. Let me see. Ah, okay. Here's one I like. It's not too long and I'll try to shorten it a bit.

"Once upon a time in on a distant Pacific Island lived a king beloved by all his people. Everyone on the island, including the king lived in grass houses, though through some feat of brilliant architecture, the people of the kingdom had built the king a two story house. The king governed strictly but fairly and everyone lived the idyllic life of an island paradise.

"Unfortunately, the neighboring island was governed by the king's brother. He ruled with an iron fist, beating people into submission and taking the majority of the crops and catches for himself and his family. He was hated and feared.

"In spite of his financial success, he was jealous of his brother. He didn't understand why his brother was so loved while he was despised.

"One day the evil king decided to attack his brother's island to wrest control and exile the good king.

"As the warriors approached, the sentries alerted the good king and he rallied his people to defeat the invaders. They pushed them back into the sea and back to their island where the brother and his forces ultimately surrendered to the good king.

"Looking at the state of affairs on his brother's island, the king convened a council of the elders of the island and together they crafted a new government where the old king would only retain a figurehead status. The evil king had reluctantly agreed since the alternative for him was severe: death. The good king would help supervise and defend the rights of the people from his neighboring island. Once everything was in place, the good king returned to his island and was met with a great celebration.

"Time went by (and I could go on and on), and one day, a large catamaran arrived with a huge package for the king. "

"I bet it's a Trojan Horse," Liz interrupted.

"Shh!"

"No. It wasn't a Trojan Horse. It was a throne. The people of the neighboring island had raised the funds to order a custom-made throne for the king. It was composed of elegant gold and heavy woods all encrusted with jewels. In reality, it was a bit much for the simple lifestyle the king embraced, but he couldn't refuse the honor. Thereafter, he held court from the throne and aside from incongruity of an ornate metal and bejeweled throne in a grass house, the two island kingdoms lived side-by-side in harmony.

"Meanwhile, the evil king was hatching a plot. He recruited several of his former guards and promised to pay them handsomely if they could steal his brother's throne. This is another area where I could drag the story out, but I'll spare you.

"Once again the good king was lucky and the thieves were routed before they could steal the throne. But after the incident, the king was worried. This throne meant a lot to the people of the other island as well as to those of his own. To protect it, he decided to stow the throne upstairs at the end of the day so that any robbers would have to get by him and his wife to reach the treasure. This worked well. Several of his strongest subjects would carry the throne upstairs at the end of the day and would then bring it down the next morning.

"One night while the king and queen were sleeping, the heavy throne fell through the ceiling and crashed down, killing them both."

"I didn't' see that coming. What a horrible story!" said Liz.

"Horrible indeed," Jim continued. "But do you know what the moral of this story is?"

"Throne king island Pacific gold crash."

"Kings with thrones shouldn't, ah."

"Okay. Here it is: People who live in grass houses –"

"Shouldn't stow thrones!" Liz, Steve, Bob and Bill all said together.

Bob thanked everyone and made his way to the door. He needed to get back to his family. After coffee and port, Bill, Steve and Jim helped with the dishes, then Bill and Steve said they had to be on their way too.

"Jim, could you stay a few minutes?" Liz asked.

"Sure."

They walked Bill and Steve to the door and watched them drive away.

"I was just hoping you could tuck me in," Liz said.

"Sure. I'd love to."

Leading him to her room, Liz invited Jim to sit in a stuffed recliner next to her bed. Grabbing a very large t-shirt that was hanging on one of the four posts of her bed, Liz said, "I'll be right back."

Jim looked around the room finding it feminine, if possible even more so than her room at her parents' house. The comforter was a subdued, delicately flowered print in blue and was trimmed in lace, as were the pillow shams. Dozens of stuffed animals lay comfortably among the pillows. An antique French clock and a porcelain lamp crowned an elegant desk. Framed posters from ballets and operas graced the walls.

Liz entered and smiling at Jim she hung her dress in her closet, moved most of the stuffed animals to the empty chair across from Jim, and crawled into bed.

"Oh, I love bed," Liz cooed, lying on her stomach with her head turned towards Jim.

Surprisingly, Jim didn't take this as an invitation. There was nothing sexual going on here. Liz was sleepy and warm and snuggling into her bed.

"So, do you like your covers tucked in loosely or tight?" Jim asked.

"Tightly, if you please. I'd really appreciate it if you could stay with me until I fall asleep. You can just go out the front door. It will lock behind you."

Jim tucked in the covers and sat on the bed next to her. He slowly and gently rubbed her back and stroked her hair. In a few minutes Liz's face relaxed into a contented smile and her breathing slowed.

Jim got up, turned out the light, kissed Liz gently on the top of the head and said quietly, "Good night, Liz. Thanks for a great evening."

He made his way to the bedroom door and turned back for one last look at the sleeping Liz, the light from the hallway casting his shadow into the room. He heard a small, sleepy, almost little-girl voice say, "I really like you, Jim."

"I like you too," Jim replied, closing her bedroom door behind him.

Jim double checked the front door after leaving to ensure it was locked, then walked down the steps to his car through the enveloping fog which had just rolled into Berkeley.

4

The training had paid off for Mike. He was ready. Over the past weeks, he and May had done the entire course except for the swim. To simulate that, they did laps in the Bay, starting and finishing at the official exit point from the swim. Together they'd learned that while Mike was a far better swimmer than May, May left him in the dust on the bike portion. For the run, they were pretty fairly matched now. That wasn't the case when they did their first training run together. May almost didn't break a sweat, and certainly didn't have to walk (or was it crawl) up the dreaded sand ladder like Mike did. But over the course of their training, they'd reached parity on their runs. She was in better shape and could probably run much further, but their speeds were comparable. Mike had complained that he thought the triathlon legs were not fair. The longest part of the race was the bike so the race favored strong cyclists. The shortest part of the race was the swim, so strong swimmers were effectively penalized. In the Escape, for the top athletes, the swim only represented about 20% of the total time. It just didn't seem fair; at least not to Mike, a stronger swimmer than cyclist. May said it was even worse with an Ironman where the swim was usually less than an hour for the top athletes, the bike was five hours, and the run a bit over three hours.

They'd discussed how they wanted to do the Escape. Neither was particularly interested in time. Mike just wanted to finish and May was actually looking at this as an easy training run for the Ironman Canada which was to be held later in the summer. For his part, Mike couldn't imagine doing a two and a half mile swim followed by a one hundred twelve mile bike and then doing a marathon. The Escape would be hard enough. But May was sure she could do the Ironman Canada and had hopes of possibly qualifying for the Hawaii Ironman in a year or two.

For the Escape, Mike and May had agreed to do the race together rather than running separate races and meeting afterwards. This was actually May's decision and it caught Mike by surprise. As he'd found out during their training, May was very competitive. But then again, she already knew she could beat him in this race since his advantage in the swim would be quickly lost during the bike leg.

The only hard part in doing the race together was the swim.

Unlike biking and running where you could easily match the pace of your partner, an open water swim with nearly two thousand other people made that impossible. Plus, although they were both in the forty to forty-four age group, the women started separately from the men. So they'd agreed that Mike would wait for May in the bike transition area, warming up and stretching before the bike leg. Mike would then set the bike pace and May would ride with him. They had considered just having May catch Mike on the bike leg and continuing together from there, but there was a chance May wouldn't see Mike in the crowd and would zip on by. They'd also do the run together and then finish together, though Mike had a feeling that May would likely try to out-sprint him at the end, and she'd probably win.

After boarding the San Francisco Belle at Pier 3, Mike looked over at May who was loosening up and stretching as were most of the athletes on board. Feeling his eyes on her, May looked up and smiled encouragingly. Over the last few weeks, they'd become good friends. In addition to both being cops, they had a lot in common. Even their backgrounds were similar. Somehow, they seemed to have arrived at the same place in life: early forties, divorced, no children, financial stability, work they loved, and perhaps most important, an understanding of people. They'd both seen real evil and violence, a lot of victims, and a surprising number of genuine people, most of whom got caught up in a mechanical justice system that valued strong argument over truth. From all of that, Mike and May had both acquired a deep cynicism. They had each lost friends to violence and this reinforced the feeling that they needed to appreciate what they had, and cherish anything special. It was beginning to look like the two of them might have something special.

As the boat slowed and turned, Mike felt a sudden queasiness. It wasn't seasickness. It was nerves. He was prepared but nervous. The adrenaline was about to flow and his body was anticipating it. He watched closely as the first groups jumped into the water and then began swimming. It looked insane. The perfectly calm San Francisco Bay had erupted into a chaos of splashing and churning as the swimmers tried to find their own places and begin their swims. There were collisions. It looked like there were a few confrontations that turned into weak punches.

But before he could analyze how he was going to avoid the

melee, it was his group's turn to go. He looked for May, but couldn't see her and then he was jumping into the water. Surprisingly, it wasn't a cold shock. With the full wetsuit and the chilly ride onto the Bay, the water felt surprisingly comfortable. Mike decided to swim. He reached out for his first stroke and was kicked in the face. Simultaneously, someone grabbed his leg from behind and pulled him back. Then someone hit him from the side and he felt arms flailing around him. Once again he started to swim and again he was kicked in the face. This time his goggles were knocked off. Mike started to panic but remembering his lifeguard training and his years as a Water Safety Instructor, he relaxed, breast-stroked away from the crowd, and looked around to make an assessment of what was going on. He saw that another wave of swimmers was about to hit the water. He scanned the horizon and realized that he could take a wider route, parallel to the pack but not in it. He readjusted his goggles and started to swim. After about twenty strokes, he found a rhythm and settled into his own contemplative world of stroking and breathing, periodically looking up to make sure he wasn't swimming wildly off course.

May watched as Mike finally settled down. She felt bad. She had forgotten to tell him about the violent swim start. She remembered her first triathlon where she thought she was going to drown. She almost gave up at the start of the swim. In later triathlons, she had learned not to try to swim with the pack, instead choosing to start wide, even if it meant a longer swim. Of course you really didn't have that option in this race. It wasn't like you could walk a few hundred yards down the beach for the start. Fortunately, Mike had figured it out. He was now passing the majority of his group. She loved to watch him swim. There was power and control, smoothness. He made it look so easy. In fact, everything with him was so easy. She'd known a lot of people in her life but had never found anyone so easy to be with. Over the course of their training, they'd had several breakfasts and lunches together and had become great friends. And friendship was a great start. As soon as she thought it, May kicked herself. She shouldn't look a gift horse in the mouth. She was lucky to have such a great friend. She shouldn't start wishing for more or she'd certainly mess things up. May didn't have time to think about that any further. It was her turn to go. She jumped.

Mike was waiting for May in the bike transition area.

"I hope I didn't keep you waiting too long," she said.

"Not as long as you might think. That first part of the swim really set me back." Mike replied, enjoying watching May strip off her wetsuit much more than he should have. He couldn't help noticing the erect nipples protruding through the thin material of her Speedo as she quickly slipped on her bike shoes.

"Ready?" she asked.

"Let's go!"

About two thirds of the way through the bike course, May pulled up alongside Mike.

"You're about 3 minutes ahead of our training pace for the bike leg. How are you feeling?"

"I'm feeling good. I'm not feeling tired at all."

"Well, don't push it too hard. The run will be harder than you think," May cautioned.

They made it to the transition area without incident and quickly changed into running shoes. They jogged the first quarter mile of the run course to shake off the wobbly feeling that a long bike ride causes and then moved into a very comfortable pace running side by side except when they had to avoid or pass someone. They reached the turnaround point on Baker Beach and it was clear that Mike was flagging.

"Doing okay? May probed.

"Ah. Yeah. I'm tired but I know I can finish."

As they approached the sand ladder, Mike slowed. "Ah shit," he moaned.

May slowed and slipped behind him. "Walk it if you have to. You don't need to set any records today."

Mike slowed to a jog. About fifty steps from the top, Mike had to walk. "I'm really sorry. I don't think I can do this."

"Sure you can. Once we get to the top, it's mostly downhill. Just walk this last bit and we'll coast to the finish. Just don't stop altogether."

The fifty steps were grueling and Mike was tempted to sit down and enjoy the view. But with May behind him, he kept moving albeit slowly. When they reached the top, May encouraged him to jog. Sure enough, less than a quarter mile later, Mike was running again. In half a mile, they were back to their training pace.

As they approached the finish line, people were cheering them on. Mike looked over at May who didn't seem tired at all. "Let's kick it in," she said as they had about a hundred yards to go.

Mike knew the only think to be kicked was his butt, but he gave it his best. At the last second, May slowed and Mike finished first, much to his surprise.

"Good job Mike!" May exclaimed, hugging him as soon as they'd cleared the finish area. "That was really impressive. I know I couldn't have done the Escape as my first triathlon. It was years and more than a dozen shorter events before I even tried it. Not only that, but if you subtract out the time you waited for me, you finished in under three hours! You should be proud of yourself."

For his part, Mike was a bit distracted. The only thing separating May's body from his was her thin Speedo. He could feel her small breasts pressing against him and he loved the odors emanating from her taught sweaty body. He buried his head in her hair. He'd been with quite a few women over the years, but he'd never felt anything like this. She was attractive and he respected her. In fact, he outright admired her. She could do things he couldn't and while she was very competitive, she was also gracious. Maybe there was a lot more here than he'd let himself think about.

"Thanks May. I've never done anything like this before. I know I couldn't have done it without you."

May squeezed a little tighter and they held each other for a bit longer before May broke the spell.

"Ready to eat?"

Letting the intensity go and trying to keep it light, Mike replied, "Sure, what did you have in mind?"

"Well, I know it has a touristy reputation, but I'd like to take you to the Cliff House. They have great breakfasts and one of the best views in the City."

"You know, I've lived here my whole life and I've never been to the Cliff House. I've always thought it was a tourist trap. But sure, I'm game."

After a quick change, they loaded the bikes onto May's car.

"Here," May said. "Have a look at this while we drive over."

Mike opened the manila folder and saw that it was a lengthy technical report regarding Bay and ocean currents.

"I got that Friday. There are no big surprises, but it may help a bit. Did you hear anything more from Vice?"

"Not really. We know that the first victim was a City College student who was dealing and had some connections in the Tenderloin, but we haven't been able to tie him to prostitution at this point. My friend's team is still trying to get someone to talk about him, but I think everyone is afraid of being implicated in his death, so they're not saying anything."

Mike turned to the report and they continued in silence. As May was pulling into a parking spot along the Great Highway, fifty yards down from the Cliff House, Mike said, "So if I read this correctly, there's a 93% chance that all of the bodies were dumped somewhere between Fort Point and Fort Mason. There really aren't too many places that are private enough to dump a body without being seen. In most places, you'd have to carry it quite a ways to the edge of the water. I guess we have the yacht club, some of the old piers at Fort Mason, and Fort Point as the most likely locations. In any case, it looks like all the victims were dumped in San Francisco –"

"Hey," May interrupted clearly irritated. "You're not going to pull the jurisdiction thing are you?"

"No, no. I'm certainly not going to cut you out of the case. We'll work together just as we have. But your victim was likely killed in the City, so assuming we catch the perp, we'll likely prosecute the whole thing here. Please don't worry. We're a team!"

May felt guilty. Why did she react so strongly? She trusted Mike. "Sorry," she said. "I overreacted. I've been cut out of cases in the past over jurisdiction. Plus, I really didn't want to stop working with you."

"Well, for my two cents," Mike began, smiling warmly. "I would hope we can spend time together beyond the work and the training. Maybe I'm on a post-race endorphin high, but I think we have something really good here. I'm not planning to screw it up."

They got out of the car and May dropped some quarters in the parking meter. As they started up the hill, Mike took May's hand. Several surfers were waiting for waves in Kelly's cove, a popular surfing spot at the north end of Ocean Beach. Mike had always loved this stretch of coastline. It was hard to believe that the city of San Francisco had such great beaches. A few miles to the south was Fort Funston where hang gliders flew whenever there was wind. The cliffs there suddenly ended and the sand dunes above the long flat beach ran all the way to Kelley's Cove next to Seal Rock and the treacherous cliffs of Land's End.

They reached the Cliff House, just above the ragged point at Land's End and were told they had a thirty minute wait. They gave Mike an electronic buzzer and said that it would work within about two hundred feet of the restaurant. May led Mike outside.

"I know you're the San Francisco native, but if you've never been to the Cliff House, you may not know what's here.'

"Actually, it's just that I've never eaten at the Cliff House. I have spent a fair amount of time on Land's End. The trail starts just beyond the Sutro Bath ruins and connects to the one we ran today. I used to hang out here as a kid. I've hiked the lower trail, which is pretty treacherous at points, and I've done fairly regular runs along the bluffs outside the Golden Gate, down to Marina Green and back. It's one of those areas that not many people, even those of us who live in San Francisco, tend to think about. Have you been out there?

"Yeah. I sometimes come into the City and often start my day with a run from here to the Marina and back followed by breakfast here. I'm surprised I haven't seen you running."

"Maybe you did. Ships passing in the night and all that."

They walked in silence for a few minutes down into the Sutro Bath ruins and out onto the point where water used to flow into the baths.

"What about the Camera Obscura?" May asked.

"Camera Obscura?"

"Gotcha! I can't believe that you haven't seen it. The prices have gotten ridiculous over the past years, but if you've never seen it, it's worth it. Let's go."

They walked back up the hill past the Cliff House and May led Mike to a funky building just to the south of the Cliff House. It was square shack with a flat roof and a cylindrical rotating object on the top. A man sat reading in the concession entrance.

May asked for two tickets and paid the fee. She took Mike's hand and said, "Prepare to be impressed!"

Mike was anything but prepared to be impressed. From the exterior, it certainly didn't look like much. There was no crowd, no line. The guy at the front looked positively bored. If this was such a great thing, why was it so empty?

They walked through the narrow entrance pushing aside a curtain. On the walls were old-fashioned holograms. Mike hadn't seen one of these in years and with the advent of modern 3-D technologies, didn't think they really stood up very well to the test of time. Still, they were interesting artifacts of the beginning of the technology age. But Mike hoped this wasn't May's idea of something cool.

As they rounded a corner, Mike spotted the disc in the center of the room that was illuminated by a beam of light from the ceiling. As he approached he saw a moving panorama of Seal Rock, the sea lions and surfers in the water, Kelly's Cove, and the north end of Ocean Beach.

Mike knew a fair amount about photography and a bit about graphics. But for all the images, photos, and films he'd seen over the years, he'd never seen such remarkable resolution. It was realer than real. Surreal didn't describe it because that word made it sound bizarre. No, this image was just intense. Once you started looking at it, you couldn't stop. Clearly the image was magnified, but there was something about it. He was drawn in not only by the image itself, but by the wonder of how anything could be so clear, so concise.

"Pretty cool, huh?" May asked.

"Quite frankly, I was prepared to be under-impressed. But this is phenomenal. Do you know how it works?"

"Well, we could probably ask Robert to come in to explain it to us, but I'll give it a try first. These things have been in existence for hundreds of years. Some people say the Chinese invented them in the 5th century. They became pretty popular in the fifteenth century, and DaVinci created a lot of sketches of his versions. The technology is pretty simple. There's a mirror or mirrors that reflect images back into a lens. That lens has an opposing lens which depending on the focal lengths allow for projection of the image onto a surface a specific distance away. In this case, they have this six foot parabolic dish, and they've put a motor on the top to rotate the 'camera'. It's really a combination of a pinhole camera and a periscope. The images are so ultra-real that in the olden days, the Catholic Church banned them in many places claiming they were works of Satan. During the Renaissance, a number of artists used them as the basis for their paintings. I don't know much about that, but I read somewhere that Vermeer achieved his almost surreal plays of light because of what he saw in his camera obscura."

They watched in comfortable silence for several minutes until the camera had made its loop a few times.

"Hungry?" May asked.

"Absolutely. Let's go check in."

The pager buzzed just as they entered the doorway to the building and they made their way to the restaurant. They handed the flashing pager to the hostess who led them to a window table with an incomparable view of the rocks at Land's End and the surfers braving what seemed like chaotic waves between the rocks.

"Mark will be your server today," the hostess said. "Enjoy your brunch!"

Within a minute a blond, well-built young man approached the table.

"Hi, I'm Mark and I'll be serving you today. Can I get you something to drink?"

"Well Mark," May began, not skipping a beat. "My friend and I just completed the Escape from Alcatraz and we're thirsty and famished. Can you start us off with water and lots of popovers?"

"Sure. I'll be right back with those. In the meantime, feel free to take your time with the menu and don't forget to look at our drink menu. You guys deserve to celebrate your success."

"Thanks Mark," May continued. "We're so hungry I'm sure we'll be ready to order by time you get back.

Mike was impressed. First May helped him through the Escape. Then she showed him places in his city that he'd never known about. Now, she was taking charge in the restaurant. A guy could get used to having someone take care of him like this. Mike couldn't remember ever meeting a woman who seemed as together and capable as May, and who was confident enough that she didn't feel she had to defer to him. And Mike didn't feel competitive with May, just very comfortable.

"So what do you recommend for breakfast," Mike asked.

"Personally, I like the Johnson Omelets," May responded. "It's three eggs with Dungeness crab, avocado and sour cream served with potatoes and fruit."

"Well, you've been right about everything so far. Let's stay on the roll."

"I'm not being too bossy, am I?"

"I spend all my days making decisions. I'm always the boss. I've always got the responsibility. It's really nice to let that go for a while. I appreciate your lead and all you've done for me with the training and helping me finish today. I couldn't have done it without you."

"Sure you could have. Hopefully though it was more fun with me around," May said, immediately kicking herself.

"It sure was, and as I started to say before, I'm hoping we can have a lot more fun together."

Mark the waiter arrived with a pitcher of water, a basket of popovers, butter and a selection of jams.

"The jams are strawberry, apricot, and a mixed berry. After burning about a million calories, I'm sure you'll make quick work of this basket of popovers, so I'll be back in five minutes or so with another one. I didn't want to bring more because I wanted to make sure that you get to eat them while they're hot. They're definitely not as good cold. I'll also leave the pitcher of water so you can refill as much as you need to. Have you made your decision on what you'd like to eat?

"We'd both like Johnson Omelets," May replied.

"And anything to drink?"

May looked over at Mike who just nodded and smiled. Clearly this was her show.

"I think we'll just stick with water for now."

"Great! I'll be back shortly with more popovers. Enjoy."

May put butter and a dollop of the mixed berry jam on her plate and reached into the basket for a popover. Tearing off a piece, she added a bit of butter, topped it with the jam and popped it into her mouth. She sighed with delight.

"Sorry! I just couldn't wait. Try one!"

Two minutes later, they'd each eaten two popovers. May took the last one, tore it in two and gave one half to Mike. Instantly, Mark the waiter appeared with another basket and set two glasses of champagne on the table.

"I know you're thirsty and probably just need hydration, but this is on the house. We thought you guys should celebrate. Your order will be out in ten minutes or so."

"Thanks Mark!" they both chimed in together.

Mike picked up both glasses of champagne and handed one to May.

"To a remarkable woman who I'd really like to get to know much, much better!"

"To a man who's comfortable with himself, who I'd like to get to know much, much better!"

5

Liz looked at Jim's card and dialed the number without hesitating. After all, if a girl wants something, she has to go for it. Jim picked up on the first ring.

"Jim Henderson."

"Hi Jim, it's Liz. I know it's the middle of your work day and I hope I'm not interrupting anything, but I was wondering if you wanted to join me for some Japanese and a French film at the Shattuck Cinema tonight."

"Liz, could you hold on one second?"

"Sure."

In the background Jim was talking to someone and it sounded like they were setting a meeting for the next day.

"Sorry about that. I didn't put you on hold because we have god-awful company promotions to greet you there. I've tried to get them to put on some blues or even some old jazz standards, but the marketing types are sure that listening to our promotions will encourage people to buy. I know it doesn't work for me, but the bottom line is that I'm not a marketing type so who am I to say?"

"No. I'm sorry if I interrupted a meeting."

"Actually we were done and just needed to confirm our follow up. Okay, dinner and a movie tonight? Let me think a minute. Ah, sure. What time?"

"You're the one who has to face commute traffic. When do you think you can get to Berkeley?"

"Ah, let's see. If I leave at six, I should be there by seven, barring no accidents. On the other hand, if I leave at 7, I can probably get there by seven forty or so. Of course that gets us started later…"

"Well, I'm sorry to put you into traffic hell, but if we do want to get both dinner and a movie, we should start as early as possible. I'll make seven-thirty reservations. We should be able to make the nine-o'clock show. "

"Okay. I'll give you a call if it looks like I'm running later."

They hung up and Jim realized that he hadn't even asked what the film was.

The rest of Jim's afternoon went quickly and with no crises at work, Jim was pleased to see that he was out the door before six o'clock. He jumped in his Subaru and dove into the evening commute traffic. It moved slowly but consistently until he was about half-way across the San Mateo Bridge at which point everything stopped. Listening to traffic reports he discovered that there was an accident about a mile ahead of where he was. Since he was on a bridge, there was nothing he could do but wait for the blockage to clear. He tried to call Liz but got her voicemail. He let her know that he had no idea when the road would clear but that he'd call again once he got across the bridge. Then he turned off his car, pulled a book out of his backpack and started reading while news and traffic droned on in the background.

Liz returned home with a new outfit for the evening. The off-the-shoulder dark blue dress contrasted nicely with her long chestnut hair while the white jacket added a bit of modesty. The shoes were to die for. She wanted to make an impression without being too overtly sexy.

She checked her voicemail and picked up Jim's message, did a quick mental calculation and realized that with the delay, a movie would be very unlikely. She'd have to come up with another idea. Hopefully Jim wouldn't find it too bold. She definitely had time to get a nice surprise to cap the evening.

After more than thirty minutes, Jim saw cars ahead starting their engines and beginning to move slowly. Twenty-five minutes later, he exited the bridge onto Highway 880. He called Liz and got her voicemail again. He left a message telling her he'd be there in about twenty minutes, but was a bit worried. Had he misunderstood about the timing for the evening? Had he ruined everything by being so late? God, he hated to be late.

Fortunately, when he pulled up in front of her house, the lights were on. The door opened before he could knock and Liz appeared, smiling and stunningly gorgeous. She kissed him quickly on the lips and said, "Sorry you had such a rough drive. I'll do my best to make the evening worth it.

"I changed the reservations to eight, so we should get going. I'll drive since I know the way. Could you take this duffle bag? Don't peek inside. It's a surprise for later."

Almost too stunned to speak, Jim replied, "Ah – of course. You look fantastic!"

"Why thank you kind sir," Liz responded teasingly. "Follow me."

Jim hefted the duffle bag and tried to imagine what might be inside. The contents seemed compact in the center of the bag and probably weighed about ten pounds.

"Remember, no peeking," Liz warned, grinning.

Liz led Jim to a cherry-red Porsche Boxer Roadster, popped the trunk so that Jim could place the duffle inside and said, 'Hop in!'"

Settling in to the soft leather seat, Jim took a deep breath and let it out slowly. The evening seemed to be going a bit too fast, and they hadn't even left Liz's house yet.

"You okay?" Liz asked.

"Yeah. I'm sorry. I'm a bit stressed. I hate being late. My father literally beat timeliness into me and I get really wired when I lose control of the time like this. Sorry about making things so rushed."

"Don't worry. Here, I'll put the top down and we'll take the scenic route. I'll even keep the speed under ninety." But seeing the panicked look on Jim's face quickly added, " Just joking. I'm sure Yoshi's will hold our reservations for a few minutes."

With the top down, Liz pulled slowly away from the curb. "Jim, just sit back and enjoy the stars. Relax. This is a no pressure evening. There are no deadlines, nothing we absolutely have to do. I'm just looking forward to spending it with you."

Jim did just that as Liz drove the Porsche smoothly up a winding road. As they reached the top, Liz pulled off and they sat in silence looking down at the entire San Francisco Bay. Ribbons of lights crossed the Bay to the north, west, and south, and Jim could see large ships coming into the Port of Oakland. They sat in silence as Jim inhaled the crisp night air. It was peaceful and quiet above the insanity of the Bay Area below. He could feel himself relaxing.

"Feel better?" Liz asked.

"Much. Thanks for slowing it down a bit."

"Since it's only five minutes from my house, I often come up here when I need to just let it all go. When I'm caught up in the pressures of daily life, it always amazes me that you can find serenity just a few minutes away."

"You're right. My house is at the base of Montara Mountain and it's just a few minutes to Devil's Slide, but for some reason, I rarely take advantage of it. I really should get out more," Jim said, smiling now.

"Hungry yet?"

"Absolutely!"

As they wound their way back down to civilization, Jim looked over at Liz. Her hair was flying back from her face and flipping upward into the wind. As she drove confidently down the hill, Jim couldn't remember ever having met such a beautiful woman who was so self-assured. And it wasn't self-assurance out of vanity. Liz knew who she was and what she wanted.

"So tell me about the car," Jim began, trying to restart the evening's conversation.

"I know it seems a bit much, but Daddy gave it to me for my graduation. I love the car. You felt how it rides and how smooth it is around the curves. I lived with a dying Honda throughout law school, so I'm really grateful to have this now. Of course there's no way to carry a hang glider on top unless I want to have someone attach huge rectangular racks to the front and rear bumpers with bars connecting them above the car.

"But I'd never do that to my baby. I'll just have to rely on the kindness of strangers for rides up and down the mountains."

"And to the mountains."

"Yes. To the mountains as well. Maybe when I finally settle down with a full time job, I can buy a 4X4 specifically for recreation."

"Sounds like a perfect plan. So, what are your plans? Graduating from Boalt, I'd think you'd have an easy time finding a high-paying job with a major firm like the one you're working for – Mansfield something, right."

"Ah, Mansfield, Mason, and Williams. That plus Daddy's connections can certainly set me up pretty much anywhere. But I don't know. Maybe it's just finally being at the end of an exhausting three years in law school, but I'm just not ready to join a big firm and try to bill a thousand hours a week. In fact, I'm beginning to question the whole law thing. Although I've been raised in it and Daddy and his friends have taught me to argue and shown me how the system works, I must admit that after seeing so many injustices done, I'm really questioning the adversary system. I understand the logic, and understand that Western systems of justice are all based on the concept, but I have to ask how we can focus more on winning than on getting to the truth. At the same time, I do love to argue and I think I'd be a good litigator. Did you have second thoughts about starting your career?

Jim thought carefully before answering. "Actually no. Once I stumbled into computer science in school, I couldn't get enough of it. I'd used computers before and had even done a bit of hacking, but once I saw the science of it, I became intrigued by the countless problems that you could solve if you really thought about new ways of doing things. I like to think the work I'm doing makes the world a better place by making information more accessible."

"God, it must be nice to have such a clear vision. I sure wish I did. I just get so confused sometimes as far as my priorities go. Plus, while you haven't seen it yet, from time to time I screw up in a big way and have to move heaven and earth and call in favors just to get back on track. But let's not go there tonight. I don't want to scare you away yet. "

"I'm probably not in a position to say this," Jim ventured somewhat sheepishly, "But if we're stuck with the adversary system, don't we need good lawyers who know how to argue and know how to work the system to protect those that get caught up in it?"

"Yeah, that's very true. Like I said, sometimes I lose sight of the goal. Anyway, that's Yoshi's," Liz pointed out as she turned into a large parking garage. "I remember when it used to be on my street in Oakland. Now it's really a big deal."

Liz wound her way up the ramps in the parking garage until she reached the top which was open to the sky. She chose a spot far away from the other cars. As Jim got out of the car, he looked up at the stars which were visible in spite of the city lights. To the northwest he could see the Bay Bridge and the lights of cars racing towards both San Francisco and Oakland.

Liz took Jim's hand and led him towards the elevator. "Have you been here before?"

"Ah, Jack London Square, yes. But it was during the day. The Port of Oakland is one of our clients. But I haven't been to Yoshi's. I've heard it's a great jazz and blues club with excellent Japanese food. That seems almost like a contradiction."

"Daddy often took the family to the one on Claremont when I was little. I remember the food but not the music. I don't think it was as much of a venue as it is now that they've moved down here."

"I've caught a few shows here and the food is exceptional. It's changed from the more standard Japanese fare I remember. I think you'll find it interesting. I didn't book us into a show since I was anticipating a movie afterwards, but maybe we could do that another time."

As the elevator doors opened on the first floor, Jim realized he was still holding Liz's hand. It felt surprisingly comfortable, almost like they'd done this before. At the same time, he felt a bit guilty. After all, he wasn't even divorced yet.

Liz made her way to the maître d'.

"Ah, Ms. Leahy. It's good to see you again. I have your table ready. Please follow me."

He led them to a table away from other diners and said, "Daniel will be your server tonight. Do enjoy your evening and give my best to your father."

"Does everyone know your father?" Jim asked, clearly impressed.

"Yes. And I'm a very lucky girl. I really have a perfect life. I just need to figure out what I'm going to do with it."

Daniel, the waiter appeared, recounted the specials for the evening and took drink orders. Liz ordered a Bellini. Jim asked what a Bellini was and after Daniel explained, he asked for the same.

"We'll also share the Hamachi Crudo and the Panko Brussels Sprouts as appetizers," Liz ordered, taking the lead.

"The Hamachi is one of my favorites," Daniel replied. "I'll be right back with your Bellinis followed by the appetizers. Take your time with the menu."

Jim looked admiringly at Liz. He couldn't help comparing her to Sharon. Liz was a classic beauty with a contagious energy. She was charismatic and people were drawn to her. Either she didn't have too many tragedies in her life, or somehow, they hadn't affected her. Sharon was haunted by demons. Liz had a family who supported and encouraged her. Sharon's dragged her down. His life had been much more like Sharon's than Liz's and Liz's seemed very enticing.

"So Jim," Liz began. "I'm going to say straight out that I'm very attracted to you and that I would really like to get to know you much better. That said, and before I jump in with both feet, can you tell me more about your marriage and pending divorce?"

"Sure. You know, it's funny. I've never really talked with anyone about it. Although my friends know what's going on, I've never given anyone the details. I'm sure that part of it is that I had hoped that we'd get back together and didn't want to say anything that might give people a bad impression of my wife Sharon or of our relationship."

Jim paused, looked at Liz and then told her the whole story, interrupted only by Daniel bringing drinks, then appetizers and then their dinners along with regular refills of hot sake.

When Jim finished, Liz asked, "Do you still love her?"

"It's funny," Jim replied. "Months have passed since we've really seen each other and things have changed. I've always told myself that I still loved her but as I look at it now, it seems quite distant. I know five months isn't a long time, but maybe it's my upbringing where I moved so often and left people behind. I remember them and I remember the feelings and experiences I had, but the immediacy is gone. Still at least with respect to Sharon's memory, I think I'll always love her, but it's almost like it's been filed away. Sorry I can't explain it better."

Jim looked down at his empty plate feeling embarrassed, thinking he'd really thrown a wet blanket on the evening. On the other hand, she did ask.

"Hey Jim," Liz said softly. "Thank you for opening up about this. I can see it was hard for you. And while you may think you've ruined our evening, you definitely haven't. I really wanted to understand where you were with all of this. Thank you for trusting me.

"You know, I've been there. While I haven't been married, I've had several long term relationships. As I look back on them, I can honestly say that I still love every one of my exes. But as you can see with Bob, Bill, and Steve, that love has evolved and all of my exes are now great friends. I'm hoping that even though the relationship with Mark just ended, that he and I will be friends for a long time too.

"From what you said, you and Sharon are still on good terms. Maybe your relationship will transform into something else. If there's one thing I've learned in my short romantic life, loving someone isn't necessarily sufficient for a long relationship and neither is just being compatible. I think (since I obviously haven't achieved it yet) that it takes a combination of the two along with something more, a fit in temperaments. You have to be able to get along on multiple levels. Sometimes these things can be worked out. Sometimes they can't. While it's not my place to say, from what you've told me, this is where your relationship with Sharon broke down. You were a great fit from your backgrounds, goals and levels of intelligence, but your inherent stability and consistency was probably very challenging for her. Sure, she could change, but in my experience, it takes life-altering events to effect this level of change. I'm really sorry it didn't work out for you and that you had to go through the pain you did. Hopefully, with each new try at a relationship we learn something and eventually find the right person."

"Does that mean you don't believe in one perfect match?" Jim asked, clearly surprised.

"With over six billion people on the planet, I find it hard to believe that there is one perfect match for each person. Plus, if you think about a given person's life, they go through major changes depending on events, experiences and their reactions to them. While I'd like to subscribe to the very romantic notion that you can find the right person and live with them happily ever after, unless they're twins who have identical experiences and identical reactions to those experiences, they're going to change in different ways. There are no guarantees that they'll be able to maintain compatibility. That's not to say you need to find someone exactly like you to be successful in a long-term relationship, but you need some basic levels of compatibility in terms of how you relate, how you react to good and bad situations, and how you grow. I think that affords the best chance of success. But life is change and you never really know. All we can do is try our best, learn from our mistakes, and keep moving forward."

Jim was stunned. Who was this woman? What was she, twenty-five? How did she arrive at such rational wisdom? Truth be told, this was very much along the lines of Jim's beliefs. After growing up as a military brat and going through so many losses of friends and dramatic changes in his life, he couldn't help but think that every change presented an opportunity. There weren't really good and bad decisions in your life, just different ones that set you on different paths – paths that affected or directed your career, your relationships, and your possible futures. Who's to say that one is better or worse than another? It was all really about tradeoffs. Tradeoffs of career choice versus free time; tradeoffs of social networking versus privacy; hell, even tradeoffs of what you choose for dinner. Clearly that was true for relationships as well.

Seeing Liz's plate empty and watching her down the last of the sake, Jim asked her whether she was interested in dessert.

"Well, although they have some pretty good desserts here, dessert is part of my surprise. Let's see. It's nine-thirty. Perfect. Let's pay the bill and go. By the way, since I invited you and forced you to face traffic, dinner's on me. Next time, maybe I can come your way."

Jim appreciated the fact that even after his tale of marital woe and expression of continued love for Sharon, Liz still wanted to see him. They tussled over the bill briefly when it arrived and in the end, Jim prevailed.

"Okay," Liz capitulated. "But there can be no question that the surprise is on me. Deal?"

"Sure."

After stopping a moment to gaze at the view arm in arm from the top of the garage, they got into Liz's Porsche. She made her way through surprisingly heavy traffic and took the freeway north, exiting on University Avenue. Liz made a left onto a street that Jim didn't recognize, then several turns onto darkened residential streets. She pulled up in front of what looked like a small house surrounded by hedges and tall plants that he couldn't identify at night.

Liz popped the trunk and asked, "Jim would you get the duffle bag out of the trunk? Same rules, no peeking!"

They walked together up the cobblestoned path and climbed the steps to the porch of a Craftsman-style house. Mounted next to the door was a sign that read: Japanese Teahouse.

Although the sign set Jim's expectations, he wasn't prepared for the beauty of the interior. The floors and walls were rich woods of varying tones. Several hand-carved exotic wooden benches, chairs, tables and hutches lined the walls. Spectacular orchids graced the room along with large murals depicting Japanese life.

"Ah, Ms. Leahy! It's been quite a while since we've seen you. I was pleased to see your reservation for tonight," greeted a middle-aged Japanese woman dressed in a classic red and gold kimono.

"Hello Miko, I'm sorry it's been so long. I'll try to get here more often in the future. I really have missed it. Miko, this is my friend Jim."

"I'm honored to meet you Jim and hope that you will enjoy

your visit with us. Ms. Leahy, I have reserved the room you requested. What type of tea would you like?"

"Let's start with the Marnier Tea. I think Jim will like that."

Miko picked up two white bundles then led them down a hallway paneled in wood and stone with more Japanese pen and ink drawings on the walls. They stopped in front of a door with a carved wooden sign saying 'Ochitsuki'. She handed the bundles to Jim and Liz, opened the door and said "Dozo".

As Jim and Liz entered, Miko said, "Please ring if you need anything. I will bring the tea in few minutes and will leave it outside your door. She closed the door behind her and Liz locked it. Seeing Jim's look of surprise, Liz soothed, "Don't worry Jim, you're not my prisoner. If you're not up for this, we can do something else. Otherwise, relax and enjoy."

As Jim's eyes adjusted to the dim light, he looked around the room. The floors, walls, and ceiling were all made of thick wood panels. A gently bubbling hot tub was off-center on the right side of the room. On the left were two doors, one with a small window. Between them was an area of stone with a stone bench and a large overhead shower. Beyond the last door was a long table with an embroidered runner. Beads of condensation sprouted from a pitcher on a tray with two glasses. The far end of the room was open with sliding shoji doors that looked onto a spectacular Japanese garden, complete with small waterfalls, bridges and exotic plants and fish. Tatami mats lined the doorway.

"It's, ah, beautiful," Jim stammered, setting the cooler down. "I didn't expect this." Then, buying time, he asked, "What does Ochitsuki mean?" I lived in Japan for a while as a kid but I don't know that word."

"Well, from what I understand," Liz began, removing her shoes and nodding to Jim to do the same, "It's a word that means tranquility and relaxation. I used to come here after exams to unwind. It's quiet and peaceful with that beautiful garden. There are only a few rooms and most look out onto the garden like this one, but they're positioned such that each has complete privacy. I don't know how they did it, but sound from one doesn't reach any of the others. I've been here many times and I've never heard anyone else even though I know others are here."

At that moment, there was a soft knock at the door.

"That's the tea."

Liz opened the door and brought in a tray with an ornate ceramic teapot and cups, cloth napkins, and a plate of small cookies. She took it over to the tatami mats in front of the garden and placed it on a small table that Jim hadn't seen from the entry. She sat down and let out a big sigh as she gazed into the garden. Jim joined her on the floor and looked at Liz's face, gently alit from the small garden lamps. She looked over at Jim and smiled wordlessly. She turned to the tray and poured two cups of tea, placing cookies on the saucers, then handed one to Jim.

"To comfort, gentleness, and tranquility," she whispered very softly, lightly brushing Jim's cup with hers.

A bit unsure of the gentleness reference, Jim replied softly, "To comfort, gentleness and tranquility."

Following Liz's lead, Jim took a sip of tea and looked silently into the garden. As he watched the movement of the water and the plants gently swaying in the breeze, he could feel the layers of stress from the day beginning to ebb. He took another sip of the tea and was suddenly aware of the complex flavors. There was orange, like the Grand Marnier it was named for, a hint of cinnamon, cloves, maybe some apple. The flavors were distinct, yet combined so well. The warmth of the tea soothed him from the inside out. He let out a deep sigh and relaxed, closing his eyes to better listen to the sounds of water and wind in the garden.

After a few minutes, he opened his eyes to find Liz smiling at him. "Better?" she asked.

"Much." Jim replied. "Do you have a plan?"

"Not so much a plan as an idea. The first door is a bathroom. We can change into the robes there and then move into sauna for a few minutes. I find that a few minutes of a good sweat to clear the pores does wonders. After the sauna, we can open my surprise and then perhaps we can soak for a while. What do you think?"

"Sounds wonderful. You know, I've never done anything like this. I've been in a few hot tubs, always with other people, but never really found it relaxing. This is very different. Thank you!"

"Why don't you bring the cooler over here and put it on the table while I change?" Liz suggested as she stood up with the bundle Miko had given her.

"Sure."

A few minutes later Liz stepped out of the bathroom wrapped

in a towel with the robe draped over her shoulders. "I'll meet you in the sauna."

Jim stepped into the bathroom and saw Liz's dress hanging on an ornate hook. He couldn't help looking under it and did confirm that she had left her bra and panties there. Was he ready for this? On the other hand, so far, nothing sexual had happened. Maybe this was just going to be a relaxing evening. He undressed, hung his clothes on the hook next to Liz's and wrapped the towel around his waist. He stepped out of the bathroom, gazed once more at the garden, then took a deep breath and entered the dimly lit sauna. The hot dry air took his breath away for an instant.

Liz was lying on one of the benches on her stomach, the towel still modestly wrapped around her. Jim stretched out on the perpendicular bench, his head near hers. They lay there in silence for a few minutes. Jim turned over on his stomach. The heat was intense and a gentle torpor descended on Jim. He barely noticed Liz getting up. She went to a large bucket of water, took the ladle and poured some water over the coals in the corner. Steam briefly filled the room and the additional humidity made it easier to breath. Liz came over to Jim, straddled him and gently massaged his back starting with the trapezius, working down and under his scapulae, then to his waist and back up. It felt great. While he had given countless massages in his life, Jim had received very few. Most of those were clumsy attempts. But Liz was good. She knew what she was doing and he told her so.

"I took a few massage classes while at Cal. I like it a lot and briefly, actually very briefly, considered giving up the Law for massage."

"I bet your father would have been unhappy with that," Jim joked lightly.

"Actually, no. I discussed it with him at the time and he was very supportive. He did ask if I could enjoy a life with so much less intellectual challenge. And as we both knew, clearly I couldn't. So it's kind of a hobby now."

Liz continued a few minutes more. "Okay. My turn," Jim proposed.

Liz lay back down on her stomach and lowered the towel to her waist. Jim started much as Liz had, working the upper back, under the shoulder blades, and down to her lower back. He moved upward and massaged her neck and head, pressing upward and outward, gently stretching, then stroking back down above her ears, onto her neck again, and then repeated the whole process very slowly.

"My God, you're good," Liz praised.

Minutes passed in quiet sensual bliss.

"I think it's time to step out and cool off," Liz suggested. "You're working far too hard for this heat. It's wonderful though. Thank you!"

Liz pulled up her towel and exited the sauna, holding the door for Jim. The comparably cool air was a bit of a shock but definitely a relief. Liz walked over to the table near the end of the room and filled the glasses with ice water. She handed one to Jim who drank greedily and then came over to refill his as Liz drank. He then refilled hers. Liz put on her robe and let the towel drop from underneath. She laid it near the hot tub. Jim did the same.

"That was perfect!" He said. "I feel wonderful. Okay. I guess I'm ready. What's the surprise?"

Liz smiled enigmatically and opened the cooler. She removed a pair of black napkins, two paper plates, and a rectangular package wrapped in white paper and tied with a green ribbon. Next, she took out two fluted champagne glasses and then a bottle of champagne. She handed Jim the bottle and asked him to open it while she unwrapped the package.

Jim noticed that it was Veuve Cliquot and tried to remember what he'd learned about opening champagne at Liz's parents' party. After removing the foil, he carefully untwisted the wire, keeping his hand over the top. He shook the wire gently to loosen the cap then removed it. He kept his hand over the top of the cork as he gently oscillated it back and forth until the cork began to move upward. He increased the pressure on the cork and as it rose slowly, he allowed a small amount of the pressure to escape with a barely audible hiss. Once the pressure eased, he removed the cork.

"Impressive!" Liz said smiling. "Not many people know how to properly open a bottle of champagne. I'll pour. Why don't you have a seat next to the garden?"

The glasses were as chilled as the champagne so Liz easily filled the glasses with the golden bubbly liquid. She turned her back to Jim to conceal what she was doing, then placed something on the paper plates.

"Ready?" she queried softly.

"Absolutely!"

Jim could see Liz pick up one of the champagne glasses. She reached for one of the paper plates then turned and said, "Surprise!"

Jim took the glass and looked closely at the contents of the plate in the dim light, barely making out two lumps of what appeared to be dark chocolate.

"They're strawberries dipped in dark chocolate and injected with Grand Marnier."

Liz picked up her plate and glass and sat down beside Jim. Taking a bite of one of her strawberries, she raised her champagne glass and toasted, "To new beginnings!"

Jim bit into one of the chocolate covered strawberries and was assaulted with the independent but complementary flavors of fresh fruit, rich chocolate, and the liqueur. He touched Liz's glass with his own and gazed into her smiling brown eyes as he sipped his champagne, washing down the bits of chocolate and strawberry in his mouth.

"Where do you work?" Liz asked almost tauntingly.

Jim started to respond but as he searched his brain for the name of his company, he realized what Liz was getting at. He was relaxed and work, which had never before left his mind for more than a few moments, was suddenly very far away – almost a distant memory.

"Who cares? Right now, I feel like this is my whole world."

Liz took the last bite of her strawberry, and a sip of champagne. Even in the dim light, Jim could see the melted chocolate on Liz's lips. As he looked at her longingly, she leaned upwards and kissed him. It was a deep, long kiss and Jim tasted chocolate, Grand Marnier, and Liz. Perhaps it was the champagne, or maybe the Grand Marnier, but Jim suddenly felt a little drunk. But it was a nice feeling, the world seemed as warm and soft as Liz's lips.

Gently pulling away, Liz looked intently at Jim. I'd really like to spend some time with you in the tub. I'll shower first."

And without giving him a chance to object, Liz stood up, carefully spread her towel and robe on the floor next to the hot tub and stepped into the shower. She turned to face him and leaned her head back into the hot stream of water, as the thoughts of Liz's shower at Elk Mountain overwhelmed Jim. She left the water running and slipped into the warm, simmering water of the hot tub.

Jim was very aroused. He was also embarrassed. He couldn't imagine walking naked to the hot tub in his current condition.

"It's okay," Liz coaxed. "It's wonderful in here. Shower and come join me. I won't look."

Jim did as he was told and true to her word, Liz didn't look. Jim slipped in beside her and they sat quietly, soaking and relaxing for several minutes, only their hands touching.

Jim didn't have to try to banish thoughts of Sharon from his mind. What he'd said before was true. At this moment, this room was his whole world. Liz was the only presence he felt.

As if sensing his thoughts, she leaned back towards him and he bent down to kiss her. If possible, this kiss was even more intense than the last. Although he had been with several women and had what he considered to be good number of sexual experiences, Jim had never felt both relaxed and excited at the same time. The urgency that arose within him came from a very deep place. He pulled Liz onto his lap, her back pressing against him. He gently stroked her breasts as he nuzzled and kissed her neck. Liz reached her hand over her head and stroked Jim's wet hair. Then she rolled over, straddled him and slipped him inside her.

They kissed without moving, then Jim eased them to the steps of the tub and up and out of the water, never losing contact with Liz. He knelt on the towel, then sat, and was then consumed by Liz, the warmth, the garden, the tranquility, and the urgency of their coupling.

6

Jim and Liz followed Steve and Bill down California's dry, flat, hot Central Valley. They stopped in Fresno, only a half an hour from their destination to fill up with gas and pick up last minute supplies and a few more cold drinks. Bill was clearly excited and Jim was a bit nervous with anticipation as he always was when he visited a new Hang Gliding site. After using the facilities, they pulled onto Highway 180 east towards King's Canyon. The terrain quickly changed from the ugly flatness of the previous hours to rolling hills which grew larger and more tree covered as they travelled further east. The Sierra Nevada loomed in the background and they could occasionally catch glimpses of snow-covered peaks, which seemed impossible given the one hundred plus degree heat. And as they pulled into the campground, Jim could, indeed smell turkey droppings.

"Do you get used to the smell?" Jim asked Steve as they stepped out of their cars to be greeted by Dan Fleming, the owner of the campground and landing area. Liz started laughing hysterically as she mouthed 'Turkey Poop' at them.

"I don't even smell it anymore," Dan replied laughing as well. "I guess this is your first time?"

"It is Jim's first time," Steve answered. "Dan, I don't know if you remember Bill and Liz, but they've flown here before too. Jim qualified for the Nationals and wanted to get a weekend in to try to understand a bit about the site before the big event."

"No one could forget Liz," Dan joked. "Bill, good to see you again. Jim, congratulations! I think you're going to like our little site. Let's step inside and we can get forms and waivers signed and I'll give you the lay of the land before you fly."

Thirty minutes later, the paperwork was done and Jim thought he had a reasonable idea where not to land and where at least a few of the good thermal areas were. Of course seeing the mountain and the terrain for real was completely different from looking at photos and a map.

"So," Steve queried. "Should we set up camp first so we don't have to do it when we get back or should we fly first?"

"Well, it's 12:30. I suggest we fly first so we don't miss the best conditions of the day," Bill proposed.

"I disagree," Liz piped in. "We really have all day. I can't imagine that it'll take more than half an hour to unload and get set up. Even if it did, the conditions will probably be good until sunset. Do you remember the last time? That evening glass off where all the air over the entire valley seemed to be going up?"

And so it was settled. They quickly unloaded their cars and set up tents; three in all as Liz and Jim were bunking together. Jim noted that neither Steve nor Bill seemed surprised. They moved some cool drinks and ice packs from the large cooler that Steve had brought into a much smaller one, loaded Jim and Liz's gliders onto Steve's 4x4 and headed up the hill.

It was a hot dusty windless day but a few cumulus clouds were popping over King's Canyon. As they rode up in companionable silence, Jim felt a bit nervous as usual when he flew a new site.

"Is there any chance one or more of us can land on top to avoid the shuttle with the cars? Jim asked to take his mind of the winding dirt Forest Service road.

"Actually, there's plenty of room up there," Steve responded. "The launch is on private land next to a house and the owners manage the launch and set the rules. Unfortunately, they've asked that no one land on top, so we're stuck with the shuttle. It's about half an hour each way, so we should be sure to leave plenty of time for the turnaround. Even with the sun not setting until eight-fifteen, daylight can get away from us and I must admit that I really don't like driving this road in the dark. I think Liz had the right idea with setting up camp first."

Trees along the road gave way to a large clearing as they neared the top of the ridge. Jim spotted microwave towers not far ahead. Steve pulled into a large dirt parking area next to a few other vehicles with hang gliding racks, but there was no one around. They got out of the car, stretched and then Steve led them to the launch.

"A ramp!" Jim exclaimed, admiring the low wooden deck-like structure that inclined off the edge of the ridge. "What a great view."

"Yeah. This is pretty nice. It makes takeoffs much easier. "See the gaggle?" Steve asked pointing upwards and a bit towards the northwest.

Sure enough, there were six gliders circling up in a thermal about a mile to the northwest, easily two thousand feet over the launch.

"Let's go!" Bill ordered.

They quickly set up and pre-flighted their gliders, added their instruments, and agreed on a frequency for their radios.

"I'm going first," Bill announced.

"Well, I'm glad I don't have to be the wind dummy today," Liz responded.

"Hell, we don't need a wind dummy. Just look at those guys!"

Bill walked his glider to the launch, clipped in, watched the brush below for movement and then ran down the ramp. Almost as soon as his feet left the ground, a thermal hit him and he began climbing. He made a few one hundred eighty degree turns back and forth across the ridge, steadily rising. A few hundred feet above the launch, he began circling.

"Yee haw! Get your butts up here!"

"As the senior pilot here, I'll go last," Steve said. "Liz, why don't you go next?"

Jim hadn't seen Liz fly. She, like Bill before her, set her glider down at the top of the ramp, clipped in, and waited patiently, eyeing the brush below the launch. Seeing what she wanted, she picked up her glider, pointed it down, parallel to the slope of the ramp, and ran down. Unlike Bill, she didn't go up right away. She turned right and sank slowly below the launch. A few hundred yards to the northwest, she turned back and passed a hundred feet below the launch as she headed south. Just as she was about to turn back, she started climbing. A few seconds into the climb, she banked the glider and circled upward rising very quickly.

"Your turn," Steve offered.

Jim walked up to the launch and was suddenly worried that he'd be the one who went straight to the landing area today. It had happened before. But he waited and waited. A few minutes later, well down the hill, he saw frantic movement of the brush. As soon as he felt the first whiff of air, he ran down the ramp and rose immediately into the thermal. He flew straight out from the launch climbing at over seven hundred feet a minute according to his variometer. When the glider surged violently upward, Jim knew he had hit the core. He banked the glider steeply and began circling up at over one thousand feet per minute. Round and round he went. The buildings near the launch got smaller and smaller. The air cooled. He spotted Liz's and Bill's gliders well below him. They were flying toward him, clearly hoping to catch his thermal, but his thermal was rapidly weakening. He looked at his altimeter and saw that he was over eight thousand feet. The view extended from the Central Valley to the west to the snow-capped mountains of the Sierra Nevada behind Mount Whitney. Jim decided to head northwest along the ridge knowing it might be a while before he caught his next thermal.

"Nice up here isn't it," he heard Steve's voice crackling in his headset.

Looking around, he saw Steve at the same altitude a bit to the east.

"How'd you get up here?" Jim queried, clearly puzzled.

"Right after launch, I caught one that went up even faster than yours. I watched you climb until you topped out not far from me. We must have hit the inversion layer. Let's spread out a bit as we head up the ridge. That way we can double our odds of finding the next good thermal."

A few miles to the north, Jim heard, "Got one!" and looked over to see Steve circling up. He quickly joined him and they circled up together, again topping out just over eight thousand feet.

They repeated this strategy which worked out well. About fifteen miles from the launch, above Pine Flat Lake, Steve suggested they turn back. The sun was lowering and the thermals seemed fewer. They found themselves at ridge level, still several miles from the landing area, scratching around in the bit of lift provided by the light breeze blowing up the ridge.

"Got a weak one," Jim announced.

Steve joined him and they circled lazily, climbing at less than three hundred feet a minute. They topped out at fifty-five hundred feet.

"Looks like the party's over," Jim lamented. "I sure hope we can make it back to the LZ!"

"I wouldn't worry too much. There aren't too many areas of sink between here and there and usually about this time the magic happens."

"Magic?" Jim wondered.

They continued south finding a few small thermals which got progressively weaker. As they reached ridge level, they transitioned into noticeably warmer air. Jim had experienced this at a few other sites. They called it the evening glass-off. The warm air of the valley seemed to rise as a whole into the cooler air above as the angle of the sun got low. Sure enough, they had an easy flight to the landing area, arriving with nearly two thousand feet of ground clearance. Steve started doing wing-overs, pulling into a dive, then leaning and pushing out through one hundred thirty degree banks. Jim followed suit but was a bit more conservative with his one hundred ten degree wingovers.

Jim watched as Steve set up for landing then did the same, touching the ground twenty feet to Steve's left.

"This is an amazing place to fly!" Jim exclaimed after unclipping and removing his helmet. "Is it like this all the time?"

"Well," Steve replied, "The road is closed to pilots most of the winter. Spring is much more punchy and you don't get the glass off, summer is like this most of the time depending on the westerly winds which blow through sometimes, and fall can be hit and miss. Still, I think it's one of the most consistent thermal sites I've flown. You can see why they chose it for the Nationals.

"Let's break down and see if Bill and Liz have done anything for dinner."

"Don't forget that we have a shuttle to do."

"Damn! That's right."

Once their gliders were broken down, they carried them over to the campsite.

Seeing Bill and Liz lounging at a picnic table with beers in one hand and cards in the other, Steve complained, "I guess we know who's going to do the shuttle. No, no, don't get up. We'll do the dirty work."

"Oh, don't worry," Liz said laughingly. "We weren't going to get up. We've been here a while and decided that since you guys got epic flights while we only got a little over an hour. You could do the shuttle."

Steve almost said that if they got down here that long ago, they could have already retrieved the car, but he held his tongue.

"Steve, let's go," Jim suggested.

"Okay, but since I'm cooking dinner, how about you guys start the fire in about thirty minutes?"

"Shit!" said Liz and Bill simultaneously.

"Sorry! We should have gotten the car. I forgot that you were cooking tonight. Everything will be ready to go when you guys get back."

Deciding they'd been sufficiently chastised, Steve got into Jim's Subaru and they headed back up the mountain.

As they turned onto the Forest Service Road, Jim asked, "So what do you think about me and Liz?"

Steve thought for a moment and then responded, "I think it's really good. You seem like a perfect fit."

"And you weren't?"

"Well, it's a long story and I don't want to go into too many of the details, but yeah, it certainly seemed like it when we got together. And it's not that things really changed. It's more like the beginnings of so-called true love didn't keep growing. We became best friends first and lovers second. I helped Liz through some difficult times and she was very supportive of me, including my upcoming move back east. I think that's when it became clear that we had more of a friendship than a long-term romantic relationship. When she started seeing Mark, I knew it wouldn't last. Although I could see the reason for the engagement, knowing Liz as well as I do, I knew that he wouldn't be enough for her even with the social connections and money."

"And you think I'm a better fit?"

"Truth be told, I don't know you that well, but I do know Liz and she's crazy about you already. From what I can see, you're headed in that direction too and I don't see too much to get in the way if you decide to pursue it."

They drove in silence for a few minutes which Jim broke with his next question. "Any words of advice?"

"I was afraid you were going to ask me that. I really don't like the idea of meddling in other people's business, but okay. My advice is to take it a bit slowly. Be sure you want to do this. While she seems strong and directed, there's a very fragile part of Liz. I've had glimpses of it, but I think you should try to see as much as you can before you make any major commitments. There are some dark sides to Liz which you haven't seen as well as some very remarkable ones."

"I think you could say that about anyone. I know I have my dark sides too. But I'll follow your advice and will take it as slowly as I can or as Liz permits."

"Don't get me wrong," Steve resumed. "I think you guys will ultimately be very good for each other. I really like you and look forward to a long friendship even after I move back to Chicago. I'd love to have you guys visit and to perhaps plan some flying trips together. And of course we can always do things without Liz, if she'll allow it."

"Yeah, IF she'll allow it," Jim said laughing.

They arrived at the launch and Steve jumped out of the car

and into his own. Clearly the sun would be setting soon, and while it might be nice to watch the sunset from the top of the ridge, neither wanted to drive down the road in the dark.

Jim decided to follow Steve down the hill, keeping a good following distance so he could avoid the dust. Steve hit the brakes hard several times on the way down and Jim saw deer bounding away in the edges of Steve's headlights. Thirty minutes later, they were back at the campground and true to their word, Liz and Bill had coals ready to go.

"If you look in the cooler, you'll find a large square foil package. Throw it into the coals and put the grill on top. I'm going to grab a quick shower and will be back in ten minutes. Liz, why don't you also open and pour the wine and break out the salad."

"Ja wohl! Mein Commandant!" Liz responded jumping to attention and snapping a military salute.

When Steve returned, Bill and Liz had covered the scarred picnic table with an elegantly embroidered table cloth and laid out both salad and dinner plates, water and wine glasses, and silverware and cloth napkins along with two votive candles. Liz poured water and wine all around while Bill served salad.

Jim handed Liz the plate of brownies that he'd brought. "Do I have time for a shower too?" He asked after seeing Steve take two large foiled-covered glass baking dishes out of the cooler.

"Yeah, if you don't take too much time. Dinner will be on the table in fifteen minutes.

When Jim returned, he watched in amazement as Steve rotated kabobs of meat and vegetables on the grill and then added marinated asparagus spears. A few minutes later, he placed three kabobs on each plate along with several asparagus spears. He removed the grill and carefully took out the foil package. Opening it up, he added several small red potatoes to each plate.

Once seated, Steve smiled at everyone and said, "I hope you enjoy the ginger, sesame, soy kabobs, the asparagus and my special garlic, cumin, cayenne and secret spiced potatoes. Now, who's going to say grace?"

Thinking this was a trick like the last dinner they'd all shared together, Jim chuckled. Everyone looked at him seriously like he'd broken a spell. Jim felt embarrassed and reddened, looking down at his plate. Then they all laughed.

"Gotcha again!" Bill roared.

"Well, I do have something to say," Liz interrupted. "I want to thank all the gods in heaven and all the powers that be for giving us this perfect day, creating the series of events that brought us all together, and for this wonderful meal that Steve has prepared. And, not to get too saccharine, but I also want to thank them for bringing me Jim. Sorry if that embarrasses anyone but that's how I feel. I know it's not Thanksgiving, but I am feeling very thankful. In fact, I'm feeling so thankful, that tomorrow I'm going to drive for you guys!"

"Can we finally eat now?" Bill asked, Liz slugging him as soon as the words left his mouth.

For his part, Jim was a bit overwhelmed. It wasn't just Liz's admission, or the exotic dinner in a rustic campground, it was the feeling of belonging. He spent most of his life apart, on his own. He had friends from work and a few from college, but they were really just acquaintances. Even in his romantic relationships, he'd kept some distance and as he thought back to Sharon. There too, even with all the closeness they'd shared as a couple, they had excluded others. He'd lived a 'me against the world' kind of life. But this was different. He belonged to this group.

Jim raised his glass and said, "Thank you all for including me. I don't want to get saccharine either, but it's made a huge difference during a difficult time in my life. To good friends!"

If possible, dinner was even better than it looked and smelled. They ate ravenously, and as usual, engaged in political discussions, this time focusing on the economy. Steve, with his economic expertise, dominated though everyone held his or her own. Exhausted and sated, they all went to bed around midnight. After another day of excellent flying, they returned to the Bay Area and tried to make the mental transition back to the work week ahead.

7

Over the course of the next weeks, Liz and Jim fell into a bit of a routine. Since both were working and their jobs were thirty miles apart and separated by the San Francisco Bay, they decided to try to spend Wednesday nights together, alternating week to week from Berkeley to Pacifica. The weeknight rendezvous were challenging as each faced commute traffic to reach the other. By the time either got through the commute, it was seven-thirty or eight o'clock and the few hours they had together seemed a bit hurried as they tried to fit in dinner, a game or television, and lovemaking. The rush to get out in the mornings was sometimes comical as neither was used to the habits of the other. They laughed at their frequent collisions and in spite of the chaos, felt increasing intimacy as they worked out timing for their morning ablutions. They had exchanged keys which permitted easy access to the other's place and facilitated a few surprise dinners, ready when the one working late arrived.

At first, Jim was apprehensive about having Liz spend the night in Pacifica. After all, this was the house he'd purchased with Sharon and although they had a property settlement in place, their divorce wasn't final. Still, they hadn't lived there together that long and Sharon had taken everything she'd brought to the relationship. And for some reason, the house in Pacifica didn't bother Liz at all. In looking at the house, all she saw was Jim. The house was decorated with his colors, his artwork, and masculine style throughout. And it didn't take much time for Liz to leave her marks. She brought clothes, makeup, lotions, a hair dryer, a curling iron, and everything she needed to sleep and get dressed there. But she also added her own touches to the decor. She was careful not to be too overwhelming, starting with semi-practical items like table cloths, napkins, and candles. And occasionally, she'd bring a small knick-knack or a favorite not-too-feminine piece of artwork like the jade sculpture Daddy had brought back from his travels in China.

Jim appreciated Liz's changes. They helped dim the memories of his life with Sharon in the house and gave him the sense of building a future with Liz.

One Tuesday night, Jim returned to Pacifica after working late and discovered Liz's car parked in front. As he entered the house, he was pleasantly surprised to see the table set with lighted candles. Liz's visit was completely unexpected and he was glad not to have to prepare dinner. Liz ran up and hugged him tightly.

"I didn't actually fix dinner," Liz confessed. "Go ahead and settle in. I brought Chinese. It's in the microwave, so it should be hot in about ten minutes."

"And to what do I owe this wonderful surprise?" Jim asked as Liz nuzzled his neck.

"We'll talk about it over dinner," she replied enigmatically and a bit somberly.

Jim put his computer and notebooks in the office and quickly checked email to see if anything urgent had happened at work. Seeing nothing significant, he went to the bedroom, took off his shoes and changed into chinos and a long-sleeved t-shirt. Returning to the dining room, food was on the table.

"I have hot and sour soup, pot stickers in chili oil, vegetable chow mein and kung pao chicken, extra spicy. I also opened a bottle of Zin from your collection. I hope you don't mind."

"Absolutely not! This is wonderful."

They served themselves and before eating, Jim toasted, "To Liz, always full of pleasant surprises!"

Liz burst into tears.

Jim jumped up, crossed to the other side of the table and hugged Liz from behind.

"I'm sorry," he said. "I'm not sure what I did to upset you, but I'm sure everything will be okay."

"No, no. It's not your fault. I have a not so pleasant surprise and your toast just caught me off guard. Let's eat a bit and then we can talk."

Jim reluctantly went back to his place. They touched glasses and sipped, Liz smiling warmly through her tears. She took a deep breath, let it out and began eating.

"How was your day?" she asked.

Not wanting to push, Jim decided to tell her about his day to distract her and to give her a chance to settle down. Once he had finished recounting two significant personnel problems and an excellent customer meeting, Liz looked at him calmly and said very matter-of-factly, "I'm pregnant."

Without even a hesitation, Jim responded, "That's wonderful!" He came around the table and hugged her from behind again. "I know it's unplanned," he continued, "but this isn't a problem. It just accelerates things a bit. I love you!"

Liz wiggled out of Jim's embrace and said, "Jim please go sit down. There's more to the story and we really do need to talk about this. I just hope you won't hate me when I finish."

"Don't be ridiculous!"

Seeing Liz's determined look, Jim once again went back to his seat and waited expectantly, a stupid grin on his face.

"Jim, I know you're excited, but I have bad news. You should prepare yourself."

Jim's giddy elation evaporated.

"Okay. I'm listening, but no matter what it is, I'll still love you."

Liz took a deep breath and began. "I'm not sure it's yours."

Seeing the look of shock on Jim's face, she swallowed and continued.

"No. I haven't cheated on you. But I did have sex with Mark the day we broke up, and it was only a few days later that you and I had that wonderful evening at the Tea House. I'm really, really sorry."

Jim tried to think quickly. Could he raise another man's child? Sure, but not like this. Mark was a giant and had dark hair and eyes. Then again, there was a good chance the child was his anyway. Was it worth the risk? He wanted to say something to Liz, but he couldn't get his mind around the scope of the situation fast enough to respond.

Seeing him thinking hard and clearly struggling with the problem, Liz broke the silence.

"Jim, I wanted to tell you about this because I don't want us to have any secrets. But the fact is, I've already made up my mind what I'm going to do. I'm just hoping you'll support me.

Seeing Jim nod a bit hesitantly, Liz continued.

"I've already made an appointment for an abortion Friday morning. I'm hoping you can take the day off and keep an eye on me afterwards."

Abortion! Jim had always supported the idea of a woman's right to choose what happened to her own body, but this might be his child. That plus the thought of Liz going through such an invasive procedure, the possibility of infection, the risk of permanent reproductive damage – no, this wasn't the right thing to do.

"Do you really think that's necessary? Abortion is radical and it carries risk. Maybe we should take some time to think about this. I'm sure we can work something out."

"Look Jim, I have thought this through. I know it's a shock for you, but ultimately, this is my decision and the decision has been made. I'm not ready to become a mother. This is a bad time in my life and I really don't want to add the stress of a baby to our nascent relationship. As for risk, for some women it's true. But the fact is I've had abortions before and have never had a problem. Plus they certainly haven't affected my fertility in any way. After all, I got pregnant this time while on the Pill. And I don't miss taking my pills."

"Abortions plural?" Jim asked sheepishly, clearly in a state of shock.

"Yes. We haven't talked about my past sexual history, but I've had four abortions. The first was when I was thirteen. If you want to go into it now, we can, but believe me when I tell you that it's not as big a deal as most people think it is. And remember, I'm six or seven weeks pregnant. We're talking about an embryo, just a few cells. There's no person there yet."

Jim was stunned. Was this one of the dark sides of Liz that Steve talked about? He looked over at Liz and watched her defiance soften. Suddenly she looked incredibly vulnerable and Jim couldn't help himself. He put his feelings aside, deciding to focus on Liz's needs, not his own. He went to her and pulled her up into his arms. Liz cried softly.

"Do you hate me?" she whispered in a husky sob.

"Of course not!"

Jim picked Liz up and took her to the bedroom. He pulled back the covers in the bed and placed her in it, covering her up. Liz rolled over onto her stomach burying her head in the pillow and Jim started massaging her back. He could feel her begin to relax. She asked him for help in removing her clothes then asked him not to stop. Twenty minutes later, Liz fell asleep. Jim got up to leave the room and looked back at Liz who seemed so vulnerable. The shadows of trees swaying the breeze seemed to caress her sleeping form. Just before he closed the door he heard a small voice say, "Jim, I love you."

"I love you too Liz."

8

Jim awoke the next morning to find Liz propped on one elbow smiling down at him.

"You're wonderful, you know."

Looking up at her, Jim felt lucky to be with the most beautiful woman in the world. As he thought back to his feelings of the night before, he realized that his anxiety had somehow been resolved while he slept. It was a new day, a bright sunny day, and he and Liz had just entered into a new phase of their relationship.

Jim was heads down at work later that morning when his phone rang.

"Jim Henderson," he answered.

"Hi Jim, it's me."

It had been several months since Jim had talked to Sharon and now she was calling. Thinking about the previous night, Jim wondered as he had several times before if women didn't have some kind of sixth sense.

"Hi Sharon. How are you?"

"Actually, I'm doing much better. After all these months, my life finally seems to be on track. But I'm not calling to bore you with my life. The divorce process is pretty much done now. We just have to sign a document called a Stipulation and Final Declaration of Disclosure. It may sound like a lot, but since we have a settlement already signed and filed, it really just needs our signatures. Once that's submitted, we should have the Final Judgment as soon as the court can turn it around. Are you by chance available tonight? Could you drop by for just a few minutes to sign it? I know it's a long way to Walnut Creek, but we do need to get this done."

Jim thought for a few minutes and decided that this would work out. He could sign the documents then spend the night with Liz in Berkeley.

"Sure. I can be there. Will seven-thirty work?"

"Perfect. See you then."

Jim called Liz and told her he had to go by Sharon's to sign some final divorce papers and that he'd be in Berkeley by eight-thirty or so. Liz said she'd have pizza waiting. The rest of Jim's day was busy but uneventful.

That evening, Jim was pleasantly surprised by the lack of heavy traffic. He called Sharon and left a voicemail to let her know that he'd probably be about thirty minutes early. If she wasn't there, he'd wait.

Jim easily found Sharon's apartment complex. Although he had her address, he'd never actually visited her before. The complex itself was a bit more difficult to navigate, and it was five after seven when Jim knocked on Sharon's door. He heard barking and Sharon's voice saying "Quiet Odie! It's just Jim."

The door opened and Jim was overwhelmed with feelings that he'd thought were long gone. Standing before him was his wife. She was gorgeous. There was a light in her eyes he hadn't seen in years and she looked content – something he'd never seen before.

"Come on in," Sharon invited. "This is Odie. Odie, this is Jim."

Jim looked down to see a small terrier mix wagging his tail frantically and looking expectantly at Jim. Jim squatted down and held out his hand towards the dog. Surprisingly, instead of sniffing it as Jim expected, Odie put his right paw in Jim's hand. Jim shook it gently and said, "Nice to meet you Odie."

If possible, Odie looked pleased. He glanced up at Sharon, looked back at Jim, then turned and walked across the room to a doggy bed which he hopped into. He lay down and looked expectantly at Sharon.

"Good boy, Odie!" Sharon praised. "Jim, I have the papers on the table. Would you like a quick tour? It will be quick because the apartment is pretty small."

Jim nodded and Sharon walked him around the apartment showing him her office, her bedroom, the master and guest baths, and the view of Mount Diablo from the living room. Jim followed her to the table and took a seat as Sharon stepped into the kitchen behind the bar. She poured two glasses of wine and brought them over, then took a seat facing Jim.

She handed him a glass and toasted, "To happier futures for both of us."

Jim touched her glass with his and repeated, "To happier futures."

"So how have you been?" Jim asked tentatively.

"Good. Actually, really good.

"I went through some hard times right after I left. My mother went insane. She called constantly and kept showing up unannounced. She just wouldn't let up on how I ruined my life and disappointed her. How no man would want me now and how I was denying her grandchildren.

"I started seeing a psychologist and that seemed to help a bit. Going by myself worked better than the sessions we tried together. Ultimately I realized that the problems were mine, not couple problems. Couple's therapy really couldn't help us.

"Anyway things got much worse and then better. I had some major abdominal pain and got really sick. I had internal bleeding from an ovarian cyst that ruptured. If someone at work hadn't dragged me to the doctor, I might have died."

Seeing Jim's look of concern, Sharon quickly continued. "Like I said, things got bad and then better. Once they diagnosed the problem, there were decisions to be made. Surgery was required, but I had several options. Ultimately, I decided to have the one ovary removed, and the Fallopian tube on the other tied off. I know it sounds drastic – I'll never be able to have kids – but there was risk of further problems and I just made the decision that I didn't want to have kids. If I change my mind, I can always adopt, like I did with Odie. That worked out well.

"Ultimately though, the best result was that it shut my Mother up. Once she found out I couldn't have kids, our relationship changed. I think she feels sorry for me. She's sure I'll be alone the rest of my life. But at least it got her off my back. That, combined with the therapy, and my new job which is working out very well, thank you very much, has made me feel peaceful and content for the first time in my life. No major stress, no major mood swings, though that also might be because of the surgery. Apparently, the bad ovary caused a lot of hormone fluctuations. Anyway, I'm really happy now. I'm sorry our time together was so rough."

"And I'm sorry that I couldn't figure out how to be a better partner for you, for us."

"Like I said Jim, it really wasn't your fault. Yes, we all have problems and can be better people, but mine were destructive to every relationship I ever had. Hopefully I can do better in the future.

"Anyway, here are the final papers. You just need to sign and date here."

Jim looked at the papers. He looked at Sharon expectantly. She smiled without giving a hint of what she really wanted. But after a moment, seeing his hesitation, she stood up, came over to him and took his hand. Jim rose and Sharon led him towards the bedroom. Sensing sudden tension she stopped, turned, and looked up into his eyes. The connection was still there. She felt it. He felt it. She turned her lips upward and they kissed. It was gentle, long and slow. Her body softened and she melted into Jim. It was all Jim could do to not pick her up and carry her into the bedroom.

Jim gently broke their embrace and looked deeply into Sharon's face.

"I'm really sorry," he said softly. "I'm seeing someone."

Surprisingly, Sharon didn't seem upset.

"I suspected as much. You're a very attractive, desirable man and I was sure that someone had snatched you up by now. Is it serious?"

Thinking about the pregnancy and the upcoming abortion, Jim had to admit that it was.

"Don't feel bad, Jim. Sometimes the timing is just not right. I think we missed our opportunity, but do keep in mind that you were my husband and there will always be a special place in my heart for you."

Jim looked at Sharon and again, tried to think quickly. Somehow he knew that this was a pivotal moment in his life. He had two very different paths to choose from. And once again, just like the previous night, Jim found it impossible to sort through all the possibilities quickly enough to make a thoughtful choice. So by default, being a man of his word, he decided that he needed to continue on his current path.

"Sharon, I'll always love you. I really mean that. But I've made some commitments that I can't just walk away from. I'm not sure exactly where my life is going but I have to give it a chance. I'm sorry. As you said, if the timing had been just a little different..."

They moved back to the table and Jim signed and dated the documents. They walked to the door together and before Jim left, they held each other one last time. The feelings were there. The connection was there. And as he walked back to his car, Jim couldn't help thinking that he'd just made the biggest mistake of his life.

9

Liz was waiting with pizza warming in the oven when Jim got back to her place. She saw guilt painted on Jim's face but chose to ignore it for the moment. She hugged him and immediately smelled the scent of another woman, but she didn't smell sex. She signed in relief. Jim had probably just hugged his soon-to-be ex.

"How'd it go?"

"It was harder than I expected. She's changed. She's better."

Then seeing the look of surprise on Liz's face, he continued. "Don't worry. I'm with you now. The timing of things just didn't work out for Sharon and me."

"You are still married. You could go back."

Jim thought about that for a moment and tried to imagine restarting his life with Sharon. Still, even with the apparent changes in her, all he could picture was their old life together, the tears, the frustration, the ups and downs. Even if she had changed, there was no way all of their issues would just automatically be fixed. And he certainly had his own baggage to deal with. No, he needed to close the door on that aspect of his past much as he'd done every time his family relocated when he was a kid. It was time to move on. With Liz he had the opportunity for a new kind of life – a life with family and friends, intellectual challenges and lively debates. It was so different from what he'd known with Sharon or before Sharon. He wanted what life with Liz promised.

"No. I don't want to. That part of my life is over. Sharon and I had our chance and didn't make it. Time has passed for both of us and we've each moved on in our own ways. I signed the final papers and that should close the door. I'm definitely free to let it go and begin anew. Thank you for being a part of my new life."

Liz smiled and hugged him tighter. She was sure that Jim wasn't completely over Sharon. But then again, she wasn't completely over Steve, or Bill, or Bob. And like her, Jim had made up his mind to move on. They'd be okay.

After pizza and a couple of beers, they got ready for bed.

"Are you sure you want to go through with this?" Jim asked warily.

Looking composed and confident, Liz replied, "Of course.

This is the best thing. And don't worry. It's really not a big deal. The worst thing is that we have to abstain from sex for a week or two – actually, that's just intercourse."

They climbed into bed and Jim gently massaged Liz's back. Within moments she was sound asleep. Jim picked up the book he'd set on the nightstand and began to read, mindlessly caressing Liz gently. After a few minutes, he turned out the lights. He marveled again at the shadows swaying across the bed cast by the streetlights outside.

"I wish she wouldn't do that," Liz said in a small voice, still clearly asleep.

"Do what, Liz?" Jim whispered.

"It doesn't matter. There's nothing you can do to stop her. Good night, Jim."

"Good night, Liz."

The next morning they had fresh bagels from Noah's, yogurt and berries for breakfast. Jim asked if Liz remembered anything about their conversation, but she didn't. She told him she often talked in her sleep.

After breakfast and light conversation about the news of the day, they drove to the clinic. Jim waited as Liz was taken back for the procedure. She returned forty-five minutes later, a bit pale but smiling.

"Everything went exactly as expected. No complications."

Seeing the concerned if not distressed look on Jim's face, Liz went to him. "Don't worry. Settle down. I'm okay! You look worse than I do!"

And it was true. Jim was nauseous. He was shaky when he stood up to meet Liz. He'd never had an invasive medical procedure and couldn't imagine what Liz had gone through. He also couldn't quite believe that this was as easy for her as it seemed. Their child, or at least their potential child, had just been aborted. Jim had always wanted children. What might have been his son or daughter was no more and Jim felt overwhelmed by sadness. It seemed like another doorway into the future had just been closed to him. He wanted to talk with Liz about his feelings but decided it was better to wait. If she had any sensitivity about this at all, it was definitely a bad time to bring up his issues. After all, this was about Liz, not him, wasn't it?

10

Several weeks later, Steve, Jim, Bill and Liz pulled up to Dunlap in Steve's 4x4, ready to compete in the US Hang Gliding National Championships. They quickly registered and then set up camp.

"Can you feel the energy here?" Steve asked, clearly excited.

"Ah yeah. I find it a bit intimidating," Jim responded very nervously. "Compared to these other pilots, I'm really just a beginner. I'm not sure I should be here."

"Of course you should be here," Liz said encouragingly. "You may not have the experience of all these guys, but you certainly have some great skills."

"Plus, as you've told us," Bill continued. "You're not expecting to win. You're just here to learn. Or was that just false modesty?"

"No. You're right. Still, look at these guys. Their equipment is top of the line and they have gadgets I've never even seen before. I definitely feel out of my league."

"C'mon," Steve ordered. "Let me introduce you around. You'll see that these guys are just like us. They love to fly and this competition is really a way to celebrate how far our sport has come. It's not a cutthroat thing. Yeah, everyone wants to win, but it's not like other sports where big money and sponsorships are on the line. Very few of these guys are what you could call professional pilots. They're like us. They still have to work for a living and flying is recreation.

"Hey Mick!"

A tall, thin, dark-haired, bearded young man in his thirties turned towards Steve smiling.

"Steve! Good to see you man," he shouted, grabbing Steve's hand and pulling him into a hug. "I knew you'd qualified and I was hoping to see you before you left for Chicago. How are you?"

"Great Mick. Yeah, I have mixed feelings about returning to the flat lands of the Midwest. Hey, I want you to meet Jim Henderson. He hasn't even been flying two years, but finished fifth at the regionals. The guy's got some natural talent. Jim, this is Mick Mickerson. He won the Nationals last year; finished third at the World's; and currently holds the open distance record at what three hundred sixty miles?"

"Three hundred sixty-eight if you're really counting. Good to meet you Jim. Welcome to the Nationals. I look forward to seeing you fly. If Steve thinks you've got talent, and you came up this quickly, you must be good. Hopefully you're one of the sane ones. I've seen a few tragedies with guys that came up a bit too fast and got themselves into trouble because they didn't read conditions well."

"Ah – no, no. I'm really very conservative. And I'm here to learn from you guys. I'm not expecting to do anything fantastic."

"Modesty. Probably a good thing to have in a pilot. Certainly much better than that guy," Mick said smiling, nodding towards a slick-looking pilot with what seemed to be groupies around him.

"Who's that?" Jim asked.

"That's Brent Powers. He's a real asshole. He's got a business selling custom GPS', variometers, communication systems, tracking systems, high end harnesses and helmets – pretty much anything that anyone could ever need in this sport, and quite a few others. His company sponsors him and he's out to make a name for himself and his company no matter who he screws. He takes chances in his flying, puts others in bad positions, and if there's one thing this sport doesn't need, it's additional risk. We already have to deal with Mother Nature's fickleness. I pity the guy that draws him in this competition. As you know, we're doing a round-robin one-on-one format.

"Anyway, if Brent has his way, Hang Gliding and Paragliding will go the way of other high-end money-rich sports. Actually, perhaps more like NASCAR. He's really trying to make it look like a much riskier sport than it is. You know, people love to watch a sport where someone could die. I really hope he fails to promote the insanity and danger. I like what we've got now. This sport is a lot safer than most, even safer than General Aviation though I'd like to see more safety in competition."

"Yeah," Jim jumped in. "When I got into the sport, I did some research into the statistics as I'm sure pretty much everyone does. I was pleasantly surprised to see that in recreational flying, fatalities really diminished over the past few years. In fact, I think the only ones last year were people who forgot to hook into their gliders, basically jumping off a cliff without their gliders. Overall, statistically, per hour of participation, it's even safer than equestrian sports and scuba diving.

"On the other hand, I saw that the number of fatalities in

competition was rising, somewhat alarmingly for a newbie like me."

"Unfortunately, that's true. We've been working on making competitions safer, but we're still learning. In the Owens Valley at the Cross Country Classic a few years ago, we lost two pilots, or really three depending on how you count it, on one day. In previous years, pilots complained that the Safety Director shouldn't be able to cancel a day's flying – that it should be up to the pilots since they clearly knew their capabilities. A skilled pilot might be able to complete the day's task when others couldn't so he should be able to make the call himself. The decision to let pilots decide was clearly a bad one."

Mick paused after looking at his watch. "Sorry guys, I have a meeting with the meet directors. I could continue this over dinner, hint, hint."

Clearly Steve's gourmet campground cookery was well known.

"Sure, come join us," Steve said laughing. "Bring a couple of friends if you like, and bring some alcoholic beverages."

"Will do!" Mick answered as he jogged off to the officials' tent.

"He seems like a really nice guy."

"Yeah, like most of the pilots here, he really is. For him, it's all about flying and promoting the sport as a fun recreational activity. If people get to see it as safe and fun, we'll be able to open more sites. Land owners will be glad to give us places to fly. Otherwise, with more accidents, danger, and jerks, sites will get closed. Our buddy Brent cost us one of the best sites in the Bay Area after swearing at a landowner and diving at his home's picture windows. I'll save that story for dinner."

"So what about this guy Brent? Should I be worried?"

"Probably not. Unfortunately as someone with so few competition points, you're very low seed. You'll likely be paired up against someone like Mick. They always pair the low seed against the top seed in the first rounds. It may seem unfair, but you're up against an experienced pilot who has the skills to watch out for you and you'll learn a lot by following him. More than likely, you'll be eliminated before you ever come up against Brent, at least in this meet. With my luck, I'll draw him. We're pretty much even on competition points, in the middle of the ranked pilots."

Steve did the rounds with Jim, introducing him to several of the world's top pilots. All of them were welcoming to the newbie.

Dinner was a feast, enjoyed by all to very high praise. Steve beamed. Jim was pleased to see that all the competitors really restricted their alcohol intake and from what he could see, no drugs were making the rounds. While there was a strong sense of camaraderie, it was clear people were psyching up for the next day's competition.

Liz and Jim zipped their sleeping bags together. They made love energetically as Liz tried to help Jim calm his nerves. Afterwards, Jim was still wide awake. He stroked Liz's hair absentmindedly as she dozed. He unzipped the tent and looked out at the shadows that the full moon cast on the campground.

"Don't worry, Jim," said a small, sleepy voice. "I know things. You'll be okay."

"Thanks, Liz. Good night."

"G'night."

The next day dawned beautiful. The weather service forecast perfect flying conditions for Dunlap. At 8am, the seventy pilots along with drivers, wind dummies, and staff showed up at the kickoff meeting. After greeting everyone, laying down the flight rules, and reminding everyone that this meet's first goal was for everyone to have fun, the officials described the day's task, a forty mile triangle route for time. Then they posted the matchups for the day.

As expected, Jim was paired with Max Johansson, one of the top seeds. And to his consternation, Steve was paired against Brent Powers and worse, they were scheduled to be the first to launch. That meant the conditions would be weaker and they'd have to work harder to even complete the course.

Liz had volunteered as a driver and Bill was scheduled to be a wind dummy. In recreational flying, the pilots who launched first into unknown conditions were called wind dummies. In competition, these were the pilots designated to help determine the quality of the conditions so the officials could decide when to start the competition, and if conditions deteriorated, when to suspend it, thus avoiding having competitors unfairly penalized when weather conditions changed.

They made their way up the mountain and the wind dummies and first ten pairs of competitors setup and pre-flighted their gliders. The officials came through and examined each competitor's equipment: glider, harness, helmet, hook knife (in case of a water or brush landing) and GPS. As the first thermals began rolling up the launch, a wind dummy took off. Unfortunately after fifteen minutes of scratching around with very little lift to be found, he ended up in the landing area. Thirty minutes later a second wind dummy launched and met much the same fate, landing in less than twenty minutes.

The strength of the thermal gusts reaching the launch seemed to be increasing as Bill took his turn as wind dummy. He scratched below launch picking up every upward movement of air to maintain his altitude, but after twenty minutes, it looked like he was on his way down as well. The pilots were getting discouraged. It had looked like such a promising day and now there were even a few cumulus clouds forming – indicators of the tops of warm, moist rising air. Why weren't the thermals better?

"Look!" Liz shouted to the group after most had walked away from the launch.

Sure enough, Bill had found a thermal. He was well below launch, but obviously climbing steadily. Within a few minutes, he was at launch and a few minutes later, he was at least a thousand feet over, headed for the base of a cumulus cloud. The meet was on.

Steve had lost the draw and had to launch first. He was really hoping for better conditions, but since it was a one-on-one heat, even if he couldn't complete the course, he only had to beat his competitor to advance. There was little doubt in his mind that he could beat Brent Powers. The guy was a loudmouth and called a lot of attention to himself, but he really wasn't a great pilot.

Seeing a promising rustle in the bushes below, Steve ran down the launch. The weak thermal lifted him for about a second and then it was gone. He started searching to no avail. Down he went searching but not finding much.

"You have thirty seconds to launch or you're disqualified," the meet director shouted to Brent Powers.

"Ah, shit!" Brent complained as he ran down the ramp.

To his pleasant surprise, Steve had caught a thermal and was climbing fast though he was still several hundred feet below the launch. Brent flew towards Steve and was rewarded with a singing variometer indicating a nice thermal. He started circling and was quickly back near launch level. But Steve was climbing faster, much faster. And as Brent reached the launch, Steve was right below him.

The rules in soaring dictate that the faster climbing pilot has right of way. With sailplanes this is important but not critical as the lower, faster climbing pilot can see above him through the glass cockpit. In hang gliding, the rule is critical as the lower pilot can't see above his glider.

But it was clear Brent Powers was not going to play by the rules.

"Don't try to pass me you motherfucker!" he shouted. "I'm grabbing my chute and I'll ram you if you do."

Everyone at the launch heard this. Unfortunately Steve didn't. Steve was completely unaware that Brent was above him as he pulled tighter into the core of the thermal. As he came around a particularly tight circle, Steve heard a crack. The upper leading edge of his wing bent and the glider slipped into a fast spin. He reached for his parachute and threw it hard but it was too late. The collision occurred only a hundred and fifty feet above the launch and with the lost time in realizing the situation, and the spin which caused the glider to fall out of the sky at over a thousand feet a minute, the parachute didn't have time to open. Many people walk away from crashes like this. Generally, a glider, with all of its sail, doesn't fall that fast. But Steve was not so lucky. Not only was he falling fast because of the spin, when he hit, the uncontrollable glider slammed Steve head first into a rock outcropping. He was killed instantly.

Brent Powers tossed his chute easily. It opened and took him and his glider down safely a few hundred yards behind the launch.

All of the pilots ran to help Steve. They unfolded the tangled glider which had enclosed him like a shroud and discovered his inert body. Liz pushed through the crowd and hugged Steve to her, crying softly. The pilots who had run to call for medical assistance were told it was no use. The rest stood there in silence, not sure what they should do.

At that point, Brent Powers strode up confidently. His shadow fell on Steve's inert form.

"Hey man, sorry about that. But I did warn you not to try to pass me up."

Liz stood up. She turned towards Brent. Jim saw a Liz he'd never seen before. The tears were gone. The woman standing there was as cold as ice. She walked up to Brent and hissed,

"You've killed him you bastard. Now it's your turn."

In thinking about it later, Jim couldn't say what it was that alerted him to a real imminent threat. He ran towards Liz and Brent and seized Liz just after she pulled the hook knife from Brent's harness and just before she sliced open Brent's jugular. He tried to hold her, saying the all-too-trite words that came into his mind, "He's not worth it Liz." But Liz threw him off with unexpected, almost superhuman strength and went after Brent again. "Don't ever try to stop me like that, Jim," she warned. The words hit Jim like ice water as he saw a side of Liz that frightened him.

For his part, Brent Powers was backing away with his hands raised.

"Hey," he pleaded. "It was an accident. I'm sorry."

"Sorry isn't going to bring Steve back but at least I can rid the world of vermin like you."

Brent turned and ran. Liz started to go after him but was wrestled to the ground by four pilots. When it was clear she couldn't overcome them, Liz's face softened. She dropped the knife and in a very small voice said, "Jim, please help me."

Jim came over and Liz looked up at him pleadingly.

"It's okay now. Jim, please tell them I won't hurt anyone."

Jim nodded at the pilots and they let her go. He picked her up in his arms and carried her to the shade of an oak tree where he set her down. Liz looked stunned. Her eyes were opened very wide, almost as if she'd awakened from a dream and didn't know where she was.

"Are you okay?" Jim asked softly.

"Yes. I'm just really sleepy. Would it be okay if I took a short nap? Could I put my head on your lap for a few minutes?"

Jim sat down and stroked Liz's head and face as she relaxed. She smiled softly. Just before she fell asleep, in her sleepy voice Liz said, "I love you Jim."

"I love you too, Liz."

At the time, Jim rationalized what had just happened. Steve, perhaps Liz's best friend in the world and her former lover, had been killed by a self-aggrandizing idiot. Of course she would get angry. He'd heard about adrenaline rushes that give people temporary superhuman strength. He'd also heard that they were usually exhausted once the adrenaline wore off and that often, they didn't remember what they'd done. So it really didn't come as a big surprise to him when Liz woke up and asked him what had happened. And Liz didn't seem surprised. It was like she was remembering as he explained it.

The meet was cancelled for the day. The directors would spend the day getting witness accounts and would hold a pilot's meeting at seven o'clock that evening. Everyone was expected to attend. Jim decided on the spot that he would drop out of the competition. In fact, he wasn't sure if he'd ever fly again. He certainly wasn't going to participate in any future competitions.

Throughout the day, people were called into the director's tent and were interviewed by the directors and by two representatives of the Fresno Sheriff's department. Liz, Bob, and Jim had a sparse and somber dinner, but opened a bottle of expensive wine that Steve had brought to celebrate their finishes at the meet. They toasted Steve and started the process of mourning by recounting stories of how they met and their many adventures together. At seven, they, along with the rest of the pilots and support staff, made their way to the director's tent. The meet director stepped out with the safety director and the two officers from the Sheriff's Department stood behind them.

"Hello everyone. It's been a devastating day for all of us. This is a risk sport and most of us know someone who's lost his or her life in pursuit of flight, especially those of us who flew in the early days before we had developed the safety equipment and training that made this one of the safer sports. Old timers like me thought that we were past all that. We still hope that we are. But while recreational flying fatalities are at an all-time low, competitive flying is seeing more fatalities than ever before. By our nature, most of us are very competitive. But competition in a high risk sport just ups the danger and we need to be more vigilant.

"I want you to know that after this meet, there will be no more sanctioned events with one-on-one formats. We're exploring other formats that will ensure fairness to the competitors and will reduce risk of accidents. We're also committed to improving safety by giving the Safety Director more direct control over who flies and under what conditions.

'Unfortunately, for this meet, we're going to continue with the current format. Many of you are looking at the Worlds and need this meet to qualify. We can't cancel the meet and unfortunately do not have the time or resources to change the format. So, tomorrow we continue.

"I probably don't need to caution you about flying safely, but for those of you who are the most competitive, please take a moment to reflect. Steve Franklin was a great pilot. He might have qualified for the Worlds. He did nothing wrong. He made no mistakes. And yet, he died today. It's not my place to eulogize Steve, but I will say that I'm going to miss him. He was a great friend and a thoughtful person.

"Our sport has a reputation for danger that we've been working hard to correct. If people think it's a safe activity, we'll have more places to fly and we'll see broader acceptance of the sport. Tragedies like this set us back years. Please don't do this to the sport and please don't do this to yourselves. Our competitions should be fun, not life-threatening. Tomorrow and for the rest of the meet, be extra careful and extra thoughtful.

"Okay. That said, I want to tell you our findings. After many interviews and much discussion, it's clear that this was no accident. The collision was intentional. Brent Powers will be banned from flying for life. In addition, the Fresno Sheriff's Department has issued an arrest warrant for Brent Powers. To my understanding, he will be charged with Voluntary Manslaughter. As some of you know, these are very serious charges with severe penalties.

"Unfortunately, Brent Powers has disappeared. His tent and camping gear are here but his car is gone. No one has seen him since the collision. We hope he will return and face up to what he has done. In the meantime, if anyone has any information that could help in finding him, please let the Sheriff's Department know.

"For the friends and family of Steve Franklin, please accept my condolences. I'm sorry to say that I can't do more than promise to do my best to ensure that this never happens again. But I will do that. I promise.

"Everyone please try to get a good night's sleep. We'll see you at eight in the morning at the Pilot's Meeting. Since several people have dropped out of the competition, we're recasting the pairings and these will be posted tomorrow."

Brent Powers was eventually arrested. Because he was a proven flight risk, he was held without bail. At the preliminary hearing, the judge, who knew nothing about hang gliding and who had a full docket and a long backlog of cases, convinced the

District Attorney to settle the case out of court. He argued that it would be hard to convince a jury (and him) that Voluntary Manslaughter occurred in a high risk sport like hang gliding.

In negotiations with the defense attorney, the DA realized that he had an unwinnable case and they agreed to reduce the charges to involuntary manslaughter and the sentence to time served, a year probation, and a ten thousand dollar fine. Brent Powers was released. With his ban from sanctioned hang gliding events and regulated sites, and the accounts of what he had done, word spread through the hang gliding community and the resulting boycott of his business forced its closure.

The deal to release Brent occurred quickly and Liz, Jim and Michael Leahy didn't get the news until it was too late. Liz swore revenge. Jim tried to calm her. Michael Leahy predicted that Brent Powers would screw up again and it wouldn't go so easy for him the next time. They considered a civil suit, but Steve's family didn't want to pursue it. They too saw hang gliding as a dangerous sport and wanted closure, not a prolonged court case far from home.

11

After a somber trip to Chicago for Steve's funeral, life got back to normal for Liz and Jim. Liz gave up hang gliding altogether, selling her glider and equipment. Jim kept his equipment, imagining perfect days circling up towards puffy cumulus clouds, but put flying on hold for a while. He turned his sporting interests back to surfing and went for runs most days of the week.

Jim's divorce became final and he and Sharon parted friends, both with regrets about life's tendency to send you opportunities at the wrong time. But both were realistic enough to know that they each needed to move on separately. As part of the settlement, Jim bought Sharon out of the house in Pacifica by refinancing. It was the first home he had ever owned and in spite of the memories of Sharon there, he really didn't want to part with this small house, its spectacular ocean view, or its easy access to Montara Mountain.

Liz continued to work at Mansfield, Mason, and Williams but without having passed the Bar, she was limited in what she could do and began to find the job boring. A few months in, she had to admit that after seeing the inner workings of a large firm, the thought of becoming an associate who had to bill a thousand hours a week to begin the climb towards partnership just didn't seem like what she ultimately wanted to do. Still, it gave her some income, added much-needed experience to her resume, and put her in contact with a lot of people who might make a difference in her career.

After three months of fighting the late afternoon commutes to each other's places during the week, Jim and Liz made the natural decision to move in together. With her upscale furniture and artwork and a strong sense of how to change Jim's house without taking the 'Jim' out of it, it wasn't long before all vestiges of Sharon had disappeared.

The third Sunday of every month Liz's parents held an afternoon party similar to the one that Jim had attended. They also invited family and close friends over for champagne brunch at least one other Sunday of the month. In spite of not really liking champagne, Jim enjoyed the brunches the most. He and Liz would bring flowers and champagne, always falling back on Veuve Cliquot, and if the weather was nice, the festivities were held outside on the deck with the spectacular views. Jim always had shaggy dog stories to tell, much to the delight of Mickey Leahy who matched them with stories of his legal wrangling over the years.

One perfect Sunday afternoon in the fall, after most of the guests had left and the sun was setting, casting long shadows, an older man stepped out onto the deck.

"Richard!" Mickey shouted, jumping up and embracing the newcomer in a bear hug slapping him on the back. "When did you get back?"

"Actually, my flight got in two hours ago and knowing you had these standing afternoon fetes, I thought I'd drop by."

"Everyone," Mickey began. "For those of you who don't know my illustrious colleague and former partner, this is Richard Johnson. He's just back from a year abroad. China, right?"

"Yes. I spent most of the year travelling in China going from place to place gathering recipes. I love Chinese food and have been toying with the idea of opening an upscale Chinese restaurant incorporating foods that most Westerners haven't seen. I've found some amazing dishes. Perhaps I could bring a few to your party next month."

"That would be fantastic," Janice said enthusiastically, standing up and taking Richard's arm. "Let me make a few introductions."

As Janice made the rounds, Mickey turned to Jim. "Richard and I have known each other for over thirty years. We went to law school together, worked together in the DA's office, and after I jumped ship to hang out a shingle, Richard joined me and later became a partner. He did pretty well financially at the firm, but four years ago came into a large inheritance. He decided to give up law and pursue a long buried passion, cooking. He spent a year taking classes from some of the best chefs in the country, then started travelling, working as an apprentice in kitchens of some great restaurants. This last trip he spent a year in China. I'm sure he'll have stories to tell for weeks to come. He's a real-life renaissance man, good at virtually everything he tries. He even set up our original network, computer and database systems."

Janice approached them with Richard on her arm.

"Richard, I'd like you to meet Liz's special friend, Jim. Jim is Vice President of Engineering at MacroData Systems, a hot

Silicon Valley startup. Jim, I'd like you to meet Richard. I'm sure you two will have lots to talk about."

"Great to meet you Jim," Richard said, warmly shaking Jim's hand. "I hope you're treating our Lizzy well."

"I certainly try."

"And Lizzy!" Richard exclaimed, stepping towards Liz and blocking her momentarily from Jim's view, "It's been years since I've seen you. You certainly have turned into a stunningly beautiful young woman."

As Richard took Liz into his arms to give her a hug, Jim noticed a change come over Liz. Her arms went limp, her eyes widened, and her face relaxed. She looked over at Jim, looked up at Richard, and in almost a whisper said, "Hello Richard. It has been a long time."

Janice broke up the embrace and led Richard away to meet the next group of guests. Liz took Jim's arm and in a small voice said, "Jim, I'm not feeling well. Can we go?"

She went over to Mickey, hugged him and said, "Daddy, I have to go. I'm not feeling well."

"Okay Pumpkin. I hope it's not something you ate. Jim, take good care of her and give us a call later to let us know how she's doing."

"Will do, Mickey!"

Liz took Jim's arm, put her head on his shoulder, and they made their way to the car. Jim said goodbye to everyone, letting many know that Liz wasn't feeling well.

Once in the car, Liz immediately fell asleep. She slept through the entire drive back to Pacifica, waking only as they pulled in the driveway.

"Feeling better?" Jim asked.

"Ah, yes," Liz responded sleepily. "What are we doing home?"

"Don't you remember? You said you weren't feeling well and we left the party.

"It must have hit me really hard. I don't remember leaving. I know I drank a lot of champagne, but I didn't think I was that out of it. Well, I'm glad to be home with you."

12

"Hi Dawn, how's the new job going?"

"Oh hi Eve! The new job is going pretty well. It's a dramatic change from my other 'job' as you can imagine, and the money isn't anywhere near as good, but I feel better about myself and what I'm doing, even if it is a bit boring."

"Boring?"

"Well, working the street is never boring. Even when I was standing around waiting for a john, there were people to watch and I did make friends with a few of the other girls. Of course their pimps didn't like me and didn't like me talking to the girls. I think they were afraid that I'd put ideas into their heads that they could work without a pimp to protect them. Of course I had Jane. She earned their respect even if she didn't work with them.

"But working in an office from nine to five is a challenge. I'm surprised at the office politics and pettiness. I thought the street was bad but it doesn't compare to what people do to each other to get ahead in business. And it's for such small amounts of money. Really! I don't get it."

"Yeah, I know. If you think it's bad in an office, you should try the University. You've heard about publish or perish, but it's much worse than that. People have to compete for grants to keep their jobs and people are willing to do anything to win those grants or get tenure. Worse, the tenured professors generally don't try as hard, at least on the teaching front. It's really sad that the most accomplished aren't usually the ones who do most of the teaching or who really interact with and mentor the students. When I worked there, I loved what I did. I also loved having summers off, and I loved the flexible schedules. But the politics, it's ugly. I suspect this is the case in almost every job.

"By the way, you mentioned Jane. What's happening with her?"

"Oh, you know Jane. She's disappeared again. As soon as I left the street, she was gone. I guess she didn't think I needed protection anymore in my new job. She's always been such a loner. As troubled as she is, I miss her."

"Did you hear about Liz? She's got a new man in her life."

"Actually, no. Even though I'm off the street, I'm not ready to show my face to the family yet. What's happening? I'd heard she'd broken it off with Mark Sinclair. I also heard about Steve.

That was very sad. From what I hear though, Liz gave up the sport. That should keep her safer. Did she take up with that guy she met hang gliding?"

"Yes, she did. He's a Silicon Valley executive in a startup and is quite nice. They make a great couple. In many ways, he reminds me of your father. He's a self-made man with a good sense of humor, motivated to succeed. From what I can see, a proposal may be coming soon and I don't think it's going to be a long engagement. Liz is in love and committed."

"Well, I hope it works out. We're a family of troubled girls. You're the only one who seems stable. I'm a whore. Jane is psychotic. Liz has been wild and has had those horrible abortions. Only Betty has escaped and we'll see what comes of her as she goes into puberty. God! I'm such a cynic sometimes."

"Well, truth be told, I'm probably more screwed up than the rest of you. I have never had any interest in sex. I'm actually still a virgin."

"God, Eve. I didn't know. I guess no one did. We really are a screwed up family. I sure hope that Liz and Betty fare better."

"Me too!"

CHAPTER 4

"To keep the fire burning brightly there's one easy rule: Keep the two logs together, near enough to keep each other warm and far enough apart - about a finger's breadth - for breathing room. Good fire, good marriage, same rule."

- Marnie Reed Crowell

1

In February, Liz passed the Bar Exam on her first try. Michael Leahy threw a big celebration at Quince in San Francisco and family and friends came to wish Liz well. Everyone asked if she was going to join her father's firm, and when she told them no, they asked if she was going to try to climb the partnership ladder at Mansfield, Mason, and Williams. Liz responded that she was planning to stay there until she determined what she really wanted to do.

Unfortunately, in the weeks that followed, now that Liz could legally practice law, the firm heaped on the work. Liz was billing over eighty hours a week and working over ninety. She hardly saw Jim.

For his part, Jim's company was about to ship a new line of products and he, too, was working ridiculous hours. It seemed that he and Liz only saw each other early in the morning and just before they fell asleep. They were too exhausted for lovemaking as they fell into bed after their long days, and too rushed when they got up in the morning.

One Friday night as Liz stumbled in to the house at nine-thirty in the evening, Jim was waiting with a glass of wine.

"Thank you, kind Sir."

"I have a surprise for you."

"Jim, I think I'm too tired for your surprise tonight. Maybe we can get up early and have a quickie before I head back into the office."

"We're getting up early, alright, but it doesn't have to be a quickie, and you don't have to head into the office. I called Jonas Mason and told him that if he didn't give you the weekend off, his partners would be prosecuting me for murder. I told my boss something similar. I made it sound as serious as possible and they agreed to give us Monday as well. I suspect we'll have to make up the hours somehow, but I think we need this. I've booked tomorrow and Sunday night at Lucia Lodge in Big Sur."

"You didn't really tell my boss you'd kill him if he didn't give me the time off, did you?"

"Well maybe not exactly, but whatever I said worked, so don't look a gift horse…"

Liz took a gulp of her wine, set her glass down and leaped into Jim's arms, kissing him deeply. They stumbled into the bedroom where they made up for lost weeks, the exhaustion falling away.

The next morning, Jim and Liz fixed breakfast and passed a leisurely morning together before heading down the coast. They stopped in Moss Landing for lunch and then made the drive past the Monterey Peninsula into Big Sur. They arrived at Lucia Lodge just as big drops of rain started to fall.

"Well there goes our weekend in Big Sur," Liz stated, clearly disappointed. Then thinking of the massive mud and rock slides that close Highway 1 regularly, "I sure hope we can get home on Monday."

"Oh, I wouldn't worry too much," Jim replied, grinning mischievously, pulling out an oversized umbrella. "I checked the weather before we came and so far things are going exactly as I expected."

Ignoring Liz's questioning look, they hurried into the store that served as the Lodge office. An attractive young woman with sparkling blue eyes and dark hair in a French braid looked up as they came in, shaking off the water.

"Hi, we have a reservation – Henderson."

"Oh yes, Jim Henderson and Elizabeth Leahy. We have you in Cottage 10 – the Honeymoon Cottage. Drive back to the driveway just north of us. There's plenty of parking and you're in the last cottage at the end of the cliff. I see you have dinner reservations for seven p.m. We'll see you then. We only have one other couple staying with us this weekend but they're dining elsewhere so you'll likely have the dining room to yourselves.

"Enjoy your stay," she said, winking at Jim surreptitiously.

"That was rude," Liz fumed as they got in the car.

"What?"

"She was clearly flirting with you."

"No, I don't think so," Jim soothed. "Let's see if we can get to the room without getting completely soaked. Wait here a minute. I'll take the bags to the room and then we can make a break for it."

A few minutes later Jim opened the passenger-side door, holding the giant umbrella over Liz as she stepped out. They fought the wind as they made their way along the cliff edge almost losing the umbrella several times. The wind and rain fell so hard that even with the intermittent protection from the umbrella, they ended up soaked by time they reached the small entry to the cottage.

Jim opened the door and urged Liz forward. He stepped in behind her and closed the door as a gust of wind shook the entire structure and the rain pounded the thin windows. It was mid-afternoon but with the black clouds looming outside, dancing firelight from the woodstove barely illuminated the room.

Liz looked around. The cottage was dominated by a large lace-canopied bed with a rustic hand-hewed wood frame. There was a small plush sofa, two stuffed chairs and burl tables. A silver ice bucket with a bottle of Dom Perignon glistened in the flickering light next to two crystal flutes and a small velvet box.

"Oh my God!" Liz exclaimed, realizing that Jonas Mason, Jim's boss, and even the receptionist at the lodge had conspired in this surprise.

Reaching for the box and dropping to one knee. Jim looked up at Liz who was dripping wet in the firelight. "Will you be my wife, Elizabeth Louise Leahy?"

They stripped off their wet clothes and were thirty minutes late for their dinner reservation.

2

James Mitchell Henderson and Elizabeth Louise Leahy were married on a spectacular October day at Michael and Janice Leahy's home. It was a moderately large wedding. Most of the guests came from Liz's side, some family and dozens of family friends. With no family of his own, Jim invited most of the people he worked with at Macrodata. Since Northern California was experiencing a classic Indian Summer, the wedding was held outside in the seventy-five degree weather. Rows of white chairs decorated with fall flowers faced the arched alter. Although both Jim and Liz were of Catholic origins, they had decided on a secular officiant who led them through their self-written vows. As the ceremony neared its end, the officiant said she had a few words for the young couple.

"Jim and Liz, as you enter into this commitment, I have a very simple request. I'm much older than you are and I've married dozens of couples. I always hope that the marriages will work out and that the couples will live happily ever after.

"The reality is that today, most marriages, even those I've performed, end in divorce. I don't mean to ruin an occasion of celebration with negative comments, but there are things I want you to think about and I want your witnesses to understand so that they can help you in your times of need – these will come.

"Our modern culture makes us want to embrace the rapid changes in our society, technologies, and our lives. We move so quickly now. Given this pace of change, in five years, you will be different people. In ten or twenty or thirty years, you will find it hard to believe you were the people we see here today.

"I can't predict whether you'll be one of the few couples that spend the rest of their lives together, but I can offer one small piece of advice that may help improve the odds. Through your marriage, you will encounter obstacles. Each of you will do your best to overcome them, but you may take different approaches. In many cases, you won't understand what the other is trying to do.

"But do remember this. You love each other. Neither of you actively wants to hurt the other. Relationships are fraught with imagined wrongs. You think you've heard the other and you're hurt. You respond in kind and the situations escalate. You fight.

"With each fight, something is lost. You find it hard to

believe that your spouse truly loves and supports you. You develop doubts and start looking for problems. You find them and the next fight pushes you further apart. A downward spiral begins and you find yourself attracted to a sympathetic ear. Maybe that person will be kinder, more understanding.

"But the reality is that in most cases, the next relationship sees the same problem. People who divorce once tend to divorce again, sometimes several times. It's not always a question of finding the 'one perfect match'. Most of the time, living with even that one perfect partner is going to be a challenge.

"So what's my one piece of advice? What is the magic answer to keep a couple together? It's going to sound simple, but the execution is hard. Here it is: Just Be NICE to each other. No matter what happens, how angry you feel, whatever wrong you think has been committed, JUST BE NICE.

"You'll be amazed at how many fights can be avoided if you just show enough respect for your spouse to be NICE.

"You'll be amazed at how many misunderstandings can be avoided if you're always NICE.

"And, you'll be amazed at how easy it is to stay close and to communicate openly if you're always NICE!

"So, in addition to the very romantic vows you've just exchanged, I ask you to make one more promise to each other.

"Do you, Elizabeth Louise Leahy promise, to the best of your ability, whatever obstacles arise before you, to always be NICE to Jim?"

"I promise," Liz answered.

"And do you, James Mitchell Henderson promise, to the best of your ability, whatever obstacles arise before you, to always be NICE to Liz?

"I so promise."

"In that case, by the powers vested in me by the State of California, I now pronounce you Husband and Wife. Congratulations!"

Jim and Liz kissed deeply. It was a bit more passionate that is often seen at weddings, but was in no way lascivious. All in attendance were warmed by the passion.

Champagne was served, the band played rock and blues, and everyone truly enjoyed the festivities.

For her part, after hearing the vows and seeing the couple kiss, Eve felt the thrill of hope. Maybe things would work out for

Liz. She certainly deserved it. It was too bad Dawn hadn't come to the wedding. She would have understood. And Jane. Maybe the ceremony would have touched her. She couldn't remember Jane being nice to anyone. Jane was tolerant of a few, but for the most part, she just distanced herself from everyone. So then again, maybe it was for the best that Jane wasn't here.

Eve caught sight of Betty during the ceremony. Betty seemed happy for Liz. She tried to catch up to her later but somehow lost her in the crowd.

This idea of being NICE was unusual, but as Eve considered it, she realized that maybe there was wisdom in those words far beyond their simplicity.

As she thought about other couples she knew, even Mickey and Janice, she realized that the successful ones seemed to consistently show that level of respect for each other. They were always nice. Of course, perhaps that was just what they projected to others. But even if that was true, as least they made an effort.

Toasts were made, dinner was served, the cake was cut and then the real festivities began.

The newlyweds danced their 'first dance' for which they had prepared with dance lessons at a San Francisco dance studio. Jim had always loved to dance but had no previous dance training. He had reluctantly agreed to the lessons but found himself intrigued by the precision of the movements required by the romantic and sexy rhumba that Liz had selected. Liz was patient, and their dance came off to applause by all in attendance. Jim promised Liz that dance would become a part of their lives.

Liz danced with Mickey and Jim with Janice who seemed to finally relax a bit. She held Jim close and told him that Elizabeth was a very special girl who needed someone strong to take care of her. Jim promised to always be there for Liz.

Hours later, completely exhausted, Liz and Jim prepared to make their way to a boutique hotel in San Francisco. Mickey and Janice made sure the party continued once everyone wished the newly married couple the best on their honeymoon.

After a leisurely morning with breakfast served in bed, Jim and Liz took a taxi to San Francisco Airport where they boarded a mid-afternoon plane for Frankfurt with a final destination of Venice.

3

A week later, Mike McKensey crossed the Golden Gate Bridge to pick up May for their now regular Saturday night out together. He was a bit nervous.

He rang the doorbell of the small house in a quiet San Rafael neighborhood and May answered immediately.

"My, my, you certainly look handsome," she praised.

Looking at May, Mike was awestruck. While both were frequently required to wear suits for court appearances, they usually dressed very casually. Tonight, wearing an elegant black sequined dress, a white bolero jacket and matching bag, May was stunning.

"Ah, ah – you're gorgeous!" Mike stuttered.

"You shouldn't sound so surprised if you want to make points with a girl," May teased, stepping forward to kiss Mike. "So what's on the agenda? This is the first time you've asked me to dress up for our Saturday night dates, so I'm really curious."

"You'll just have to be patient. It's a surprise."

Mike opened the passenger door of his freshly detailed 1973 BMW 2002ti and held May's hand as she sat down and swung her stocking-clad, very fit legs in. He raced around to the driver's side, hopped in, started the car and made his way towards Highway 101.

"If I'd known we were headed to the City, I could have picked you up," May began.

"No way! That would have spoiled the surprise."

Now it was May's turn to be nervous. She and Mike had been seeing each other for quite a while. Perhaps it was their ages and what they'd each been through before, but in spite of the stress of their jobs, the unreasonable schedules, and the regular interruptions which often brought both dates and intimate occasions to premature endings, they got along incredibly well. Patience. That seemed to be the magic word. Each was quietly patient with the other. Maybe having seen so much violence, so many people struggling just to get by, they had learned that in a special relationship, you need to allow for mistakes and misunderstandings and be patient enough not to overreact. It certainly worked well for them. After all this time, they'd never fought. They had become lovers but remained best friends.

They'd discussed living together and agreed that it would

happen, but they hadn't set a date. With their work schedules in two different cities, their current living situation was convenient. Neither had to commute. On the other hand, May realized that if they were to live together it should probably be at Mike's place since she'd have a reverse commute. She found that she could make it from Mike's home in the Western Addition to her place in twenty minutes with no traffic. She'd owned her house for years. Was she prepared to give it up? Could she live in the City?

May looked over at Mike who was uncharacteristically quiet. He was nervous. She knew what was coming tonight and it wasn't just because she was a detective. Any woman would know.

Living together was one thing. She could always go back home if things didn't work out. And given her track record, things usually didn't work out. Clearly civilians like her ex were bad partners. And the few cops she'd dated had competitive macho problems. Mike was different. They really did get along. But marriage? .

May cleared her mind, closed her eyes, and relaxed for just a moment.

She was surprised when Mike nudged her gently.

"We're here. Sorry to have woken you. You look so beautifully peaceful when you sleep."

May hadn't realized she'd fallen asleep. She looked around and realized that they were parked on Pier 3. This is where they'd boarded the San Francisco Belle for the swim leg of the Escape from Alcatraz triathlon.

"We started the Escape from Alcatraz here and I thought it would be nice to put a different spin on it by booking a dinner cruise."

"What a wonderful idea, Mike. I've never done anything like this."

Neither had Mike. The evening started off with drinks as the boat pulled away from the pier to the sounds of piano music. Mike and May held hands and toured the decks, marveling at vistas that could only be viewed from the water. As the lights of the City, the Golden Gate Bridge and the Bay Bridge came up, dinner was called and the couple was led to an elegant table on the third deck next to a large window. A bottle of champagne awaited in an ornate ice bucket next to the table.

Almost instantly, a perky young blond approached, opening

the bottle of champagne as she introduced herself. "May and Mike, I'm Janet and I'll be serving you this evening."

Pouring the champagne, she continued, "I want to make this a truly memorable experience for you so if there's anything you want or need, don't hesitate to let me know. I won't be far away.

"Here are the menus. You can choose from the multiple appetizers, entrees and desserts. While most people wait until after dinner to step out onto the dance floor, as you can see, there are always a few couples who dance before and between courses. Feel free to join them.

"And last and not least, here's our wine list. If you need any suggestions, I can help you with wine pairings depending on your dinner choices.

"Please take your time and enjoy your champagne. Look my way when you're ready to order or if you have any questions."

As Janet stepped away, Mike pick up his glass of champagne, looked at May and said, "To a special evening. Thank you for letting me be a part of your life."

May smiled warmly, already feeling more relaxed after her earlier cocktail. "To us," she said encouragingly, almost expectantly. "I think we have something very special."

"Feel like dancing?" Mike proposed.

"Sure, let's go."

They made their way to the dance floor and rocked sensually to a Frank Sinatra song, holding each other for a moment after the tune ended, then politely turning to applaud the orchestra.

May led Mike back to their table as the boat made its way under the Bay Bridge next to Treasure Island. The strands of lights on the bridge reflected off the water as they passed. They sipped champagne as they made their dinner choices

Dinner and the service were beyond what they expected. And as Janet had suggested, they did get up to dance between courses. As always, their conversation went smoothly and surprisingly even on a romantic outing, discussion of work seemed unable to disrupt their rhythm.

"You know, if not for these murders, we'd never have met. Now that they've stopped, I can't help thinking that if the timing had been a bit different, we wouldn't be here tonight. I feel very lucky," Mike began.

"Yeah, I know what you mean. We lucked into a very strange case. I copied you on my query to the profiler. Did you see his response that nothing in this case made sense, particularly now that the murders have stopped?"

"Yes, I did. But I don't think I mentioned that my friend in Vice finally got back to me after all this time. Apparently there was a young hooker that no one messed with, but she's disappeared. There's no real correlation, but she didn't have a pimp and still garnered a lot of respect from even some of the hard core down there. I can't help thinking that that kind of respect has to be backed up by violence. But at this point, we're at a dead end – with the case I mean."

They finished their dinners, relished the dessert and decided to sip their after dinner drinks – a Tawny Port for May and a Grand Marnier for Mike – outside on the deck as they passed under the Golden Gate bridge, infinite dark ocean to the west merging with stars at the horizon.

"May, I'm not the most romantic guy in the world and tend to be overly practical at times, so this question may seem a bit awkward, but what would you think about us getting married?"

May looked up at Mike and smiled. Yes, he could have dropped to one knee and offered a ring, but that wasn't Mike. Their relationship thus far had been one of equals. It made sense that he'd want to discuss this with her; that they'd arrive together at a decision for their future.

"Mike, this has been a very romantic evening. It's an evening I'll remember for the rest of my life."

Seeing Mike's look of disappointment, May wrapped her arms around his neck.

"Of course we should get married. We're a perfect team. And, we're not going into this blindly. On top of all that, let me be the first to say it out loud: I love you Mike McKensey."

"I love you too, May."

Mike McKensey and May Reeves were married two weeks later on top of Mount Tamalpais at sunrise. The officiant pronounced them husband and wife just as the sun peeked above the soft blanket of white fog several hundred feet below them.

4

Every year, MacroData Systems held a holiday party in early December. The company usually rented a large space in a San Francisco hotel for the celebration. They hired a band, provided a sumptuous dinner buffet with multiple stations and offered an open bar. They even had a group of students available at the end of the evening to ensure that those who'd had a bit too much to drink got home safely.

The band was already playing when Liz and Jim arrived. They found a table filled with Jim's engineers and their wives and chatted briefly before making the rounds of the buffets. Liz was particularly taken by the sushi bar and loaded up multiple plates with exotic sushi rolls.

Wines from the Napa and Shenandoah Valleys of California were featured this evening and several of the vintners were present to discuss their particular varietals. Returning to their table, Liz and Jim ate greedily and made several trips to the buffets.

During dinner, Jim got into a serious discussion with one of his engineers. While the rest of the wives rolled their eyes and waited for the conversation to turn back to something more civilized than database design and query languages, Liz excused herself and started making rounds of the tables, greeting everyone she knew and relying on them to make introductions to those she didn't.

At one point, Rajiv Kumar, founder of MacroData Systems interrupted a light conversation Liz was having with one of the engineers' wives and asked Liz to dance. They made their way to the dance floor where they danced a fast swing dance followed by a chaste foxtrot. Leading Liz back to his table, Rajiv reintroduced his wife Vinaya. Wine, multiple desserts, and several coffees later, the three were deeply ensconced in serious discussions about MacroData and its position in the industry.

For his part, Jim was having a great time. He wasn't worried about Liz. He knew that she had social skills that far surpassed those of anyone in the room, so he relaxed and savored spending time with his engineers in a non-work setting, getting to know them better and listening attentively to their wives and their perceptions of MacroData and their husbands' roles in the company.

As the evening progressed and more wine and mixed drinks were consumed, Jim was surprised as large groups of his engineers and their wives moved to the dance floor. Although he recognized that many of his compatriots were of Indian descent, this was the first time that he saw their cultural roots emerge. The orchestra changed the music and as he looked towards the dance floor, Jim had to ask himself how he'd ended up in a Bollywood production. His engineers and their wives were dancing in concert, choreography perfectly synchronized as dozens of them moved together on the dance floor.

Many people talked about the Asian influence on the Silicon Valley. Most referred to the 'Asian Pride' movements in schools where huge number of Chinese immigrants' children worked much harder than their lazy American counterparts and graduated at the tops of their classes. But Jim now realized that at the same time, the Indian immigrants and their children, native English speakers, were having an even greater influence. They seemed to fit in better. There was a relaxed sense that helped them integrate into the American culture more quickly than their Chinese counterparts. Nonetheless, they were a force to be reckoned with and were, without a doubt, becoming very influential in the Silicon Valley. Look at Rajiv. He came from India twenty years before as a graduate student in Computer Science, and today, he was President and CEO of a successful startup.

Jim looked around and was not surprised to see Liz laughing with Rajiv and his wife Vinaya a few tables away. Since the majority of his table was on the dance floor, he made his way over.

"I see you've charmed my wife into abandoning me," Jim joked.

"Oh, no. I think it was the other way around," Rajiv replied. "Liz has captivated our attention with her mesmerizing presence and witty conversation. We've ignored the rest of our guests. Why don't you take Liz out onto the dance floor and we'll make our rounds?"

"Well, I would, and though I've learned quite a few new dances, these Indian steps boggle my mind."

"Don't worry. The band will certainly transition to something more American shortly."

And almost as if they'd heard Rajiv's pronouncement, the band moved smoothly into a Nat King Cole tune. As ordered by his CEO, Jim led Liz onto the dance floor where they did a good job of faking a foxtrot with their rhumba moves. Swing followed, with another foxtrot after that.

Liz and Jim danced the night away, switching from wine to tonic and club sodas respectively, sobering quickly and relishing their time together on the dance floor.

The evening wound down and after saying goodbye to his team and thanking Rajiv and Vinaya for a great evening, Jim and Liz stepped outside into the brisk San Francisco night and asked the valet to retrieve their car.

"There's something I need to tell you," Liz began.

"What, you're leaving me for Rajiv?" Jim quipped.

"No. This is serious. We do need to talk."

"Okay. I'm ready. Knock me over," Jim continued.

Liz stopped Jim, took both of his hand and looked into his eyes seriously.

"Rajiv offered me a job as company counsel and I've tentatively accepted – I've told him I need to talk to you about it first."

The valet arrived and Jim gave her a generous tip after she opened the door for Liz and brought the keys to Jim.

Jim waited for Liz to fasten her seatbelt, then pulled away wordlessly.

Liz gave him a few minutes of silence, and then said, "So what do you think? I really like the idea, but I won't take the offer if you think I shouldn't. I love the thought of us working together, commuting together, getting to finally work on the same schedule and pushing toward for the same goals. What do you think?"

Jim wasn't sure what he thought. He didn't know why, but this pissed him off. He tried to think back to their wedding ceremony. Just be NICE. Just be Nice. Just be nice.

The mantra played over and over in his mind and he tried to suppress his unreasonable anger. Liz was clearly waiting, impatient.

"Ah, I really wish we'd had a chance to discuss this before you talked to Rajiv," Jim stated flatly.

"I didn't have much of a choice. We were talking, jumping back and forth between the situation at MacroData and my job at Mansfield, Mason and Williams. I'm sure this is partly my fault as I surely did say that I wasn't having fun there billing huge numbers of hours with boring work, mostly research.

"Rajiv and Vinaya both asked me my opinions about several MacroData issues and you know me, I love to offer my opinion.

"I guess, I must have said something that hit home, because they both, almost simultaneously, asked me if I'd considered working for a company like MacroData. After a while, they pressed me on it and ultimately offered me a job.

"I must admit that I was and still am intrigued. I've envied your job: a startup with technology that might change the world. I'd love to be a part of that. It certainly beats writing briefs for spurious lawsuits that don't really settle anything.

"But you're right. I should have talked to you about it before saying anything. It just didn't work out that way. I'm not sure how I could have pushed them off more than I did. Please think about it, and please forgive me for overstepping my bounds. I don't want to interfere in your career. At the same time, this looks like a great opportunity for me. I know that if you weren't working for MacroData, I would have accepted on the spot.

"So, please don't be mad. Think about it and how it will be to work together. Sleep on it and let's discuss it tomorrow. We have the whole weekend to get comfortable with the idea. If you're not in agreement by Monday, I'll call Rajiv and make my excuses. What do you think?"

Jim considered her proposal. He certainly hadn't expected this. He'd always thought that his career and Liz's would be separate. Was this too much intimacy? Could two people work at the same company and keep a marriage together? Could he escape the feeling that Liz was invading his space? Be Nice. Be Nice.

"Okay Liz. I can't say I'm happy about this. MacroData is mine. At least I've thought of it that way. I've always thought that you'd have your career and I'd have mine and that we'd have a lot to talk about when we came home. I'd be learning from you and you'd be hearing my stories. I just never imagined that we'd - - that we'd be working together.

"So, it's my turn to ask you. Please be patient with me and give me the weekend to think about it. Let's not talk about it until Sunday night. I know that's a lot to ask and that you're excited about it, but please give me that time to try to get comfortable with the idea."

Not being a terribly patient person, Liz almost lashed out, telling Jim that she deserved the position and didn't need his permission to take it, that she'd earned the offer on her own merits. But she too went back to the officiant's advice. Be NICE. Be nice.

"Okay. I understand that this is a surprise and is totally unexpected. I'll try to leave it alone until Sunday night. I'm kind of excited about it so I'm not sure I'll succeed, but I'll try."

When they got home, Liz was exhausted. Jim needed a few minutes to unwind after the drive and after Liz's proposal.

Jim tucked Liz into bed and gently stroked her back as she drifted off to sleep. He turned out the light and watched mesmerized as the streetlights once again cast the wavering shadows of the trees onto Liz's sleeping form.

"I don't think she should do this," Liz said in her small sleepy voice.

"What do you mean?" Jim asked.

But Liz was asleep and Jim never got an answer.

5

Liz did go to work for MacroData as Chief Legal Counsel and quickly made her presence felt. When she didn't have the answer to a question, she reached into her network of connections, often contacting Michael Leahy. She proved to be valuable beyond Rajiv's expectations.

For his part, Jim was pleased that things were going so well for Liz. As it turned out, even though they worked for the same company, most of Liz's time was spent on matters that didn't concern Jim. It was almost as if they had different careers, but at the end of the day, when they came home and discussed their respective days, they had a lot of common ground. Liz soaked up Jim's accounts of technology decisions while Jim learned that he really had no idea of how complex the legal issues could be for a startup like MacroData.

Life was good and Jim was happier than he could ever remember being. He had it all: a great job, a wife who shared his interests, plenty of money, and a new extended family and group of friends that provided a social life Jim had only dreamed of.

In late November, after an elegant Thanksgiving dinner with the in-laws, Liz led Jim to her former room.

"It's snowing in the mountains," she began.

"Yeah, I've heard this is going to be a great season up there."

"Well, if I recall, you never learned to ski or snowboard, right?"

"No," Jim replied a bit sheepishly. "My family didn't ski and quite frankly we never had the money to do sports like that."

"How'd you like to learn? We have the money now and I really miss skiing. I haven't been up since law school started. It would be fun to teach you to ski. Of course snowboarding might be more to your liking given your surfing background, but I couldn't help you with that."

"Sure. I'm game. Don't your parents have a place at Bear Valley?"

"Yes, they do, but I really don't want to stay there. Bear is pretty much intermediate skiing. I'd like to take you to Kirkwood. They have great beginner slopes and it's easy to progress. The conditions and slopes are predictable. How about we go up next weekend?"

They went up that weekend and the next, and the next and

then spent the week between Christmas and New Year's at Kirkwood. By the end of January, Jim was skiing groomed black diamond slopes. Liz had proven to be an excellent teacher, never taking Jim to places that were beyond his skill level; never pushing him too hard, but encouraging him to face his fears by giving him techniques that would help him advance.

One day in early February, they stopped at the bottom of a black diamond run.

"I think it's time you learned about moguls," Liz proposed. "You're going to fall, and it's going to be challenging, but it's a great thing to learn and I think once you master it, you'll have more confidence in exploring other terrain and you'll discover a whole new aspect to skiing."

"Okay. I'm game. What do I do?"

"As you can see, to our left is a very bumpy area of the slope. Since this is the beginning of an intermediate trail, it's not terribly steep and since they groom this almost every night, the moguls aren't too big. I think it's a good place to start.

"Mogul skiing requires a different technique. Your tendency will be to try to turn around all the bumps. That's really not possible. It's hard to turn that fast. The proper technique is to ski right at a bump with your weight forward. When you reach the top, because the bump is essentially round on top, you can pivot your skis in any direction very quickly since it's down in all directions. With weight forward, push your skis down and aim for the next bump. Let the bumps slow you down, not your edges. And whatever you do, don't lean back, as much as you may think you need to."

"I don't think I can remember all that, but I'll try."

"Okay. Try to follow me and imitate what I do."

Liz headed into the field of bumps and Jim followed, committed to do what she had suggested. She skied up the first bump and slid down the other side, the tips of her skis never leaving the snow. As she dropped down the second mogul, Jim hit the first. He tried to keep his weight forward but as he reached the top of the first mogul, the unusual upward motion threw him off balance and his weight went back. He tried to do a quick turn but the tails of his skis crossed and down he went, losing a ski and a pole. He found a flat spot, put on his ski and looked warily at the mogul field below.

"As you approach the bump, reach forward with your pole,

touch the bump and bring yourself up and around the pole, then repeat."

Jim tried that, made it over one mogul, but on the second one, fell again.

"Don't get frustrated. It takes practice."

"Why don't I meet you at the lift? I should probably experiment with this a bit on my own."

"At the pace you're going, I'll do another run and meet you here or at the lift if you make it that far before I get here."

And off she went. Jim watched in awe as Liz skied the bumps almost as if they weren't there. Her upper body was quiet and her legs moved up and down smoothly with her skis never leaving the snow. It looked amazingly graceful.

Jim successfully traversed two bumps, then fell again. Two more; the same. Then three. Then four. As he was nearing the end of the mogul field, Liz skied past him saying, "Looking good!"

Jim fell again.

"Damn! Just when I thought was getting it."

Liz stopped. "Don't worry. You are. You're a natural. Your body will learn. Just don't overanalyze it."

At the end of the day, Jim was exhausted. They replenished themselves with a decent meal at the Kirkwood Inn, washed down with an Amador County Zinfandel.

Warmed by the glow of physical exhaustion and fine wine, they went to bed early. Jim rubbed Liz's back. He loved feeling her relax into his hands. The moonlight cast shadows onto their bed creating an incredibly romantic atmosphere.

"You were really good today," Liz said in her sleepy voice.

"I felt completely uncoordinated and got really frustrated. At the same time, I'm excited about learning something new. I think I'm going to be able to do this and I might even become a decent skier."

"Don't worry about that. You're going to be good. I'm so happy to see you two fitting together so perfectly."

"You two?" Jim asked, surprised. "Don't you mean us?"

"Are you awake or asleep?"

"I'm asleep and of course I mean us. I'm just so sleepy. I love you Jim!"

"I love you too, Liz."

A week later, Liz and Jim made an offer on a cabin about

thirty minutes from Kirkwood. The south-facing A-frame sat on three acres with views to the Central Valley. Because the south side was mostly glass, even on the coldest winter days, the house was warmed by the sun. The land bordered national forest property and there were trails and old logging roads that extended for miles, crossing creeks, passing old abandoned gold mines, and offering serenity and solitary beauty for Jim's runs and the couple's hikes during the spring, summer and fall. The Mokelumne River was only ten minutes away and Liz and Jim could often be found cavorting naked in remote swimming holes in the river canyon on warm days.

One warm spring day as they were about to give the icy snow-melt of the river a try, Jim spotted a pair of fly fishermen making their way towards them. As they got close, Jim realized that one was a woman. He watched fascinated as their lines arced gracefully forward and back, landed far away on the river and drifted downstream. Every so often, one would catch a fish, pulling it in by the fly line, then release it downstream. It looked like a peaceful meditation as they brought together the air, their skill, and the cascading river.

When they were about to leave, Jim approached and asked about the sport. Like most people who love what they do, the couple was happy to share their experiences and to give Jim advice on how to get started. A year later, Jim was a competent, if not expert fly fisherman. For her part, Liz preferred to just watch Jim work his magic and soak up the sun nearby.

Aside from the fact that they always seemed to have less money than Jim expected, life was perfect. They discussed putting together a budget, but they were never really short of money, so it didn't seem urgent.

6

As Liz gained experience at MacroData, Rajiv became increasingly comfortable letting her negotiate deals on her own. Long gone were the days where he was present in every meeting with a prospective customer, supplier, or strategic partner. Instead, Rajiv and his counterpart would lay out the basic terms of a deal and then turn it over to Liz and her counterpart to draft the agreements and iron out the details. Occasionally, Rajiv would be drawn back in as major terms changed or unforeseen concessions had to be granted. But even there, Liz proved to be a tough negotiator and it was rare that MacroData had to make concessions. Plus, the business was growing fast and Rajiv was thinking about an Initial Public Offering. He needed to leverage his time as best he could and offloading much of the legal wrangling saved a lot of time.

Eighteen months into Liz's tenure, Rajiv introduced her to Martin Davies, CEO of Majormajormajor, a software company that worked in the medical records area. Marty was a former roommate from grad school and obviously a big fan of Joseph Heller's Catch-22, claiming the book kept him from taking himself too seriously. He wanted to license MacroData's database system to streamline record retrieval and analysis.

"Liz, Marty and I have laid out the general terms and I'd like you to work with him and his legal guru to finalize this contract. I think it's going to be strategic for MacroData, helping us get deeper into the healthcare industry."

"And I think this is a match made in heaven," Marty agreed enthusiastically. "With your technology, we'll become market leaders in our space."

A week later, Rajiv called Liz into his office.

"Where are we with the Majormajormajor contract? "

"Well, I'm still negotiating. I'm having a hard time getting them to bend on licensing issues."

"But those issues were decided between Marty and me. You don't need to negotiate that."

"Look Rajiv, you've hired me to look out for the best interests of the company. If this deal is as big as you think it will be, we should take as much as possible in royalties. We certainly shouldn't be giving them the break you proposed."

"Liz, I didn't *propose* the terms, I *promised* them. It's not your place to second guess me. Just finish the contract with the terms Marty and I agreed on and do it quickly."

Liz's eyes flared. She stood up dramatically and stormed out of Rajiv's office, heading straight for Jim's where she slammed the door.

"That son-of-a-bitch! I've put ridiculous hours working to protect this company and now he's ready to throw it all away."

"Slow down," Jim proposed soothingly. "Tell me what happened."

After recounting the situation, barely containing a rage that Jim couldn't understand, Liz looked at Jim intently and said, "You have to talk to him!"

"Liz, I'm sorry. I can't do that. This is not my area. It's something you and he need to work out."

"I knew you'd take his side. You men always stick together!"

"Liz, where is that coming from? You know that's not true. But though you don't want to hear it, Rajiv is the CEO, and he can make any decision he wants. He has overruled me many times on the development front and I've learned I need to trust him. I don't always like it, but he is the boss and it's his company."

"You've got no balls, Jim."

Before he could respond, Liz was gone.

When it was time to leave work, Jim looked for Liz but she was nowhere to be found. He went to the parking lot and the car was gone. Since no one at MacroData lived nearby, Jim had no choice but to take a very expensive cab ride home.

The car was in the driveway but the house was dark.

"Liz?" Jim called on entering.

"Leave me alone!" Liz shouted from behind the closed bedroom door.

"But Liz, let's talk about this."

"Just leave me the fuck alone!"

Figuring she needed time to cool down, Jim fixed himself a dinner of scrambled eggs and watched TV. About midnight, he made his way into the dark bedroom, undressed, and slipped into bed beside Liz.

"She's right you know," Liz said in her small sleepy voice.

"Who's right?" Jim asked, surprised Liz was speaking to him.

"Liz," replied the sleepy voice.

"But you're Liz," Jim protested.

"I'm the sleeping Liz. The waking Liz is right though. Rajiv should do what she says."

Not sure whether this was a game to let them talk on a different level, Jim decided to play along.

"Well, she may be right, but sometimes, we have to trust others to make decisions. Sometimes there are considerations that we don't see. And in the case of Rajiv, he's the boss and it's his decision to make."

"Couldn't you just talk to Rajiv and maybe find out what these considerations are? If we explain them to Liz, maybe she'll go along."

"Well," Jim began, more puzzled than ever by this conversation. "I could do that, but it would be a breach of protocol in the company. It's not my area. I have no involvement in this deal and probably shouldn't even know about it. Worse, it would look like I'm protecting you – ah, Liz - and giving her special treatment that other employees don't get. That would create problems for Liz and me down the line."

"Hmm," mused the little voice. "I see."

Jim was lost in thought during the silence that ensued. He thought Liz was sound asleep and that this was the end of it.

"I'll fix it," said the sleepy voice. "Goodnight Jim."

"Goodnight."

When Jim awoke in the morning, Liz was not in bed. Her car was gone too.

Jim showered, dressed, wolfed down a banana and made his way to the office unsure of what the day would bring, trying to understand what had happened to Liz and to their perfect relationship.

Surprisingly, the day progressed normally. Late in the afternoon, Rajiv called a company meeting and announced the deal with Majormajormajor. While the engineers made a few jokes about the company's name, everyone was excited about the prospects of breaking into a new industry.

7

Jim left the office early and picked up champagne, flowers, salmon, and salad fixings. Frank Sinatra was playing and dinner would be ready just minutes after Liz got home.

Walking through the door, Liz beamed as Jim handed her a glass of champagne. "Why thank you kind sir!"

"Let's not fight ever again," Jim toasted.

"Let's not!"

Liz and Jim made love after a quiet dinner and a slow dance.

Basking in the afterglow, Liz confessed, "Jim, I've always had a problem with authority. I got in trouble constantly in school, but Mom always defended me and my rights. I wonder if that didn't make me too bold. In high school, I got arrested after I punched a cop."

"You what?!!"

"Yeah, I see now that I was spoiled, but when that cop insisted I had run a stop sign that I definitely stopped at, I lost it and punched him. I actually don't remember doing it, but he had a bloody nose, and Daddy had to bail me out of jail. Fortunately, he got the charges dropped."

"Well, in business, unless you run your own company, you have to answer to your boss. Hey, even if you do run your own company, you have investors, customers, and employees to answer to. Pushing back against authority can be a good thing at times, but you need to know when to back off."

"Yeah, I know," Liz replied sheepishly. "I just get so focused on the goal. I want to see MacroData be the best it can be and when I see a decision taking us the wrong way, I just have to block it. I've actually negotiated far beyond what Rajiv asked for several times and I can tell you that it has benefited the company tremendously."

"Liz, you can't do that. He's the boss. He has the vision and as employees, we sign up to follow his lead. We provide input but it's his right to make the final decision. If we really don't like his leadership, we can leave. But so far, Macrodata is doing well and there may even be an IPO in our future."

"We could leave, though," Liz proposed thoughtfully. "We could start our own company. You'd be a great CEO."

"Maybe someday, but with the company doing so well, I really can't see leaving anytime soon."

Over the next month, things seemed to be back to normal. MacroData was going well, and at least to outside appearances, Rajiv had regained confidence in Liz. Jim assumed that Liz had apologized to Rajiv, but when he'd asked her about it, she just changed the subject.

One Friday afternoon as Jim was wrapping up review of a design specification, he heard raised voices coming though the wall that separated his office from Rajiv's. Rajiv was such a peaceful person that Jim couldn't remember hearing him shout before. He also was pretty sure he heard Liz yelling at Rajiv. As the argument escalated, Jim decided to see what was going on. Stepping outside his office he saw that Megan, his and Rajiv's shared administrative assistant, was clearly alarmed and didn't know what to do.

Jim knocked on the door but the shouting didn't cease. He opened the door just as Liz slammed Rajiv against the wall.

"Liz!" he yelled.

As Rajiv fell to the floor, clearly terrified, Liz turned towards Jim, her eyes and nostrils flaring. Then suddenly her face changed. Her eyes went wide as she looked around the room. She pushed past Jim and ran to her office, closing the door behind her.

Jim went to Rajiv and helped him up.

"What happened?"

Standing up and straightening his clothes, Rajiv looked stunned.

"It started out over a contract issue again," he began. "As it escalated, I realized that I had lost control of the discussion and myself. I can't remember losing my temper like that before – at least not since I was a kid.

"Anyway, when I recognized that I was part of the problem, I reached out to touch her to try to calm the situation. At that point, she completely lost it and slammed me against the wall. I think she would have really hurt me if you hadn't come in.

"Jim, I obviously haven't had the time to give this much thought but clearly Liz can't work here anymore. I'm sure we can work out some arrangement, but at the very least, I suggest you get her some counseling. She clearly has anger management and authority issues. Are you two having problems at home? Is there some family issue that's causing her to act out?"

"I really don't know," Jim replied, embarrassed and

concerned. "I'm really sorry this happened. I'd better get her home and see what's going on. I'll see you Monday."

By now, Rajiv had recovered his composure. "Good luck, Jim," he said, draping his arm over Jim's shoulder and walking him to his office door. "I hope this won't change our working relationship. I've never believed in husbands and wives working together, but I made an exception because Liz seemed so ah - exceptional. The company will do whatever we can to support you. See you Monday."

Jim made his way to Liz's office and knocked softly. Getting no response, he entered and found Liz asleep at her desk.

"We need to go home, Liz."

"We blew it, didn't we?" said the small sleepy voice.

"Yes. We did."

They made their way to the car in silence. Arriving home, Jim fixed a light dinner and they watched TV until ten when Jim noticed that Liz had fallen asleep next to him. He guided her to bed, helped her undress and tucked her in. As he stroked her face gently, running his hand from her forehead back into her hair, the small voice said, "I'm sorry, Jim. I really thought we had it under control. She's going to lose her job, isn't she?"

"I'm afraid so. You really crossed a line. You can't have physical violence in the workplace. Maybe with some counseling, if we could show some progress, you could get your job back. On the other hand, I never really thought it was a good idea for us to both work for MacroData. So, I think it would be best if we looked for something else.

"Either way, I think counseling is essential. If you can lose control that way with someone like Rajiv, how do we know it won't happen elsewhere or that the consequences won't be worse. Liz, I think this is really important."

"I don't think she'll agree to counseling. She really hates shrinks. She had to see one years ago and it didn't go well."

"Why do you keep saying 'she'? You're Liz, right?"

"Well, sort of. Like I said, I'm the sleeping Liz."

"So you're only here when Liz is sleeping?"

"Usually then, but not just then."

"When else?"

"Well, sometimes when things get really difficult for Liz, she goes to sleep and I take over."

"Like this afternoon when I came into the room?"

185

"Yes. That was me. I was a bit surprised to see Rajiv on the floor. I saw the look on your face and decided to get us out of there."

"Have there been other times?"

"Yes. I talked to Rajiv after the last incident and apologized. There have been some times with the family or in school or – like I said, when it gets too difficult for Liz, I sometimes take over to help her out of a bad situation."

"Does anyone else know you're different from the main Liz?"

Liz wrinkled her nose and frowned for a second.

"Right now, no. You're the only one I trust to talk to. She really loves you, you know. And I love you too. I think you're a good person and are the person Liz is meant to be with."

"You said 'right now'. Did you talk to other people? Did others know you were different?"

"Well, I did talk to Steve. I really liked him. Liz did too. He was her best friend. It wasn't like with you. Steve and Liz weren't destined to be together. But we talked, usually when Liz was in bed."

Jim sat on the bed in silence for a while, continuing to stroke Liz's face and head. When he heard her breathing slow and knew she was asleep, he made his way back to the living room where he picked up his laptop and began writing down his thoughts, hoping to put some sense to the situation. This wasn't the Liz he knew. But then again, did he really know that much about her? He wished Steve were still around so that he could talk to him and get his perspective. Steve, too, seemed to think that Liz and Jim were meant to be together. He had helped bring them closer in his own way.

Jim continued typing. He described all he could remember about their meeting, the evolution of their relationship, the major events, friends, family, and work situations. He remembered the look on Liz's face at the Nationals when she seemed ready to kill Brent Powers. He remembered family gatherings where Liz needed to leave suddenly and he now recognized that he had seen the wide-eyed 'sleepy Liz's several times before. There were often times when Liz didn't remember what had just happened. Even when they first met, there was that kill-that-baby incident. He'd discounted it at the time but maybe it was one of many clues he'd ignored. He thought back to their countless late night conversations. Recently, they even talked about Liz in the third person. What was going on? How had he missed all of this?

Jim's mind was squirrel caging. He got up, went to the kitchen and poured himself a glass of wine. Returning to his laptop, he reviewed his notes. Then he began internet searches. He found an online version of the Diagnostic and Statistical Manual of Mental Disorders, also called the DSM, and spent the next few hours reading about personality disorders. It was confusing. Maybe Liz was suffering from Histrionic Personality, or maybe it was Borderline Personality Disorder. He didn't think she was schizophrenic, but maybe the 'sleeping Liz's and the waking Liz were two different people and Liz suffered from Dissociative Identity Disorder, formerly called Multiple Personality Disorder. That kind of seemed to fit, so he continued reading articles about some very strange cases, and then discovered that there were several books, and even movies made about the subject.

Unfortunately one thing really didn't fit. According to what he'd read about these multiple personalities, the main personality was usually docile and self-effacing, other personalities exhibited the more aggressive, outrageous behaviors. Liz, at least the main Liz (he couldn't stop thinking of her that way), was confident, outgoing, and friendly. This didn't match up with any of the cases he'd read about. It must be something else.

Towards dawn, Jim was exhausted. He made his way to bed, slipped in next to the sleeping Liz, and quickly fell into a very sound sleep.

Sometime later, Jim awoke suddenly, realizing it was very light and that Liz wasn't in bed. He looked at the clock and saw that it was after noon. Getting up, calling Liz's name, Jim made his way to the kitchen where he found a note on the table. Liz had gone to her parents for the day but would be back in time for dinner. She needed some time to sort things out. He probably did too.

Thinking back on his research, he was even more confused than ever. His unconscious mind hadn't done its job. Even if he were on the right track, how would he and Liz deal with this? The 'sleepy Liz' had said that Liz would refuse counseling. A psychiatrist would certainly be out of the question.

And maybe he was on the wrong track anyway. After all, her family and friends had lived with Liz her entire life and they hadn't noticed anything. Or had they? Then again, maybe this was a recent change. Maybe it was a hormonal thing like Sharon said she encountered with her ovarian cyst. Maybe it was some sort of psychological problem that was recently triggered. Too many maybes. Jim needed to find out more about Liz when she was younger to see if the signs were already there.

Jim thought about who he could talk to and sensed that Mickey was his best choice. He sent an email to him requesting a one-on-one lunch meeting for some time that next week. In the meantime, he'd just try to see if things between him and Liz could get back to normal, whatever that was. He certainly hoped that this wasn't the new normal.

8

Liz got home that evening loaded with fragrant containers.

"I brought Thai," she announced to a wary Jim.

"How are you feeling?" he asked cautiously helping her set the table.

"I'm okay. Are you?"

"As you might imagine, I'm really concerned. We need to talk about what happened. Are you up for it?"

Seeing her nod, Jim continued.

"I don't know how much you remember, but you got violent with Rajiv. You slammed him against the wall and my impression was that if I hadn't come into the room, you would have hurt him seriously.

"Surprisingly, Rajiv, while a bit shook up, seemed to think that the escalating argument was at least in part his fault. But your sudden violence caught him off guard. It scared him, but more than anything, after he recovered, it concerned him. Between your lack of respect for authority, and what appear to be anger issues, Rajiv is concerned that you will have problems being successful. He suggested you get into counseling ASAP.

"Quite frankly, he is probably within his rights to have you arrested."

Liz nodded, her eyes filling with tears. "I spent the day with my parents and told them what happened. They reminded me of times this has happened before and Daddy suggested I consider counseling. I suspect you feel the same way, but I'm not ready for that. I'm sure we can figure this out and that I can work it out on my own. So for now, I'm asking you to be patient and let me see if I can get myself together.

"I'm going to take some time off, start working out, eating better, and I'm going to write. I'm hoping that this will help me organize my thoughts and become better able to look at my moods and actions objectively. Will you support me in this?"

Jim thought about her proposal. Many psychiatrists were touting the benefits of healthy diet and exercise for mental illnesses. The journal idea was a good one. It would give Liz a good way to look at her moods and behaviors. In the worst case, it would document Liz's thinking for a while. Maybe some patterns would emerge. If she didn't get better they could seek some help.

"Okay. I agree, but with a few conditions."

Seeing Liz start to get angry, Jim held up his hand and continued. "Look Liz, what you did to Rajiv was unacceptable. Not just in a business environment, but ever, except in the case of self-defense."

"But I don't remember doing anything to him. We were discussing that new contract, and it did get a little heated, but it certainly wasn't anything to get violent about."

"Liz, I saw you. The fact that you don't remember what happened should be of concern to you. It certainly is to me. I'm willing to give your proposal a try, but here are my conditions, and I'm sorry if that offends you, but we are married, we're a team, and we need to work on this together. I am impacted by what you do. My relationship with Rajiv will be much more difficult now. Rajiv is hoping that he and I can move past this and get back to our normal business relationship, but I know that some part of this is going to be contingent on you getting some help.

"I don't want to leave MacroData. I helped build the company and it's becoming successful. I'd like to share in that success. You are more important to me than my career, but I'd sure like to keep both. You and I need to find a way to make that possible and a big part of that is going to be our working together to get you into a more stable place.

"So, first, I agree to wait one month. You will write in your journal every day. I don't need to see what you've written, but I want to see that you have written. As for diet, sure, let's go vegan for that month and let's cut out alcohol as well. A month long cleanse certainly won't hurt either of us. As for exercise, find something fun that you can do most days of the weeks, and if you want me there, I'll join you whenever possible. We can certainly make sure our weekends are active.

"At the end of the month, let's sit down and talk about how it's gone. I'd like to read and discuss your journal. We might find some helpful things. Then, we can talk further about the need for counseling. With luck, it won't come to that. But if I'm not convinced, you need to agree now that you'll at least give it a try."

"Okay, Jim. Let's do it. I know I have problems, but you're right. We're a team and we can solve this together. I love you, Jim!"

Jim began to believe it was possible. Liz might be okay. And in the worst case, he had her promise that they'd seek counseling if things weren't going well. One month shouldn't make a huge difference.

"I love you too, Liz."

9

Jim met Mickey at Café Claude, a well-known French restaurant in San Francisco. They decided to lunch late to avoid the rush. Mickey was already seated at a table outside when Jim walked up. Mickey leaped to his feet, seized Jim's hand, and pulled him into a bear hug.

"How's my favorite son-in-law?" he asked enthusiastically.

"I'm your only son-in-law," Jim replied smiling.

"Still my favorite though," Mickey quipped. "You look exhausted. Sit down and let's catch up over a fine lunch."

Jim perused the menu desultorily and when the waiter came to take their orders, Jim asked for les pates aux champignons.

"And can you make that vegan – végétalien?"

"Bien sûr," replied the waiter.

"Vegan?" Mickey queried.

"Yeah. It's something that Liz and I are going to do for the next month – sort of a cleanse. She's also going to be exercising and keeping a journal. We're hoping the combination will help her get things together.

"She told you what happened, right?"

"Well, yes. She did," Mickey replied gravely. "But being a good jurist, I'd like to hear your version. Not that I think it will differ substantially, but sometimes multiple perspectives help us understand."

"That's exactly why I'm here, Mickey. I love Liz and am planning to spend the rest of my life with her no matter what problems we have to face."

"I admire and respect your commitment. Now go ahead. Tell me what happened."

When Jim had finished, Mickey mused, "I didn't think it was that bad. You honestly believe she would have seriously injured him?"

"As much as it scares me to say it, and as much as I'd love to deny it, there's no doubt in my mind. If I hadn't come into the room and called her name, Liz would be in jail."

The waiter brought salad for Jim and soup for Mickey and they ate in silence for a few moments.

"Mickey, I'm Liz's husband and considering my commitment, I'm hoping you'll help me understand some things about Liz, particularly things that might have happened when she was younger. I'm not trying to play shrink; I just need to see if there's a pattern or if this is just recent behavior. And of course, if it's a pattern, is it getting worse or is this just something that happens once in a while?"

After a thoughtful moment, Mickey took a deep breath. His open smiling face went dark and he began to speak quietly, almost as if he didn't want to hear himself.

"Children are a blessing and a challenge, particularly to a marriage. Elizabeth has been the biggest issue in our relationship. You know how I feel about her. I'm incredibly proud of her and proud to be her father. But she has some major issues. Janice and I have done our best. And while I may be a force in the courtroom, I hate to admit that my Sicilian wife kicks my arse at home. So when we've had disagreements about Elizabeth, Janice has made the decisions. It's been her decision that we keep Elizabeth's problems in the family, that we protect her.

"I've done more than I probably should have. There have been incidents of violence before, and drug use, and drunkenness, and disappearances. Janice tries to write them off as cases of adolescent exuberance. When Elizabeth lived at home, we could keep an eye on her and the rescues were pretty easy. In college, some of the situations were worse, and were much harder to contain. Now that she's on her own in the world – I don't mean completely alone – she has you. But now that she's not living under our protection, I fear for her safety and quite frankly, for the safety of others.

"Having been involved in psychiatric commitment proceedings, I truly know the significance of that that phrase, 'a danger to themselves or others'. It frightens me that I can make such a pronouncement about my own daughter."

Mickey paused. He avoided Jim's gaze as he picked at the meal the waiter had brought a few minutes before.

"Mickey, I know this is difficult, but has Liz always been like this? Was she like this as a little girl?"

Mickey reflected for a moment, then looked Jim and smiled.

"No. Absolutely not. She was a wonderful little girl. Brilliant. Clever. Always ready with a smile and wanting to please me and Janice.

"So when did it change?"

"Well, I guess she was about twelve or thirteen. Elizabeth developed early. That puts the fear of God into every father's heart. But the boys she brought home were respectful. Elizabeth was happy and didn't seem to take them too seriously. They were just good friends. She always had an entourage of friends."

"I hate to interrupt, but didn't she have an abortion at thirteen?"

"She had just turned thirteen," he replied somberly. "We still don't know who the father was. Elizabeth never told us. I grilled every one of her friends but none seemed guilty. And as you know, I have certain skills in adversarial situations like that. No. We never found out.

"The changes started a several months before that incident though. Elizabeth had become morose and reclusive. She avoided the family gatherings, excusing herself as soon as it was acceptable, and spent a lot of time alone in her room or out walking. We tried therapy, but she clammed up as soon as she entered the therapists' offices. She refused to speak.

"Then there was the abortion. She insisted on it. She wouldn't even consider the alternative. And since the doctors felt it would be risky for her to carry a child to term, we reluctantly agreed. Given her mental state, we thought it would make things worse. But surprisingly, Elizabeth got better. In most ways she was back to her own self after the abortion – at least most of the time.

"A couple times a year, something would happen that seemed totally out of character. She'd be stopped by the police and I'd get a call. It might be underage drinking or small acts of vandalism. Later it was drugs, including cocaine, and there were a couple incidents of violence.

"I begged Janice to get Elizabeth some professional help, but she refused."

"This is probably going to sound rude," Jim began diplomatically. "But did you consider the possibility of rape?"

"I appreciate your efforts to make this easier, but sometimes you just have to look at a problem head-on. God knows I haven't done that over the years. Yes. We did consider rape. But we couldn't come up with any way it could have happened. Elizabeth never came home with bruises or injuries, except from some of her sports, and I believe that if a stranger attacked her, she would have put up a fight."

"And if it wasn't a stranger?"

Mickey looked surprised.

"We never even considered that. But here we are more than a decade later. I don't know how we'd find out. Liz either doesn't know or for some reason won't tell. I had several deep father-daughter talks with her after the abortion. And my truth-sniffing nose believes that she has no clue who the father was."

They finished their lunch in silence. Mickey picked up the check and they made their way back to Jim's car, where Jim held out his hand.

"You've given me a lot to think about," he said. "Thank you for being so candid. I'm sure there's a solution here. It may take a while, but we'll find it."

Mickey pulled Jim into another bear hug.

"She was wise to choose you, Jim. I'll do whatever I can. I can't say the same for Janice. We may run into a roadblock there, but I'll do my best."

"That's all any of us can do," Jim replied.

"You have wisdom beyond your years, son-in-law."

10

The month started off well. Liz took up cross-fit and began training. Within just a few days, her body began to change, becoming tighter and stronger. Her attitude seemed to improve too. Aside from the fact that Liz wasn't working, life for Jim and Liz seemed to get back to normal. With the vegan, alcohol-free diet, even Jim had to admit he felt better.

Some mornings before work, Liz would join him on his runs up Montara Mountain. He could see her getting more fit. She even expressed an interest in learning to surf, so they purchased a longboard and wetsuit and on days when the waves were small, he took her out to Linda Mar beach and pushed her board into waves. She quickly learned to stand up and it wasn't long before she was catching waves on her own. Jim had always fantasized about having a woman he could surf with. It would open the door to more shared experiences and travel to exotic surf locations around the world.

Periodically, Jim would ask to look at Liz's journal. She kept it on her laptop in an unencrypted file. Jim did his best to honor his word and he made it clear to Liz that he would respect her privacy and that per their agreement, he wouldn't read it until the month was over. In the meantime, he just looked at dates and verified that she was writing every day. From what he could see, she was writing quite a bit, usually multiple pages with each entry. He was curious, but he knew he could wait.

One late night as he was about to go to sleep, Jim heard the small sleepy voice.

"I don't think she can keep this up," it said softly, clearly concerned.

"But things are going so well. Liz and I are having more fun than we ever have. She's looking great, and seems to be getting herself together."

"Yes, I know it seems that way on the outside, but on the inside, something is not right. I think things that need to come out are going to and all these good actions are just a lid on something that's going to overflow."

"What sorts of things?"

"I don't have any way of explaining it. It's too complicated. But be careful Jim."

"Careful?"

But Liz was sound asleep and he heard nothing more that night.

When he awoke the next morning, Liz was gone. No note; nothing to indicate where she might be.

Jim, hoping for the best, assumed that Liz went off to one of her workouts. But when he returned that evening, Liz wasn't there. He tried her cell and it went to voicemail after several rings, meaning she wasn't picking up. He called Mickey but got no answer. He left a message. He called Janice and again, left her voicemail.

A few hours later, Janice returned his call and said that she hadn't heard from Liz and neither had Mickey. They had called Bill and some of Liz's other friends but no one had heard from her. They weren't prepared to call the police because Liz had only been gone for the day. Maybe she needed some time alone. Maybe she was in the mountains. That was something Jim hadn't thought of. All agreed they'd talk again the next night if Liz hadn't reappeared.

Jim called the cabin in the mountains but only got the answering machine. That really didn't tell him anything. If Liz wasn't answering her cell phone when he called, she probably wouldn't answer the phone up there either.

Jim went back to the computer where he buried himself in more research about psychological disorders. He thought back to his conversation with Mickey and to the changes that took place in Liz as she entered adolescence. It was probably reasonable that her parents wrote off her behavior as associated with puberty and adolescent angst. But what if they were wrong? What if something really terrible had happened to Liz and they never knew about it? The psychological consequences could have been dire and could explain her current behavior. He dug deeper.

Well after midnight, he heard a car pull into the driveway. He went to the door and stepped outside. The fog had rolled in and the street lights glowed fuzzily through the moisture. The shadows from power lines and neighboring trees seemed to float on the mist, never quite reaching the ground. The car door opened and Liz stepped out. She made her way to the stairway, staggering a bit.

"Oh, Jim, I love you so much!" Liz shouted into a night so quiet a whisper would have been heard a block away. "Take me to bed!"

Jim half carried her up the stairs and guided her to the bedroom where she collapsed on the bed. He helped her undress and tucked her in. She didn't wake up. He stroked her head, hoping to hear from the sleepy Liz, but he was rewarded with soft snores instead.

11

The next morning, Jim was pleased to see that Liz was still in bed beside him. He got up and made a breakfast of oatmeal with raisins and cinnamon, toast, and fresh squeezed orange juice. As he entered the bedroom carrying their breakfast, Liz awoke.

"How'd I get here?" she asked sleepily.

"You drove yourself home last night, but since you could barely walk, I suspect driving wasn't the best idea. How much do you remember about yesterday?"

Jim moved some pillows behind Liz as she sat up and placed the tray in her lap. Then he sat beside her cross-legged and looked at her expectantly as she ate a spoonful of oatmeal, took a bite of toast, and sipped her orange juice. Jim took his bowl and spoon from the tray and took a bite as well. He hadn't eaten the night before and was hungrier than he had thought.

"I'm sorry, Jim. I just couldn't take it anymore. This vegan thing. No alcohol. Being good all the time. That's just not me. I awoke yesterday and I was done with it. I went out and had eggs and sausage for breakfast, a huge cheeseburger and milkshake for lunch, and a steak, very rare, for dinner. And yes, I went to a bar in the City and drank quite a bit. I must admit that in spite of a bit of a headache and some dehydration, I feel better than I have since we started this fiasco."

Jim wasn't sure how to react. They'd had a deal. Should he confront her and demand that she start counseling? Somehow, this didn't seem to be the right time.

"Okay," he began cautiously. "Where do we go from here?"

"I've been thinking about that a lot these past few weeks. I can see that I really didn't belong at MacroData. In fact, I don't think I'm the kind of person that can work for anyone else."

"So are you thinking you'll start your own firm? Hang out a shingle as they say?"

"Well, I suppose I could, but I think it makes more sense for you and me to work together. We're a good team and I don't think we'd have the kind of disagreements that I had with Rajiv. I'd like you to give notice at MacroData so we can start our own company. You'll be great. I know it."

"Liz, as we discussed before, I don't want to leave MacroData. I helped build the company and now that it's doing well, I want to share in its success. I want to reap some of the rewards for my efforts."

"But don't you see that it's over there? They're going to look at you differently now that your crazy wife has attacked the CEO. We'll never be able to socialize with anyone in the company and it is a very social group. That's what helps keep it running smoothly and why everyone gives so much.

"I know it's my fault, but it's for the best. You need to leave."

"Liz…"

"Jim, at least promise me you'll think about it. Talk to Rajiv. I think he'll probably agree that the current situation is not workable. You guys can work out a transition."

Jim realized that much of what Liz said made sense. At the same time it really bothered him that Liz would just assume that he would do what she said. Even worse, she didn't seem to care that he would have to give up the work that had been his passion for years, that she was asking him to start over when he was so close to a major success. She was asking too much.

"Liz, I don't think I can do that. MacroData has been my life for a long time. I'm not willing to just throw it all away. I will think about it and I will talk to Rajiv, but don't get your hopes up."

"Jim, this is non-negotiable. You made a commitment to me and our marriage and I don't see us succeeding if you keep working for MacroData. Think carefully."

Jim got up and left for work. He was angry.

He did talk to Rajiv and Rajiv didn't think the situation with Liz would be a problem. As far as he was concerned, the incident was forgotten. From what he could tell, the other employees felt the same way. Only Megan had actually seen that Liz had gotten violent and neither she nor Rajiv had discussed it with anyone else. As far as the company was concerned, Liz and Rajiv had a major disagreement on the business and Liz had decided to leave. There were no hard feelings.

When Jim got home, the house was dark. He did find a note in the kitchen saying that Liz was at her parents' and would be back late. Jim shouldn't wait up.

Near midnight, Jim went to bed but he couldn't sleep. Liz eventually came home and she slipped into bed, never touching him. Jim could smell the alcohol again. He rolled away and eventually fell asleep.

The next morning Jim woke to the smell of bacon and eggs.

Clearly the vegan diet was a thing of the past. Still, he was pleasantly surprised that Liz had made breakfast.

Sitting down at the table, he looked up to see a smiling Liz setting a plate before him laden with eggs, hash browns and bacon. She poured both of them glasses of orange juice then sat down across from him.

"How'd it go with your parents?" he asked?

"Good. Really good. They think it a great idea for you to start your own company and are convinced you'll be a great success. How'd it go with Rajiv?"

"It went very well. We had a long discussion and he wanted me to tell you that he holds no grudges. He feels that he was a big contributor to what happened and wants to apologize for his part in it. Other than Megan, no one in the office knows what happened that day and no one ever will. He's made it clear to the team that you decided to leave and that the two of you had worked out an arrangement though he hadn't been happy with it originally – implying that that was what the disagreement was about.

"Anyway, he thinks there will be no problems with social situations – it will be like it was before you joined MacroData."

"Jim, don't you see that he's just saying this to keep you? He knows how valuable you are and that you'll be a threat in your own business. You didn't buy this, did you?"

"Yes, I did and do. I love working at MacroData and don't see any reason to leave."

"Jim, you need to think about this more and understand what's really at stake here. I'm going to start spending more time at the cabin so you can be alone for a while to reconsider."

With that, Liz stood up, stormed out and drove away. Jim sat there too stunned to finish his breakfast. How could what seemed like a perfect marriage be disintegrating so fast?

That evening, Jim returned home from work to a darkened house once again. Liz had left a note stating that she wanted to be left alone for a few days. He was invited to come up to the cabin for the weekend.

12

Friday night after the commute traffic had settled down, Jim headed up to the mountains. He and Liz had exchanged a few emails and Liz seemed genuinely excited that he was coming up for the weekend. She promised to have a late dinner waiting.

It was a warm summer evening in the mountains. Floodlights illuminated the driveway and cast the shadows of countless circling moths and passing bats onto the driveway. Jim could make out a candle on the deck and what appeared to be a table set for dinner outside. The lights of Stockton shimmered four thousand feet below and more than fifty miles away. A full moon had just risen in the east.

Jim climbed the steps to the deck, a bit stiff after his three-hour drive and a bit cautious about what kind of reception he'd get from Liz. Was their marriage really in trouble?

As he approached the table, Liz raced out of the house, ran to Jim and literally leaped into his arms, wrapping her legs around him and almost toppling them both. That could have been a disaster as the deck sat thirty feet above the sloping hillside.

"Jim, you don't know how much I've missed you!" Liz shouted enthusiastically. "Remember our first dinner together?"

"Pizza in Upper Lake?" Jim asked tentatively.

"No, Silly. The first time I cooked for you!"

"Spaghetti Carbonara?" Jim queried, his stomach suddenly growling loudly in anticipation.

"Exactly right. Sit! I've got salad first, garlic bread ready for the broiler, and a nice bottle of Zin from the Shenandoah Valley just down the hill."

"Ah – okay," Jim replied, confused by Liz's enthusiasm. "Just let me pee and put my stuff down. Liz kissed him gently, then slid down his body lasciviously before stepping away, wordlessly promising things to come.

A few minutes later, Jim returned to the deck. The moon was higher and the pine and fir trees cast long shadows across the deck. It almost seemed like daytime. Liz was waiting at the table expectantly. She'd poured the wine and served the salads and Jim could smell the garlic bread toasting in the oven.

"To my husband, the Love of my Life!" Liz toasted. "Although we didn't say it in our ceremony, I want to be with you until death parts us. I'm sorry for being so difficult.

Sometimes I don't understand why I do the things I do. I hope you'll want to stay with me too."

"Liz, you are the love of my life and I do want to be with you for the rest of my life," Jim replied, touched.

They sipped the excellent Amador Zinfandel and Jim took a bite of his salad as Liz looked on expectantly.

"Oh my God!" Jim exclaimed. "Did you make this? I've never had a salad this good. It's kale, right?"

"Kale tossed with lemon grass, sliced olives, crushed red pepper and a bit of olive oil. Pretty good, huh?"

"Unbelievable. I thought you couldn't cook."

Jim regretted the words as soon as they left his mouth, but Liz laughed at Jim's discomfort.

"I would never have admitted it, but it's true. Aside from the Spaghetti Carbonara, I really couldn't cook. But now that I have time, I'm finding that reading recipes and trying them out is very meditative. I like it. If I take more time off, I might become a great cook. Maybe I'll give up the Law and become a chef. No. I'm just kidding."

They ate in silence for a few moments as the moon rose higher and the shadows retreated. Liz excused herself somewhat formally and went into the house. She returned with a huge bowl of the Carbonara, garlic bread and freshly grated parmesan cheese.

"So will you be coming home soon?" Jim asked tentatively.

"We can talk about that more later, but for now, let me just say that I don't feel like I'm completely in control of myself. We tried our vegan, no alcohol, exercise thing and I almost went crazy. Quite frankly, I have problems and I need to try to sort them out on my own. If I can't, I'm committed to seeking help. But I don't know that our marriage will survive the process of us trying to fix me. So I'm asking you to be patient with me. Give me some time. Come up on weekends. It's peaceful here and it's away from things that seem to set me off. Let's see if I can find some stability.

"Excuse me again. I have to put dessert in the oven."

Upon her return, they talked quietly about Liz's family and discussed ideas for the future, one of which included Liz setting up her own practice. They shared long comfortable silences, gazing out at the trees and the lights of the Central Valley in the distance.

When they had their fill of the Carbonara, Liz refilled their wine glasses, cleared their plates and went back to the kitchen to get dessert. Jim felt better. This was the marriage he wanted to have. It was possible. It might take some work, and patience, but they could do it. He was sure of it.

Liz returned and placed a plate in front of Jim.

"Ma pièce de résistance," she announced. "I've always loved Lava Cake and didn't realize it was so easy to make. I know you'll like it and it's perfect with the Zin."

And it was. The hot rich chocolate cake and dark molten center contrasted perfectly with the dollop of vanilla bean ice cream while the fruitiness of the Zin set off the chocolate flavors. This was one of the best home-cooked meals Jim had ever had.

After dinner they made their way up to the loft where they made love. Jim dozed for a while then came fully awake. He looked over at Liz's naked body basking in the light of the full moon and was instantly aroused. He tentatively stroked Liz who responded and woke slowly.

"Would you like to try something a little different?" she whispered seductively.

"Ah – sure. What did you have in mind?"

Liz sat up quickly, her full breasts swaying sensually, and reached into the drawer of the nightstand. She pulled out a joint and a lighter, licked her lips and slipped the joint between them. She lit the joint, inhaled deeply and held it. She exhaled and offered the joint to Jim who was clearly shocked and caught off guard.

"You've done this before, right?" Liz asked.

"Ah – actually, I was a straight shooter in high school. I did try it in college, but I got ridiculously paranoid and quite frankly, haven't tried it since. It scared me. I don't have objections to people smoking weed, except that it's illegal here and I don't like the idea of supporting dealers."

"Well this is home-grown by a friend of mine, so no dealers. I've always found that it enhances lovemaking. Every sensation seems to last forever. Give it a try. I promise to take care of you."

Jim reluctantly took the joint and inhaled deeply, holding it until his lungs felt like they would burst. He passed it back to Liz, who took another hit and who then passed it back to him. One more long hit each and she put the joint out.

They began to make love. Jim could feel the drug taking effect. Things seemed to slow down. He savored the taste of Liz as he kissed every part of her body. When he buried his face between her thighs, she moaned. He became completely focused on the warmth and wetness and on subtle movements of her hips.

He could feel her getting excited and knew that she was about to cum. Her hips thrust upward and she whispered huskily, "A little to the left."

Jim froze. A little to the left? Was he doing something wrong? Had he hurt her? Had he not heard her the first time she asked? Had he spent too much time to the right? God, he was a terrible lover.

"Don't stop!" Liz commanded.

So Jim did as he was told. He focused on the left, but not too much. Or was it too much too? Or maybe not enough? He couldn't keep his mind from squirrel caging. He couldn't stop thinking about one thing at a time. He'd lost touch with the world around him as he was consumed by one thought, one sensation. It seemed like the world as he had always perceived it was gone. Now he only saw a single tunnel or maybe it was that his thoughts and feelings were locked into a tunnel, moving forward without his control. He wanted his perception of the world back. Looking at one thing was interesting for an instant, but to not sense the rest of the world was frightening. It was like being blind in the middle of a busy freeway where you could only hear the cars and trucks, not see them, feel the wind, or have the ability to move out of the way.

For her part Liz didn't seem to notice and sometime later (Jim didn't know whether it was seconds or hours), Liz had a crashing orgasm, screaming loudly. Would someone call the police? Would they think a woman was being murdered? Would he go to jail? What would it be like in jail? Would he be raped?

"Take me now, Jim!" Liz commanded.

Jim climbed on top and tried to enter her but he'd lost his erection at the thought of being raped in jail.

"Can you make it stop?" he pleaded.

"Make what stop, Lover?" Liz asked languidly.

"I can't control my thoughts. I keep doing everything wrong. I can't stop it. Help me!"

Liz shook off her torpor and looked closely at Jim. She'd

heard about people reacting this way, but had never seen it and certainly couldn't imagine this happening on two hits with the good home-grown shit they'd smoked.

"It'll be okay," she soothed. "Here. Put this up one of your nostrils and sniff hard like you're not supposed to do with a nasal spray."

Too frightened to question her, Jim did as he was told. Something in the small vial that Liz had handed him shot up his right nostril and he felt a burning, then an acrid taste in the back of his throat.

"Now the other one."

Jim sniffed the substance into his left nostril and let Liz guide him onto his back.

"Now close your eyes and try to relax. Think of hang gl- no; think of skiing down a freshly groomed slope with its corduroy. Envision each of the turns and feel your legs flex and extend as you glide, glide, and glide.

Sure enough, the haze from the weed started to clear. He could picture himself skiing. In fact, the more he skied down that imaginary hill, the clearer the image became. When he reached the bottom, he opened his eyes and saw Liz looking at him lovingly.

"I think that's the first time you've ever let me really take care of you," she said. "I like it and it makes me feel good that when you're frightened, you can trust me."

"What was it?" Jim asked tentatively, knowing, but dreading the answer.

"That was Coke silly. Haven't you ever done Coke before? Don't you feel the effects? Don't you feel a clarity that you don't normally feel?"

Jim thought about it for a moment, looking around the room, at Liz, at the moonlit trees outside. He felt normal again. His mind had quit squirrel-caging and he could change his focus again at will.

"No. I haven't. As you can see, I'm a lightweight when it comes to drugs. I've avoided painkillers, even after serious surfing accidents. Just a bit of local anesthetic makes me nauseous and shaky as the epinephrine affects me too strongly. I just drink a bit of alcohol in moderation from time to time. I don't do other drugs and you can see why."

Liz rolled Jim over onto his stomach and straddled him. She

started to massage his neck and shoulders as she talked about skiing, hiking, swimming in the rivers, anything that would put beautiful thoughts into Jim's mind. After a while, Jim fell asleep. Liz got up and went down to the kitchen where she poured herself a few fingers of brandy. She stepped out onto the deck and took a seat at the table, peacefully sipping her brandy naked in the warm moonlit night.

The next morning, Jim woke up confused. Liz fixed him a light breakfast of cereal and fruit and for a few moments, Jim would feel normal. Then it was back. He'd lock onto something and couldn't control his thoughts. It was as if he were stoned all over again. Fortunately it only lasted a few minutes. By noon, it was happening less and less frequently, but Jim became exhausted and took a long nap. It was late when he woke up and he was hungry. Liz was working outside and looked pleased to see him when he stepped onto the deck.

"Feeling better?"

"I think so. Will this keep happening? I won't be able to work if I feel like this on Monday."

"Actually, I'm not sure. I've never seen anyone so affected by two hits of weed. But I do know that blood tests generally won't show anything after twenty-four hours, so I would think that you'll be fine tomorrow."

Jim didn't want to think about how Liz knew about the duration of cannabis elements in the blood. Clearly there was a side to Liz that he hadn't seen before. Was this the woman he married?

"So," Liz continued. "How about dinner? I was thinking about the Union Hotel in Volcano."

Putting aside his growing unease, Jim agreed. They had a very pleasant dinner on the garden patio and drank another excellent Amador County Zinfandel from the Shenandoah Valley.

Back to their normal ritual, with Jim pretty much recovered, Jim tucked Liz into bed and gently stroked her head as she fell asleep. Liz was certainly an enigma. Life with her would never be boring. But would it be too exciting? Too dangerous?

As if she'd heard his internal questions, the small sleepy voice asked, "Are you okay, Jim? I wish she hadn't given you drugs."

"I'm okay now, but it was really scary for me. I can handle fear in my sports and in business, but at home, when I think I'm safe, it was really hard. Does Liz use drugs often? " Jim asked, surprised that he hadn't even had to think about referring to Liz in the third person.

"Well, you've seen her drink. Sometimes she gets very hyper and drinks or smokes pot to calm her down. Sometimes she gets very depressed and uses cocaine to bring her up again. Other times, she seems to be okay, often for weeks at a time, but I do worry because there are these cycles where it seems she's up, then down, then up."

"Do you think she might be bipolar? From my reading, it sounds like it. Do you ever have these ups and downs?"

"She might be bipolar, but I'm not. I'm very even-tempered," the little voice said proudly.

"Yes. You seem to be. What do you think I should do? How can I help Liz?"

Liz was silent for a while and Jim thought she had fallen back to sleep when the voice said, "I don't think you can help her now. Things are happening that I can't completely explain, but until Liz is ready, I think the best thing you can do is to be patient and understanding; that may not be easy."

"What do you mean?" Jim asked.

But the voice was gone and this time, Liz was completely asleep.

13

Dawn was exhausted. She'd only had three clients this evening, but she was done. She just didn't have any energy. Maybe she'd lost the touch, being out of the life for these past several months. But it didn't feel like that. She felt like her whole body was just tired and weak. Maybe she was getting sick. Some warm soup before bed sounded good.

Dawn didn't regret being back on the street. She had to admit that her office job just didn't do it for her. The politics were petty. People did terrible things to each other to gain a bit more recognition for that next raise or promotion. She just didn't see the point. You didn't make much money and there wasn't much satisfaction in the work. At least in the Life, she made a lot of money and felt some satisfaction over leaving her clients happy. She controlled it all. Maybe that was it. Here she had control. In the office she had none.

Suddenly, she was slammed from the side and someone grabbed her purse. Fortunately, or perhaps unfortunately, it had a strap which went over her head, and the purse itself was tucked under her arm. Thinking this was just an attempted purse snatch, Dawn almost smiled. But when the purse didn't come loose, her assailant wrapped his arms around her, lifted her off the ground and carried her into a nearby alley where he threw her to the ground.

Dawn looked up and recognized Jimmy. The girls talked about him. Those he ran seemed to live in constant fear and usually displayed bruises where he'd beaten them. Most didn't survive long on the street as he didn't manage their drug intake well and they quickly degenerated into junkies. A few had died of overdoses.

"Hey, sweetness," he said slimily. "I heard you were back. Still think you can work without protection? Well, you're wrong. You're working for me now. Gimme your bag. I want to see how much you made tonight. Then you and I can go have some fun. I want to see what you've got that makes you so damned special."

Dawn sat up, stunned. What was she going to do now? She lifted her purse strap over her head and handed it to him holding on so he could pull her to her feet. Maybe he'd just take the money and would leave her alone.

Jimmy opened the purse and pulled the money out of her wallet and threw it and her purse to the ground.

"Three bills? That's it? I heard you did better than the other girls but this is just chicken shit. You're going to have to do a lot better than this in the future. But you can give me a little something more right here and now," he ordered, grabbing her arm and slamming her against the wall.

Jane saw Jimmy attack Dawn. She knew she should have been closer. She was supposed to protect Dawn. That was the only job she had ever been good at and she'd clearly screwed up. What was wrong with her? Why had it gotten this far? Dawn was about to get hurt. Jane hurried.

"I don't know if Dawn has anything to give you, but I do," she said triumphantly, slipping her shiv accurately between Jimmy's ribs directly into his heart.

A few hours later, having watched Jane efficiently move and dispose of Jimmy's body in the Bay, Dawn broke her stunned silence.

"You've done this before, haven't you?"

"Yes. I have. I don't like that you've chosen this line of work, but Jimmy was right. You do need protection. There are a lot of scumbag men out there and I have no problem eliminating them if they try to hurt you. They don't deserve to be on this planet."

"I knew you were around to protect me. But I didn't know you killed them. This is wrong, Jane."

"Dawn, some part of you knew. You're the only girl on the street without a man. How do you think you've been able to stay that way? Until Jimmy, they've all been afraid of you or actually, of me. The problem was that you were gone for so long that many forgot what happened to men who messed with you. But you're back, and I'm here. I'm sure Jimmy bragged about what he was going to do. Now that he's disappeared, the others will think twice before they try anything with you."

"How many?"

"I don't know. It doesn't matter. Would you ask me how many mosquitos I killed if they were swarming on you? Any man who hurts you deserves what I give him. This is a good thing, nothing for you to worry about."

Dawn thought back through her clients and those that got rough with her or who threatened her. There was also that dealer who disappeared. Did Jane kill them all? Several were nasty people. Maybe they did deserve what they got. But there was one client. He kept calling her a name. What was it? He wanted her to pretend to be his ex-wife. He was sad and desperate. He said that she looked just like his wife when she was younger. She remembered him getting overexcited and forcing her head down onto him causing her to gag. He didn't hurt her, but she did run away.

"Do you remember a middle-aged, nicely dressed guy that I was going down on? He got too excited and forced my head down. He was angry with his ex-wife and I was pretending to be her. Did you kill him too?

"I don't remember these assholes. If they hurt you, they die."

"But he didn't really hurt me and he wasn't a threat. I slipped away and as I left, I heard him crying. He was very upset by what he'd done and I think he was just seeking some help, some escape from a life that had become unbearable for him. He'd lost everything that mattered."

"Well then, I did a good thing by putting him out of his misery."

Dawn was too stunned to speak.

They rode home in silence.

CHAPTER 5

"Chaos is the score upon which reality is written."

-Henry Miller

1

As Jim drove home from the mountains Sunday night, he couldn't help asking himself if he was in over his head. He loved Liz. And he was falling in love with the little sleepy voice too. Of course she was a part of Liz, so there wasn't anything wrong with that. But the drugs, the mood swings, living apart. Was this the life he pictured when they'd married? Clearly not. Was Liz mentally ill? That seemed like a big jump. She'd gotten through her life thus far without being declared incompetent. And most of the time she was intelligent, thoughtful, and charming. But could he say that? Was it still most of the time? Something had changed. He wasn't sure when or where, but something had definitely changed and it seemed like Liz was heading downhill. Even she sensed it. So did the little voice.

But how could he best help her? She was unwilling to seek psychological help. He certainly wasn't in a position to force her. From what Mickey had said, Janice wouldn't be supportive and it was unlikely Mickey would go up against Janice where Liz was concerned – at least he hadn't so far. And what did Jim have to go on anyway? The sleepy voice wasn't anything significant. Lots of people talked in their sleep and didn't remember what they'd said when they woke up. The incident with Rajiv could very well have been just a very bad day. He didn't know exactly what went on in that office and while he doubted that Rajiv would have behaved inappropriately, it was possible that Liz was only protecting herself. No. He really had nothing substantial. Maybe it was the drugs. The little voice had said that Liz had used drugs for a long time. Perhaps what they were seeing was caused by the drugs.

When he got home, Jim called the cabin to let Liz know he'd arrived home safely. He was greeted by the sleepy voice.

"Sorry. Did I wake you?" he asked.

"Yes. But it's okay. I'm glad to know you made it home safely. Jim, I love you, you know. Liz loves you too. I'll do my best to take care of her when you're not here. Don't worry too much."

"I love you too," Jim replied, more confused than ever. "I'll call tomorrow evening after work. Good night!"

"Night."

After hanging up, Jim logged on to their bank to review their bank statements. Before he met Liz, Jim had been pretty frugal. He'd tracked his income against his expenses, made sure he was saving money and contributed as much as possible to his 401K. Each month, he plugged everything into QuickBooks so that he could do month-to-month and year-to-year comparisons.

Perhaps it was Liz, her lifestyle, the money her family had, or perhaps he had just been in denial, but Jim had quit tracking their expenses. He certainly hadn't touched QuickBooks since their marriage. He made a good salary and so had Liz. The 401K contributions were their primary savings and they lived a very comfortable life. They had agreed to purchase whatever possible with credit cards and to pay the cards off every month. This allowed them to take the float on their expenses and to avoid carrying much cash. It also would have allowed them to track their expenses closely, but since there always seemed to be plenty of money, Jim he had never followed through with that. Now it was time to catch up.

Four hours later, Jim had entered all of their transactions, splitting out his, Liz's, and their joint expenses, and had reconciled their bank and credit card transactions. Then he started running reports.

The first thing he noticed was that they ate out a lot. The cost of eating out was far beyond what they spent on groceries. They also bought a lot of alcohol. He was aware of the champagne they bought for the family parties and of the wine they bought regularly as part of their frequent tours of wineries in Northern California, but Liz had made regular purchases from several liquor stores, many for several hundred dollars.

Clothing expenses were high, but this wasn't unusual. He liked to see Liz dressed nicely and they often went shopping together. Jim loved to watch her model clothes.

But most disturbing, beyond the alcohol purchases, were the large amounts of cash that Liz was withdrawing. It amounted to thousands every month. Was this her drug money? Did she have a habit that cost thousands a months? Add in the alcohol and it was clear that Liz had a major drug and alcohol problem. This could certainly explain her behavior. But how should he address it?

2

The next evening, Jim called Liz as promised. She seemed up and engaged. Jim told her about his day, but didn't dwell on it too much as he knew she still felt resentment towards MacroData. They hadn't discussed his leaving the company since the night Liz stormed out. Now Liz seemed to be holding her tongue to avoid pressing Jim again.

Instead, Liz talked about her gardening projects. She'd been making trips to the river and collecting stones to build decorative edges to pathways into the garden. She was battling the deer that seemed to eat everything.

Screwing up his courage, Jim decided to broach the subject of money.

"Liz, I decided to go through our finances to see where we are."

"And we're fine, right?" Liz asked or perhaps insisted.

"Well, yes. We're okay, but we are spending a lot more than I thought we were. We have two houses now so it makes sense to think about tightening things up a bit."

"And with me not working, right?"

"Actually, no. That's not my primary concern. We should be able to do okay on my salary alone for a while."

"Okay. What is your concern?" Liz demanded.

"Well, I'm concerned that a lot of our money is going towards alcohol purchases and that most of your cash withdrawals are going towards drugs. It's one thing that these drugs are illegal, but I'm also worried about their effects on you. Maybe this explains some of your behavior lately like the incident with Rajiv."

"My behavior? You're in no position to question my behavior. Yes, I drink and I use drugs recreationally. I've been doing it for years and I've made it this far, thank you very much."

"Liz, we talked about this. You admitted you have some issues. We're married. We're a team and I want to help."

"Yes. We're married. But marriage implies trust. We have discussed this situation and I said I'd take care of it. But you've gone off searching through our bank and credit card statements clearly looking for damning evidence. You don't trust me, you won't give the the space I need, even for a short while. I'm done. Now leave me the fuck alone!"

Liz hung up abruptly.

Maybe she was right. They had agreed that Liz would have the time to work on her problems. But that was the original agreement. Then she broke that agreement. Then he discovered the drug use. That had come as a complete surprise. How could he have known her so long, lived with her, married her, and not seen her drug use? Maybe he was overreacting. On the other hand, why was she hiding it? What was she afraid of? Then again, how would he feel if she had been going through all his purchases? Granted, he had nothing to hide, but he had to admit that it would feel invasive. Jim decided to give her some time.

He didn't call the next night or the one after and Liz didn't call him. Friday morning, he drove to Albany, a village next to Berkeley, and found the chocolate shop where Liz had purchased the chocolate-covered strawberries they'd shared at the Japanese teahouse spa. He placed them and a bottle of Veuve Cliquot in the cooler he'd brought and made his way to the mountains.

Pulling into the driveway behind Liz's car, Jim noticed that all the windows were open. He could hear voices, but not very clearly. As he climbed the steps to the deck, he heard a woman's voice with a British accent say, "But Dawn, it can't be as serious as all that."

Another voice he didn't recognize replied, "But Eve it's VERY serious. She's killed people."

Jim rounded the corner of the deck and looked into the large windows. A shiver raced down his spine.

Liz spoke in a British accent to someone in front of her who clearly wasn't there "Dawn, you can't possibly mean that she has literally KILLED someone."

Liz took a step forward, turned around and said in the other voice, "Eve I saw her kill someone and dispose of the body. She's very efficient. She admitted to killing anyone who threatened me. I believe there have been several."

Jim dropped the cooler in shock. Liz turned towards the sound and seeing Jim, her face changed before his eyes. The first looked like Liz but somehow more sexy. The second had a definite British air with eyebrows raised critically. The third was the face he'd seen in Rajiv's office, wide-eyed and surprised. The small voice said, "Jim, give us a few minutes. Could you go to the car and then come back?"

Jim nodded, not sure if he should come back. He felt an

overwhelming desire to run far away. Killed people? Who was Liz talking about? Why the voices? He searched frantically for a logical explanation and all he could come up with was that Liz was trying out for the local theatre company in Volcano. That would make sense. But the presence of the small voice told him it was much more serious than that. What had she said? That she came out to get Liz out of difficult situations? Jim was frightened.

"Jim," Liz called from the deck in her normal voice. "You wonderful man. Did you bring the chocolate-covered strawberries and champagne?"

He turned and saw a smiling Liz. This was the woman he'd married. She looked happy to see him and completely normal. Was it possible that she had no recollection of what had just happened? Had she really not seen him standing on the deck?

"Yes," he responded a bit warily. "I realize I was a jerk not trusting you and going through your expenses. I wanted to apologize and get an early start on our weekend together."

"Fantastic. Give me a minute and let's do a picnic down by the river. I've discovered some really cool places during my rock hunts. Grab your fly fishing stuff."

"Ah Liz, what was happening inside a few minutes ago?"

"What do you mean? I saw the cooler on the deck, looked out back and saw your car and wondered why you'd left the cooler. Was it meant to be a surprise?"

Jim considered carefully before responding. He was pretty sure that Liz didn't remember the exchange she was having with herself. Clearly, now was not the time to confront her. Jim tried to push what he'd just seen from his mind. If Liz was back, he needed to try to reconnect with her.

"Absolutely!" he replied as enthusiastically as possible. "I'm just glad you're not still mad at me."

"Jim, you're the love of my life and I couldn't possibly stay mad at you!"

They packed up a few more things and made their way to the river where they sipped champagne and fed each other chocolate-covered strawberries. Jim began to relax, caught up in the fantasy of their previous life. Maybe the bad part was over, done. Maybe it would be like this going forward. Jim wanted to believe, and for just a while, he did.

They made slow sensuous love in the full sunlight as the river cascaded by. After laying there peacefully enjoying the sounds of the river, the birds, and the wind in the trees, they went for a swim in a deep pool just downstream.

They dried off and dressed, comfortable in their shared silence. Jim picked up his fly fishing gear and walked further down the river, planning to work his way back up as Liz started searching the river banks for rocks. Jim focused on his casts. He settled into the meditative rhythm of fly fishing.

Sometime later, the sun dipped below the hillside and long shadows cooled the banks of the river. Jim had moderate success, catching and releasing several small rainbow trout. When he returned to their picnic blanket, he discovered that Liz had created quite a pile of rocks nearby.

"Cool rocks, huh?" she said, proudly.

Indeed, Liz had found quartz rocks flecked with fool's gold, heavy iron-ore rocks, volcanic rocks, and even some jadeite and large pieces of obsidian.

"I assume you expect me to haul all this to the car?" he teased.

"Hey, I do this all by myself every day. I'm sure you can manage and can probably use the exercise anyway."

Forty-five minutes later, the car was loaded with rock. Jim and Liz were both hot and sweaty, so before leaving, they decided on one more swim. Liz did a swan dive from a ten-foot boulder over the deep pool and Jim followed with a forward one and a half, entering the water smoothly with almost no splash.

"I didn't know you could dive," Liz marveled.

"I have talents that will surprise you," Jim promised, taking the naked Liz into his arms sensually, then suddenly dunking her.

They played in the water until each was refreshed and then they made their way to the car. Dinner at the Union Inn in Volcano was as good as ever. Jim tried not to think about the drugs, alcohol, uncontrolled anger or the conversation he'd witnessed. This was the old Liz. This was the marriage they'd planned. This was how it started and this was how it was going to be. Jim was almost convinced.

Arriving home, Liz admitted to being exhausted. Jim tucked her in and stoked her head, hoping to hear the small voice. Just as he was about to give up, she spoke. "You've been waiting for me. Haven't you, Jim?"

"Yes. I have. I didn't want to talk to Liz about what happened this afternoon until I'd talked to you. Can you help me understand? Liz has Dissociative Identity Disorder, doesn't she?"

"I don't know what dissociative whatever is, but yes, Liz is not alone in her body. She shares it with me and others."

"How many are there?"

The little voice was silent for a moment then responded thoughtfully. "I don't know for sure. I think there are five of us including Liz."

"But who are they and how does it work? Does everyone have a different name?"

Liz frowned. "Well let me see if I can explain. We all see Liz, but Liz can't see us. We can sometimes see each other, but not always. Imagine being in a theater with a spotlight. We sit in the wings until it's our turn, then we step into the spotlight. The only really strange thing is that Liz never watches the rest of us. She kind of goes to sleep when one of us is on."

"Okay. I know about you. I thought you were just a sleepy Liz, which I guess you are. Today, I saw a British woman who I think is called Eve, and another woman who I think is called Dawn. What's weird is that they actually looked different from Liz. So do you, come to think of it."

"Of course we look different. We're different people, silly."

"So what about the names? Who are these people? Do you have a different name?"

"Well, I always answer to Liz, but my name is Betty. I'm Liz's baby sister. Dawn is Liz's younger sister and Eve is our cousin."

Jim processed this for a moment and counted silently.

"That makes four of you. Who's the fifth?"

"I really don't want to talk about her. I don't know her. I've just heard about her, so I don't want to say anything. It could be very wrong."

Jim decided not to press.

"You know," Jim began. "I've done some reading on this. Most people only have one personality. You have several. Psychiatrists call this Dissociative Identity Disorder, though many don't believe it actually exists. It seems to be caused by a major traumatic event when you're young. Unfortunately, each personality is only a part of the whole person. They may think that they are complete people, but there are really just parts of the original person that have split and gone their own ways. There are therapies to reintegrate the personalities."

"That scares me, Jim."

"Why would that scare you? Wouldn't you want to be a complete person? Wouldn't you want Liz to be a complete person?"

"I am a complete person!" Betty insisted. "If we get reintegrated, what happens to me? I die, don't I?"

"No, of course not," Jim replied a little unsure of himself. "You'd still be there, but you'd be part of Liz."

Jim sat there for a few moments hoping to talk about this more, but he ultimately realized that Betty had no more to say to him tonight. He got up, grabbed a beer, and went out onto the moonlit deck where the impact of his situation struck him. Could he live with multiple personalities? How would they see him? What about that conversation he'd overheard? Weren't they talking about a murderer? Was that the fifth personality? Was Liz a murderer? No. That was just too crazy. Of course she wasn't. He hadn't read about any cases where one of the personalities was a murderer. It didn't seem likely. But where would they go from here? He loved Liz and fully expected to support her in sickness and in health, even though that hadn't been part of their vows. But how would they get past this? It was bigger than they were. Jim wasn't dealing with one other person; he was going to have to deal with five.

The next morning over breakfast, Jim brought up what had happened the day before and told Liz about his conversation with Betty.

"Daddy used to call me Betty when I was a little girl," Liz mused. "I'm Elizabeth, I now shorten it to Liz, but Daddy really liked to call me Betty."

Alarm bells went off in Jim's head. Had Mickey molested Liz and caused this break? No. That wasn't likely. Mickey had appeared confused about the changes that had taken place in Liz. It wasn't Mickey.

"But what about the British voice?" he asked.

"Well, I used to pretend to be British in college. It was a game, a change, trying on something new."

"Liz, I really think you may suffer from Dissociative Identity Disorder; it used to be called Multiple Personality Disorder."

"Jim, Jim, Jim," Liz chuckled, not at all upset. "First it was alcohol and drugs, now multiple personalities? I think you're reaching pretty far to try to explain my behavior with Rajiv. I admit it was bad, but come on, multiple personalities?"

"Tell me Liz," Jim began, clearly confrontational. "Do you remember actually slamming Rajiv against the wall?"

"Well no," Liz responded somewhat tentatively.

"How about pulling his knife and trying to stab Brent Powers after he crashed into Steve?"

"Ah no," Liz replied reluctantly, clearly becoming frightened.

"And yesterday, do you remember me standing on the deck watching you talk to yourself?" Jim insisted even more vehemently.

"Jim, please stop. You're scaring me."

Liz burst into tears and ran into the bedroom throwing herself on the bed and sobbing uncontrollably.

Jim came in and gently stroked her head.

"It will be okay," he soothed.

"I really don't think you should pick on her like that," Betty chastised.

"But she – you – really need help. And you're not going to get it if you don't recognize that there's a problem."

"Jim, you need to let us figure this out. If you press, you're only going to make things worse. Please stop. Finish your weekend together and go home. Come back next weekend and let's see where we are. Otherwise, you're going to cause Liz to get hurt."

It was all he could do to control himself. Jim had become successful by identifying problems and pushing until he resolved them. He was on to something here and he knew he could solve this. He could work with Betty to find out what the traumatic event was that caused the split. He could help with the reintegration. Liz would be whole again.

But then again, he wasn't a psychiatrist. He didn't know what he was doing. He was in over his head and his meddling might very well make things worse. Although she seemed to be very young, Betty was wise. He'd back off. The week away would do him good. He could step back, do some research, maybe consult a psychiatrist. He could make a plan. He'd find a way to bring things back under control.

3

Jim gave Liz a safe arrival call when he returned home Sunday afternoon then he called her Monday evening and again on Tuesday after work. Something was wrong. Liz seemed depressed. Their usually lively conversations had turned desultory. It was hard to get Liz to tell him about her day and even her recent enthusiasm about the rocks she was finding had evaporated.

"Jim, I'm tired. These calls exhaust me even more. I don't think I'm getting sick but I just don't want to be bothered. I'm sorry if that hurts your feelings, but we talked about me working on myself and I need to do that without your interference. Again, I'm sorry if that upsets you.

"I know you were planning to come up this next weekend, but I think I need a few weeks to myself. If I can't get myself together by then, we can talk about me getting some help. For now, I'm asking you to be patient and understanding and to try not to worry."

Jim reluctantly agreed. He wondered if he wasn't responsible for what appeared to be a deterioration of Liz's condition. Was he wrong to have confronted her with the multiple personality theory? Certainly it was a mistake to scare her with her lapses of memory. What would it be like to think it was normal to have gaps in your memory? We all have times we can't remember things like what we had for breakfast a few days ago or the name of the movie we saw last week. Somehow that doesn't seem odd to us and usually, given time to think about it, or reminded of some related details, we remember. Could Liz's experience be similar? Was it natural for her to not remember hours at a time or maybe even days when another personality was on stage?

Over the next weeks, Jim filled his free time working out, either surfing, running or cycling. He had found that if he exhausted himself, he could usually sleep through the night. And somehow, the regular exercise made him more optimistic and hopeful. As he'd read while doing his research on psychological disorders, exercise seemed to help most people stay sane.

One Sunday night after having spent the entire day working out, Jim wolfed down a medium pizza which he chased with two beers. He was asleep by nine o'clock. Near eleven, he awoke with a start; sure something had happened to Liz. He dialed the cabin and a sleepy voice answered.

"Are you okay?" he asked.

"Yes we are, Jim," Betty replied.

"I'm sorry I woke you. I just had a bad feeling. I thought something was wrong."

"No, Jim. We're okay. You should go back to sleep."

"Betty?"

"Yes, Jim"

"Do you think Liz will want to see me soon? I miss her terribly. I miss all the good times we had. I miss holding her when we go to sleep at night."

"I'm sorry, Jim. I miss you and I know Liz does too, but we do have problems and it's still not time to get back together. Try to be patient."

"Can't you talk to Liz? Can't you tell her I should come up?"

"No, Jim. Liz and I don't talk. Remember, Liz doesn't see or hear the rest of us. I'm sorry, but there's nothing I can do. Liz needs to get to a place where she either gives up trying to fix herself or accepts how she is – we are – and then decides to go back to your marriage."

"Back to our marriage?" Jim asked, frightened by Betty's implications.

"Don't worry, Jim. It will be okay. I do know things. Try to get some sleep."

But Jim couldn't get back to sleep. He got up, went to his computer and dove into research on Dissociative Identity Disorder and tried to find psychiatrists who had experience treating it. There weren't very many. In fact a large percentage of the psychiatric community seemed to doubt its existence. Or at least they didn't think there were actually multiple personalities; they attributed these patients' behavior to other conditions. Jim thought he could change their minds if they met Liz and her personalities.

Jim then read several case studies about reintegration. He was surprised at how few documented cases of reintegration there were. Was Liz's disorder that rare? Was there hope for Liz and their marriage? Could he live with these multiple personalities? Could they live with him?

He'd posed these questions before, but now he felt a new clarity. Liz needed to reintegrate. She was damaged. Some traumatic event had caused the split and she needed to be put back together again. She may have been able to make do before, but something had changed. Liz had lost her drive, lost her focus and enthusiasm, and seemed... completely lost. Liz's main personality was suffering. Even though he knew her personality had split, even the pieces seemed to be unravelling. Jim hoped this wouldn't become a Humpty Dumpty story.

With what seemed to be a dearth of psychiatrists trained to handle this disorder, Jim seriously considered continuing his research and attempting the reintegration himself. But he thought about what happened after he confronted Liz and the fact that they hadn't seen each other since. Maybe it was because he was too close. Maybe he just didn't have the expertise. He had to find someone who could help. But how? All that he read said that the patient needed to at least admit that they had the condition. God! Now he was thinking of her as a patient. He clearly wasn't cut out for this. Maybe he was going a little crazy too.

Dawn was breaking so Jim grabbed his board and wetsuit and drove up to Ocean Beach to surf. In less than an hour, the tide had dropped and ruined the waves. Jim wasn't anywhere near tired and his brain was still squirrel caging, so he decided to go for a run up Montara Mountain. At the end of the run, he felt a full-body fatigue. The surfing had exercised his upper body and the run his lower.

Stepping out of the shower, Jim felt relaxed and optimistic. Somehow this would work out. He and Liz were meant to be together.

4

"Mike, we've got another one!"

"Another what, honey?" Mike McKensey asked. He was still trying on pet names. Honey seemed trite, but May didn't mind and she'd started calling him 'Honey' as well. Ah, the wonders of being a newlywed. Since they'd been married less than a year, they still qualified.

"Another body, HONEY!" May replied, trying to emphasize that 'Honey' probably should be reserved for private time and wasn't appropriate for work. Men did require some training.

"But it's been how long? Eighteen months?"

"Yeah, about that. But there's no question. It's the same MO. This one washed up on Stinson this morning and a jogger found it. It's pretty unrecognizable, but it's on the way to the ME, so I'm hoping he'll be able to help us with an ID. Want to sit in on the autopsy?"

Mike only thought about it for a few seconds. While he hated autopsies, and bodies pulled out of the water were the worst, this would be the first new clue on a long-idle case. "I'll be there in twenty minutes."

Suited, masked and gloved, Mike and May still cringed as the ME sliced open the victim's chest. It was worse when he opened the stomach and intestines.

"Looks like he had Mexican Food within a couple of hours of his death."

Mike and May looked at each other in surprise, both at the fact that the ME could recognize something out of the mush in the stomach, but also in coincidence that one of the other victims also had eaten Mexican food shortly before his demise as well. Could there be a connection?

"That may be helpful," May began. "One of the other vics had just eaten Mexican food as well. This is probably a stupid question, but you couldn't narrow down the restaurant he ate at, could you?"

Mike elbowed her in the ribs.

"It's not as stupid a question as you might think Detective McKensey. May might be on to something here. I see black beans – that might help narrow it a bit, and bits of chipotle. Again, that might help too. Otherwise, the rest looks like mush to me."

"Any clues to his age?" Mike asked.

"I'd guess mid-fifties. You should be able to get an ID off this one soon enough. He was in the water for less than a day, so we got prints and they're already being processed. I'd be surprised if you didn't know who our victim was in an hour or two."

Mike and May thanked the ME, leaving him to the even more disgusting parts of the autopsy, which likely wouldn't give them any new information. They stepped out, removed their suits, masks, and gloves, and made their way back to May's office where they discovered it would be an hour or so before the fingerprint search results would be back. Mike could only marvel at the efficiency of the Marin County Sheriff's Office. In San Francisco, it would have taken days to get anything done.

"I know it's probably not the best thing after an autopsy, but are you interested in lunch?" May asked. "I've got a few ideas I'd like to bounce around."

"Absolutely, Hon-" Mike began, realizing that this was the first time they'd worked together since their marriage. "Sorry about that. I've stopped thinking of you as a cop. I'll try to be better."

"That's probably the best compliment I've had in years," May replied. "I'm glad you could forget that I'm a cop and think of me as woman. But, yes. When we're on the job together, I think we need to treat each other like coworkers and maintain a bit of formality. We don't have to carry it to an extreme, since most everyone knows we're married, but particularly for me, I don't want the other cops to think of me as anything but a cop and familiarity will undermine that."

Mike agreed. They needed to separate work and marriage.

Mike and May made their way to the same café they'd first had lunch at.

May kicked off the discussion. "The ME said chipotle and I know that there are a lot of Mexican restaurants that serve black beans and chipotle, but our other vic had eaten at Chevy's and I'd be willing to bet that this one did too."

"Yeah, I was thinking the same thing. Chevy's is about half way between Moscone and the Tenderloin. If this one attended a conference at Moscone, I think our theory of the murderer being a hooker or a pimp makes sense."

"Could you go back to your friend in Vice to see if anyone has seen that hooker they talked about?"

"Sure." Mike replied, definitely in work-mode now. "I'll do that. It'll probably take a day or two."

When they returned to May's office Mike was astounded that not only had the Marin County Sheriffs ID'd the vic through fingerprints, they'd confirmed he was staying at a Financial District hotel, attended the current conference at Moscone, and that he'd had dinner at Chevy's. Of even more significance was that one of the busboys had seen him walking, or stumbling a bit after four margaritas, towards the Tenderloin. The hooker/pimp theory was getting legs.

Two days later, Mike called May.

"May, I've got something good!"

"What, no sweet words, no 'Honey', Honey?" May teased.

Mike was confused and a bit pissed-off. He wasn't sure why he was reacting to her teasing but this clearly wasn't the time. This was work time and he had something important to discuss.

"Look May, this is the first case we've worked together on since we've been married. I was confused at first about how we should behave, but as we discussed a couple days ago, when we're working together, we're just cops working together. The personal stuff needs to stay at home.

"It's difficult when you kid me like this because I'm not sure what you really want," Mike almost snapped. "Do you really want me to be romantic on the job? "

"Of course not Mike," May replied suitably chastened. "I'm sorry. I was just teasing and I can see how it would be inappropriate and confusing. You're absolutely right. At work, we need to be two cops, not a married couple. Please accept my apology. I won't do it again.

"So, what's the good news?"

Mike felt bad for almost losing his temper, but decided to act like a cop and put it aside.

"Well, my friend from Vice got back to me and yes, that hooker is back."

"That is good news. Have her picked up. She's the best lead we've got so far."

"Apparently, it's not that easy. She not consistent, they've seen her a couple of times a week, but she doesn't have any real pattern – it's not like she works specific days or times. They're thinking she's a college student, in it to pick up a few extra bucks when she feels like it."

"Of course. It's never that easy. I assume you've got the Tenderloin staked out."

"Yeah. We also pulled in a couple of the other hookers down there and have what we think is a pretty good sketch. We've circulated it and have asked that we get a call if anyone sees here – in exchange for a few favors of course."

"Of course. We don't have your level of prostitution up here in Marin, but we, too, make deals with our informants," May said, sounding a bit discouraged.

"But May, I've been saving the best part for last. I guess you can call it 'best'. It's certainly good for our theory."

"I'm ready to hear something good about this case."

"About two weeks ago, a guy named Jimmy, one of the new, very young pimps with a reputation for violence, bragged that he was going to bring this hooker into his stable whatever it took. Apparently, he's disappeared.

"Digging deeper, my friend asked about the other vics. You remember that college student who was doing some dealing? Apparently, he was a big supplier for several of the pimps down there. Since he looked young and innocent, one of the pimps offered him some extra cash if he'd rough up that same hooker. He figured he could ride in on a white horse, rescue the girl and she'd be forever grateful.

"Anyway, my guy questioned that pimp who said he was lucky he didn't do the dirty work himself. Apparently, until Jimmy got it into his head, everyone had learned that you didn't mess with this girl. But she'd been out of the life for so long, and the street has a short memory."

"So she offs at least two bad guys. Maybe we should give her a medal."

"Yeah, but what about the other guys?"

"Well, if they're frequenting prostitutes, they're probably not stellar citizens. Hmm, I'll tell you what. Now that we're pretty sure that each was associated with prostitution, I'll do some research into that aspect of our other victims. Maybe there's something that ties them together.

"By the way. Does this hooker have a name?"

"She calls herself Dawn. Of course no one knows if that's her real name. If she's a college student or part-timer, it's likely not."

"Dawn.   Okay.   That'll do for now.   Can you fax me the sketch?"

"Sure."

5

Liz just couldn't handle it anymore. Something was definitely wrong with her. After Jim questioned her about her memory, she started paying attention. Jim had frightened her, but once he was gone and she began to think about it, she suspected that the fear came from the possibility he might be right. Something he said made sense to some part of her.

Liz decided to be meticulous about writing in her journal several times a day. Usually she wrote when she got up in the morning, trying to remember her dreams. Then she wrote at lunch, mid-day, at dinner, and at bedtime. Most often she didn't go back and read previous entries; she just picked up where she left off. That was really easy to do on a computer. Yesterday, something had possessed her to go back and review what she'd written and Liz had discovered big gaps. Sometimes multiple days had lapsed between entries and she had no idea how that could be possible. She was diligent about her journal.

Liz called home and reached her mother.

"Hi Mamasita, I'm still up her in the mountains trying to sort things out."

"Hi Liz. You know you're welcome here. Your room is waiting."

"Mama, I can't come home right now. I'm trying to sort things out."

"Are you having problems with Jim? Is that what's going on?"

"No, Mama. Jim is wonderful but I've got some major problems. I'm trying to figure out what's wrong with me."

"What do you mean, 'wrong with you'?"

"Well, Jim –"

"No! Don't tell me what Jim thinks," Janice interrupted abruptly. "You can't let a man tell you what's going on with you or what your problems are. What do you think is wrong?"

Liz hesitated. Her mother almost never talked to her this way. She was chastising her and Liz hadn't even gotten started.

"Mama, did something bad happen to me when I was little? Something I don't remember?"

The line was silent for what seemed to be an eternity.

"Mama?" Liz asked tentatively, almost wondering if the line had gone dead.

"There are always bad things that happen to us when we're young," Janice finally replied.

Liz was getting nervous. Why was her mother being evasive? Or was Liz just being paranoid? Everything seemed to frighten her lately.

"Mama, I have to go. I'll talk to you later. I love you!"

"But Liz—"

Liz suddenly felt overwhelmingly tired. She sat down on the sofa and was instantly asleep.

Liz dreamed she was a little girl again. Life was wonderful. Daddy loved her, played with her and teased her. But she teased him back. She could make him smile. Even when he came home in a bad mood, usually after losing an argument in court, she could make him laugh and forget about his day. God how she loved Daddy.

She also loved skiing. Daddy had worked for the Ski Patrol for many years and had taught her to ski almost as soon as she could walk. Now she could ski on her own and she was fast. She had earned the respect of the older kids at Bear Valley because she beat most of them in the slalom and giant slalom races that the resort sponsored regularly. She also skied moguls effortlessly, even at her tender age.

In her dream, she had just finished a full day of skiing. Company was coming for dinner and Mama had told her not to be late. She took the last lift of the day up to the top of the mountain and quickly skied to the Home Run trail that led from the Mount Reba Ski Area back to Bear Valley village. It was a long trail, but Liz could usually get home in twenty minutes or sometimes much less.

As she headed down the trail, the snow got stickier and stickier. She could barely make her skis move forward. It seemed to take forever. And now, the trail had changed. She didn't recognize any of the normal landmarks. It was growing dark, Liz started to panic. She was a little girl all alone, lost on a snowy mountain.

Liz awoke with a start, trembling with fear and very cold even though it must have been eighty-five degrees. It was already dark in the cabin and Liz cursed as she tripped over one of the feet of the coffee table. She realized she was a bit disoriented but managed to make her way to the kitchen where she turned on a light that was suddenly too harsh. She closed her eyes then opened them slowly. She filled a glass with well-water from the tap and drank thirstily. She couldn't remember ever being so thirsty.

As she finished her glass of water, Liz's nerves calmed. She stopped shaking. Sitting back down on the sofa, Liz picked up her laptop. She opened her journal to write about her dream and in front of her in all caps were words she had never written:

LIZ, DON'T WORRY. TRUST JIM. EVERYTHING WILL BE OKAY. I KNOW THINGS.

BETTY

This time, Liz couldn't contain her panic. Her thoughts were out of control. Her mind looked for a simple answer, but there was none. Was this really a message from her younger self or was it one of her other personalities trying to talk to her through the journal? Or was it just her subconscious sending her a message? Was she writing in her sleep like some people talk or walk in their sleep? For all she knew, she did all of that and more. What was she going to do?

This was just too much. She couldn't handle it. Maybe she should just end it all and save herself and everyone else a lot of grief. And embarrassment. Oh God. Her mother would be so embarrassed!

Suicide seemed like a better and better option. Something inside her almost shouted 'No'. And Liz was instantly asleep.

When she woke, it was after midnight. Liz was on her back looking up at the stars. She had no memory of stepping outside and lying down, but the stars were beautiful on this moonless night and Liz almost succumbed to the tranquil depth of the infinite sky.

Almost.

Liz panicked again. She leapt to her feet and ran to the phone. She called Jim.

"Hello?" a sleepy voice answered.

"Jim! Help me!" Liz cried desperately.

"Liz? What's wrong?"

"Oh Jim, I'm going crazy. I think I may hurt myself. Please come get me now. Take me to a hospital where I can get some help. Make it close to home."

"Do you want to come home?"

"No, Jim, I think I might hurt you. We talked about my getting help. Now please come get me. I'll do my best to be here when you get here but I'm having blackouts and I don't know what I'm going to do next. Please hurry!"

"Okay. I'll call the hospital and then I'll call you back during the drive."

Liz hung up, grabbed her car keys and threw them off the deck into the brush below. She'd never find them tonight. That was one small piece of insurance. She needed something to occupy her mind while she waited for Jim. She started to write in her journal but suddenly became afraid that once she finished, she'd fall asleep and would wake up to a new message from within. That terrified her. This couldn't be happening. It couldn't. She just needed to stay calm and the doctors would figure out what was wrong with her and she'd be fine. She just had to keep telling herself that.

Liz closed her journal file and opened a game of Sudoku. That should keep her mind occupied until Jim arrived.

For his part, Jim leapt up out of bed, slipped on jeans, a t-shirt and sandals, grabbed his phone and drove like a maniac towards the mountains. With light traffic and no stops they usually made it there in two and a half hours. Tonight, he would beat that.

On the way, he called San Francisco Community Hospital and asked for the Psych Ward. He was directed to Psychiatric Emergency Services.

"Hi, my wife is having some sort of psychotic episode and has asked me to bring her to the hospital. She says she may hurt herself or others."

"Hello Sir, my name is Ann. May I speak with your wife?" asked a concerned voice at the other end of the line.

"I'm sorry, but she's at our place in the mountains. I'm driving up to bring her back to the Bay Area. I should be back to San Francisco Community about six a.m. Will there be someone there to admit her?"

"Of course sir. Can you give me your name and your wife's name?"

"Sure. I'm Jim Henderson and my wife is Liz Leahy. She kept her maiden name," Jim replied, feeling stupid for stating the obvious.

"Thanks, Jim. I know this is a difficult time and we're here to help you. Can you tell me more about what's going on with Liz?"

"I probably could make some guesses, but I haven't seen her in a few weeks and we haven't spoken until tonight when I got a panicked phone call. She's terribly frightened. I think it's better if you evaluate her without my uneducated opinions."

"Uneducated, maybe," Ann began very soothingly. "But you've lived with her and have a better perspective than we're going to get in a night or a few days of observation. Don't worry. Everything you say is confidential and we certainly take into account the situation and background before leaping to conclusions. In reality, we never leap. We're quite conservative."

Feeling reassured, Jim almost told them about his theory of Dissociative Identity Disorder but thought they might confine him instead of Liz if he explained his reasoning. Instead he just gave the facts. "A few months back, Liz and I were both working in a Silicon Valley software company. Things were going well for the most part, but one day, she physically attacked our CEO. Needless to say, she resigned afterwards and said she needed to work on herself, so she moved to our place in the mountains. I could tell you more, but I think it's best if I call Liz and keep her company until I get there."

"Okay Jim. But if you feel you can't handle it, feel that Liz may harm herself, please have her call me or you call me back and I'll talk to her until you get there or for the entire trip back here if necessary."

"Thanks, Ann. I'll do that."

Jim called Liz and she answered on the first ring.

"Jim! Are you almost here?" Liz asked frantically.

"No Liz. It's only been about half an hour. It'll be a while. But I'll stay on the line until I lose service outside Pine Grove. At that point, when the phone goes dead, don't worry. It's good news – I'll only be ten to fifteen minutes away.

"I spoke to a very nice lady at San Francisco Community. Her name is Ann, and she's expecting you. She's also available to talk to you now if you'd like to talk to her instead of me."

"No, Jim. I need you. Please just keep me company."

"Okay Liz. Please write down her number. If you need her, Ann can talk to you during that fifteen minutes that I'll be out of cell coverage."

But Liz believed that she'd be okay as long as Jim was on the line and that she could wait the fifteen minutes when Jim's cell wouldn't work.

The drive went quickly. Their conversation was mundane. They didn't talk about what was happening to Liz. Instead, they stayed off-topic and Jim asked Liz to tell him about each of her best rocks. When the conversation started to run thin, Liz described her Sudoku puzzle and Jim tried to imagine the squares. Although he really didn't help her solve it, it did help keep him awake.

The drive back was similar for most of the way. Liz was afraid to go to sleep, so they talked, then turned on an oldies station and sang along for a while. Just before they reached the East Bay, Liz dozed off.

"I'm not sure this is the best idea," Betty stated flatly.

"Should we be doing something else?" Jim asked calmly, finding himself surprisingly comfortable discussing Liz with Betty.

'I don't really know. Of course since no one has objected, maybe everyone thinks this is best for Liz. Ever since you told her about us, it's been really bad for her."

"So it's my fault," Jim stated, resigned in his guilt.

"Not completely. There were ripples. Things going wrong. Plus, there's that other thing. I think that's the real problem."

"What other thing?"

"Dawn is really upset. She feels guilty. She thinks she's been responsible for some very, very bad things. She's been thinking about killing herself and some of these feelings might be affecting Liz."

"What sorts of bad things?"

"I can't go into that. Let's see if the doctors can help Liz. Good night Jim."

"But Betty, can't you tell me more?"

Betty was gone.

Jim called Ann and got directions, letting her know they were almost there and that Liz was holding her own. She was sleeping now. He gave her contact information and Liz's social security number so Ann could get the paperwork started to speed admission. A few minutes later, Jim pulled up to San Francisco Community. He woke Liz gently. They walked into the hospital and made their way to Psychiatric Emergency Services. Jim completed the missing portions of the forms with Liz's help and then Ann explained the nature of voluntary commitment. Liz could leave at any time. She could contact friends and family by phone, but while in the facility, would be expected to follow certain rules. The attending psychiatrist would meet with her sometime later that morning. In the meantime, Ann would conduct a preliminary evaluation.

Liz signed the consent form without reading it (Jim read the whole thing). Ann turned to Jim and said, "We'll take good care of her, Jim. I'm sure you'll be hearing from Liz shortly. Don't worry if there's a gap in communication. That's normal. Now, why don't you go home and get some sleep."

Jim thanked Ann and looked on longingly as she led a clearly frightened Liz away. Liz turned back to him and her face changed. "It'll be okay, Jim," Betty said. And she was gone.

6

"The son-of-bitch did it!" Janice shouted to Mickey who was in the shower.

"What son-of-a-bitch did what?" Mickey asked, always surprised, even after all these years of marriage at how his wife just assumed he knew what she was talking about.

"Jim! He put Liz in the psych ward at San Francisco Community."

"It's an excellent facility. I'm sure they'll be able to help her."

"Michael Patrick Leahy! I don't know who's the bigger son-of-a-bitch, you or our son-in-law. You know Liz doesn't need to be in a psych ward. You're going to help me get her out."

Mickey thought carefully before answering. Having faced his Sicilian wife's anger many times, he knew he had to choose his battles. The Irish were also known for tempers, but theirs were usually over as quickly as they started. If his wife was any indication, you should never cross a Sicilian. Their anger didn't subside until they'd had their revenge.

Still, he'd ducked this issue for years. This may be one of the battles that had to be fought.

Drying off as he stepped out of the shower, Mickey maintained an air of non-chalance which just fueled his wife's frustration. He tried to take her in his arms but she quickly pulled away.

"So what exactly did Jim say? I assume he called?"

"You assume correctly. I can't believe he had the balls to call me and tell me he'd had our daughter committed."

"Something's not right here," Mickey mused in his best courtroom manner. "A husband can't commit a wife, just like that. Tell me what he said."

Faced with the objective lawyer standing almost naked before her, Janice responded honestly. "Okay, well, he said Liz called him in a panic after midnight and asked him to come to the mountains to take her to the psych ward in San Francisco. He said he raced up there, helped her stay together on the trip back, and that she admitted herself, a voluntary admission."

"That sounds more reasonable. And what, exactly, did Jim do wrong here?"

"He should have called me BEFORE he took her to the hospital. Liz hates psychiatrists. You know what happened the last time. She shouldn't have to deal with those people."

Mickey did, indeed, recall what had happened the last time. Liz was fourteen and therapy seemed like a good option for his recently disturbed little girl. The first few sessions seemed to go well, but then Liz lost control and attacked the male psychotherapist who was treating her. The injuries were severe enough to send him to the hospital. Janice had decided there would be no more shrinks in Liz's life. And fortunately, until recently, aside from a few slips from which she recovered quickly, Liz did seem to be doing okay. It may have taken her a while, but she graduated from one of the most prestigious law schools in the country, so things couldn't have been that bad, right? Or could they?

"At this point, if Liz actually thinks that she needs professional help, don't you think we should trust her on this?"

"But what if Jim is pushing her to do this? I talked to her yesterday and she seemed fine except that she said something about Jim having theories about her problems."

"Did she actually say that?" Mickey urged in his gentle mode of cross-examination.

"Well, actually, no. She didn't. I told her not to listen to Jim."

"Alright, let me get this straight," Mickey continued, moving in for the kill. "Liz calls you yesterday and after you tell her not to listen to Jim, she later calls him and asks him to take her to the psych ward. She didn't call you back and ask you to help her. She went to her husband instead.

"Is it possible, even slightly possible, that you're not really angry at Jim because he didn't call you first, but you're angry at him because Liz called him instead of you when she felt she was in deep trouble, when she was desperate for a kind of help we always avoided? Is it even a tiny bit possible?"

Janice hated her husband at moments like this. He was too damned smart and too smooth. She also loved him more than any man she'd ever known. As angry as she was, she still had to admit that he had a point. Jim hadn't done anything obviously wrong here, but Janice couldn't help but feel that he was part of the problem, that if he hadn't come into Liz's life, Liz wouldn't be in a psych ward.

"Okay," she reluctantly admitted. "It's possible. I'll try to think about it objectively. But I have this feeling there's more going on here and that Jim is at fault. I'm going to get to the bottom of this and I'm going to save our little girl."

'Janice, my love, Liz has had problems since she became a teenager. We've known all along that it wasn't just adolescent angst. I fear that we're the ones at fault here for not addressing the problem sooner. Liz has been a very strong person, but also very fragile. That fragility makes her very vulnerable."

"That's why we have to protect her!"

"I'm not so sure. I think Liz needs to be stronger. Avoiding whatever these problems are just increases the probability of a major disaster ahead. We won't always be there to protect her, you know."

She did know. But she had sworn an oath to protect her little girl until death prevented her from doing so.

After Mickey left for work, Janice called the hospital and asked to speak to Liz.

"I'm sorry Ma'am," replied the voice on the other end of the line. "I'm not permitted to say who is here and who isn't."

"But I'm her mother. I know she would want to talk with me."

"Again, I'm sorry, but if your daughter were here, she'd need to authorize us to tell you that. I have no such authorizations from an Elizabeth Leahy. Try not to worry, Ma'am. If she is here, I'm sure she'll call you when she's ready."

"She can do that?"

"Of course. Our patients have access to phones and to authorized visitors."

"Then I'll come visit. What are your visiting hours?"

"Again, Ma'am, even if your daughter is here, you wouldn't be able to visit unless she's authorized it. At this point, you'd be wasting your time. We couldn't give you any access to the facility and you'd be asked to leave.

"I know this is hard, but if your daughter is here, it's likely for a good reason. Give her time to settle in and I'm sure she'll contact you if she's here."

"May I speak with your supervisor, please?"

"Of course, Ma'am," she responded, not sounding the least bit offended.

The supervisor came on the line and repeated the same story. No he could not tell her if her daughter were there. No, she could not visit. He reassured her that if her daughter were there and wanted to speak to her mother she would call. Janice hung up fuming. What had Jim done?

7

The intake procedure went well. Ann had taken away most of Liz's belongings making a detailed list which Liz signed for. Ann then placed them in a secure place outside the main part of the facility. Liz would get everything back when she left. Ann took all of Liz's vitals and then went through an extensive questionnaire about medical history and medications. She asked about alcohol and drug use but didn't seem at all judgmental when Liz described her somewhat heavy usage. Ann explained how the facility worked and the rules that Liz would have to follow during her stay. The stay was confidential and unless Liz wanted people to know she was there, no one would know. Liz filled out a Release of Information form for Jim, and told Ann that for now, she'd prefer that only Jim know she was there.

Ann showed her around the facility, introduced her to a few other nurses and patients, then led her to her room. She would be sharing it with a few other women, but this didn't bother her. The room was light and airy with plants and soothing artwork on the walls. She showed her the community phone which was occupied and which had a line of patients waiting to use it, and before leaving, told Liz that Doctor Karmere would be interviewing her later that morning.

Liz perused the small library in the community room and picked an innocuous-looking novel to read. Then she got in line for the phone. An hour later, she finally reached Jim. "Are you okay?" he asked, clearly nervous. "I was getting worried."

"I'm as okay as I can be right now. The place is nice, Ann is nice. I'm supposed to meet my doctor later today. I don't know how long I'll be here. I hope they can figure out what is wrong."

Jim decided not to probe. "I'm glad you're doing this. It takes a lot of courage and I'm proud of you."

Liz felt warmed by Jim's words, but still quite unsure that she'd done the right thing. At the same time, she felt peaceful for the first time in many months. It was almost as if the conflicting forces inside her had gone to sleep for a while.

"Jim, can you do me a favor – actually two?"

"Absolutely! What do you need?"

"Could you bring me a couple changes of clothes – underwear, bras, some sweats and some t-shirts?"

"Definitely! What's the second thing?"

"Could you not tell my parents about this yet?"

"Whoops! It's too late. I called them this morning. Your mother was quite upset. I'm sure she's already on the phone, but from what Ann told me before I left, they won't confirm that you're there or give her any information unless you authorize it. And of course, you can call her anytime."

"Oh – okay," Liz replied somewhat discouraged. "I'm sure it will be okay. Jim, there are people waiting for the phone and I have to go."

"I'm sorry. I thought your parents should know where you were. We didn't get a chance to discuss this before I left. I'll come during visiting hours with your clothes. I love you."

"I love you too, Jim!"

Liz handed off the phone and made her way back to her room where she sat and read until a nurse came and said that Doctor Karmere would see her. Liz and the nurse made their way to an interview room where Liz was asked to take a seat. "The Doctor will be right with you," she said as she closed the door behind her. Liz went back to her book.

A few minutes later there was a knock at the door and a tall, physically fit doctor of about fifty walked in.

"Hi Ms. Leahy. My name is Ken Karmere. You can call me Ken."

"And you can call me Liz. Does your middle name begin with a 'K' as well?"

"Why yes, it does. My parents loved alliteration though I'm not sure I like having the initials 'KKK'."

"Yes, my personalized license plate has 'LLL' in it for Liz Louise Leahy. I had to cheat a bit since my first name is actually Elizabeth, but most people do call me Liz."

"Then I will too. Give me a minute to go through your file."

Liz watched as he read. He chewed the side of his mouth as he concentrated and played with his pen. Periodically, he would frown at something he read and dimples would appear at the side of his mouth.

"Okay, Liz. I'm going to spend about 30 minutes with you today to see if we can begin to determine what's bothering you. Please note that this is a teaching hospital, so some of my interns and residents may be on the other side of that rather obvious non-mirror. Also, the conversations in these rooms are recorded, primarily so I can go back through them when I write up my notes. Any questions before we get started?"

Liz shook her head.

"So, what seems to be the problem?"

"I wish I knew. Over the last months, I've had fits of uncontrolled violence which I don't actually remember. I also feel like something is going on inside me. I can't really describe it, but I feel like I'm sitting on the outside of a raging internal conflict. My husband Jim says he heard me talking to myself in two different voices a while back, but I have no recollection of that. Also, he says he talks to a younger version of me when I'm asleep. At first I discounted it. But yesterday, I found a note in my journal that wasn't written by me. It was signed 'Betty'. That's what my father called me when I was a little girl. This really upset me and since then, I don't feel I can control my thoughts. Now I see that for some time, there have been gaps. I didn't really think about them before but I do lose track of time. I find myself in places and have no idea how I got there. I'm getting really frightened and I thought it might be a good idea to get professional help."

"What did the note say?"

"It said, 'Liz, don't worry. Trust Jim. Everything will be okay. I know things. Betty'"

"And you didn't write it?"

"Well obviously, I did. No one had access to the house or to the computer, even remotely. But I don't remember writing it."

"And what about these voices that Jim heard?"

"He said they were two different people. One was a British woman named Eve, and the other was named Dawn. They were apparently discussing someone else, someone who may have committed a murder. They stopped suddenly when Jim came into view. He said that Betty took over and that I came out a bit later.

"Do you think this is even possible? Jim thinks I suffer from Dissociative Identity Disorder."

Eve and Dawn, opposite sides of the day, Ken mused. "It's very unlikely. I've been practicing almost thirty years and after working with thousands of patients, I've never seen it. Most of us don't think it actually exists. Yes, we've read a few case studies, but without seeing it, it's kind of hard to believe.

"More often there is a kind of a split. People have psychotic episodes and don't remember what happened during them. They also forget in order to protect themselves from unpleasant events or memories. Sometimes they pretend to be other people to escape themselves and their demons. But separate personalities? I can't rule it out, but I really don't think it's likely.

"Of more concern to me right now is the violence you've talked about. Can you tell me more?"

"The most recent one was that I attacked my boss. I have no recollection of what happened. We were having a lively discussion over a contract matter – I'm an attorney, you know – and the next thing I knew, Jim was standing there shouting at me to stop. Rajiv, my boss was slumped to the floor and I had clearly just slammed him against the wall and pummeled him."

"Why was Jim there?"

"We work – worked at the same company and he was in the office next to the CEOs when he heard the commotion. He and Rajiv's secretary opened the door and saw what I was doing."

"And you have no memory of this?"

"None."

"Has this happened before?"

"Which, the memory lapses or the violence?" Seeing him just nod, Liz continued. "Well, as I mentioned I really just noticed the memory lapses. But yes. There have been several times in my life where I've become violent and didn't remember. According to Jim and some other friends, I almost killed a guy who had killed my best friend. Also, when I was much younger, I attacked a therapist – a psychiatrist. My mother vowed I would never see another one after my overreaction, but here I am."

"Do you remember why you were seeing him?"

"My parents saw some big changes in me when I was thirteen or fourteen and were concerned. I guess they decided I was okay after all."

Ken thought about what he had heard for a few moments.

"Okay, Liz. Here's what we're going to do. We'll keep an eye on you for a few days to see if we spot anything unusual in your behavior. We'll also get you involved in both group and individual therapy sessions. Sometimes things come out there. We'll see if we can figure out what's triggering your episodes. At this point, I'm not going to recommend any medication. You're here voluntarily and quite frankly, you seem to be a perfectly rational young woman. Believe me. After my decades of practice, I'm pretty good at spotting people with major issues, and you don't seem to be one of them. But we'll take a little time away from your normal world. That alone may do you some good. In a few days to a week, we can sit down and make a determination.

"How does that sound?"

"I guess it will be okay. Do you think you'll find something in these therapy sessions?"

"We usually do."

Standing up, Ken made his way to the door. As if as an afterthought, he turned back and took Liz's hand in what appeared to be a friendly handshake.

"Liz?"

"Yes, Ken?"

"What if I changed my mind, determined that you were unstable and decided to keep you here indefinitely?"

Ken watched as Liz's face changed. If he didn't know better, he would have thought a different person had entered the room and taken Liz's place. Her jaw clenched. Her eyes flared. The cords of her neck muscles looked like they could burst. Her shoulders curved forward and her arms flexed. She looked ready to leap upon him like a wild animal and rip him to shreds. He knew she could smell his fear.

Jane took control of the situation. There was no way she was going to let this asshole lock her away in this looney bin. She knew what went on here. Electroshock, drugs, nighttime molestations and rapes. It wasn't going to happen.

She leapt upon the sleazy shrink, knocking him to the ground and began slamming his head into the floor screaming, "You're never locking me up you son-of-a-bitch. I'll kill you first!"

"Help!" he cried, doing his best to protect his head from the next impact. "Security!"

In seconds, two members of the security team and two strong young residents seized Liz. Each took a limb and pulled her off the doctor. "Seclusion!" he gasped.

They took Liz to a seclusion room and released her inside. She made moves to attack them but the security team forced her back as they exited the room. For the next thirty minutes, Jane slammed herself against the padded walls, screaming, "Let me out of this shithole!" She pounded on the door, threw herself onto the floor, beat at the walls, leapt towards the ceiling and continued shouting and battering everything around her until she fell in a heap, physically exhausted.

Recovering from his ordeal, Ken looked on through the hidden video camera. "You knew, didn't you?" his former chief resident Samantha asked.

"No. I didn't really know, but something told me she wasn't as normal as she seemed. No obvious signs of psychosis, but something…"

They continued watching, fascinated. A few minutes after the collapse, Liz sat up, looked around as if surprised, straightened her clothes, made her way to the bed and sat primly, looking expectantly directly at the hidden video camera.

"Want to join me?" he asked.

Knowing that most patients became calm after a few minutes in the seclusion rooms, Sam tentatively agreed.

They approached the room and used the intercom to speak to Liz.

"Liz, are you calm now? Will you stay on the bed if we come in?"

"I'll be good," said a small voice.

They entered and saw yet a different Liz. This one had big wide eyes and relaxed demeanor. If possible, she looked several years younger than Liz.

"Liz, do you remember what happened?"

"Liz isn't here, but I saw what happened."

"And you are?"

"I'm Betty. I know you want to help Liz, and most of us think this is a good idea. But it was a mistake to threaten us with being locked up here. Jane can't stand to be confined."

"Jane?"

"You met her. You never want to meet Jane. No one does. She's dangerous."

"Can I talk to Liz?"

"I don't know. I'm not sure I should be talking with you. We need to decide what happens next and if we stay here or not. I'm sleepy. I'm going to take a nap."

And that's exactly what she did. Ken and Sam stepped out of the seclusion room.

"Did I see what I think I saw?" Sam asked, completely intrigued.

"I'm not sure. Let's not jump to any conclusions," he advised conservatively even though both of them knew they'd already taken the big leap.

"I'm going to order Assaultive Behavior Precautions with pharmacological restraint if she acts up again. We'll emphasize an anti-psychotic as part of the Rapid Tranquilization procedure. We certainly can't have 'Jane' hurting people. I'm also writing up a 5150. That will give us three days to figure out where we go from here. In the meantime, just to cover our bases, let's do some research on Dissociative Identity Disorder. I'd like to get together with you tomorrow morning to see if we can come up with something resembling a treatment plan, though I suspect we're breaking new ground here."

"I'll get right on it boss," Sam replied enthusiastically. Sam had recently completed her last year of residency at the hospital and Doctor Karmere had taken her on part time while she got her own practice going nearby. Who would have thought she'd stumble onto a case like this so early in her nascent career?

8

After determining that Liz was no longer an immediate threat, two nurses guided her back to her room. She slept soundlessly and dreamlessly until ten the next morning.

Jim was told that Liz was sleeping when he dropped off her clothes. He was worried, but trusted that Liz was in good hands. Plus, he knew she could leave whenever she wanted to. He headed home, did a double workout and fell into an exhausted sleep.

"Why don't you shower and we'll get you some breakfast?" a nurse suggested seeing Liz back among the living the next morning.

Both sounded excellent to Liz. Sunlight streamed through the windows and Liz was feeling optimistic.

"That sounds great. Then I think I'll sign myself out and get on with my life," Liz replied.

"No, Honey. That won't be happening. Doctor Karmere signed an order and we'll be keeping you for a while."

Jane jumped from the bed, ready to strangle the nurse, but two attendants restrained Liz as the nurse administered the prescribed medication. Liz fell back onto the bed, sound asleep.

Nurse Buckley had seen it before but she still marveled at the power of these anti-psychotics.

Almost two hours later, Liz woke up.

"Want to try again, Honey?" Nurse Buckley asked.

"What did I do for Doctor Karmere to order me to stay? We were having a nice conversation and I thought I might see him as an outpatient."

"From what I hear, you physically attacked him. It took four people to pull you off. You really don't remember?"

"No," Liz replied forlornly.

"Don't worry. It's only a seventy-two hour hold, so in a bit more than two days, you can go home if you like. In the meantime, I suggest you try to relax and accept that we're trying to help you."

Liz did as she was told. She showered, had lunch, watched a little television, sat in on the group therapy session where other than introducing herself, she just observed and finally went back to her room. She took the medication that was offered to her.

Late in the day, Nurse Buckley let her know that Doctors

Karmere and Louis would like to see her. She took Liz to a different interview room. Liz was surprised to see that Ken was already there and was accompanied by a woman of about her own age.

"Hi Liz, I'm Samantha Louis – Sam. We met briefly yesterday, but I suspect you don't remember."

Liz flushed, embarrassed by what she'd heard about her behavior. The whole hospital had probably heard about what she'd done.

"It's okay, Liz," Ken soothed. "These things happen sometimes and I know that you, Liz, didn't mean to hurt me. Sam was my Chief Psychiatric Resident until last June and I've hired her part time until she gets her private practice going. If you don't mind, I'd like to have her involved in our discussions. She may be able to see you on an outpatient basis with me consulting."

The word 'outpatient' reassured Liz. It didn't sound like they were planning to commit her. She looked from one to the other expectantly.

"Liz, do you know someone named Jane?" Ken queried gently.

Liz racked her brain which seemed to be moving a bit more slowly than normal. "No, I don't think so," she replied.

"Well, after the events of yesterday, we're beginning to think that perhaps you do suffer from Dissociative Identity Disorder. This is quite rare, but from what we've read, it's quite curable as well. It's not a brain dysfunction so it typically doesn't require long-term medication. It tends to be resolved best through therapy called reintegration.

"In most cases, patients have suffered from a very traumatic event when they were young. To protect the fragile psyche, the personality effectively splits. The main personality is protected by the others though it usually is missing some parts of a complete personality. Often that main person is quiet, reserved, and self-effacing. You seem to be quite the opposite, so your case is obviously different.

"From what we understand, the first step in reintegration is to find out what that traumatic event was. Once the personalities see the problem, we have to convince them to reintegrate. The process can take months or years."

"Are there doctors who specialize in this?" Liz asked,

frightened but intrigued.

"Well, not really. True DID is so rare that most psychiatrists never see it in their entire careers, and those rare ones who do usually see it only once."

"So you're thinking that you can treat me? Won't I be a guinea pig? What if you make a mistake?"

Ken and Sam had discussed this. They thought back to the philosophy of 'first do no harm' and wondered if they were up to it.

Ken responded. "Sam and I have talked about this. We're confident we can get to the bottom of the originating traumatic event. We've done that many times before with quite a few patients. From the literature, the reintegration is more of a challenge. We're not sure about that. Quite frankly, from the studies we've read, the psychiatrists aren't actively involved in resolving the problem. There is no magic formula for reintegration. Each case is different.

"We offer a safe place and person you can trust as we guide you through the therapy. We challenge thoughts and feelings along the way while allowing you to decide how you want to proceed and at what pace. We're there to help where we can."

Ken and Sam watched as Liz processed this. After a few minutes, her face changed. It softened. Her eyes widened. At least ten years disappeared. "We die, don't we?" said the small voice they'd heard the day before.

Neither Ken nor Sam knew how to respond.

"You don't really die," Sam began. "You become part of the whole Liz."

"Like when you die, you're buried and become part of the trees and plants around us?" Betty asked.

"Ah – I guess so," Sam replied thoughtfully.

"So, if I asked you to die so that you could become part of the world around us, would you volunteer?"

Ken and Sam stared at Betty too stunned to speak.

"I'd like to go back to my room now, if that's okay," she said.

Liz didn't remember how she got back to her room. "Did I hurt someone again?" she asked Nurse Buckley.

"No Honey. You didn't. You had a nice chat with the doctors and came back her on your own."

Liz breathed a sigh of relief then got in line for the phone.

"Mama, I need you to come get me," Liz said matter-of-factly when her mother answered.

"I'll be right there!"

"No Mama. They have me in here on a 5150 – a seventy-two hour hold. I need you to come get me the day after tomorrow in the afternoon. Can you do that?"

"They have you on what? I'll get our lawyers down there to get you out immediately."

"No Mama," Liz replied calmly. "It won't work, and even it if did, the order would expire before they could do anything. I'm okay here. But I will be ready to leave when the order expires."

"How could they do this to you?"

"Well Mama, you remember that psychiatrist I saw for a while when I was younger?"

Janice flashed back to the event. They'd had to cover the quack's hospital bills.

"Well, I did the same thing. I attacked the doctor."

"He probably deserved it," Janice fumed.

"I don't think so, Mama. But I don't want to talk about it. Just come get me, and please don't tell Jim."

9

The next two days were boring for Liz, but she was patient. She called Jim daily and reassured him. She told him the doctors thought that she did, indeed, suffer from Dissociative Identity Disorder. They had proposed an outpatient treatment and she was considering it. In the meantime, she was relaxing and talking to the doctors.

On her last day in the hospital, Ken and Sam asked to see her again. She had made it clear to the staff that she would be leaving that afternoon.

"Are you sure that you don't want to give us a chance?" Sam asked tentatively.

"I'm sure. The more I think about it, the more I believe that you are on the wrong track. I don't have DID. I suspect the memory issues and perhaps even the violence are due to my drug and alcohol use. I think you've been caught up in my husband's fantasies about DID. In the meantime, I'm going to go on a cleanse and see if things get better."

"But—", Sam started but stopped when Ken raised his hand.

"Liz, whether it's DID or not, you have some psychological issues. People in good mental health don't suddenly attack others. Will you at least stay on the anti-psychotic medication I prescribed?"

"I'll think about it," Liz responded getting up to go. "I'm sorry for any trouble that I've caused you."

Sam turned to Ken and said incredulously, "You're letting her go?"

"I'm afraid I don't have any choice. You saw her determination. Somehow, the other personalities have convinced her that she doesn't need treatment. I suspect she'll be back, hopefully before she hurts anyone."

Janice was waiting when they released Liz.

"Oh my poor baby! Are you okay?"

"Yes, Mama. I'm fine. I want to ask a really big favor."

"Anything!"

"Could you take me up to the cabin? My car is there and I want to go back. It's so peaceful there. I'm going to see if I can get off the alcohol and drugs and if that will fix the problem."

"Liz, I think you should come home and stay with me. I can take care of you. And you don't have any problems. You're perfect the way you are!"

"No Mama, I'm not. I see that I have problems. Jim and the doctors seem to think I suffer from a multiple personality disorder, but I don't think that's it."

"Baby girl, I think Jim is gaslighting you and that he's convinced the doctors that you're crazy. Please come home!"

"Jim hasn't even talked to the doctors, so I don't think that's it. I also don't think Jim is trying to drive me crazy like Charles Boyer did to Ingrid Bergman. He's trying to find a solution to the problems I obviously have.

"I don't want to hurt you Mama, but I can't come home because I think that home may be part of the problem. Please trust me. I'm going to try to get better and save my marriage. And don't blame Jim. This is not his fault. I asked him to take me to the hospital. He never suggested it in any way."

Janice was stunned. Liz turned on some music and they drove without speaking until they reached the cabin.

"I love you, Mama," Liz said as she got out of the car.

"I love you too, Baby Girl. Don't you think –".

"No, I don't. Goodbye Mama. Drive carefully."

Janice fumed all the way home.

10

Jim called the hospital and was told that Liz had checked herself out. He asked if he could speak with one of Liz's doctors. He was put on hold as the nurse verified Liz's Release of Information and tried to reach Doctor Karmere.

When she came back on the line, she said that although she found it a bit unusual, Doctor Karmere was willing to meet with him at 10am the next day. Jim quickly agreed and thanked her. He then immediately called Janice.

"Liz is not here," she shouted at him defiantly. "This is all your fault."

And she hung up.

Jim tried to call back but got no answer, just their machine. He left a message saying he thought it would be a good idea for everyone to get together to talk, but Janice didn't pick up and didn't call back. He tried Mickey's office and Mickey called him back late in the afternoon.

"Jim," Mickey began. "I'm sorry it's come to this. Janice is a wreck and she's blaming you. Liz is in the mountains, but I'm not sure that you should go see her. I think things need to settle down a bit."

"But Mickey, I'm afraid Liz will hurt herself or someone else."

"Well, the doctors released her, so they don't seem to share the same concern. I think that for now, the best thing is, as I said, to let things settle down. Definitely avoid Janice. She has a temper. I'll try to work on her over the next few days and maybe then we can get together to reassess the situation."

Not having much else to suggest, Jim capitulated, said goodbye, and spent the rest of the day and all night waiting for the meeting with Doctor Karmere. This time it took three workouts, surfing, biking, and running to wear him out enough to finally get some sound sleep.

At ten the next morning, Jim was taken to Doctor Karmere's office by Ann, the nurse who had spoken with him the night he'd brought Liz in. She offered him water on the way, which he gratefully accepted, but she wouldn't answer questions about Liz. That was for Doctor Karmere.

Jim entered the office and was greeted by a fit and friendly man in his fifties. He also noticed an attractive young woman about Liz's age who stood up expectantly.

"Jim, I'm Ken Karmere – call me Ken, and this is Doctor Samantha Louis – Sam."

Jim shook hands with each and they motioned him to a chair at a small conference table where they joined him.

"First, let me say that we're sorry for what you're going through. It has to be very challenging. I understand from Liz that you've done some research on Dissociative Identity Disorder?"

"Actually, quite a bit."

"Good, good. Well. We were a bit skeptical when we admitted Liz, but then she attacked me. Or rather Jane attacked me."

"Jane?"

"I guess you haven't met Jane," Ken mused.

"Ah no." I've really only talked to Betty, and of course Liz. But I did see Liz talking to herself in two different voices with two very different looks. They called themselves Eve and Dawn, and Betty confirmed their identities to me. Eve is their cousin from England and Dawn is Liz's younger sister. Betty wouldn't talk about the other personality, but she said that she thought there were five of them in total.

"Eve and Dawn were discussing someone who Dawn said committed a murder. She said that this person may have killed several people – anyone who threatened Dawn. Could Liz be a murderer? Could she have killed multiple people?"

Ken and Sam looked at each other, not sure what to say.

"It's possible," Ken admitted. "In almost all cases of DID, there is a violent personality that acts as the protector. Some of these have been murderers."

"So does that mean Liz could be convicted of murder?"

"I'm not a lawyer, but I have read quite a bit on the subject. There have been many cases of claims of Multiple Personality or DID in murder trials. One study I read found that almost ten percent of murderers suffer from DID. I find that hard to believe, and apparently, so does our legal system. The vast majority of DID defenses fail. There have been a few that succeeded, but the defense needed to convince the jury that the defendant suffered from DID and that the personality that committed the murders couldn't tell right from wrong. The first has proved to be a tall order as there was a period where DID became a standard insanity defense. Prosecutors easily found psychiatrists who would testify that not only did the defendant not have DID, but that DID itself didn't exist.

"In the few cases that did succeed, the defense was able to show that multiple personality behavior existed long before the murders. Too many defenses were used after the fact."

"So if we can prove that Liz suffered from DID before the murder or murders, she might not go to jail?"

"Well, first off, we don't know that Liz committed any murders. Let's not jump to any conclusions at this point." Then looking at Sam, Ken continued, "Actually, if we had evidence that Liz had committed a murder and might commit more, we might have to contact the authorities. This is something Sam and I should discuss, but right now, I don't think we have any direct evidence and what you heard could be interpreted in multiple ways.

"Sorry to do this, but I think we'll leave that to you for now. You can decide if you want to contact the authorities. I suspect that with no concrete evidence – names, dates, places, etc., you won't get too far."

Jim thought about this for a moment. If Liz was a murderer and might kill again, shouldn't she be stopped?

"Couldn't you have kept her here? That would have protected her and perhaps others. Isn't there something about being able to keep people if they're a risk to themselves or others?"

"Yes, and we did that – but for seventy-two hours. To keep someone longer, it takes really solid evidence and people on the outside have to be supportive of the decision. From what we understand, Liz's mother would fight us on this and it would likely become a protracted process."

"So what can we do?" Jim asked desperately.

"Sam and I have discussed this. Sam, why don't you take over."

"Jim," Sam began, trying to sound more confident than she felt. "We believe that the other personalities have convinced Liz that she doesn't suffer from DID. I know that sounds strange, but we think they've influenced her without being identified. They didn't actually talk to Liz, they just created feelings.

"At this point, we think the likelihood of her recommitting herself is small. Quite frankly, we probably wouldn't have kept her here on an inpatient basis anyway. We also suspect that Liz will never be able to work with a male psychiatrist. She apparently attacked one before.

"Before I go further, I should ask if you're aware of any significant trauma that occurred when Liz was younger."

"No. However, I spoke with Liz's father and he saw a dramatic change in Liz when she was twelve or thirteen. At first, Mickey and Janice – Liz's parents – thought it was just puberty coming on. But over time, they saw significant problems. Liz got pregnant at thirteen, you know."

Seeing them shake their heads negatively, Jim continued. "Apparently, they never found out who the father was. Mickey is a skilled interrogator – a trial attorney – and he is convinced that Liz's boyfriend was not at fault. He thinks something bad occurred, probably a rape, and pushed for therapy – hence the incident with the other psychiatrist. Janice has fought him on this for years. Then, with Liz's success in school, she pretty much convinced Mickey that Liz was really okay.

"I'm pretty sure that whatever happened, it wasn't Mickey. But unfortunately, Liz doesn't remember, neither does Betty, and Janice refuses to even consider that something damaging happened to Liz."

"Jim, that's very helpful," Sam replied encouragingly. "We'd like to get Liz back into therapy and we're thinking the easiest way to do that would be to use the excuse of marriage counseling. That's something that Liz could easily agree to even though she would probably see through it. It would give the other personalities an excuse. They want to help Liz – they let her come here before – and I think they want your marriage to be okay. It seems important to Liz.

"I have extensive training in couple's therapy and was planning to make that the focus of my private practice. We're hoping you can convince Liz that the two of you should start seeing me for couple's counseling. We think that might open some doors.

"I know it sounds like a stretch, but we believe that some part or parts of Liz will realize that they need help and that this will be an easy way to start. What do you think?"

"But what about the violence and possible murders?" Jim asked nervously.

"Ken put Liz on an anti-psychotic that will suppress violent tendencies. If she stays on it, we're hoping that won't be much of an issue. Plus, our guess is that since it's the protector who is violent, the violence is probably in defense of Liz or one of the others. If Liz is not put into dangerous situations, the violence shouldn't occur."

"But our boss Rajiv isn't – wasn't dangerous," Jim argued. "He wasn't a threat."

"Do you know if he touched her?"

"Ah, no."

"Perhaps if Liz was in a heated discussion or argument and a man touched her, Jane could have perceived that as a threat," Sam suggested.

"Rajiv does touch people he's trying to connect with," Jim said thoughtfully. "I guess it's possible. I'll ask him."

They sat in silence for a few moments, each thinking about how to go forward. Sam broke the silence. "So, Jim, do you think you could talk to Liz about coming to see me for couple's counseling?"

"Okay. I'm skeptical, but I'll give it a try."

They exchanged contact information and Jim left, more confused and worried than ever.

11

Liz didn't stay on her medication though she did medicate herself with alcohol when she was hyper and cocaine when she was feeling down. She was back at the cabin feeling better than she had in quite a while. Writing in her journal at least three times a day, Liz checked for messages written by someone else and looked for gaps but didn't see anything unusual. It started to feel like the last few months were just a bad period. Maybe it was the drugs and alcohol. She promised she would wean herself as best she could. Now, if Jim could put these crazy ideas out of his head, they could get back to their normal life.

Her thoughts were interrupted by the sound of a car coming down the shared private road. She couldn't see the car yet, but since theirs was the last house on the road, it was certainly coming to the cabin. Hopefully it was Jim. Liz missed him.

It was Jim and he pulled his car up behind Liz', pleased that she was there. He'd thought long and hard about how he'd broach the subject of starting marriage counseling with the psychiatrist that had seen Liz in the hospital and had decided to take it slowly. He needed to see if the 'old Liz' was back. He was nervous as he stepped out of the car and called Liz's name.

Getting no response, Jim continued onto the deck and looked in the window, calling Liz's name again before entering the cabin. As he reached for the door handle, his right arm was grabbed from behind and twisted behind his back. He was slammed against the closed door by a very powerful person he couldn't see.

"What the fuck are you doing here, asshole?"

The voice was deep and husky, commanding. It almost sounded like Liz but it wasn't.

"Are you Jane?" Jim asked, trying to sound confident, swallowing the fear that was threatening to overwhelm him.

Ignoring him, Jane ordered Jim to respond. "I said, what the fuck are you doing here?"

"I – ah – came to ask Liz if we could see a marriage counselor."

Jane laughed. It was a masculine laugh, the kind of laugh he'd heard in war movies when interrogators tortured their victims.

"Bullshit. You're here to kill us, aren't you?"

"Of course not," Jim replied, outraged. "I'd never hurt Liz."

"Well, you've been pushing this multiple personality shit,

right? You and those doctors want to do reintegration. That's murder plain as day. Reintegration would kill us and I'm not going to let that happen. Now hit the road asshole and don't come up here unannounced again or I'll kill you."

Jim knew it wasn't an idle threat.

Jane pulled him away from the door, forced him to the edge of the steps and pushed him down them. Jim landed hard, the gravel of the driveway scratching the side of his face.

"Please tell Liz why I came," he stated evenly as he stood up, brushed himself off and made his way to the car.

"I don't talk to Liz. Neither does anyone else. If you're so damned smart, you should know that. Now get the fuck out of here."

12

It had been a few weeks since Dawn had been back to the Tenderloin. After the last murder, Dawn had promised herself she wouldn't return. She had been noticed. The regulars and the pimps looked at her suspiciously then looked away quickly. She also didn't want Jane to kill anyone else. It was all too much. Still, she couldn't stop herself from coming. She had to do this.

It wasn't the sex, though she had to admit that she enjoyed the sex with most of her clients. No. It was the control. She was in control. She decided when and where, with whom and what would happen. Often, she made the johns beg. They wanted her and they'd do whatever she asked to be able to touch her. Yes. It was the control. She'd never felt it anywhere else. In other jobs, there was always a boss who told her what to do. On the street, she was the boss.

Dawn pulled her car into the alley where she always parked. It was a few blocks away from the main action, but the car was safe here and it was one of those rare places in San Francisco where you could almost always be assured of a parking spot – but only at night.

She stepped out of the car, locked the door and dropped the keys into her small handbag.

"What did you do to Jimmy?" a raucous voice shouted at her.

Jane saw the attacker reach for the knife in his belt and instinct took over. She let him approach, trying to appear cowered and frightened, turning away in self-defense. As he seized her shoulder to spin her around, Jane accurately inserted her knife between his ribs, killing him instantly.

Eve, Dawn and Betty watched horrified but fascinated as Jane went through her disposal ritual.

"I told you she killed people," Dawn whined as Jane was patiently waiting for the tides.

"Betty, you shouldn't be here," Eve counseled.

"No," Betty replied. "I needed to see this too. Now I know that Jane is a killer."

"I can hear you, Ladies," Jane responded sarcastically. "Don't think of me as a killer, think of me as law enforcement. I'm ridding the streets of scum like this piece of shit."

"But what if the police arrest us?" Eve asked. "You barbaric Californians have the death penalty. We'd be executed."

"They'll never catch us," Jane responded coolly. "I never leave any clues."

When Jane was finished, they made their way back to the mountains. That night, Dawn dreamt about Mitch Stern.

"Why did you kill me, Margaret?" he asked pleadingly. "I'm so sorry I forced your head down. I got carried away with the fantasy."

Dawn remembered the sad-looking man that she'd approached that night so long ago. He looked broken and desperate. He'd told her he'd never done anything like this before, and she believed him. When she said he could call her whatever he wanted, he looked so happy, like a little boy who was just granted his Christmas wish. He called her Margaret. What was it he'd said to Jane? That he was sorry? That his wife had just left him? That he was trying to imagine being with her again?

"Why did you kill me?" the dream figure asked again? "I think I might have been okay after all. I would have survived the divorce."

Dawn awoke feeling terribly guilty. So did Eve, Betty, and Liz who shared the dream. Keeping up with her journal, Liz wrote down what she remembered, but like most of her dreams, it didn't make any sense to her.

A few days later, Dawn was back in the City. She parked the car in her usual spot and made her way to the Tenderloin. As she turned the corner, she saw one of the older pimps nod to two somewhat disheveled-looking men who began to walk towards her.

"Miss Dawn?" the older one asked with a bit of a southern accent. "We're with the police and we need to speak with you. Can you come with us please?"

Jane thought quickly. She continued towards them, trying to appear surprised.

"Certainly, officers, she responded graciously. "Can you tell me what this is about?"

The two officers relaxed, reassured that Dawn was going to cooperate. Plus, she wasn't even five foot six and couldn't have weighed more than one hundred twenty pounds. She clearly wasn't a threat. She certainly couldn't have killed and disposed of the much larger male victims. But maybe she knew something that would help. "There have been some murders and we have some questions for you," the oldest one replied, clearly the senior cop.

Jane continued smiling and tried to look curious. She stepped between them and looked reassuringly at each in turn as they started down the street together towards their waiting car. "I'll be whatever help I can be," she said.

Without warning, Jane lifted her arms behind the two cops, seized their necks, one in each hand, stepped quickly back and slammed their heads together. She grabbed the younger one and pushed him into the other, forcing them violently into and through a storefront window. Then she kicked off her shoes and ran as the pimps, hookers and passers-by looked on, along with Eve, Dawn, and Betty.

"We're going to be arrested. We're going to jail. We're going to be executed. All because of you, Jane. All because of you," Dawn accused.

But Jane was in survival mode. She ignored them, cautiously making her way back to the car, ensuring that no one was following.

13

They had just finished dinner and were washing dishes together when the call came. Mike seemed excited, quickly rinsing and drying his hands. He stepped into the living room where he grabbed his notebook and a pen and began asking questions. He scribbled furiously as May finished up the dishes and joined him, beginning to get caught up in the excitement. She picked up bits and pieces of the conversation, determining that it was about the murders, but saw Mike's enthusiasm turn to disappointment just before he hung up.

"Fuck, fuck, fuck!" Mike railed. "They let her get away!"

"Dawn?"

"Of course, Dawn. What did you think – "

Then he stopped himself. This was May. He wasn't pissed at her. He was just pissed.

"I'm sorry. Give me a second to calm down."

May got up and poured Mike a finger of Grand Marnier which she popped in the microwave for ten seconds. She poured herself a small glass of port, returned to the living room, and encouraged the rapidly pacing Mike to sit down beside her.

Mike looked at her like she was crazy but sat down. He inhaled deeply and tried to calm down as he let his breath out slowly. He cautiously sniffed the warm Grand Marnier, then took a sip. He rolled the warm, viscous liquid slowly on his tongue and felt himself relax a bit as the orange brandy flavor filled his head.

"They had her and she got away," he said morosely.

"Start from the beginning. Tell me what happened."

"Well, a few days ago, a pimp named Maurice, disappeared. He was one of Jimmy's 'associates' and had been bragging that he was going to get revenge on this Dawn. Over the last several weeks, he spent most of his time looking for her. When he disappeared a couple of days ago, one of our informants let us know that he suspected Dawn was back on the streets. We put a rotating team of guys in the Tenderloin waiting for her to show. They spotted her tonight.

"Unfortunately, they underestimated her. She's small and looked harmless. She appeared cooperative and was walking to their car between them when she just exploded. Jack Martin is in the hospital with a mild concussion and lacerations on his face. His partner, Stephen Larson was briefly unconscious, but they released him. He told the investigators that she hit them with superhuman strength. She slammed their heads together and threw them through a window.

"God, I hope we haven't lost her for good. Now she knows the police are onto her. I doubt that she'll be back in the Tenderloin anytime soon."

"Any evidence left behind? Trace evidence?" May asked.

"It sounds ridiculous, but we have her shoes – red pumps."

"Her shoes?" she asked, surprised. Then thinking like a female cop continued, "Yeah, that makes sense. A hooker would wear pumps of some sort and she certainly couldn't run in them. Maybe you'll get a print off of them, maybe DNA, at least you can chase the brand and maybe find the store where they were bought. It's not hopeless."

"Yeah, well this is no Cinderella story either. There are over seven million people in the Bay Area and we're going to have a hell of a time finding out who this shoe fits. But maybe we'll get lucky. A print or DNA. You'd think we'd be able to get one or the other off the shoes."

They sipped their drinks quietly, each silently laying out their next steps.

"We'll get her," Mike stated confidently. "We'll definitely get her!"

14

Unbeknownst to Liz, Betty, Eve, and Dawn had been arguing non-stop for two days.

"We have to turn ourselves in," Betty argued. "It's the right thing to do."

"Well, I haven't done anything wrong," Eve argued. "I'm not going to submit to your so-called American Justice. We won't get a fair trial."

"I may have done bad things," Dawn complained. "But I never hurt anyone. And I really can't help what I do. I don't want to be locked up or executed or thrown into the looney bin."

"And what about Liz?" Eve posed reasonably. "She certainly didn't do anything wrong. She's just married a wonderful man, has a new career, and a very promising life ahead of her. If we turn ourselves in, we'll ruin Liz's life."

"If we turn ourselves in, Liz can plead insanity. After treatment, she'll be able to get on with her life," Betty continued.

"Treatment?" Dawn almost shouted. "Are you talking about that reintegration stuff? We'd be killed. We'd cease to exist. It's no different than being executed in the gas chamber or whatever they do now."

"But Liz would live and so would a part of us," Betty reasoned.

"Betty, don't give us the tired cycle of life story. When you're dead, you're dead. And if we go through the reintegration process, we'll most certainly be dead."

And so the discussions went. Betty tried to be patient. Eve was outraged. Dawn was frightened. Jane was absent.

At the end of another night of the same, Betty came back to the subject of Liz again. "Look what we're doing to Liz. She's suffering. We're confused and arguing and Liz is beginning to fall apart. We're ruining her marriage. We need to do something, but we can't keep going on like this."

"It's all Jane's fault," Dawn lamented. "If not for Jane, the police wouldn't be after us."

"If not for Jane, you'd be hurt, dead, or a heroin addict. She saved you from violent men," Eve observed objectively.

"Yeah, but did she have to kill them?"

"I don't know. But she may be right. These men were trying

to hurt you. It sounds like they were what she called them, scumbags. Jane has done the world a favor by ridding us of these vermin."

"I guess you're right. But there was one. His name was Mitch. He was a nice guy."

"A nice guy who frequents hookers?" Eve snorted.

"It was his first time. His wife had left him and he was lonely. I looked like her. You remember the dream? I keep having it. I feel bad."

Liz awoke frightened and confused. She couldn't think of any specific reason, but she also felt like she hadn't slept at all. It was almost ten in the morning and she'd been in bed for nearly twelve hours. She didn't remember getting up or tossing and turning, but she was exhausted. This was the second day in a row she'd woken up feeling this way. It was a far cry from the confidence she'd felt only a few days before. Where was Jim? She needed him.

Almost on cue, the phone rang.

"Hi Liz," Jim began cautiously. "How are you? I miss you."

"I miss you terribly, Jim. Can I come home? I'm not doing too well. I seem to spend all my time sleeping. I have weird dreams and even after all the sleep, I feel exhausted."

"God, it would be great to have you home. Do you want me to come get you?"

"No. I can do the drive. I'll see you soon."

But it wasn't soon. There was some debate before everyone agreed that Liz should go home. Betty ultimately prevailed with her romantic arguments that Jim and Liz needed each other.

Jim was getting worried. It was almost dark and a light rain had begun to fall. Could something have happened to Liz? Could she have changed her mind? Could one of the others have interfered?

He was relieved a few minutes later when Liz's car pulled into the driveway. She raced up the steps as he opened the door and leapt into his arms. "I've missed you," she cried, pulling him tighter.

Jim carried her to the sofa where they held each other as the rain intensified outside. Feeling warmed by Jim and more relaxed than she'd been in weeks, Liz asked, "Are you hungry?"

Jim realized that he was. "There's really nothing in the house. Would you be okay with Alberti's?"

"Absolutely."

Twenty minutes later, they were the seated in the tiny Italian restaurant in Pacifica. It was an old-fashioned place with red-checkered table cloths, candles, and signed straw Chianti bottles lining the walls. Tony, the owner and waiter, poured them two glasses of Chianti as soon as they were seated, and without even looking at the menu, they ordered salads and a two-person order of Spaghetti Margharita.

"To our marriage," Liz toasted. "I don't ever want us to be apart. I know I've been a problem. I'm sorry I left. We should stay together and work things out together."

"To our marriage," Jim responded feeling guilty for what he was about to say. "I've missed you terribly. I think our marriage has suffered. I want to work on making ours the best marriage ever. I know we were meant to be together and I don't want to let that go.

"We are meant to be together and I'll do anything to make us a stronger couple."

"Does that include counseling? Marriage counseling?"

A flash of anger clouded Liz's face for an instant but was quickly gone. Liz looked beyond Jim pensively. She turned back to him and looked probingly into his eyes. "Is this a ploy to get me committed?"

"Absolutely not. I don't want you committed. I want you with me. I'm hoping counseling will help us work things out together. We're both aware that you have some issues. I'm sure I do too, and I'm sure I'm not dealing with your issues in the best way. Sure, you could go into therapy like you've tried before, but we know how that worked out. If we go together, which is what happens with marriage counseling, we work on us. If issues arise, I'll be there. It won't be you alone against some doctor."

Somehow, what Jim said made sense. Liz supposed it wasn't really marriage counseling; it was counseling for her. At the same time, it would be different. It would be about their marriage and how they could cope with Liz's problems. It might offer a safer venue to examine those problems as well. Jim loved her. He would be there to protect her."

"Okay. I'll do it. But I have one condition. "We don't discuss the multiple personality thing."

Jim hesitated, thinking quickly. "Agreed. I won't bring it up unless you do."

"Do you have someone in mind?"

This was the big one. Would she agree?

"It may sound strange, and please don't react until you've thought about it, but I met with your doctors at SF Community after you left. Sam, the woman psychiatrist, suggested that we see her. She does couples therapy when she's not working at the hospital. She suggested we avoid the whole DID thing and focus on the relationship and our problems."

Liz thought about this. At first she started to get angry. This was a trick. Jim wanted her back under control of the shrinks. They were going to pursue this multiple personality theory. But then another part of her thought about this woman, Sam. She was Liz's age and seemed to sympathize. She did need help. If they really could stay off the DID topic, maybe it would be useful. If Sam really did couples therapy, she probably could help them cope with the problems they both brought to the marriage, especially hers.

"Okay. Deal. Our main goal will be to help our marriage become strong enough to survive our difficulties. If Sam can also help me resolve some of my problems, all the better. She may also be able to help you solve some of yours."

Rather than rising to the bait, Jim decided to play it cool. Maybe just maybe they could get through this.

"I certainly have my share of problems," he agreed. Then, thinking of the possibility that Jane was a murderer, he continued, "Our goal will be to strengthen our marriage so we can handle whatever comes our way."

He held out his hand and they shook firmly to seal the bargain.

CHAPTER 6

"Life can be easy, it is only a question of choosing between solutions and illusions."

- Didier D'haese

1

Home life for Liz and Jim returned to normal. They awoke early each morning and either went for a run or a surf session before breakfast. Jim left for work and Liz occupied herself with improving the house and working in the garden. They had put together a long list of projects which Liz could pursue and which Jim could help with on the weekends.

Jim was looking forward to their first appointment with Samantha Louis, Liz was dreading it.

They drove to Samantha's office in the Haight Ashbury district of San Francisco. Her office was located on the second floor of an older building above a French bakery. The scent of freshly baking bread was everywhere.

"How can you stand it?" Liz asked as Samantha led them into her office.

"I know, right? I think I've put on ten pounds since I rented this office. And that's not from eating the bread and pastries. I think the scents are calorie laden and inhaling them all day is probably as bad as partaking."

"You don't really expect us to believe that you don't partake of their bread and pastries, do you?" Liz teased.

"Well, I try to put up a good front. A number of my patients are fighting eating disorders and this may not have been the best choice for an office location. But I do love it. And I do love their breads.

"So, what brings you to me today?"

"Jim just won't do what I tell him to and it's putting a strain on our marriage. I'm hoping you can convince him that he needs to follow my orders to the letter. That way we'll never fight and we'll always be happy."

"Hmm, that's a new approach I haven't considered offering my patients. I'll have to give it some thought. Being a woman, I can see how that might make some sense. If we could implement it on a larger scale and all the men did what we told them to, we could eliminate hunger and create world peace."

Jim watched the interchange with amusement. Samantha seemed more like a college friend than a therapist. Maybe this would work.

"Whirled peas?" Liz joked. "I don't like whirled peas. They get really mushy."

"Well then, maybe we should table that plan for the moment. Maybe Jim has some ideas"

"Don't get me started," Liz continued lightly. "Jim has lots of ideas. We're here to see if we can keep his ideas from driving me crazy and to see if we can hold our marriage together through the difficulties that are going to come from my craziness."

Liz turned serious, almost tearful, and looked expectantly at Sam.

"Okay," Sam began. "First some ground rules. I'm not here as a judge. I'm here as a facilitator. For couples or marriage counseling, my job is to help you two communicate. You can ask me questions, but really, this is about the two of you learning to talk to each other in ways that increase your mutual understanding, facilitate discussion and resolution of problems that arise, and strengthen your relationship. You'll be talking to each other more than to me. I may serve as referee from time to time, but I'm not here to tell you that one of you is right and the other is wrong on any issue. That's for you to decide. My role is to act as a guide. Also, except in some rare circumstances that I don't foresee, I'll always see you together. Not separately. This is very important. Our sessions are about you two. Not about either one of you separately.

"Are we ready to get started?"

Liz was pleasantly surprised. There had been no mention of her behavioral problems. Sam was focused on the relationship, their marriage.

"I'm ready," Liz replied.

"Me too," Jim agreed.

"Okay. Let's do a top down kind of thing. What would you say is the biggest issue in your relationship right now? Jim, we haven't heard much from you. Why don't you start?"

Sam had caught Jim off guard. Where should he begin? For him, the biggest issue was that his wife was likely a murderer and might be caught and put in prison.

Jim looked at Sam and she smiled encouragingly. He could almost read her thoughts. She seemed to be saying, 'stay with the program'. He thought about their relationship as if he were someone watching from outside. And then he knew where to begin.

"Well," he said tentatively looking back and forth between Liz and Sam. "We've been separated for quite a while. Liz has been living in the mountains by herself and I've been at our home in Pacifica spending my time going to work and then working out to help keep my sanity. I've really missed Liz. I had such great hopes for our marriage. I know we're meant to be together, but it has really hurt my feelings that Liz left me."

"Jim, say that to Liz, please."

Jim looked at Liz and realized that he was on the verge of tears. "Liz, it really hurt my feelings that you left our home."

And then he did cry. It all hit him at once. He was afraid. Afraid of losing Liz, afraid of losing his job, afraid of losing the wonderful life they had planned. Frightened of the unknown, what the future would bring.

He didn't say any of this. Liz moved closer and took him in her arms and she was crying too. "It will be okay, Jim. We'll figure it out. I love you."

When their time was up, Sam was quite pleased. This first session had gone better than she expected. They were building trust. The issue of separation was on the table and they each seemed to understand the impact it had on their relationship.

For their part, Liz and Jim were drained, exhausted. And yet, there was an underlying feeling of relief. They felt hopeful.

"Same time next week?" Sam proposed.

"Could we do twice a week?" Liz countered as Jim nodded his assent.

"Sure. Let's do Tuesdays and Fridays if that works for you." Seeing them nod, Sam continued. "This has been a good start. I look forward to seeing you Friday."

Liz and Jim thanked her and made their way downstairs. They decided to have lunch at the bakery, sandwiches made to order with bread right out of the oven. Jim thought about taking the afternoon off, but decided that he needed to recover from the morning's session and work would provide a good distraction.

After a quiet lunch, Jim dropped Liz at home and made his way to the office. Liz changed her clothes and spent the afternoon working in the garden, savoring the feel of the earth in her hands as she tended her plants.

2

"That went surprisingly well," Eve observed.

"Yes. It did," Dawn agreed.

"I told you it would be a good thing," Betty boasted.

"Yes, but it doesn't get to the root of the problem. Does it?" Eve chided. "Maybe the counseling will help Liz and Jim cope with the situation, but they don't know that the police are after us, that Jane has committed murders, and that Liz will likely go to jail."

"It's all my fault," Dawn moaned.

"Stop feeling sorry for yourself, Dawn," Eve continued. "It doesn't matter who is at fault. We need to have a plan."

"I still think we should turn ourselves in to the police," Betty reiterated. "It is the right thing to do."

"It may be the right thing to do morally," Eve replied. "But they will lock us up, they will convict us of serial murders, and they will likely give us the death penalty. No one will believe an insanity plea after our arrest."

"Then we should do the reintegration," Betty stated flatly.

"I don't want to die," Dawn whined.

"Enough Dawn, none of us do. But what are our alternatives? We could run away, but it doesn't solve the fundamental problem. You're a slut who can't control herself and Jane is an efficient serial killer who has no conscience. Even if we run away, it's just going to happen again somewhere else. On one point, I agree with Betty. Morally, this can't continue. We just need to figure out a solution."

"Well I'm convinced that reintegration is the right thing to do," Betty stated firmly.

"You'd die," said Dawn. "We all would."

"I just don't see an alternative," Betty argued. Maybe we deserve to die. We are responsible for the deaths of several people."

"Most of them were scumbags and deserved what they got," Dawn insisted.

"Not that man Mitch. Don't you feel bad about him? It was wrong of Jane to kill him. If we don't do the reintegration, we could be executed for murder and we all die, including Liz. This way, at least parts of us live on inside Liz."

"You don't know that," Eve countered. "No one knows if

reintegration works. It may make things worse. Plus, Jane would never go for it. She's not going to die and she's not going to let any of us get hurt. She'd kill the therapist and Jim first."

They all considered that in silence for a few moments.

"Look, we need some time to figure this out. For now, Dawn, you need to stay off the street. Can you do that?"

"I'm not sure. I really can't do anything else. I can't stand to do any other kind of work. The street is all I know and all I'm good at."

"You certainly can't go back into the Tenderloin. Really, you can't go anywhere. The police will be looking for you. You're a prostitute. They know you'll avoid San Francisco, so they'll likely be looking everywhere in the Bay Area. You just have to stop for a while. Think of it as a vacation."

"I'll try. I'll do my best. But sometimes... You're right. I can't control myself. I'm sorry."

"Don't be sorry. Don't risk all of our lives. Think about Liz. You hold the key to her life."

3

Two days later around three-thirty, Jim got the munchies. This wasn't unusual. With his daily workouts, a light breakfast, and a minimal lunch at his desk, Jim usually found himself hungry in the middle of the afternoon. He made his way downstairs to the small café on the first floor of their building where he picked out a slice of vegan carrot cake from the assortment of healthy pastries, and grabbed a Kombucha from the large refrigerator. As he made his way to the counter to pay, he inadvertently caught sight of the front page of the San Francisco Chronicle abandoned on one of the small tables.

There on the front page was a sketch of someone who looked very much like Liz. Her hair was different and she had a sexy, enticing look, but it really looked like Liz. As he approached, he saw the headline, "Hooker sought for questioning in serial murders."

He dropped the Kombucha and fell into a chair. He retrieved the bottle which had rolled several feet, quickly paid the cashier and then sat down and read the article. While it didn't say the hooker had killed anyone, the piece implied that the police wanted her for more than questioning. Not only had five bodies been found, they suspected that there had been several more murders where the victims were not found. The murders seemed to take place when this particular hooker, known only as 'Dawn' was working the streets, and when the police had tried to question her, she had attacked two officers, sending both to the hospital while making her escape.

Jim's mind reeled. It was true. Liz had killed people. Liz was a prostitute. There was no way their marriage could survive this.

In the City, Mike McKensey had just called May.

"Did you see the Chronicle?" he asked enthusiastically.

"No. I get my news online and the Chronicle isn't something I read. Why?"

"We got the sketch of Dawn on the front page. This will flesh her out."

"What about the shoes? Did you get anything off of them?"

"We got some DNA. It's going to take several weeks to see if we can find a match. If Dawn has been picked up in the last several years, we should be able to find her. As for prints, we only got a partial thumb and it doesn't look like we're going to get anything from that. How can someone put on shoes and not leave prints?"

May thought for a second. "Well, she's a woman who's dressing up. I must admit that if I put on shiny pumps, first, I slide them on with my hand underneath. I might or might not touch the sides and top. However, if I do, and even if I don't, if I'm trying to look my best, I always wipe them off or do a last-minute buff to make sure there are no smudges and they shine enough to attract attention."

Mike wondered again about women and shoes. Here was May, a cop, and like most other women he knew, shoes were a big deal for her. Her idea of wiping the shoes down made sense, though. He had to admit that he'd done the same thing when he was required to dress for a formal meeting.

"We've also circulated the sketch all over the Bay Area. Every vice cop within fifty miles will be looking for her. If she surfaces, we'll get her, and this time, we won't underestimate her."

4

Jim didn't know what to do. He called Sam and asked to meet. She was reluctant to see him without Liz, but after trying unsuccessfully to calm him down, she agreed to meet him for coffee at the bakery downstairs.

Thirty minutes later, Jim walked in with a newspaper under his arm. He was clearly agitated and his eyes searched the mostly empty bakery before settling on Sam. He didn't even smile. He just hurried over.

"I don't know what to do. We're in big trouble," he said desperately, laying the paper before her.

Sam took a deep breath. This was what she and Ken had feared. To buy time, she slowly and carefully read the article. It identified Dawn by name. With the sketch, there was little doubt. Liz was a suspected serial killer. Fortunately, the article just said she was wanted for questioning.

But what should she do? Ethically, she should probably identify Liz to the police. On the other hand, her official sessions with Liz had been for marriage counseling and there had been no discussion of anyone named Dawn. The sketch looked like Liz, but like any sketch, it was a rough approximation and there were definite differences. If someone told her it was Liz, she'd believe them, but would she have come to that conclusion if she didn't know about Dawn, if she'd just seen the sketch on the front page without reading the article? Probably not. Seeing 'hooker sought', she probably would have just ignored it. So Dawn was a hooker?

Seeing her look up after finishing the article, Jim asked, "So what do we do? And Liz is a hooker? I don't know how I can handle that."

"Jim, you've done your homework on DID. Liz is not a hooker. Dawn is. Liz is not Dawn. They're separate people. I think you need to try to focus on that. This article brings things to a head. I think we're going to have to come up with a strategy to move into the DID therapy more quickly. Are you still on board?"

"God. She's a murderer and a prostitute. How can I live with that?"

"Is the Liz you married a murderer and a prostitute?"

"No. Definitely not. But these others share her body. I have to believe that the law would look at the others as part of Liz, even if they believed that she suffered from DID. I have a hard time separating it and I've done the research. I can't image a jury could ever let Liz go."

"Well, for now, let's hold on to the idea that the police are looking to question her. They haven't accused her of murder. Maybe there's someone else."

"There's no one else," Jim stated confidently. "You and I both know it's Jane. When she attacked me, I knew she was capable of murder without a thought. I'm not sure why she let me go. She said she'd kill me."

"I didn't know you met Jane."

"Yeah. I made the mistake of going up to the cabin unannounced and Jane greeted me and made me leave."

"So let me ask you, Jim. Was it Liz that made you leave?"

Jim thought about the seething violence that was directed at him when Jane slammed him against the door, twisting his arm. He again heard the commanding voice, cold, unemotional, calculating. He felt his fear resurface just at the thought of the person who'd assaulted him. "Ah, okay. I see what you're getting at. Jane bears no resemblance to Liz. I had no sense of Liz being there. It's true. Jane is a separate person. A violent person. She's like those killers for hire in the movies, devoid of emotion. That's not Liz.

"I guess I have to start thinking of all of them as separate. It's hard since Betty really does seem to be a part of Liz. She's a younger Liz, but I really feel she's Liz. I have to work on this and it won't be easy. Sorry!"

"Don't be sorry. Now we just have to figure out how to change the course of things. I'm tempted to have you show Liz the article in our next session. You could say you need help addressing this sort of issue. Unfortunately, I suspect that it will be too much of a shock. Bring it anyway, just in case. I'll discuss this with Ken and we'll see if we can come up with a plan. You're pretty astute, so just follow my lead."

"Okay," Jim replied, resolute but skeptical. "What about the police? Are you going to notify them?"

"I have a few ideas on that and I'll discuss them with Ken as well. Don't worry, Jim. We'll figure this out. See you tomorrow."

Sam closed up her office, picked up a copy of the Chronicle, and made her way to the hospital. Ken was waiting. After he read the article, he got up and started pacing. Sam knew this was his way of working out a problem.

"There are several issues here," he began. "We have the obvious one of duty to warn. Court cases require us to breach patient confidentiality to inform a likely victim or law enforcement if violence is imminent. There are arguments against this as that breach of confidentiality typically terminates a therapist-patient relationship that might have prevented the violence.

"There's also the question of imminence. In this case, we don't have any such knowledge. Quite frankly, we have no indication that our patient has committed murders, but even if she has, we have no indication that the murders will continue or that anyone in particular is in imminent danger. No, I think we're okay on that one.

"I have no idea how you're going to move from marriage counseling into this. It's too abrupt. You've promised not to bring up DID, to focus on the marriage, but you've seen this article. Still, I don't think you should break that trust.

"Maybe you can have Jim do that out of concern for Liz or for the marriage. That too seems a bit sketchy and I'm still afraid that it's too much too soon. However, we do need to see if we can find a way to protect Liz and the public. What are your thoughts?"

Sam had been thinking along the same lines. "I'm not sure how we're going to bring it up, but we need to accelerate the schedule. If, in the next couple of sessions, we can get Liz to accept that we have a problem that needs to be addressed and that there's risk of more violence, perhaps I can get her to agree to medication. That should reduce the risk somewhat, make Jim feel a bit more comfortable, and buy us some time."

As Jim was driving home after his meeting with Sam, Liz was at the market buying groceries for dinner. Standing in line, she caught sight of the Chronicle. As she started to move closer, Betty took over. She saw Dawn's picture. Everyone in the Bay Area and perhaps across the country was now looking for them. When it was her turn in line, she paid for the groceries and carried them to the car. Liz drove home unaware of the few missing minutes. But something was bothering her. The uneasy feeling was back. It was like that feeling of almost having to vomit. You know you'll feel better but you just can't quite make it happen. Liz placed the groceries on the counter when she got home, made her way to the bedroom and curled up in a ball, waiting for Jim to come home.

5

Jim was nervous as he and Liz drove in an uncomfortable silence to Sam's office. He didn't know how they were going to raise the DID issue. Would Liz storm out and leave him for good? Would she kill someone else?

For her part, Liz was frightened. It was happening again. She felt disconnected, like there were gaps in her memory. Something inside her seemed to want to get out. She felt like she was going to lose control and marriage counseling was not what she needed.

As they made their way up the stairs, even the redolence of fresh baking bread couldn't lighten their moods. Sam greeted them warmly, offered coffee and soft drinks and motioned them to take a seat.

"So how are you two doing?" Sam probed gently. "Did you work on some of the communication techniques we discussed last time?"

Seeing that Sam wasn't going to bring up the DID, Jim responded. "Yes. We were exhausted after the last session, but I think we see the benefit. Liz?"

"I'm sorry," Liz said nervously. "I'm not doing well today. I'm not sure I should be here at all."

"And what do you mean by not doing well?" Sam asked.

Liz looked at her feet which were tapping rapidly.

"Liz?"

The tapping stopped and Liz seemed to straighten herself. She sat up like she was just called on in a classroom and raised her head. Her face was younger, her brown eyes wide.

"It's not Liz that doesn't want to be here. It's the others," Betty answered. "I want to do something and the others don't want me to and won't participate."

"What is it you want to do?" Sam asked gently.

"We saw the article in the paper. Liz didn't. I protected her from that. But things are out of control. Jane has put us all at risk. I don't want us to go to jail or to be executed. I think our only way out is this reintegration thing you talked about. I'd like to do it. It scares me but I think it's our only choice. I think Eve may be leaning that way, but Dawn is too frightened."

"And Jane?"

"No one has talked to Jane. But we're afraid that if we might die through this integration thing, Jane will try to protect us and could hurt you and Jim. No one wants that. We also don't want anything bad to happen to Liz because of us. Dawn feels horribly guilty. She thinks her actions caused Jane to do what she did and now all of us are in big trouble, even Liz who knows nothing about us or what's been happening. Dawn and Eve are trying to figure out some solution. I'm convinced this reintegration is the only way, so I want to start it. What do we have to do?"

"Well," Sam began gently. "We need Liz to be aware that she has DID, and we need her to want to do the reintegration. That will mean finding out what happened to cause the split of personalities. Do you understand?"

"Yes. I do. I can access the Internet too, you know," Betty replied a bit huffily.

"Of course you can. So, how do we get Liz involved? She didn't want to hear anything about multiple personalities."

"That's our fault. We made her reject the idea."

"How do you do that?"

"It's kind of hard to describe. Since none of us actually talk to Liz, we can't convince her that way. Instead, sometimes we intervene by taking over so that she doesn't see or hear something. Other times, we can push feelings her way to make her like or not like something she sees or hears. It doesn't work perfectly all the time, but we've had a lot of practice over the years and that's what we did with her feelings about multiple personalities."

"So you'll do something like that in reverse?"

"No. It requires all of us to focus on Liz to change her mind. Since I'm the only one who wants to go this way, I'll have to do something more direct. It will be okay. I know what I'm doing. Can you meet with us on short notice?"

"Yes. I'll do whatever is necessary to be available. Jim has my numbers. When do you think you can have Liz here?"

"I'm hoping for tomorrow. Let me get Liz."

Betty looked at her feet which began tapping. Her posture changed from that of an enthusiastic student in a classroom to one of an exhausted young woman.

"Did I fall asleep?" Liz asked.

"Sort of," Jim replied gently. "Sam had an emergency come up and asked if we could reschedule for tomorrow. Would that be okay?"

'Yeah. I'm exhausted. Can you take me home, Jim?"

6

Once home, Liz seemed to alternate between sleeping, eating desultorily, and writing in her journal. She seemed depressed. Late in the evening they went to bed and Jim fell into a deep sleep. He was awakened in the morning by the smell of eggs, toast, and coffee.

"Time to get up, sleepy-head," Liz said happily.

"What time is it?"

"You must have been really tired. It's after nine. It's a gorgeous day and I'm feeling much better. Let's eat!"

After a relaxing breakfast on the deck outside, Liz went to work on her journal while Jim sipped his coffee.

"Jim, could you come here please," Liz called.

Jim went back into the house where he joined Liz at her computer.

"It's happened again. There's a message from Betty. Look!"

In all caps, Betty had written:

LIZ, DON'T BE AFRAID. THIS IS BETTY. WE TRIED TO CONVINCE YOU THAT YOU DON'T HAVE MULTIPLE PERSONALITIES BUT YOU DO. SOME BAD THINGS HAVE HAPPENED AND WE NEED TO FIX THEM. YOU NEED TO TALK TO JIM AND SAM ABOUT THE MULTIPLE PERSONALITIES. I KNOW THINGS AND I KNOW THAT NO MATTER WHAT YOU SEE OR HEAR, NO MATTER HOW FRIGHTENING THEY MAY BE, YOU'RE MY STRONG OLDER SISTER AND YOU'LL BE OKAY. TRUST ME.
YOU CAN TALK TO ME TROUGH YOUR JOURNAL. WRITE SOMETHING AND I'LL WRITE BACK. BETTY

"So, it's true?" Liz asked, more curious than frightened.

"Yes. It is. This has to be scary for you. Are you okay?"

"I'm not sure why, but I think some part of me knew that I had this DID thing. I couldn't really rationally explain the lapses of memory and the gaps in my journal. I think I just tried to forget them, to put them aside. Can I really talk to Betty?"

"If she says you can, I think it will work. Betty is a younger version of you. She's nice, and seems innocent, but she's been this younger version of you since your personality split many years ago, so she's pretty wise for someone her age. I'll leave you alone for a while. Why don't you two have a chat?"

"Jim, can you stay for a few minutes?"

"Sure."

Jim watched as Liz typed:

> Hi Betty, this seems very strange to me. I don't know you, but you know me. How does that work?

Jim watched fascinated as Liz briefly closed her eyes and Betty appeared. Betty smiled at Jim reassuringly, turned to the computer setting caps lock, and began typing:

IT IS A LITTLE STRANGE, BUT I CAN SEE YOU AND WHAT YOU DO BUT YOU CAN'T SEE ME. I'M ALWAYS HERE AND I COME OUT WHEN YOU NEED HELP AND SOMETIMES WHEN YOU'RE SLEEPING.

Betty briefly closed her eyes and Liz returned. She read what Betty had written and her eyes went wide.

"There really are two of me, aren't there?"

"You should ask Betty," Jim replied cautiously. "I'm going to leave you for a while so you two can get to know each other and can discuss whatever you want."

Liz looked back at the keyboard, her face suddenly focused and directed. Curiosity had clearly trumped her apprehension. She began typing as Jim got up and left the room.

Two hours later, a very excited Liz sat down next to Jim.

"That was fascinating. At first it almost scared me to death, but then it was fun. I always wanted a sister. I hated being an only child. Well, that's probably not true. I was spoiled and I loved it. Have you met the others?"

"Not really. I saw Eve and Dawn that day at the cabin when I dropped the ice chest in surprise. And Jane chased me away one day when I came up unannounced, but I didn't talk to her. She just ordered me gone."

"I guess it's nice to know I have a protector. It's kind of like a guardian angel."

"I wouldn't go that far," Jim replied a bit ominously.

Liz missed his tone and continued happily.

"So what do we do next? Betty thinks we need to see Sam and lay all this out. What do you think?"

"I think that's a good idea. There's more that you should know but I think it needs to come from Sam. She said she'd be available today if we needed to see her. Are you game?"

Liz nodded and Jim called Sam. An hour later they stopped at the bakery downstairs and bought pastries which they carried up to Sam's office.

When Sam opened the door, Liz gave her a big hug before she could even say hello.

"Sam, I'm so glad to see you! I've got so much to tell you!"

Sam looked at Jim questioningly. Jim just smiled and nodded. They took their seats and for the next half hour, Liz talked uninterrupted about her conversation with Betty and how exciting this was. Then she asked the hard question that Jim and Sam knew was coming.

"So. I've lived my life for a long time as multiple people. I didn't know about them but they knew about me. They are each their own person. It's kind of like having family with me all the time. It's fascinating. Now that I know about them and have a way to communicate with them, I really feel enriched. I'm looking forward to getting to know them all. Is there any reason that I can't just live a normal life like this?"

"Liz," Sam began, talking slowly, trying to change the cadence of the conversation. "Dissociative Identity Disorder or DID, is caused by a severe emotional trauma. It's so severe that the psyche tries to protect itself by splitting into different entities who can avoid dealing with what has happened. Generally none of the personalities remember what the trauma was, but in their own ways, they protect themselves and the main personality from experiencing that trauma.

"I know it seems fascinating. It's fascinating to me too. I've never seen a DID case before and most of my professors didn't believe it actually existed. But the reality is that each of the personalities is damaged. As they've developed over the years, that damage has manifested itself in different ways, many of them unhealthy.

"In your case, it's gone to an extreme and has become dangerous for you and others."

Liz's enthusiasm evaporated. She wasn't frightened but she suddenly became serious and concerned. "Have I done something bad again?" she asked.

"First, Liz, you need to know that you, LIZ, didn't do anything bad, but it's possible that some of the others have. You and Jim have talked about some events in your past, injuring a therapist, attacking a traffic cop, slamming your boss against the wall, and a few other incidents. As far as I know, you don't remember doing any of these things. That's because it wasn't you who did them. You took the blame, but none of these actions were your fault."

"It's really bad, isn't it, whatever I did?"

"Liz, it's going to be hard for you to accept, but it wasn't you that did anything wrong. If I told you that your cousin had robbed a store but that you had to go to jail for it, would you think that was fair?"

Seeing Liz shake her head, Sam continued. "Well then whatever the other personalities did is not your fault and you shouldn't be punished for it."

Liz's legal mind, on hold for several weeks jumped into high gear. She ran through several scenarios in her mind and then asked, "So you're saying that if I committed a crime, or rather if one of the other personalities committed a crime, I could plead not-guilty by reason of insanity? You know, I don't think so. For insanity, I would have to not have known difference between right and wrong, but I do. Of course that might not be the case for the other personalities. I don't remember any specific cases about multiple personalities, but I do remember that it was a popular defense for a while. I don't think it succeeded too often because in most cases, the defense couldn't prove that the DID even existed or that the defendant wasn't malingering – pretending. And even if they could, there's still that issue of knowing right from wrong. I don't know. I think I could be in jeopardy here if one of the personalities did something criminal. Maybe we should get Daddy's help. He's one of the best defense attorneys in the world."

Sam was fascinated by Liz's departure from the real issue. Somehow she was able to focus on the legal aspects, not the psychological ones. At the same time, she recognized this as Liz's attempt to wrest control and to avoid the potentially crippling repercussions of her situation.

"Liz, at this point, I think we should look at reintegration. The legal aspect may or may not be relevant. I've spoken with Ken, and we agree that as long as we don't think there's any imminent danger to anyone, we don't need to go to the police. If we can solve the problem and the person responsible for the crimes has been rehabilitated, we may never have to report it. Plus, from what little we know, there is no evidence that would stand up in court. The police are looking to question you, not to arrest you. That must mean that they don't have evidence tying you to the crimes."

"Okay," Liz challenged. "We've danced around the issue. I'm ready. I know I didn't do whatever it was, so give it to me straight. I've got my legal hat on and I'm prepared to look at it objectively. My client did the crime. Not me."

Jim looked at Sam nervously, but Sam didn't hesitate. She reached into her desk, pulled out Chronicle, and handed it to Liz. Jim literally held his breath as Liz read the article.

"Dawn is a hooker? I'm a hooker?" she exclaimed.

"It appears Dawn is a hooker. Remember, you're not."

Liz digested this for a moment. "So they just want to question Dawn about these murders of johns in the Tenderloin. I don't think I see what the problem is. They're not going to arrest me for prostitution."

"Liz," Jim said gently. "It's worse than that. We think Jane is responsible for the murders."

Liz dropped the paper and Betty appeared.

"I think Liz needed a break."

"So you can just take over?" Sam asked.

"No, not really. Liz didn't want to deal with the possibility of being a murderer so I took over to help her out. She just needs to rest a bit. This whole thing is so new to her."

"You know, Betty, you can't just bail Liz out all the time. I know you're protecting her, but she has to learn to deal with difficult issues on her own. Do you think you can let her do that?"

"I don't know, Sam. I've protected Liz for so long. It's kind of a habit and it's part of who I am. Is this part of reintegration?"

"I think it will be," Sam replied encouragingly. "Betty, how old are you?"

"I'm twelve."

"And how long have you been twelve?"

"Well, since my twelfth birthday, of course."

"Did you ever wonder why you've never gotten older after all these years?"

"Not really. Is that important?"

"Yes, Betty. It is. You, Liz, and the others share memories up to a point where something bad happened. After that, you each develop your own memories. I suspect that Eve, Dawn, and even Jane have gotten older. But you haven't. You're Liz before the bad thing happened. Plus you have a lot of Liz and the other's experiences. But don't you find it interesting that you're still twelve?"

"Sam, that's very confusing. I never thought about it. Why don't I get older?"

"Betty, I think if you got older, you would encounter the event that caused all this. If that happens you won't be Betty anymore. You'll become who Liz would have been at twelve or thirteen when the trauma happened, except you'll remember. This might be a big step towards reintegration if you want to pursue it."

"But Sam, that scares me. I can't get older. I can't. I don't know how to remember something in the future. Do you?"

"Betty, I can't remember the future because it hasn't happened to me yet. However, your future is Liz's past so we know that your future has happened, you just don't remember it and neither does Liz. Does anyone else know what happened?"

"I know that Eve and Dawn don't remember. I don't know about Jane. I think Liz is ready to come back now. Ask her to let you see her journal. She brought it today. Bye."

Liz looked a bit surprised to be back. "Was Betty here?"

"Yes. She was. How did you know?"

"Well, I talked to Betty – actually we exchanged messages in my journal – and she told me she came out when I got into trouble or needed to escape. I remembered how I felt afterwards: a bit surprised not to be where I was, but also relieved, safe. I feel that way now."

"Liz, Betty suggested I read your journal. Would that be okay?"

"It's on my laptop. Do you have a jump drive?"

Liz booted her laptop and Sam made a copy of the journal.

"I'm not sure what Betty wanted me to see, but I suspect there's a clue in there somewhere. I'll read it tonight. How are you feeling?"

"I was intrigued by having a family inside me. Now, if I've killed someone – I know, you'll say it wasn't me, but I'm worried. I'm afraid it will happen again. How can we prevent that? How can we be sure I won't hurt Jim?

"There are no guarantees, but I have something that might help. We have a powerful antipsychotic that we gave you when you were in the hospital. From what the nurses told me, it was quite effective in quelling your violent impulses. I'll rewrite your prescription and you should be faithful about taking it. I'm not absolutely sure it will prevent another attack, but I think it might help. Also, as far as we know, the only people who have been killed are Dawn's clients. If Dawn can stay off the streets, that shouldn't be a problem. Plus, you can avoid the police. Dawn needs to stay off the streets."

"I can take a few days off of work and stay with Liz round the clock if you think that would help."

"Jim, that sounds wonderful," Liz replied. "We really haven't seen each other much. Maybe you can join me in the garden for part of the day and I can work out with you. Maybe we can even surf."

"Okay. It sounds like we have a plan. Can you two meet me again on Monday?"

They agreed to meet Monday. In the meantime, Sam was going to go through Liz's journal and Jim was going to keep Liz company, hoping he could keep Dawn from going back to the streets. Liz was planning to have more conversations with Betty, focusing on getting to know the others if possible.

7

Since both of them had put in a long day and neither was in the mood to cook, Mike and May decided to meet at a Mamounia, a well-known Moroccan restaurant in the Western Addition. It was quiet and they could talk without the noise of the Irish Pubs Mike tended to frequent after a hard day.

The restaurant's interior was plush with curtains covering the walls, thick carpets, low tables, and dim light. They were led to a small table and sat on cushions on the floor. One of the servers came with a pitcher of warm water and an ornate silver bowl. He poured the water over their hands in preparation for their Moroccan feast.

"So, what did you find out about the vics?" Mike asked after they'd placed their orders.

"It's interesting. I was able to dig into the pasts of each one. There is a pattern. All but one had a history of frequenting prostitutes and of violence against women. Most either had restraining orders from former significant others or had actually been cited for domestic violence. And of course we have the drug dealer.

"It sounds like Dawn, or whoever has been protecting her, is doing the world a favor."

"Yeah. Sometimes I wish we could let some of these vigilante types help us clean things up a bit. But you know as well as I do that we can't let that happen. The courts decide who gets punished for their crimes, not us, and certainly not a private citizen.

"What about the other guy, the one exception?"

"I have a feeling he was in the wrong place at the wrong time. It was this guy, Mitch Stern, the fourth victim. He was at a conference at Moscone and for some reason, decided to visit the Tenderloin after dinner at Chevy's. Apparently he'd had a few, so that might have influenced his judgment. From everything I can find, he was in the middle of a difficult divorce – difficult for him – his wife just dumped him after the kids were gone. According to his workmates, he was incredibly depressed, almost suicidal, and just couldn't accept that his marriage was over. He came to San Francisco to get away and clear his head."

"Poor guy. I can't help but feel sorry for him."

"Yeah. One more reason that we can't let people do our

jobs."

Dinner arrived. The waiter brought a sumptuous dish of Pastilla, a chicken and vegetable filled pastry, followed by steaming Vegetarian Couscous. The complex spices contrasted nicely with fresh mint leaves.

Mike and May ate ravenously with their right hands, regularly reaching into a large basket for pieces of bread to help scoop up the food.

"So what about you?" May asked between bites. "Any luck with the prints, DNA or the press?"

"Well, we've had a lot of calls, but none have panned out. One was even from an engineer at a high tech company in the valley who said our sketch looked like a lawyer who worked at the company. We'll go through all of them, but as usual, we're starting with the most likely.

"Unfortunately, Dawn hasn't been seen in the Tenderloin, or in Oakland, or in San Jose. I think we scared her into hiding. Hopefully we haven't lost her for good. She probably needs to earn a living and will be back on the streets somewhere at some point.

"We got the DNA results back and couldn't find a match. She apparently hasn't been arrested recently. And as for the partial print, it's a dead end too. It might be used for confirmation purposes once we have her in custody, but it's not going to identify her for us."

"I know you're discouraged, Mike, but we'll get her. People don't commit perfect crimes. Something will turn up."

The finished their dinner and shared Halwa Shebakia, a sticky pretzel-like desert made of dough deep-fried and dipped in honey. After going through the hand washing ritual again, the server poured hot mint tea from several feet over their heads into glass cups.

Even though he'd eaten at Moroccan restaurants for years, Mike continued to marvel at the skill of these servers as they didn't spill a single drop.

8

First thing Sunday morning, Liz and Jim did a run up to the top of Montara Mountain and back. They ate a light breakfast and worked in the garden for a few hours, then spent an hour surfing at Linda Mar Beach. After showering and sharing a lunch of deli salads they'd picked up on their way back, Liz went to work on her journal while Jim sat outside and read. Just before sunset, they went for a long walk on the beach and were surprised to catch a glimpse of the renowned green flash just as the last bits of the sun dipped below the ocean's horizon. They made their way to Alberti's to share a romantic Italian dinner again.

"I don't want to intrude. I know you have a lot of work to do on your own, but how's it going with Betty? Are you learning a lot?"

"Oh yes, Jim," Liz replied, hardly able to contain her enthusiasm. "I know I should be frightened but I can't help being fascinated. Betty is wonderful. I really like her. And, I met Eve and Dawn."

Jim was surprised. He didn't suspect that Liz would make this much progress.

"Eve was very reserved. She's nice, but was distant when we started. Dawn was clearly frightened. Not just of me and what was happening, but frightened that I'd judge her and what she did for a living. Of course, Daddy raised me well, and I do know how to put people at ease. It took a while, but I won them both over.

"We're all friends now. Eve is still a bit reserved, but that may be because she's British. Dawn sees me as her older sister and seems to admire my success in getting through law school. They're both sorry for what's happened and the exposure we have. I think they're beginning to realize that reintegration is our only way out. I think my having a direct conversation with them, getting to know them, me letting them know that I respect them, and us becoming friends is making it easier. I think Sam will be fascinated with them and the conversations we've had. I'm going to show her my journal tomorrow."

Jim himself was fascinated by his amazing wife. He couldn't imagine anyone else who could accept her situation and deal with it so adeptly. She'd employed her charm, the charm she'd inherited from her father, and had won over these reluctant personalities. Liz was truly a marvel.

The next morning, Jim called Sam and let her know that they'd be coming by half an hour early to drop off Liz's journal. He thought she'd be surprised at what had transpired in less than a day. He and Liz would grab breakfast at the bakery downstairs and Jim promised to bring warm chocolate croissants and coffee upstairs when they were done. Sam tried to refuse, but ultimately succumbed to the temptation.

When they were finally seated together in Sam's office and Sam had wolfed down half of her first croissant, Sam turned to Liz and asked, "So Liz, how are you feeling?"

"I'm feeling very excited. I feel like something good is going to happen. There's still a lot I don't know, and I'm sure there are some scary things to come, but somehow, it's like I'm not alone in this. It's not just Jim and you, it's my ah - family. They want to help and protect me. After meeting them all, I really think we'll be able to get through this."

"You said 'All'. Have you met Jane?"

Liz turned somber for a moment. "No, I haven't. From what I understand from the others, Jane rarely talks to anyone. As they say, she's a woman of action, not words. It's funny, as a lawyer and my father's daughter, I've always thought of myself as a woman of words."

"That's good Liz. Now, how are you feeling on the medication? Notice any differences?"

"Not really. I feel a bit more tired than usual, but I'm not sure it's related. Otherwise, no. I can't say I've really noticed anything. Do you think it's working?"

"It should be. I'm glad to see it's not having any side effects.

"Now, I've read your journal, and I find it fascinating. The latest entries are amazing. It's stunning to see your interaction with Dawn, Eve, and Betty. I see you guys coming together. You seem to be uniting. It's not like reintegration, but your beliefs about your situation seem to be coming into line.

"I wanted to talk to you, and possibly the others about some of the other things I've read. Do you think I'll be able to talk to the others? Can they talk to me directly?"

"I think so. When I'm writing in my journal, I finish what I'm saying and I kind of clear my mind, almost like meditation. Then, a few minutes later, I see that one of them has written to me. I suspect this will work similarly with you, assuming they want to talk to you. I know Betty does. I think Eve and Dawn will."

"Okay. I want to start with some of the dreams you wrote about. I'm wondering if the others share your dreams."

"I really don't know. Which dreams are you referring to?"

"Well, there are two that really stand out for me. One is about someone named Mitch, who asks why you killed him. The other is about trying to ski home and not getting there."

Liz tried to remember her dreams. Sam passed her laptop to Liz and showed her the entries.

"I kind of remember them, but neither one makes sense to me at all."

"Okay. Do you think I could talk to Betty?"

Liz closed her eyes, took a deep breath, and relaxed. Betty appeared.

"Hi, Sam. Hi, Jim."

"Hi Betty," they both responded at once.

"Tell me Betty," Sam began. "Do you all share the same dreams?"

"I think we share most of them. I certainly remember the two you're talking about. I was confused by the first one you mentioned; the one about that man, Mitch. I think it was Dawn's dream. The second one was mine and it really scared me. I've never had a dream that frightened me that much."

"Thank you, Betty. Let's save your dream for later. Do you think Dawn would be willing to talk to me?"

Betty nodded, then closed her eyes and took a deep breath like Liz did a few moments before. But this time, she sat there with her eyes closed.

"Dawn?" Sam asked.

Aside from an almost imperceptible shaking of the head, Liz/Betty/Dawn/Eve remained silent with her eyes closed.

"Dawn?" Sam asked again.

Still no response other than a shaking of the head from side to side.

"Dawn, would you be more comfortable talking to me if Jim weren't here?"

Dawn nodded.

"Jim, I have a feeling that Dawn is embarrassed to meet you. Could you step outside for a few minutes?"

"Ah – sure. But do tell Dawn that she has nothing to be embarrassed about. I don't have anything against her."

Jim stepped out into the hallway and took a seat on the bench outside.

"Dawn?" Sam probed again.

This time Dawn opened her eyes. Her posture changed and you could almost feel the sexual energy emanate from her body.

"Hello, Sam," Dawn said offering her hand, which Sam shook.

"Dawn, why didn't you want to meet Jim?"

"I ah - just thought he wouldn't like me. I'm a whore and in his eyes, I've turned Liz into a whore too. Plus, my whoring is why we're all in this mess. He must hate me."

"I don't think Jim hates you Dawn. He's a remarkable young man. He truly loves Liz and he somehow has been able to see you all as different people. He also knows, like I do, that you're not the cause of all the problems you all are facing. It goes back to whatever that traumatic event was that caused the split.

"Something horrible happened to a young Liz; something so horrible that her mind couldn't accept it. Whoever did that horrible thing is the one who's truly responsible for this situation. Not you. Not Liz. Not even Jane. HE, and I'm pretty sure it's a man; HE is responsible."

Dawn sat silently for a minute. This had never occurred to her, or to Eve or Betty. They needed to find out who this was so he could be punished. She would talk to Eve about that.

"Dawn, can you tell me about the dream? Who was Mitch?"

"Oh, God. It was horrible. I'm so sorry. In my profession, most of the johns are okay. They're just lonely guys or guys out for a good time when they're away from home. Every once in a while I meet a sicko that I don't recognize until it's too late. That's when Jane intervenes to protect me. In every case, she saved me from being severely hurt. Every case but one. This Mitch guy was just a lonely guy whose wife had left him. He'd never been with a hooker before, but I guess I looked a lot like his ex. So when I propositioned him, he threw caution to the wind and we pretended I was his wife. Unfortunately, he got a bit carried away in the fantasy and got angry at his wife. He wouldn't have hurt me, but Jane jumped in too quickly. She killed him.

"You know, I knew what Jane was doing, but quite frankly, I believe that the other johns got what they deserved. I kind of looked the other way. Jane was ridding the world of some very bad people who would not just have hurt me, they would have hurt others, and probably did before.

"But this guy Mitch. He keeps coming back to me in my dreams and I feel terribly, terribly guilty. He didn't deserve to die. It's all my fault."

And Dawn burst into tears.

"It's okay, Dawn. It's not your fault. In this case, I think it's partly Jane's fault for hurting an innocent person, but as we discussed, ultimately, it's really the fault of whoever caused the original damage to Liz. It's his fault not yours."

"Do you think Eve would be willing to speak with me?"

Dawn wiped away the tears and tried to muster a smile. She nodded, then repeated the ritual that Liz and Betty had done earlier.

"Eve?" Sam asked.

Dawn's posture changed. She sat up straight. Her chin was tucked with her cheeks a bit pinched. When Eve opened her eyes, Sam saw that she was now with Liz's British cousin.

"Hello Samantha," Eve said in an upper-class British accent as she extended her hand. "You're quite good, you know."

"Thank you. I'm still a bit new at this, but I do love it. I'm a strong proponent of therapy, prescribing drugs conservatively. I try to exhaust other methods first though sometimes, people need medication just to cope for a while. These are the sad cases, patients who can't function without medication or are dangerous when they're not on medication."

Sam wasn't sure why she felt she had to explain herself to Eve.

"Eve, would you mind if I brought Jim back into the room? I suspect you can reveal some things that he needs to hear."

"I agree," Eve replied.

Sam opened the door and Jim joined them. Introductions were made as Eve shook Jim's had firmly and formally. Sam continued.

"Eve, from the journal, I gather that you are the objective one in this family. You've observed what's happened, and you seem to be the conservative one who brings common sense to any situation that puts the others at risk."

"You don't need to flatter me needlessly, doctor. Please get to your point."

"And please call me Sam.

"I'd like to know where you are with this process we've started. What are your thoughts on reintegration?"

"Doctor – Samantha, I've been undecided about this for a while. We were living together as a somewhat dysfunctional family, but we were getting by. Liz was becoming successful, Dawn did her thing – she really can't help herself, you know – I lived a sexless life, and Betty was just Betty, young, innocent, and surprisingly wise. Betty protected Liz and Jane protected Dawn.

"I think what destabilised the situation was this Mitch incident. All of a sudden, Dawn felt guilty. She couldn't stop thinking about it, dreaming about it. She became fearful of the violence. All of this created ripples which destabilised us all.

"Quite frankly, I have never considered what caused us to come into existence. I just accepted that we were who we were. But your theory about some trauma makes sense, and at this moment, I agree that we need to get to the root of it. I'll be supportive of the reintegration effort."

"Thank you Eve. Would you mind if I spoke to Betty now?"

Eve stood up and shook each of their hands in turn. "It was good to meet you both," she said before sitting down and closing her eyes.

Betty joined them.

"Okay Betty, it seems like everyone is on board for this reintegration. As we've discussed, the first step is to find out what happened to you all. Liz and the others don't remember. Perhaps Jane does. But I think you may be able to help us get to the bottom of this. It will be scary, but you're a strong young woman, and you know that getting through this will help Liz, right?"

"Okay! I'm ready," Betty replied in a can-do voice.

"Betty, do you remember the dream about skiing?"

"Yes. I never had a dream like that before and it scared me. I can't stop thinking about it. Do you think it's important?"

"Yes. I do. So you're twelve years old and you're quite a skier."

"Yes. I am quite good," Betty responded proudly.

"In your dream, you're skiing home, but you can't quite get there. The snow is sticky, then you're lost. You're afraid."

"What are you afraid of?"

"Well, I'm just a little girl. It would be frightening to anyone to be lost in the snow as it's getting dark."

"Yes. That's true. But in your dream, you're supposed to be meeting some friends of your parents at your house. Is that what frightened you? Is that why you can't go home?"

Betty looked puzzled for a minute. Then she changed. All of the muscles in her face tensed and became drawn. Her shoulder arched forward as her upper back muscles expanded. Jane leaped out of her chair and put her hands around Sam's neck.

"You bitch. You can't make them remember HIM. You'll kill us all!"

Jim raced over to help Sam, but there was really no need. Jane slumped to the floor, dazed, inert. Jim picked her up and placed her on the sofa. He and Sam waited patiently.

"Jane?" Sam asked. "Jane?"

"What the fuck did you do to me? I feel weak as a kitten."

"It's the anti-psychotic. If you get violent, it will completely enervate you. Can you settle down and talk to me for a few moments? I'm not trying to hurt anyone."

Jane glared at Sam, then looked at Jim with obvious disgust. She pouted, then said, "Okay. But HE can't be here."

Jim nodded and left the room again.

"Jane," Sam began gently. "How do you feel about the murders?"

"How do I feel? How do I feel? I don't feel anything. I have a job to do and I do it well."

"Don't you feel that it was wrong to kill these people?"

"There is no right and wrong. They were scum and needed to be eliminated."

"And what about this guy, Mitch? Did he deserve to be eliminated?"

"Collateral damage. It couldn't be helped. He took his chances when he solicited Dawn. He lost."

"You don't feel any guilt over that?"

"Absolutely not."

"And what about its effect on everyone else? How do you feel about that?"

"It's unfortunate. They're all wimps. I don't see why they can't put it behind them."

"Do you see that as Eve puts it, it's destabilized everyone?"

"Yes."

"Do you see that Dawn feels so guilty that she's going to get you all caught?"

"I do see that, yes."

"If you're caught, at the very least you go to prison. You may even get the death penalty. If that happens, you haven't done a very good job of protecting everyone, have you?"

Jane started to jump from the sofa. She looked like she could kill Sam. But as soon as she got to her feet, she fell back, trying to fight off the effects of the drug.

When she relaxed up a few minute later, Sam continued. "Look Jane. You know what you're doing. You understand the risks. For years, you did what needed to be done to protect Dawn, Liz, and the others. But now, you must see that your actions, and any future violence is going to bring the police down upon you. Your picture is in the paper and has been circulated to law enforcement across the country. There's nowhere to hide.

"Your job is done. If you do anything else, you jeopardize everyone."

Jane thought about this. She was at a dead end. Her sole purpose in life was gone. She was the protector. Now, anything she did would put everyone at risk. No. She couldn't do that. What good was she if she couldn't protect the others, if her every action put them in greater jeopardy? Her mission had to come to an end.

"Okay. You're right. I'm done. If I continue, they'll suffer. My purpose is gone. What do I do?"

"Do you know what happened to Liz when she was twelve? Did it have to do with this skiing dream?"

Jane raised her head and looked up towards the ceiling. She clenched her jaw and pursed her lips. Then she turned towards Sam, the decision made.

"I guess I'm giving you the keys to this reintegration process. And I guess I'm facilitating my own demise here. Okay. Here goes.

"Liz did ski back on the Home Run from Mount Reba. She did get to their cabin at Bear Valley well before dark. Her parents were gone, but her father's best friend, Richard Johnson, was waiting. He'd helped himself to a few drinks while Mickey and Janice were out for groceries. Liz came in, greeted her 'uncle Richard', kissing him on the cheek, then said she was going to take a shower and get cleaned up for dinner.

While washing her hair, the shower door suddenly opened and Richard seized her from behind, telling her how beautiful she was and how he'd always loved playing with her. Then he bent her over and raped her from behind. It was over quickly and Liz fell to the floor in tears. She didn't know what had happened or why. Richard told her that it was her fault. That she shouldn't have been naked in the house with her parents gone. She shouldn't have kissed him. He threatened that if she told her parents, he would tell them that she had come on to him, that she was a flirt and wanted him. Liz was stunned.

"At that point, Liz withdrew. She went down to dinner and didn't say a thing. She went to bed early. The next day, she said she didn't feel like skiing. Richard, Mickey and Janice left for Mt Reba. In the middle of the day, Richard came in and raped her again, threatening to tell her parents what a slut she was.

"When the family returned home to Orinda, Liz tried to talk to Janice about Richard and what he had done, but Janice just refused to listen. This hurt Liz almost as much as the rapes. She tried to bring it up with Mickey, but Janice always seemed to be there and stopped Liz from talking about her 'sexual fantasies about Richard'.

"The abuse continued for several months. Richard forced her to perform oral sex and raped her anally as well. Then Liz got pregnant and Richard stopped. Liz had deteriorated over the months of abuse, but something broke with the abortion. I became the protector."

It was a story that Sam had heard before. The women she'd met who'd been through similar abuse were all damaged for life. Most never fully recovered. But this was the first time that she'd seen DID as a result. What was different? Did it matter?

"Jane, there are a couple things I don't understand. First, do you know why Janice refused to let Liz tell what had happened?"

"I've thought about that for years, and the only thing I can come up with is that perhaps Janice was having an affair with Richard. Perhaps he threatened to reveal the affair if Janice didn't keep Liz from talking. Perhaps Janice just wouldn't let herself believe that Richard would want her daughter instead of her. Or maybe she did see Liz as competition, not just for Richard, but for Mickey as well. Mickey and Liz were always closer than Janice and Liz."

"Thank you, Jane. You're a very smart woman. I glad you were able to protect them as long as you did."

"You said you had a couple of questions," Jane continued.

"Yes. The other one – well, I don't mean to insult or challenge you in any way, so please take it as something I just don't understand. You killed these assholes who hurt Dawn. Why didn't you kill this Richard Johnson?"

"God knows I tried. I think I scared him. He did leave Mickey's practice and ended up spending a lot of time out of the country. But when I got near him, he'd look at me with this knowing smile, like he could see me naked, like he was relishing images of what he'd done to me – ah – Liz, and I got frightened and couldn't go through with it. I'm sorry. Maybe if I could have killed him, we wouldn't be in this mess."

Sam felt sorry for Jane. Behind the violence was a woman who'd witnessed the worst. "Jane, it wasn't your fault. It was Richard's fault. Can I speak to Betty now?"

An exhausted Jane nodded, closed her eyes and Betty appeared.

"Hi Betty. You heard what Jane said, right?"

"Yes. Everyone did – except Liz, of course."

"I'm going to get Jim. It's important he hears this."

9

As Sam explained it to Jim, knowing what had happened was useful, but it wasn't going to cause reintegration by itself. Liz needed to remember what had happened as did Dawn, Eve, and Betty. Then each needed to process what had happened and understand their parts. The fact that Liz could communicate with them would accelerate the process, but it would likely be months, possibly years before Liz was complete again.

After trying for days to get Janice to see him, Jim finally convinced Mickey that it was urgent. Since Janice refused a meeting, Mickey suggested that Jim show up that evening. He would handle Janice.

Mickey answered the door and invited Jim in. When Janice saw him, she shouted, "What the hell is he doing here?"

"I asked him to come," Mickey replied calmly. "He has some important things to tell us about Elizabeth."

"What have you done to Liz? I haven't heard from her. Are you keeping her from us?"

"No Janice. Liz has been in therapy. She decided to pursue it. It was her choice."

"Bull. We know what happens with therapists. It's dangerous."

"This is a woman psychiatrist and she has made significant progress. I think you need to hear about it."

"I don't want to hear anything you or some quack has to say about Liz. She's just fine. This is all your fault. If you hadn't come along with your wild theories, Liz would be practicing law and wouldn't be married to you!"

Jim laid the somewhat aging copy of the Chronicle before Janice and Mickey. Their eyes grew wide. Mickey picked up the paper and read the article, then handed it to Janice who was transfixed by Liz's picture on the front page.

"So Elizabeth is a prostitute?" Mickey asked incredulous.

"Actually it's worse than that. It appears that she is involved in the murders as well."

"That's impossible!" Janice screamed. "I'm not going to listen to any more of this."

Mickey's face went red with anger. The man who was always in control in the courtroom was about to lose it. If Janice had seen that look before, it was rare. "Sit down," he hissed. Then turning to Jim he softened a bit. "Jim, I'm not sure I want to hear this either, but I have a feeling we've avoided this for far too long and this situation is our fault for not getting Elizabeth the help she needed. Please tell us what you know."

Jim recounted the events of the last several weeks. He talked about Liz's journal, the therapy sessions, and the discovery of the multiple personalities. He described each of the personalities, including Jane who had admitted to the murders. Then he talked about how a traumatic event is the root cause of this Dissociative Identity Disorder or DID. And finally, he told them that while neither Liz, nor Betty, nor Eve, nor Dawn remembered the trauma, Jane the protector did. He wanted to talk to them about that.

Janice got up to leave.

"Sit!" Mickey commanded.

"Liz's psychiatrist, Samantha Louis, now knows the cause of the dissociation. She will begin what could be a lengthy process of reintegration of the personalities. If this is successful, Jane, who has no sense of right and wrong, will cease to exist. From her perspective, she will die for her crimes. The others now communicate with Liz though her journal and their personalities will become part of Liz. Liz is nervous and excited about this. Sam believes that by getting the personalities to remember what happened, they can start to deal with it and the healing will begin.

"But ultimately, I suspect that Liz and the others, including Jane, will benefit the most if the perpetrator of the trauma is recognized and punished. They've been afraid of him for years, even Jane. I think, though I'm no psychiatrist, but I believe that they will heal faster if he's no longer a threat.

"This is going to come as a shock to you, so I suggest you prepare yourselves."

Seeing Mickey nod gravely, Jim continued.

"The trauma occurred at your place in Bear Valley when Liz was twelve."

Mickey started to stand but Jim raised his hand.

"Please let me finish. This is difficult for me to describe and it's going to be even more difficult for you to hear.

"Liz skied back from Mount Reba and arrived at your place but you were out. Mickey, your friend Richard Johnson was there. When Liz went to take a shower, Richard raped her in the shower and threatened to tell you that she had seduced him if she said anything to you."

"He what?" Mickey screamed. "I'll kill the son-of-a-bitch!"

Janice sat stone-faced.

"Mickey, there's more and it gets worse. I know this is hard, but you need to hear the whole story."

"Hard? Hard? I will kill him. I will."

Seeing Mickey finally get control of himself, Jim continued.

"It wasn't just the one time. The next day, Liz didn't want to ski. The three of you left together, but Richard returned in the middle of the day and raped her again. Liz tried to talk with Janice about what happened, but from what Jane says, Janice wouldn't listen. When you returned home to Orinda, Richard would find ways to get Liz alone. He would molest her and would force her to perform sexual acts. Liz tried to approach you, Mickey, but again, from what Jane says, Janice always seemed to prevent her from broaching the subject. After months of abuse, Liz became pregnant. Fearing exposure, Richard stopped. Apparently the personality split happened after the abortion."

Mickey stared intently at Janice who sat there silent and cold. She displayed no emotion whatsoever. After a few minutes, he stated a fact, "You knew, didn't you?"

"Of course not!" Janice replied, clearly lying.

"Jim," Mickey began gently. "Janice and I need to talk. In a few minutes I'm going to ask you to leave. But before I do, what do you know about the police investigation?"

"At this point, other than the sketch, the police have no clues. If Dawn goes back to the streets, she'll most assuredly get caught, but I think we've convinced her to stay away. You're the lawyer, but from what Liz tells me and from the research I've done, if Liz does get caught, you'll have to prove that she does suffer from DID, AND that the personality that committed the murders didn't know the difference between right and wrong. However given the number of times this defense appears to have failed, this is going to be difficult.

"Sam and I are hoping that with Dawn off the street, Liz will not be caught. Liz and the others will join, and the hooker and her protector will cease to exist. It's a lot to hope for, but like I said, from everything we can find out, the police have no evidence that Dawn actually committed the murders. Apparently the physical evidence is non-existent."

"I'll tap some of my sources and see if I can find anything to the contrary," Mickey stated, all lawyer. "Thank you, Jim. Now it's time for me and Janice to talk."

10

Weeks went by and the reintegration process was going well. Jane was the first to go. She didn't say goodbye. According to the others, she just disappeared.

For several days, Liz seemed to have more fits of temper, especially when confronted by aggressive men. But then, Mickey announced that Richard Johnson had been arrested. Janice admitted to an affair with Richard. He had threatened to reveal it to Mickey if Janice mentioned anything about his relationship with Liz. He had called it a relationship and had told Janice that Liz had seduced him. She had chosen to believe him.

Upon further investigation, which Mickey drove forward through his good friends in several police departments, it was discovered that Richard had molested other girls. There was little doubt that he would be put away for a long time.

As Jim predicted, Betty, Eve, and Dawn suddenly felt safer. In their next session with Sam, Betty was led to the point where she actually remembered what had happened and she gently dissolved into Liz, with no obvious changes to Liz, other than a more child-like mischievousness that seemed to arise from time to time.

Not long afterwards, Dawn and Eve said goodbye, and they, too, dissolved seamlessly into Liz. Liz continued therapy after remembering what had happened to her. She was relieved at the arrest of Richard Johnson, and was working through post-traumatic stress over the rapes and molestation, learning to deal with her urges and with her attitudes toward men – attitudes she'd inherited from her former 'family'.

Liz was saddened by what was happening in her parents' marriage. They were now in counseling, but given the gravity of her mother's sins, she doubted that her father would ever forgive Janice.

Liz decided to 'hang out a shingle' and began practicing law, focusing on helping abused women. She worked long hours for little pay, but found the work therapeutic and rewarding.

After several bumpy weeks with the emotional rollercoaster of Liz's reintegration, things finally settled down for Liz and Jim. They worked out together, played together often, and shared stories of their careers. As things stabilized, they began discussion of having children.

One evening, as they were sitting down for dinner, there was a knock at the door. Liz went to answer it and discovered two plainclothes policemen.

"Sorry to disturb your dinner, Ma'am," said the taller one. I'm Detective Bob Simpson, and this is my partner, Nick Gammon and we'd like to ask you a few questions if you don't mind."
"Certainly, officers – ah, Detectives. Please come in."

Jim stood up from the table and introductions were made. The moved to the living room where Liz and Jim sat on the sofa as the detectives took seats in the facing chairs.

"Can we offer you something? Coffee, a soft drink?" Liz asked.

"No, this should only take a few minutes. We're investigating several homicides and we're looking for someone who we think has information about them. We put out a sketch, and one of your former coworkers at MacroData called and said that the sketch looked like you."

He placed the sketch on the coffee table and waited expectantly.

"Wow!" Liz exclaimed. "She certainly does look like me. What's her name?"

"The only name we have for her is Dawn. She was working the streets in the Tenderloin over the last few years."

"You mean she's a prostitute?" Liz asked.

"It appears so, Ma'am."

"Please call me Liz."

"Well Liz, can you tell me what you do for a living?"

"I'm an attorney."

"And how long have you been practicing law?"

"A few years now. I worked for a large firm, then got recruited by the CEO of Jim's company. We decided that it wasn't a great idea for husbands and wives to work together, so I quit and started my own firm."

"I hate to ask this, Ma'am – Liz, but have you ever worked as a prostitute?"

Liz and Jim laughed together.

"No Detective, I never have and never will. I'm very happily married to the most wonderful man in the world," she said, pulling Jim closer.

The detectives looked from Jim to Liz and back again. They stood up, and Detective Simpson said, "Thanks for your time. I guess we'll just have to keep looking. Have a good evening."

They all shook hands and Jim wished them the best of luck in their investigation.

"What do you think?" Liz asked.

"I think you're wonderful."

11

"Nothing!" Mike said to May when he got home that evening. "We've gone through every lead, even the most far-fetched, and we've come up with nothing. The DNA is worthless as is the partial print. We've got nothing."

"And I assume there's no sign of Dawn?"

"None. She's just disappeared. "The murders have stopped again. I hate this!"

"Yeah, I understand. We just have to be patient. She's probably moved to another city. Of course, she may not be the perp. She may just be involved, or maybe it was just a coincidence. But the killer will turn up somewhere. Once they start something like this, they don't completely stop until they're caught or they're dead."

"I guess you're right. I just felt like we were so close. And I do hate the idea that someone could get away with so-called perfect crimes."

"Yeah. Me too."

going into the Golden Gate. The first basket of popovers disappeared almost as soon as they arrived.

Mike and May kept looking at each other, wordlessly surprised at Liz's appearance.

"So what do you guys do for a living?" Mike asked.

"Jim's VP of Engineering at a high tech company and I'm an attorney," Liz replied. "And you?"

"We're homicide detectives," May answered.

It was Liz and Jim's turn to exchange wordless glances.

The conversation turned to sports and the two couples enjoyed each other's company over a sumptuous breakfast, hoping to see each other again at a future triathlon.

As they made their way back to their car, May turned to Mike. "Spooky, huh?"

"God, yes. She sure looks like that sketch. Lawyer, married to a Silicon Valley exec and obviously happily married? It just doesn't fit. We'll have to keep looking."

Other Books by Steve Jackowski

The Silicon Lathe (2013)

ABOUT THE AUTHOR

Writer, extreme sports enthusiast, serial entrepreneur, technologist.

Born into a military family, Steve traveled extensively throughout the US and overseas, attending fifteen schools before graduating from High School. After studying mathematics, computer science, comparative literature and French at the University of California, Steve began his career with IBM as a software engineer. He later founded three successful high-tech startups.

A former competition hang glider pilot, Steve continues to surf, ski, kayak whitewater, and dance Salsa with his wife Karen whenever possible.

Steve divides his time between Santa Cruz, California and the Basque Region of France.